SHERLOCK HOLMES
& The
THREE WINTER TERRORS

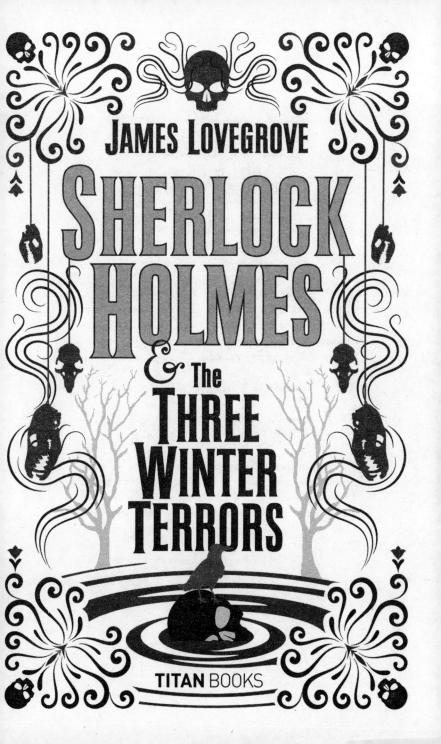

JAMES LOVEGROVE

SHERLOCK HOLMES

& THE THREE WINTER TERRORS

TITAN BOOKS

Sherlock Holmes and the Three Winter Terrors
Paperback edition ISBN: 9781789096736
E-book edition ISBN: 9781789096729

Published by Titan Books
A division of Titan Publishing Group Ltd
144 Southwark St, London SE1 0UP
www.titanbooks.com

First paperback edition: September 2022
10 9 8 7 6 5 4 3 2

A CIP catalogue record for this title is available from the British Library.

Printed and bound by CPI Group (UK) Ltd, Croydon CR0 4YY.

This book is dedicated to the memory of the late, great

JEREMY BRETT

unquestionably the best onscreen Sherlock Holmes.
(Others may disagree, but they are wrong.)

SHERLOCK HOLMES
& The
# THREE WINTER TERRORS

FOREWORD

by John H. Watson, MD

I take up my pen to write again after a lengthy fallow period. There have been too many other demands on my time and attention. First came the late hostilities, during which I renewed my commission as an officer with the Royal Army Medical Corps and worked at the Queen Alexandra Military Hospital at Millbank, treating soldiers afflicted with "Blighty" wounds. The hours were long, and constant exposure to the suffering of those poor, brave injured men took its toll on my energies, so that at the end of each day I had little left in reserve to devote to any other activity.

Following the Armistice, I resumed my duties as a general practitioner, just in time to face the Spanish 'flu pandemic that swept the world during the last year and most of this one. My caseload tripled, and again I was stretched to the point of exhaustion. Readers will be well aware that fully half of London was infected, hospital wards brimmed, and the death toll was appalling, with the mortality rate standing at 2.5%. I myself was laid low by the disease, ending up bedridden for a month and severely debilitated for a number of weeks thereafter, and I am lucky to have survived.

For those concerned as to the welfare of my great friend Mr Sherlock Holmes, he remained ensconced in his farmhouse on the Sussex coast for the duration of the pandemic, having little contact with others, as is his wont these days. Therefore he was spared from exposure and he remains, as ever, in good health.

It is only now, in the winter of 1919, that I feel recovered enough – and once more have sufficient leisure – to set about relating another of the criminal investigations undertaken by the aforesaid Sherlock Holmes. In this instance, it is actually not a single case but three, which took place during the winters of 1889, 1890 and 1894 respectively.

Initially I was uncertain whether I should prepare an account of these episodes for publication, as it entails revealing certain truths that hitherto have not been a matter of public record and casting light upon deeds which the doers might have preferred to remain unilluminated. However, since those directly involved are all now dead, more than one of them a victim of the Spanish 'flu, I feel I need not fear legal repercussions.

Each case, taken on its own merits, is worthy of being chronicled; but, moreover, they share the unique and interesting attribute of together forming what is effectively a single narrative. The common thread is the Agius family – the industrialist Eustace Agius, his wife Faye, and their son Vernon – who happened to find themselves associated with every one of the three incidents.

A second common thread is that the cases all involved phantasmagorical elements and grotesque horrors the nature of which may induce perturbation and even distress in readers of a more sensitive nature. It is not my place to counsel you to be cautious when perusing the pages that follow. Susceptibility to such things varies, and I leave it to your own judgement whether or not you have the appropriate mental fortitude. All I will say is that you may consider yourself warned.

J.H.W., LONDON, 1919

The First Terror

THE WITCH'S CURSE

1889

Chapter One

AN EXTRAORDINARY COINCIDENCE
AND AN OLD ACQUAINTANCE

T he last thing I was expecting, as Mary and I made our way home after an evening out, was a cry for help.

Until that moment, we had been having a thoroughly pleasant time of it. We had attended a performance of the latest Gilbert and Sullivan operetta, *The Gondoliers*, which had just opened at the Savoy Theatre. I myself was no great aficionado of the pair's work – too jaunty and frivolous for my taste – but my wife was and had adored this one in particular. Walking westward down the Strand, huddled together against the cold, I listened as she happily trilled Tessa's aria "When a Merry Maiden Marries", or as much of it as she could remember after a single listening. Mary's singing voice was strong and sweet, and the sound warmed me inwardly, offering a stark contrast to the chill of the night air. London in December is never delightful, and the winter of 1889 was proving a damp and frigid one indeed.

All the passing cabs were taken, but we knew there would be some waiting in the rank outside Charing Cross Station. Before we got there, however, a hoarse, desperate imprecation reached our ears. The cry came from close by, audible to no other pedestrians in the vicinity but us. Its point of origin was an alley leading down to the Victoria Embankment, and Mary and I halted at the entrance to the narrow thoroughfare, exchanging alarmed looks.

The cry was repeated. Somebody, a man, was pleading for succour. "Someone. Anyone! I beg of you. They mean to rob me. Please!"

This was followed by a muttered growl from another man. The words were unclear but the sense was not. They were addressed to the fellow under attack, who was being urged to hush, on pain of punishment.

I looked at Mary again. She saw the need in my eyes.

"There are no police around…" I began.

"Go, John," she said, disengaging her arm from mine. "I know better than to try to stop you."

"But I cannot leave you here on the street alone."

"There are plenty of passers-by. I shall remain in the light of this gas lamp. I shall be safe."

"But still…"

"Go," my wife urged me again. "I beg you, though, take care."

"I shall, you may count on it."

So saying, I dashed into the alley.

Illumination from the street penetrated barely half a dozen yards into the alley's darkness. Yet I was just able to make out the figures of three men ahead of me, silhouetted amid the gloom. One of them had his back against the alley wall, cowering. The other two loomed over him in intimidating postures. One of these pair was brandishing a stubby implement, a cudgel of some sort, while his other hand grasped their victim's shirtfront. From him came the menacing words: "Now then, no more of this snivelling. Your wallet. Hand it over, or it will go hard for you."

For a fleeting instant I wished I had my service revolver with me. But then, when going out for an evening's entertainment with one's wife, one hardly considers it necessary to leave the house armed.

Something I did have on my person that I might employ as a weapon, however, was my walking stick. It was a handsome piece of polished hickory, a gift from Mary on my last birthday, and as I hurried towards the threesome, I hoisted it aloft.

"Halloa, you blackguards!" I said in my loudest, fiercest voice. "Leave him alone!"

All three of them turned their faces to me. In the dim light I could discern that each looked startled by my sudden appearance. The two assailants, however, swiftly recovered their composure. The one who did not have the cudgel moved towards me, bringing up his fists.

I did not break my step. Rather, I increased pace, drawing the walking stick back as I went. The moment I was within range, I swung it at the man. He attempted to ward off the blow with a forearm, but this was a grave miscalculation on his part, failing to take into account both the sturdiness of the implement itself and the considerable momentum behind it. The head of the stick met the point of his elbow with an almighty, jarring *crack*. If the impact did not break the joint, it was sufficient nonetheless to put the miscreant out of action, for the elbow is a highly sensitive spot, filled with nerve endings. He recoiled away, moaning in distress, arm hanging limp.

His colleague abandoned their victim. "What do we have here?" he sneered, taking the measure of me. "A hero, is it?" He slapped the cudgel into his open palm.

"No hero," I replied in an even tone. "Merely a concerned citizen. One, I might add, who is holding a weapon with greater reach than yours. You may come at me, sir, but should you do so, you will find yourself as easily incapacitated as your crony was. I suggest you depart at once, you and he both. Or else."

The fellow gave a show of weighing up my admonition. By this time, my eyes had adjusted to the gloom, and I could see that not only was he tall and brawny, far more so than his accomplice, but he had the look of someone who had known his fair share of physical altercations, at least if his two missing upper incisors and the scar above his left eyebrow were anything to go by. He was not frightened of me, and in light of this, I found that my initial surge of righteous indignation, which had carried me along thus far like a rolling wave, began to abate. In its place came the first stirrings of trepidation. Perhaps I had erred. Perhaps I had allowed gallantry to overcome common sense.

"Ach," the big man spat, as if in disgust. "It's not worth it. Come on, you." He seized his accomplice by the scruff of the neck. "Let's be gone. There'll be easier pickings up Soho way, if we play it right."

So did those two rogues sidle off along the alleyway in the direction of the Thames, disappearing from view and indeed from this narrative altogether, for I never saw them again nor would I learn anything about them other than the obvious, that they were common street thieves. I was left alone with the object of their malicious designs.

The man was leaning against the wall, hunched over, panting hard.

"Are you all right?" I enquired.

"Y-yes," he stammered. "Yes, I think so. The brutes ill-used me but did not hurt me. God knows what they might have done, though, if you had not happened along. You have my undying gratitude, sir."

"Think nothing of it. Come, let's get you out into the street where the light is better, so that I can look you over. I'm a doctor, as it happens."

"I assure you I am fine," said the man, but no sooner had he taken a couple of steps than he swooned and, if I had not caught him, would have collapsed.

"You are far from fine," I told him firmly. "You have suffered a considerable shock. Here, put your arm around my shoulders. That's it. Now, one foot in front of the other. This way."

We emerged onto the Strand. Mary's relief at seeing me safe and sound was palpable. Her brow furrowed in concern as she turned her gaze to the man I was supporting.

"I take it this is the fellow you have rescued, John. How is he?"

"We shall know in a moment." I helped him sit down on the pavement and tilted his face up so that I could take a good look at him.

It was then that I felt a sudden thrill of recognition.

"By thunder," I exclaimed. "It can't be. Can it? Is that you, Rascal?"

The man blinked up at me in astonishment. "Rascal? Nobody has called me that name in years."

"'Ragged Rascal' Wragge. Bless me, it *is* you!"

"You have me at a disadvantage," said the other with perplexity. "You know me, but I am afraid I haven't the faintest idea who you…" He faltered. "Wait. The lady called you John. And now that I think of it, you do look familiar. John… as in John Watson?"

"The very same."

"Heavens above." A wan smile appeared on his face. "What an extraordinary thing."

"Isn't it?"

"Dearest," said Mary, "am I to take it that the two of you know each other?"

"At one time we did," said I in reply, "and indeed very well. But it has been – how long? – twenty years or more since last we were in each other's presence. Mary, unless I am much mistaken, this is Timothy Wragge, a schoolmate of mine. We were at Saltings House Preparatory together."

"Good old 'Whatzat'," said Wragge. "How nice it is to see you again, after all this time."

"Would that it were under more auspicious circumstances," I said. "But we must get you in the warm, Wragge, after your ordeal. A nip of brandy, too, would not go amiss, I'd wager."

Wragge began to protest feebly, but I would not countenance it.

"Not a word," I declared. "Do you think you can make it as far as that cab rank?"

"I can try."

"Good man," I said, and presently the three of us were snugly ensconced in a brougham and trundling towards Paddington.

Chapter Two

WHATZAT!

I made Wragge comfortable in an armchair in the drawing room. Mary, meanwhile, poured him a brandy, then said she was going to make tea for us. I told her to get the maid to do it, but she pointed out that it was late, the servants were all in bed, and it seemed unreasonable to wake them.

I proceeded to subject my old school friend to a thorough medical examination – eye motion, flexibility of joints, palpating for areas of tenderness. Wragge was, as he had said, unhurt, but he remained badly shaken. It wasn't until I had plied him with a second glass of brandy that his hands finally ceased to tremble.

"I don't get up to London much," he said. "Is it always this dangerous?"

"Only for those who go down alleys where no sane person would venture after dark," I replied.

"It seemed a useful shortcut."

"A shortcut to getting your throat cut."

Wragge looked aghast. "You mean I might have died?"

"No, no," I hastened to reassure him. "I was exaggerating, for effect. All the same, there's a good chance those two scoundrels would not have stopped at taking your wallet. I would not be surprised if they had roughed you up further, purely for the fun of it."

Wragge shuddered. "What a fool I was."

"Inexperienced, Wragge, that's all. Not foolish."

Mary returned with the tea and poured Wragge and me a cup each. "Mr Wragge, you'll be spending the night with us," said she. "I will prepare a room for you."

"I couldn't possibly impose on you, madam," came the reply. "When I am recovered, I shall go and find a hotel."

"I don't think you understand, Wragge," I said. "Mary is not asking a question. She is making a statement of fact. You are staying, and there is an end of it."

Wragge looked set to offer another polite demurral, but then, at a stern glance from Mary, relented. "If it isn't too much trouble."

"None at all," Mary said, and left to make up the bed in the spare room.

"Well, Watson," said Wragge, "she seems an excellent woman, no doubt about it. Beautiful, too, if I may say so."

"I am luckier than I deserve."

"And you yourself seem in good health. You have not changed much. Apart from that moustache and a touch of grey at the temples, I see clearly the John Watson I used to know."

"The same may be said for you." Indeed, Wragge retained the fine-boned features I remembered from our early youth, and the intelligent green eyes, not to mention the full, slightly girlish lips. His flaxen hair had thinned somewhat and he had developed a small paunch, but otherwise the years had been kind to him. As schoolboys he and I had not been the closest of friends, but we had shared several interests, including cricket and a fondness for the works of Dumas and Poe, and we had often sat at adjacent desks in class owing to the alphabetical proximity of our surnames.

He glanced about the room. "Generally, you are prospering. Nice house. Loving wife. You are in general practice, then?"

"Since leaving the army, yes."

"The army. So a man of action as well as a man of medicine. Hence you were not intimidated by those two louts."

"I wouldn't say I was not intimidated, but I have faced a fair few villains in my time. When my blood is up, I refuse to be cowed."

"How fortunate for me that that is the case. It's funny, though. I always thought you would become a writer. As I recall, you were constantly scribbling down stories in notebooks in the dormitory before lights out."

"It so happens I have had a book published, just the year before last."

"You don't say!"

"Yes, and it met with some success."

"My congratulations. I apologise for not knowing that, but then, living where I do, I am rather out of touch."

"And where is that?"

Wragge gave a soft chuckle. "You may not believe this, but Saltings House."

"You are employed at the school?"

"I have been a master there these past five years, teaching Latin, Greek and Ancient History, as well as a bit of cricket coaching. Before that, I had a position up in Yorkshire at a place called the Priory School."

"A schoolmaster," I said. "Yes, I can see how that might suit you, Wragge. You were always far more studious than I. But the school holidays do not start for another week. What, pray, has brought you up to town on a weekday during term time? It must be some urgent errand."

"Very urgent." Wragge's expression clouded. "One, indeed, that requires the involvement of Scotland Yard, no less."

"Were you intending to visit the Yard tonight? The hour is far too late for that. I doubt you would find more than a couple of constables on duty, and certainly no inspectors."

"I planned to stop by there first thing in the morning," said Wragge. "I was unable to get away from Saltings House until late, you see. I had to oversee evening prep, and then lights out in the dormitories. Once I had discharged those duties, I caught the last train up to London. My intention was to find myself a hotel for the night, as near to the Yard as possible so that I could call there early and be back at school in time for first lesson. It was while I was seeking said hotel that those two men waylaid me."

"Ah. And this matter cannot be dealt with by your local constabulary?"

"I think not. The business is more serious than that."

"Goodness me. Well, would you care to expound?"

At the back of my mind, a thought was forming. I knew of someone whose services one might engage when it came to investigating "serious business", and whose powers of deduction and analysis were infinitely superior to those of any policeman.

"I cannot see the harm, I suppose," said Wragge. "It so happens there has been a death at the school."

"Heavens," I declared.

"Yes. A death in suspicious circumstances. Just last week, one of the pupils was found drowned in the lake. Only thirteen, in his final year."

"How awful."

"Quite," said Wragge, with feeling. "Mr Gormley – that's the headmaster – insists it was nothing other than a tragic accident. I, however, have my doubts."

"Tell me more," I said, then amended, "Actually, don't. I have a better idea."

"What's that?"

"Wragge, I don't suppose you've heard of a fellow called Sherlock Holmes."

He frowned. "The name doesn't ring a bell. Should I have?"

At that time, Holmes's career as a consulting detective was almost a decade old, but his fame had yet to spread much beyond the limits of London, and even then was largely restricted to certain social circles within the capital and of course, in a different way, to the criminal underworld. My accounts of his exploits would do much to bolster his reputation both nationally and internationally, but as yet, only the first of them, *A Study in Scarlet*, had appeared in print.

"It does not matter," I said. "What matters is that, if you have a problem of an abstruse or delicate nature, Sherlock Holmes is your man. You would be far better seeing him about it than anyone at the Yard."

"Are you sure?"

"Quite sure. I will take you to him first thing tomorrow."

Having shown Wragge to the spare room, I retired to bed. Mary had waited up for me, and enquired after Wragge's wellbeing. I recounted our conversation, and she agreed that, if Wragge felt there was something amiss with regard to the drowned pupil, it was worthwhile bringing Holmes in on it.

"Mr Holmes will prove him right," she said, "or he will be able to allay his misgivings. In either case, it will bring him satisfaction."

"My thinking precisely."

"One question, dear." She gave a quizzical smile. "'Whatzat'?"

"Oh, you know how schoolboys are, Mary," I said, with a small blush. "You only have to do something once to earn a nickname, and then you're stuck with it until you leave. In my case, I used to get rather enthusiastic when calling a batsman out during cricket matches, and one day I accidentally yelled 'whatzat' instead of 'howzat'. Because it sounded a bit like my actual name, everyone started calling me that instead. It's a little embarrassing."

"No, it isn't," Mary said. "It's sweet. Now turn out the lamp and get some sleep, John. I rather suspect that 'Whatzat' Watson and 'Ragged Rascal' Wragge have a busy day ahead of them."

Chapter Three

THE MARK OF THE SEASONED ACADEMIC

As Wragge and I walked to Baker Street the next morning, he enquired tentatively whether this "consulting detective" friend of mine was a professional and, if so, was he expensive.

"A teacher's salary is modest," said he. "I have little to spare, and everything costs more in London."

"Do not give it a second thought," I said. "Holmes often renders his services for free, if he feels the cause is worthy and the case interesting enough. Even if that does not happen in this instance, I shall enjoin him to give you a preferential rate. Failing that, I will pay his fee myself."

"You would do that for me?"

"What are old school friends for?"

Upon entry into Holmes's rooms, I could tell straight away that my friend was absorbed in some thorny conundrum. Newspapers, reference books and notes jotted on scraps of paper littered the floor, while the atmosphere was thick with pipe smoke. Holmes himself was seated in his favourite chair with his knees drawn up and that faraway look in his keen grey eyes that betokened deep thought. I daresay he had been up all night, pondering.

"Watson," he said, the vaguest of greetings. "Forgive me, but I cannot speak to you right this moment. I am awaiting a telegram from my brother that will determine whether my hypothesis about a rather important case is correct or not. You and the gentleman with you make yourselves at home. You know where the tobacco is. It shouldn't be too long."

Wragge and I did as bidden, and for a while we all sat in silence, the only sounds the clatter of carriage wheels and horse hooves on the cobbles outside, the sonorous tick of the mantel clock, and the occasional tap of pipe bowl on ashtray.

Then the doorbell rang and a messenger came up with the anticipated telegram. Holmes scanned the slip of paper, whereupon a smile tweaked the corners of his mouth. He penned a reply, and the boy took this and his payment and scurried off.

Holmes then passed the telegram to me. "Take a look at that, old fellow."

The message was brief, comprising a mere three words:

NO SHIP SHERLOCK

"What do you make of it?"

"What am I expected to make of it?" I said. "Without context, the sentence is meaningless."

"Ah yes. I imagine you have not been keeping up with events

in the *Farthingale* affair. Well, there is no reason you should have, I suppose."

"You are referring to the steam clipper *Farthingale*, which sank in heavy seas in the Bay of Biscay last month, with the loss of all hands. I read about it in the papers. It was just another terrible maritime disaster, was it not?"

"There is a little more to it than that," said Holmes. "The *Farthingale* was carrying valuable cargo – gold bullion – and doubts have been raised at Lloyd's of London as to whether she sank at all."

"You mean insurance fraud could be involved?"

"That and more. Mycroft tasked me with finding out the truth, on behalf of several Lloyd's Names who are intimates of his. As a result of my investigations, I was able to ascertain that everything hinged upon the existence, or otherwise, of a clipper by the name of *Nightingale* that is more or less identical to the *Farthingale*. Now, the harbourmaster at Bilbao, on the north coast of Spain, stated that a ship called the *Nightingale* entered his port on the fourteenth of November. That is the day before the *Farthingale* is alleged to have sunk."

"Could the *Nightingale* have been the *Farthingale*, refitted and given a slightly different name?"

"Just so, and in that case, it is likely there was misconduct. The cargo of bullion had already been unloaded elsewhere, doubtless to be fenced through some criminal network, and then the *Farthingale*, rather than being scuppered, was repurposed as a 'new' ship and an insurance claim lodged."

"Two thefts for the price of one."

"Ha! Very droll, Watson, but also quite correct. I asked Mycroft to confirm, via his extensive network of sources, whether a *Nightingale* did put in at Bilbao on that date."

"And by 'No ship Sherlock' he is stating, in typically terse manner, that she did not."

"She did not," said Holmes with a shrug. "There is, in fact, no such vessel. It was the *Farthingale* all along. The Spanish harbourmaster simply confused the words *Nightingale* and *Farthingale*, and wrote down the former when he meant the latter. An easy mistake to make if English is not your first language. The *Farthingale* did then go down the next day, as was believed all along, and therefore Lloyd's must pay out. It was not too tricky a mystery to solve, but it required thought and patience. Now then, to what do I owe the honour of this visit? I can only assume that our friend here – a schoolmaster from rural Kent, if I do not miss my guess – has need of me."

I looked at Wragge, fully expecting to see astonishment writ large upon his face. This was the customary reaction whenever Sherlock Holmes made one of his detailed, accurate deductions about a person's circumstances based on physical appearance alone.

Wragge, however, evinced little in the way of surprise.

"Aren't you curious as to how Holmes knows what you do for a living and where you live, Wragge?" I said, feeling somewhat crestfallen. I had been hoping that the display of my friend's talents would impress him.

"Oh," said Wragge. "I presumed you wired Mr Holmes late last night, in advance of this meeting, and informed him about me. You mean to say you didn't?"

"No."

Wragge canted his head to one side, pursing his lips. "Well then, that is deuced clever of you, Mr Holmes, I must admit."

"A mere trifle," said Holmes, with a dismissive wave of the hand.

"How are you able to draw these inferences about me?"

"The rural part of it is easy. Your jacket is made of green houndstooth tweed, a fabric rarely if ever worn in the city. It is, moreover, cut in a style which is no longer fashionable in the capital – those narrow lapels, that double buttonhole – but which persists in the country. Furthermore, the uppers of your shoes bear traces of mud that is too pale to have come from London's streets."

"Fair enough," said Wragge. "My clothing betrays me. But how did you know I am from Kent specifically?"

"You have a copy of volume one of *Bradshaw's* in your pocket," said Holmes. "The title is just visible, peeking out. That section of the railway handbook covers London and its immediate environs, from Kent to Devon, with the Isle of Wight and the Channel Islands thrown in. The pale mud I referred to a moment ago is the type known as London Clay and, outside the capital, is found primarily in the marshlands of the Thames and Medway estuaries in northern Kent."

"But could it not have adhered to my shoes since I arrived in London, not before?"

"The alluvial deposits of London Clay in London itself are deep-seated. The city has been built over them and they are visible solely on the bed of the river when the tide is out. The mud on London's streets is of a quite different composition. Ergo, unless you have been trudging along the Thames foreshore, which I doubt, you came by your mud stains elsewhere."

"Very well." Wragge seemed satisfied with Holmes's elucidation. "But what about the schoolmaster part?"

"You have a certain way about you," Holmes replied, "an air which I can only describe as professorial. A slight stoop, a way of peering. It is almost invariably the mark of the seasoned academic. Add to that the light powdering of chalk dust upon your right sleeve, doubtless gained from resting your arm against a blackboard as you write on it, and the supposition becomes a certainty."

"All of that might mean I was a university lecturer, though, just as easily as it might mean I was a schoolmaster."

"True. However, you appear in reasonably good physical condition, and the great majority of university lecturers are not. They shun exercise and the outdoors. Schoolmasters, on the other hand, are often required to be outside, coaching their pupils in various sporting endeavours."

Wragge leaned back. "You are insightful indeed, sir. Watson speaks highly of your prowess, and with some justification, it would seem."

It was time for me to make formal introductions. "This, Holmes, is Timothy Wragge, a contemporary of mine at prep school, who now teaches there."

"Saltings House, eh?" said Holmes. "Then, Mr Wragge, I can only assume you have come to see me regarding the death of one Hector Robinson, a pupil in your charge."

Wragge's eyebrows shot up. "How can you know that?"

He turned to me, a mistrustful expression stealing over him. "Are you sure you did not contact Mr Holmes last night, Watson?"

"You think this is a ploy he and I have concocted between us?" I said. "Some kind of trick?"

"It has crossed my mind."

"To what end?"

"To win me over and ensure my custom."

I was somewhat offended. Wragge was impugning my honour, and Holmes's. Yet his suspicions were, I supposed, forgivable, and I reined in my indignation.

"Really, Wragge," I assured him, "it is no trick. Did you tell me that the boy was called Hector Robinson?"

"Come to think of it, I did not."

"No, you didn't. So I could hardly have imparted that information to Holmes, then, could I? That said, Holmes, it is my turn to be mystified. How did you know the boy's name?"

"Nothing to it," said Holmes. "As you can see from the state of the floor around me, I read the newspapers. A lot of newspapers. I subscribe not only to the national dailies but to many of the regional organs as well, not least those hailing from the immediate environs of London. One such is *The Kentish Gleaner*, in whose pages it was reported that a boy, name of Hector Robinson, met his death by drowning at Saltings House School the Tuesday before last. I have the sort of mind that is apt to retain data, not least those pertaining to the more morbid aspects of life. It is a prerequisite for one in my vocation. My mind is yet more apt to retain a particular datum if it has a connection, however thin, to my dearest friend in the world – if, for instance, it pertains to a school where he spent several of his formative years. In point of fact, Watson, I was going to draw your attention to the *Gleaner* article when next we met, if purely as a curiosity. It would appear fate has closed that circle in a different fashion. Mr Wragge, young Robinson's drowning is believed to have been death by misadventure. Such is the view of the local police and also of your headmaster, as quoted in the paper. You would not be here, however, if you did not disagree."

"Indeed so, Mr Holmes."

"Then, sir," said Holmes, placing his palms together and adopting an attitude of great attentiveness, "I would be obliged if you would regale me with the facts of the matter."

Chapter Four

THE FACTS OF THE MATTER

"Hector Robinson," Wragge began, "was not what you might call popular at Saltings House." He leaned forward in his seat a little nervously, resting his elbows on the arms and interlacing his fingers. "Rather, he was one of those boys who seem to rub people up the wrong way. His peers tended to dislike him. The majority of the teachers were unimpressed with his scholastic achievements, which were average at best. He was sallow-skinned and sickly looking – hardly resembling the Greek hero with whom he shared a name – and he exhibited a kind of surly diffidence that was deeply unappealing. It isn't that he was mean-spirited in any way, or deliberately gave offence. There was nevertheless something offensive about him."

"Some people are like that," said Holmes. "They have the misfortune to radiate disagreeability, like a bad odour."

"I try to see the best in all my pupils, but with Robinson I cannot deny I struggled. Harsh as it may sound, the lad had few redeeming qualities. It may not surprise you to learn that he was unhappy at Saltings House; nor that, given his character, his unhappiness was compounded by being the object of bullying. Now, of course, bullying is commonplace at all schools…"

"Indeed," I said. "As I recall, we ourselves were rather mean to several of our contemporaries, weren't we? Percy Phelps, for instance. Remember him? 'Tadpole' Phelps. We used to chevy him all the time. It did him no lasting harm, though. He went on to Cambridge and then the Foreign Office, where he has had a glittering career."

The last part was not entirely true. I refrained from mentioning that, earlier in the year, Holmes and I had come to Phelps's aid when an important naval treaty went missing from under his nose. I would later publish an account of this exploit, but at the time the theft and recovery of the document remained a state secret and I was bound by confidentiality laws from discussing it.

"Phelps had a brilliant mind and great reserves of self-assurance," said Wragge. "He could cope. Not so Hector Robinson. Moreover, the treatment Robinson received was unduly vicious. Two boys in particular, Jeremy Pugh and Hosea Wyatt, took it upon themselves to persecute him relentlessly, finding all manner of ways to torment him. Sometimes it would simply be tripping him up as he walked or giving him an unexpected cuff round the ear. Other times it would be humiliation, such as emptying an inkwell over him, tipping his lunch into his lap or slipping a dead mouse between his bedcovers. Then there was the verbal abuse, subtler but no less insidious. Name-calling. Making insinuations about his parents. Accusing him of deviant behaviour. Whenever I witnessed it personally, I did what I could to curb it, but I cannot control what goes on when I am not present. Besides, Pugh is a great all-rounder, both academically and on the sporting field, and is currently Head Boy. Big things are expected of him in the future. As for the Honourable Hosea Wyatt, he is somewhat less gifted, but his father is Lord Gilhampton, the Member of Parliament for Woking and a senior Minister of the Crown. Both lads are the apples of Headmaster Gormley's eye and can do no wrong in his book, so whatever complaints I made to him about their mistreatment of Robinson were met with stony indifference."

"Everything you have said so far might lead one to the conclusion that Robinson's drowning was self-inflicted," said Holmes. "He had been made miserable by the attentions of these two bullies, becoming so downcast that he saw no alternative but to take his own life."

"I agree. You can imagine it, can't you? Day in, day out, a constant scratch, scratch, scratch of cruelty, eroding his confidence, undermining his sense of his own worth. It could easily have driven him to suicide."

"But you still think not."

"I would not put it beyond Pugh and Wyatt to have dragged Robinson out to the lake, forced him into the water and held him under. It may not have been their intention to kill him. Perhaps they meant it as a prank and things got out of hand."

"Manslaughter, not murder."

"That does not make them any less culpable, as far as I'm concerned."

"You have no proof of this, though."

"None whatsoever. Just a strong instinct that Robinson did not kill himself and that his death was not a mishap either."

"Very well," said Holmes. I could see that, as yet, he was far from convinced there was a mystery to be solved here. "It would help if you could tell me a little more about the actual circumstances of his drowning. All I know from the newspaper, whose report was rather skimpy on detail, is that the lad was found floating face down in the school lake."

"I was not there when the body was recovered from the water."

"Who did find it?"

"The groundskeeper, Talbot."

"Not 'God' Talbot!" I ejaculated. "Is he still there? He must be a hundred years old by now."

"Still there, and still as cantankerous as he was when we were boys," said Wragge. "Still as fond of a drink, too."

"He was known as 'God'," I explained to Holmes, "because he had a bad leg and—"

"And therefore moved in a mysterious way," Holmes finished for me, his tone impatient. "Yes, yes, I get it. Very witty. Now, if we may confine ourselves to the case and leave these schooldays reminiscences of yours for another time… Thank you. Go on, Mr Wragge."

"Attempts were made to revive Robinson, so I am told," said Wragge. "The school matron, Mrs Harries, employed a kind of resuscitation technique, pressing repeatedly on his stomach, but to no avail. He was clearly dead and had been so some while. Mr Gormley, who arrived on the scene not long after Mrs Harries had abandoned her efforts, immediately pronounced that Robinson had drowned by accident. 'The boy went swimming,' he said, 'got into difficulties, and perished. It was his own fault.' But I ask you, gentlemen, who in his right mind would go swimming in a lake before dawn on a December morning when the water was freezing cold? Gormley's contention is preposterous."

"You say 'in his right mind'," said Holmes, "but it is conceivable that a youngster whose life was being made a living hell by his tormentors would be anything *but* in his right mind."

"Granted, but you should have seen Pugh and Wyatt, Mr Holmes, when the tragedy was announced by Mr Gormley at assembly that morning. I was watching them, looking for a reaction, and they were dismayed and horrified. Their behaviour since has, I admit, been much the same as usual, but in that moment, I saw it on their faces. I swear I did. Guilt."

"Guilt, or simply the bully's remorse, which he is wont to suffer when events bring home to him the full import of his actions. Robinson drowned himself, and Pugh and Wyatt realised they had driven him to it through their hounding and harassment, and were suitably chastened. In that case, they are not answerable in a court of law for the outcome of their transgressions, although one hopes that a higher power will hold them to account for it in the life hereafter."

"But what if they did actively kill him?"

"Then that is a very different story."

"And if Watson is to be believed, you are the man to prove it," said Wragge earnestly. "You must understand, Mr Holmes, the entire school is in a ferment right now."

"With good reason. An awful thing has happened."

"No, I mean that the atmosphere at the place is poisonous. The boys are recalcitrant and refractory. They cannot concentrate on their studies. At times they are downright mutinous, and no amount of disciplining by members of staff will bring them back into line. It is all to do with the witch's curse, you see."

"Gracious," I interjected. "Of course. I had forgotten all about that."

Holmes leaned back in his chair. "The witch's curse," he echoed sardonically. "Whatever can that be, eh?"

"It is a legend," said Wragge, "dating back to the school's founding and beyond."

"But you are probably not interested in hearing about it, Holmes," I said. My tone was, I will admit, somewhat peevish. "After all, you are so contemptuous of these 'schooldays reminiscences' of ours."

"Oh, Watson," said my friend, feigning contrition. "I'm sorry if I hurt your feelings earlier. I should very much like to know about this curse and what bearing, if any, it has on Hector Robinson's death."

"I must warn you," I said to Wragge, "Holmes has no truck with the paranormal. He reserves his deepest scorn for anything that carries even the faintest whiff of ghosts, magic or the unearthly."

"To the rigorously logical brain," Holmes said, "such things are anathema."

"I share that view," said Wragge, "to a degree. There is no question, however, that drownings have been a recurring theme at Saltings House, or rather on the land Saltings House is built on, and it all relates to a witch called Old Sarah."

Chapter Five

THE TERRIBLE TALE OF OLD SARAH

At this point, Mrs Hudson appeared with a pot of coffee on a tray.

"I had a feeling you might be after a pick-me-up, Mr Holmes," said that good lady. "I have made enough for Dr Watson too, and your guest."

"Your prescience borders on the uncanny, Mrs Hudson," said Holmes. "I was just on the point of calling down for coffee, and here you are, anticipating my wishes. Are you certain you are not clairvoyant, madam? A witch, even?"

He framed the query teasingly, and Mrs Hudson took it in that spirit, albeit with some puzzlement. "If by clairvoyant you mean sensitive to the needs of others," she replied, "then that is true of almost all women, and regrettably few men. I also know when my lodger has been up all night, working, and could do with a morning restorative."

She poured us each a cup and left.

"Now then, Mr Wragge," said Holmes, taking an appreciative

sip, "tell me about Sarah the witch. I am in the mood for something that tingles the spine."

I gave Wragge a look, hoping to convey apology for Holmes's facetiousness.

Wragge merely shrugged and said, "Back in the early seventeenth century, at the height of the witch-hunt mania that seized this country and most of Europe, a coven was unearthed in the north Kent countryside. Five women were accused of practising black magic, consorting with imps and demons, holding blasphemous midnight rituals and the like – everything short of riding broomsticks through the air. They were arrested by constables and held at the county assizes in Gravesend until a witch-finder could be found to verify the truth. It so happened that one lived close by, a local squire by the name of William Chapman, a devout Puritan with a particular passion for seeking out and executing witches. He wasted no time in subjecting the five to so-called trials in order to get them to confess. This entailed various forms of torture that were standard in most witch-hunts. The women were refused food and water and kept awake for hours on end until they were so exhausted their thoughts became addled and they did not know what they were saying. They were cut with blunt knives, and when they did not bleed, this was deemed proof of unholy powers. They were stripped bare and their bodies searched for the 'Devil's mark', a birthmark, perhaps, or a mole, the presence of which was conclusive evidence that Satan was their lord and master."

"Hardly empirical methods, any of those," said Holmes.

"Well, quite. Methods designed, rather, to bewilder, hurt

and demean, until the alleged offenders became so cowed and wretched that they would admit to anything, simply to make it stop. Then came the drownings. The five witches – they were inarguably that now, for each had signed a confession admitting her guilt – were taken to Saltings. That's the name of the area of marshland where the school is sited and where, furthermore, Chapman had his manor house. There, they were dragged to one of the inlets that leads to the Thames estuary, and one after another they were thrown into the water with their thumbs tied together and their big toes likewise. This was the final test of their witchy powers. If they bobbed to the surface and swam, plainly the Devil was helping them, and as a result they would be hauled back out and hanged. And if they sank…"

"They drowned, and the point was moot."

"The supposed head of the coven was called Sarah. Her surname is lost to the mists of time, and she was known to all in the area just as Old Sarah. She was the most senior among the five and had served for decades as a midwife and a healer in the region. Chapman decided she must be the ringleader because she had been the least cooperative. That is to say, she held out the longest under torture before breaking. The night before she was subjected to the water test, a priest visited the room where she was being held, in order to bring her the comfort of the scriptures. Sarah remained defiant. She told the priest that her confession to Chapman was invalid because it had been made under duress. It was a position she maintained right to the end."

"And she was not wrong to do so."

"She claimed that she and the others were the victims of malicious gossip. They were friends who enjoyed a spirited get-together from time to time, and there was no harm in that. But women who convened in the company of their own sex exclusively were, it seemed, not to be trusted. They must be up to no good, and the likeliest explanation was that they were witches. You need to bear in mind that the country was in upheaval in the wake of the Reformation. There was a collective moral panic, and people were looking for a scapegoat, something to blame for the nation's ills. They decided the answer was witchcraft, and soon everyone was seeing witches everywhere. If a woman did not behave as a woman ought, if she showed a spark of unconventionality or rebelliousness, then there could be only one cause for it: she was in league with Lucifer."

"You seem well-versed in the topic, Mr Wragge," Holmes observed.

"I read up about the Saltings witch trials not so long ago. I teach Ancient History, but history in general is a subject for which I have a real passion, and shortly after I took up my post at the school, I recalled the legend and felt moved to do some research. Old Sarah, at any rate, was the last of the five to be thrown into the water. What happened to the other four is not recorded, at least not in any of the local archives I consulted. My assumption is that they did not rise to the surface."

"Or did, but Chapman had no interest in rescuing them. He simply left them to drown."

"Yes. Otherwise they would have been pulled from the water and undergone formal execution, and there would be some official documentation of that. As I was saying, Old Sarah was the last of them, and just as she was about to be flung into the inlet, she addressed the assembled company. She denied any wrongdoing, called William Chapman a fraud and a monster, and she said that if she did have a witch's powers, she would use them now to call down a curse upon his head. She would beg the Devil to ensure that Chapman met with the same fate that she was about to suffer. One can only imagine the reception this got."

"Chapman, I should think, professed himself impervious," I said, "being convinced that he had God on his side and that his faith would protect him."

"I should think so too," said Wragge. "And then Old Sarah joined her fellow 'witches' in the water, and doubtless like them strove her hardest to stay alive but, hobbled as she was, could not for long. Meanwhile, Chapman and the others in the small crowd that had gathered to watch the proceedings looked on from the shore, perhaps congratulating themselves on ridding the world of an evil."

"And what became of Chapman in the end?" said Holmes.

"That's the thing, Mr Holmes. Not a year later, what should happen but that he did drown, just as Old Sarah had wished for, and, what's more, in that selfsame stretch of water. He was out in a rowing boat with his family. It was clement weather, and yet, for no apparent reason, the boat capsized. Chapman's wife and two sons made it safely to shore, aided by some of the locals. He himself did not. His body was recovered the next day."

"Poetic justice," my friend averred.

"And an ironic end to the story," said Wragge. "Or it would have been, had not two subsequent owners of Chapman's house died in a similar manner. One was a privateer, John Markby, who plundered foreign ships in the Caribbean on behalf of Queen Anne. The other was an admiral, Hatherthwaite, who had served at Trafalgar under Nelson and was in charge of the naval dockyard at Chatham. Both perished at sea."

"Statistically speaking, that is not an unlikely demise for a man in the nautical profession."

Wragge acknowledged the remark with a nod of the head. "Regardless, it came to be believed that not only had Old Sarah's final words incited dark forces to weigh against William Chapman, but her curse had somehow infected his home too, so that anyone who lived there was liable to die just as he had. In consequence, the manor house came to be shunned. It was tendered for sale but nobody would buy it, and gradually it fell into rack and ruin and had to be demolished. Sometime around the turn of the century, a new house was built on the land, and this, in due course, became Saltings House School."

I cut in. "The man who built the new house – his name currently escapes me – was aware of the curse of Old Sarah and took steps to mitigate its effects. He had a priest bless the grounds, and he erected a memorial to Old Sarah as well, an obelisk with her name carved on it."

"That's right," said Wragge. "He was a shipping magnate, name of Obadiah Jackson, and the obelisk has come to be known as Old Sarah's Needle. Jackson's son Quentin sold the property in order to pay the death duties on his father's estate, and that was when it was turned into a school. Old Sarah's Needle is still there, and has been regarded with a kind of superstitious awe by generation after generation of Saltings House pupils. According to schoolboy lore, on Halloween night the ghost of Old Sarah emerges from the marshes, crosses the school grounds and vanishes into the obelisk, cackling to herself all the while. As she goes by, her feet squelch, and she leaves a trail of sodden grass behind her."

"Yes, that was the story, wasn't it?" I mimed a shudder, but it was not wholly an act. How well I recalled being told about Old Sarah's ghost by a senior boy, our dormitory captain, on one of my first nights at Saltings House. I scarcely slept a wink that night, and when October 31st came round and we went to bed, I huddled under the covers with my hands pressed to my ears so that I might not hear those damp footfalls on the lawn outside and that dread cackling. I was only eight, but my terror was pure and genuine; and so indelibly was this terror imprinted in my psyche that I felt it again now, an echo of it at least, as I cast my mind back.

"No one knows who first dreamed up the yarn, but it persists still," said Wragge. "Many's the boy in my charge who has come up to me and jabbered on about Old Sarah's ghost, having himself learned of it for the first time. Many's the boy, too, who will not go near Old Sarah's Needle, not even in broad daylight, such is the hold her legend has over the school."

"Obadiah Jackson did not die of drowning, I trust," said Holmes.

"No. He died in bed. It was cancer that carried him off."

Holmes gave a mordant chuckle. "Then his act of propitiation worked, and its influence has held fast."

"So it would seem."

"Until now, that is."

"Mr Holmes," said Wragge, rising to his feet. He began pacing back and forth on the bearskin hearthrug. "I fully understand your scepticism. I am not asking you to believe that Saltings House labours under a curse from a long-dead witch. What I am trying to do is explain why the mood at the school is so febrile at present. You have a hundred and fifty boys aged eight to thirteen, every one of whom knows about Old Sarah, knows that witches were drowned close by the school some two and a half centuries ago, has been reliably informed by their peers that the ghost of one of these women habitually haunts the place, and is altogether so impressionable that he regards these fancies as fact." He stopped pacing long enough to run an anxious hand through his thinning hair, then started again. "Then what should happen but one of their number drowns. Appalling as that event is, it is made all the more appalling by the supernatural connotations it evokes. The pupils, almost without exception, are convinced that Old Sarah's curse has struck once again, and are in a state of heightened tension. When they are not being mulish, they are having tantrums, and when they are not having tantrums, they are breaking down in tears. This has been going on for over a week, and has risen to such a pitch that it is now little short of hysteria. Mr Gormley has been trying to keep a lid on things, but his approach to governance revolves around the repeated application of the cane. I am not against corporal punishment – 'spare the rod, spoil the child' and all that – but it can often have the effect of making a situation worse, not better, especially if used to excess."

"The more you beat them, the more it compounds their agitation."

"Exactly. Exactly!" Wragge halted, pointing a forefinger at my friend. "Several of the boys' parents have got wind of Robinson's death and written to Gormley to express their disquiet. He has assured them that it was just an accident and will not be repeated. None of them yet know about the turmoil that has erupted at the school, but God help us when they find out – and they will, and sooner rather than later, for term ends this Saturday and the boys will be going for Christmas. These people pay a great deal of money to have their offspring well educated, groomed for public school and success in life thereafter. They will not be pleased to discover that the headmaster is losing control and chaos looms. Doubtless many of them will withdraw their children, and the school's name will be mud. That, I think, is what Mr Gormley fears most, that the reputation of Saltings House will suffer, and so, by association, will his."

"What about Robinson's own parents?" Holmes asked. "How have they taken the news?"

"As well as can be expected. I saw them briefly when they came to collect his belongings, and I offered them my condolences. Both were clearly in a state of profound shock and grief."

"And they are content that their son drowned by accident?"

"I overheard Mrs Robinson talking to Mr Gormley. She said something to the effect that her Hector had always been a poor swimmer, and she cannot think what must have got into him, going out into the lake on his own and at such an ungodly hour. Gormley merely made sympathetic noises. As I think about it, it makes me quite cross. He must know there is at least a chance that Pugh and Wyatt had some hand in it, even if he won't admit as much. If only he had not been so negligent, so in thrall to Pugh's accomplishments and Wyatt's family status…"

"Mr Wragge," said Holmes, "I can see that you are quite sincere in your concern, and I am loath to play devil's advocate but feel I must. How can my involvement possibly stem the tide of panic that is sweeping the school? If I am able to prove that Hector Robinson was the victim of foul play, how will that help? Might it not even have the opposite result? Think about it. Say someone at Saltings House has young Robinson's blood on his hands. I identify the culprit, he is duly arrested, but the fact remains, a killing took place on the school grounds. Life will not go back to normal, not for some while."

"Won't it?" I said. "Won't knowing who was responsible and seeing him brought to justice offer relief, like lancing a boil?"

"I concur with Watson," said Wragge. "If it is shown that human agency was behind Robinson's death, and not some ancient curse, the boys will at least have a rational explanation for what has occurred. It will no longer prey on their minds in the same way, no longer touch on their deepest, darkest fears. Likewise their parents will be less inclined to withdraw them from the school. I mean, murder is terrible, but at least it is explicable and is rarely repeated. Dread of the supernatural, on the other hand, can persist, and even the rich are not immune from superstition."

"More importantly," I added, "if the killer is found and punished, a wrong will have been righted, and the culprit will no longer be around to cause ructions."

"That's it," Wragge said, gesticulating at me to show agreement. "What Watson said. Setting aside witches, curses and the rest, that is what really matters here."

"But what if, after all that, it turns out that Robinson did kill himself?" said Holmes. "Or that his death was, as your headmaster maintains, an accident?"

Wragge shook his head. "I don't know. I don't know. I just think it will help having somebody come in from outside and pronounce authoritatively on the whole business one way or the other, that's all."

"If it is not you, Holmes," I said, "it will be a Scotland Yarder. Wragge came up to London yesterday with the express intent of recruiting a police inspector. It was only by dint of the two of us bumping into each other first, before he got to the Yard, that he is here with you now."

"Bumping into each other," Wragge echoed wryly. "Again, Watson, I must tender you my thanks."

Holmes looked from Wragge to me and back again, narrowing his eyes. "There is something you haven't told me, old friend."

"Nothing much." Briefly I recounted the circumstances of my meeting with Wragge the previous evening.

Holmes whistled. "Ever the knight in shining armour! This is why I value my Watson so. He is as doughty as he is valiant. So what you are telling me is that if I do not take the case, it will default to an inspector in Her Majesty's constabulary."

"That would be my next step," said Wragge. "I only agreed to consult you, rather than the police, because Watson spoke so highly of you." A note in his voice suggested he was rueing his decision, since Holmes had as yet shown no great enthusiasm for helping him.

"The capable hands of Sherlock Holmes," I said, "or the clumsier hands of Lestrade, Gregson or another of those worthies whom you hold in such low esteem. Which is it to be, Holmes?"

"Hum!" said Holmes. "You are blatantly appealing to my vanity, Watson."

"Is it working?"

"A little, yes. And whether he realises it or not, Mr Wragge has piqued my curiosity. The affair boasts those outré elements I find so irresistible. A drowning. A witch's curse. An outbreak of hysteria. Very well then. Where's the harm in it?" Holmes clapped his hands together, and I could see that he had made up his mind. "A jaunt to the Kent marshes beckons, and along with it the opportunity to visit friend Watson's alma mater. Mr Wragge, consult your *Bradshaw's*, if you would. When is the next train?"

Chapter Six

POTENT OLFACTORY REMINDERS

So it was that we boarded the mid-morning express from St. Pancras to Gravesend. Mrs Hudson had obligingly prepared beef paste sandwiches, which we unwrapped and ate during this first leg of the journey.

At Gravesend, well past noon, we caught the branch-line stopping service that would take us to Larksham, the nearest village to Saltings House with a station. I could not help but think back to the numerous times I had, as a boy, travelled along this very stretch of track, in a compartment of a South Eastern Railway carriage much like the one Holmes, Wragge and I now occupied. The company's livery colour had switched from green to black during the intervening years, but little else about its rolling stock had changed, down to the jolting lurch of the wheels and the uncomfortable seats.

Outside, the landscape was likewise as I remembered it, dotted with hamlets and smallholdings and growing increasingly flat the further east one went, with the broad, grey sweep of the

Thames estuary forever just visible and, past that, the shores of Essex on the horizon. I remembered how I would be filled with both excitement and foreboding, perhaps more of the latter than the former, as I journeyed towards school all those times; and conversely how I would be filled with exhilaration and elation as I went the other way, homeward, for exeats and the holidays.

On that wintry afternoon, every tree was bare and lofted its frost-rimmed branches to the sky as if in supplication, like a naked beggar asking for clothes, while the edges of the canal that ran parallel to the track were fringed with ice, white as an old man's beard. It all spoke to me of loneliness and an inexpressible longing, and I fell into a subdued mood, contemplating both the passage of time and the passing of youth. No amount of cajoling from Holmes or polite entreaty from Wragge could stir me from this brown study of mine, and only when we finally alighted at Larksham did I rouse myself, conscious that childhood was long behind me and that I was a grown man, here on a grown man's business.

We drove to Saltings House in a hired dog-cart, and as we neared the school, once again melancholy threatened to overwhelm me. I had not been wholly unhappy as a pupil there, but I associated the place with separation and absence: separation from family, absence of parental love. I had not even had the benefit of my brother attending the school with me, for he had been five years my elder and, by the time I began at Saltings, had moved on.

However, when the gates came into view, all at once these feelings vanished. Those wrought-iron portals, each with the school crest worked into its bars, had once seemed lofty and vaulting. They were actually, it transpired, rather small and unimposing. Likewise the school itself. The main building, which I remembered being as large as a castle, was just a rambling, rather indistinct Gothic Revival house with mean little arched windows peering out from walls of knapped flint. Those chimneys, in memory so numerous and towering, were fewer and stubbier. The cedar that loomed over the front drive, a viridian-fronded giant in its day, was merely a taller than average evergreen. I almost laughed.

On the other hand, the tidal saltmarshes that lay beyond the school looked just as they had when I was small. There was not the same sense of diminution; adulthood did not bring a change of perspective to them. They reached away towards the estuary in endless rolling procession, small islands of cordgrass and reed amid a maze of water channels. From them, carried to us by an onshore breeze blowing straight off the North Sea, came a silty, brackish smell that was intensely familiar. It was the smell of freedom denied, for the marshes, although open country, were also a barrier. It had been instilled into us pupils that we were forbidden to venture onto them, on pain of punishment. One might get lost out there. One might get stuck in the mud. One might even be swamped by the incoming tide, which, when it rose, rose fast. The dangers were great and many, and woe betide the boy caught breaking bounds and risking his neck to explore that terra incognita.

As we climbed down from the dog-cart, Wragge said, "Mr Gormley will be furious that I have brought you here, Mr Holmes.

I suppose I should go and see him first, to own up. With luck, I may be able to convince him it is a good idea."

"Watson and I shall come with you," said Holmes. "I am sure the fellow can be made to see sense, and it will make life easier if I have his blessing to investigate Robinson's death, rather than be forced to skulk furtively around the school."

The scent of floor polish hit me as we entered the hallway, and like the smell of the marshes it was another potent olfactory reminder of my time here as a boy. I recalled how polish would be applied to the parquet flooring in every corridor on a twice-weekly basis. It seemed this tradition was still being maintained, for the floor was buffed to a shine and as slippery underfoot as a skating pond.

As we proceeded towards the headmaster's study, I became aware of noise echoing through the building. At this hour the entire pupil body must have been in class, quietly and diligently learning. Nonetheless, from all directions came uproar – chatter, cries, high-pitched wails, interspersed with deeper voices raised in anger. These gruff, masculine tones belonged, I could only assume, to the masters as they essayed rebuke and reprimand, seemingly in vain. Wragge had spoken of near-hysteria, and here was aural evidence of it. Where there should have been the hushed orderliness of a normal school day, there was barely suppressed pandemonium.

The door to the headmaster's study bore a brass plaque announcing that the occupant therein was 'Mr Kester Gormley, MA Hons (Cantab)'. In answer to Wragge's knock, we were curtly invited to enter.

Gormley proved to be a slight, bony, dark-complexioned man with enormously bushy eyebrows and a hunched, intense way about him. He sat at his desk, enveloped in the folds of a black academic gown, with paperwork in front of him and a large tabby cat seated on his lap. He was stroking the creature distractedly, running a hand over its fur as though he might somehow smooth the stripes off it. The cat appeared accustomed to such brusque handling and had its ears flattened and its eyes half closed, a picture of feline forbearance.

"Wragge!" Gormley barked, those sizeable eyebrows of his knitting like two storm clouds gathering. "Damn it all, man, where have you been? I've had to ask Yeowell to cover your lessons for you. You'd better have a good explanation for this unannounced absence."

"I apologise, Headmaster," said Wragge. "I was in London on business. I had hoped to return here in time to teach as usual, but, for one reason and another, that proved impossible."

"You could at least have wired, saying you were going to be absent."

"Again, I can only apologise. It slipped my mind."

Gormley seemed mollified, if only a little. "And would I be right in thinking that that 'business' has something to do with these two gentlemen?" He sized up Holmes and me speculatively.

"It does. May I introduce Mr Sherlock Holmes and Dr John Watson. Dr Watson, I'll have you know, is an Old Saltingian."

My connection with the school seemed of little significance to Gormley, but the identity of my friend was. "Sherlock Holmes.

Sherlock Holmes. Where have I heard that name? Ah yes, the detective fellow." His frown deepened to a scowl. "Oh, Wragge, don't tell me you've engaged him in connection with Hector Robinson. You have, haven't you? Good grief, the impertinence! After I have made it quite clear that Robinson met with an accident. Did I not say so? Several times?"

"You did."

"And yet Timothy Wragge knows better." The headmaster's tone was deeply sarcastic. "So he decides to take matters into his own hands, and off he trots to London, where he finds himself some wretched amateur sleuth, a charlatan who swans around thinking he can do better than the police."

I saw Holmes visibly struggle to contain his annoyance. "Mr Gormley," he said, with all the suavity he could muster, "Mr Wragge did originally plan to call in someone from Scotland Yard. He plumped for me instead for the simple reason that I, as a civilian, may conduct my enquiries discreetly and anonymously, without arousing undue attention. Whereas the presence of an officer of the law at Saltings House – a member of the London Met, moreover – will inevitably bring publicity, which I imagine you do not want."

It was a slight misrepresentation of Wragge's actions, but neither Wragge nor I felt moved to gainsay it.

"What I do not want, Mr Holmes," Gormley replied, "is a busybody poking around into matters that are no concern of his."

Again Holmes showed restraint. "That is understandable, but look at it this way. If I am able to establish that there are no suspicious circumstances attaching to young Robinson's death, what have you lost by allowing me to, as you put it, 'poke around'? Nothing. Rather, you have gained confirmation that you were right all along."

"Confirmation from a source that has no accredited professional standing."

"Regardless," Holmes continued, imperturbably, "it will help lift any shadow of shame from the school and perhaps quell the mood of consternation prevailing among your pupils. And that is what I fully intend to do: demonstrate beyond doubt that Hector Robinson went swimming unsupervised, entirely of his own volition, with calamitous results."

The other man eyed him circumspectly. "Is that so? You believe my theory of events?"

"Nothing Mr Wragge has told me leads me to think otherwise. I may only be an 'amateur sleuth', but if you know anything about me, you will know that my pronouncements carry weight."

"That is true, that is true," said Gormley. "I have seen, when your name crops up in the press, that certain high-placed officials hold you in some regard." He stroked his cat a little less forcefully than before, while he mused on Holmes's words. "What do we think, Thomas Aquinas?"

It took me a moment to realise that he was now addressing the cat, which, in response to hearing its name, raised its head and let out an inquisitive little meow.

"Should we allow Mr Holmes free rein?" he continued, still speaking to the animal. "Do we believe he will be of use?"

The cat stood and arched its back, curling its tail around

Mr Gormley's hand. This seemed to be the affirmation the headmaster was seeking.

"Very well, Mr Holmes," he said. "I will permit you to make your enquiries. With the greatest reluctance, mind. As for you, Wragge…" He jabbed a finger at my former schoolmate. "This is not over. We shall have words later, you and I. You have overstepped the bounds of your position, and also been remiss in your duties. There will be consequences. Grave ones."

"Yes, Headmaster," Wragge said. "I understand. I am hoping that, once Mr Holmes has ascertained the truth, you will be able to see your way to absolving me."

Mr Gormley harrumphed. "That remains to be seen. In the meantime, you are dismissed."

So saying, he resumed stroking Thomas Aquinas, while we left his study, Wragge with a somewhat hangdog air, Holmes with a wry smile playing about his lips.

"It's amazing," Holmes said outside, "how easy it is to mollify a man, even one as intemperate as Mr Kester Gormley, simply by telling him what he wants to hear."

"I just hope he does not dismiss me after all this," Wragge muttered gloomily. "From the sound of it, he may. I knew there would be a price for going over his head. I just did not realise it would be quite so steep."

I tried to lift his spirits. "I'm sure you are an excellent teacher, Wragge, and should it come to it, you will have no trouble finding a situation at another school."

"Not if any prospective employer asks Gormley for a recommendation. He is a spiteful sort."

"But is Thomas Aquinas? That is the question. Gormley values the cat's counsel. As long as Thomas Aquinas looks on you with favour, you will be fine."

Wragge chuckled, in spite of himself. "Honestly, the affection he lavishes on that pet. Would that he were half as considerate towards the boys in his charge. Speaking of which, I really ought to go and take over my class. Vincent Yeowell is a games master and knows nothing about the ancient Greeks or Romans or, indeed, anything. He's unfit to teach any academic subject. He's also," he added, with feeling, "an absolute brute, and I dread to think what he is putting my lot through right now."

"I would ask you, Wragge," said Holmes, "to put your pedagogical commitments on hold for a little longer."

"Why?"

"It would be helpful to have you on hand as a guide and go-between, effecting introductions where necessary. Could you do that?"

Wragge deliberated, then assented. "There are only a couple more lessons to go today anyway. Whatever damage Yeowell has done is already done. More to the point, I am probably in line for the sack, so it makes little difference whether or not I show up for class. Where would you like to go?"

"You mentioned that the school matron tried to revive Robinson after he was pulled from the lake."

"Yes. Mrs Harries."

"I should like to interview her first."

"Follow me," said Wragge. "Her surgery lies this way."

Chapter Seven

THE REDOUBTABLE MATRON HARRIES

The matron's surgery was a small first-floor room lined with shelves bearing bottles of cough syrup, castor oil, cod liver oil, carminative and more, the full panoply of children's medicines. The matron herself, Mrs Harries, was one of those short, stout women of a certain age who, on first acquaintance, seem formidable and even fearsome but soon reveal themselves to be kind-hearted and caring. This, to me, made her ideal for the role, more so than Matron Ives, that bony old termagant who had been responsible for the health of the school in my day and whose remedy for most complaints was to tell the sufferer that he should stop being so feeble and buck up his ideas. I felt that Mrs Harries would brook no nonsense but would, when necessary, act as a surrogate mother for young boys who were missing their real mothers.

"My goodness," she said, in answer to Holmes's prompting, "it was horrible, gentlemen. Horrible! I can hardly bring myself to recall it."

"Compose yourself, madam," Holmes said. "Take your time. I realise it must be unpleasant to revisit the episode, but you must if we are to get to the bottom of it."

Mrs Harries settled herself in the surgery's only chair. We three men remained standing, rubbing shoulders in those cramped confines.

"The first I knew anything about anything," said she eventually, "was Talbot hammering on the door to my room. This was around six o'clock in the morning. 'Matron Harries, come quick!' he cried. 'The lake. There's a boy what's in bad shape. He's been drowned, I think.'"

"That is Talbot the groundskeeper."

"Yes. He sounded quite frantic. I threw on a dressing gown and followed him out to the lake. There, sure enough, was a boy's body, lying on the bank. Talbot said he had come across it on his morning rounds. He'd seen something in the water, he told me, a pale shape. At first he thought it was a bundle of clothing. He had waded in to pull it out, and that was when he made the dreadful discovery. 'You must do something,' he said to me, gesturing at the body. 'Give him medicine or something. Bring him round.' Well, I could tell at a glance that no medicine, or any other treatment, was going to return vigour to that lifeless shell."

She put a hand to her mouth, her shoulders shaking. Then, the fit of emotion having run its course, she resumed her narrative.

"Looking at that pale little face, I recognised Hector Robinson," she said. "He lay on his back, limbs akimbo, and he was still – so still. Nevertheless I felt that if there was even the remotest chance of saving him, I must try. I asked Talbot to find something to elevate his legs. He took off his overcoat, rolled it up and laid it under the boy's feet. Then I knelt and began pumping Robinson's abdomen with both hands. I used to work in a hospital, in Canterbury, where I learned of this technique of resuscitation. It was developed by doctors in Amsterdam during the last century. They have plenty of drownings there, what with all those canals. If you can expel the water from the lungs, it is possible that the natural physiological processes will start up again and normal breathing may be restored."

"I've read about a German surgeon called Friedrich Maass who suggests that chest compression could be used as a method of resuscitation in cases of drowning," I said.

"Well, I was unaware of that. I did what I thought best, anyway."

"I meant no slight on your abilities, Matron. I was merely offering the benefit of my own medical expertise. I am sure you did your utmost."

"I did, sir, but it was all for nothing. I pumped at that poor thing's belly for a good five minutes, until at last I gave it up. It was making no difference. All that came out of his mouth was a little water, laced with threads of blood."

"Blood," said Holmes.

"Evidence of pulmonary oedema," I said. "Common in drownings. Excess fluid causes injury to the delicate air sacs in the lungs."

"I know that. I simply felt it was worth remarking upon. And 'a little water', you say, Mrs Harries. How much?"

"Perhaps no more than half a pint's worth," the matron said. "Is that significant?"

"I am not sure. It may be. Is there anything else you can tell me? You strike me as a highly observant woman. Were there any aspects to the body that you found odd or noteworthy? Were there, for instance, any bruises or lacerations visible?"

Mrs Harries pondered a moment. "None that I recall seeing."

"No signs of violence at all?"

"No. Ah, but wait. Yes, there was one thing. His fingernails."

"What about them?"

"Several of them were splintered," she said, "right down to the quick. A couple, indeed, had broken off altogether."

"How singular. Did you draw anyone's attention to this fact?"

"I did not. At the time, I was too upset; and since then, I have tried to put the whole event out of my mind. Can you imagine it, Mr Holmes? A thirteen-year-old's life snuffed out. And such an unhappy boy, too, at least here at the school. Friendless, cheerless, solitary. I tried to take him under my wing. I do that with the pupils who are having a hard time, and often it helps them. But Robinson – he was difficult to approach. I never quite got the measure of him, and he never warmed to me, so my efforts came to naught. All the same, to find him dead like that, his sopping pyjamas clinging to his limbs, his skin so cold and white… It might have been a consolation if he had known some joy during his brief span of years. Somehow it was worse, for he seemed to have known none."

"He was dressed in his pyjamas," said Holmes.

"Yes."

"So far, no one has mentioned that. Did you know, Wragge?"

"No," said Wragge. "I wasn't present when the body was pulled from the water, remember, and it has never occurred to me since to ask what he was wearing."

Holmes turned back to the Mrs Harries. "You said you saw no signs of violence on Robinson's body."

"Yes."

"But the fact that he was wearing pyjamas does mean you could not have seen all of his body."

"That is true," said Mrs Harries. "I unbuttoned his pyjama jacket before I started pumping his belly, however, and there were no bruises on his torso, I could swear to it. Likewise his face and hands."

"Chest, face and hands – those are the likeliest places where such marks of violence might be found," Holmes allowed.

"I noted only the broken fingernails, nothing else."

"What about Gormley? Does he know about the pyjamas?"

"It is conceivable that he does not. I had Talbot fetch a blanket to cover Robinson with, and the blanket remained in place until the police came with a wagon to take the body away. I don't suppose Mr Gormley thought to peek under it."

"That is interesting. Gormley was not in the least curious?"

"Would you be?"

"In my profession, I cannot afford *not* to be curious. Distasteful as it might have been, I would have looked."

"Well, Mr Gormley elected not to," said Mrs Harries, "and one cannot blame him for that. Besides, both Talbot and I told him that it was Hector Robinson and that the boy had drowned. He had no reason to doubt us."

"So he never checked for himself?"

"I stayed with the body right up until it was removed. It was the least I could do. Somebody had to keep watch over it and keep prying eyes away from it. At no time did Mr Gormley look beneath the blanket. He hardly went near, in point of fact."

"Is it material, Holmes," said Wragge, "whether or not Mr Gormley looked at the body?"

"Might he not have wanted to see young Robinson's face at least, to confirm what had happened? Rather than simply taking someone else's word for it?"

"I suppose so. Equally, he might have been squeamish, and if that is the case – well, as Mrs Harries says, who can blame him?"

"Are you implying what I think you're implying?" I said to Holmes.

"I don't know, Watson," came the reply. "What do you think I'm implying?"

I hesitated, but felt it must be said. "That Gormley might have already known both that it was Hector Robinson and that he had drowned, simply because he himself might have been the one responsible?"

Both Wragge and Mrs Harries let out a gasp.

"Not necessarily," said Holmes, making a patting gesture with both hands, as if to stop things from becoming heated. "I am merely raising a possibility, in a speculative spirit. However, since Watson has seen fit to drag this particular notion out into the open… Mr Wragge, Mrs Harries, can either of you tell me whether the headmaster was present at the school on the night in question?"

"Oh, he was," Mrs Harries stated. "I can vouch for that. Mr Gormley is wedded to Saltings House. He goes nowhere."

Wragge nodded. "In so far as I saw him that night, not long after lights out, making for his room, then he was here, yes."

"Very well. And tell me, what have the local police made of it all? They came to collect Robinson's body. They must have had questions."

"Very few," said Mrs Harries. "They seemed to take everything at face value. Mr Gormley spoke to a sergeant at some length. He expressed his belief that Robinson had drowned by accident. He was quite insistent on it, and the sergeant seemed convinced."

"I imagine the fellow concerned was the straightforward type, with a keen interest in making life easy for himself," said Holmes. "Many a regional police official is like that. Many a metropolitan one too, for that matter. A couple more questions, Mrs Harries, if I may, and then we shall leave you in peace. First of all, was there a bathing towel anywhere in sight? Lying near the lake, perhaps?"

"Not that I'm aware of."

"Much as I thought. And the body – what sort of condition was it in? I mean other than sodden. Was it clean? Dirty?"

"I do fancy it was quite clean. A strand or two of weed attached to it, that's all."

"Not mud-stained?"

"Not as I noticed."

"That is helpful to know. Thank you, my dear lady, for your time. I am sorry if this interrogation has caused you undue distress."

"You are kind, Mr Holmes. Handling that body is not an experience I would care to repeat, but I am recovered from it, more or less."

So she said, but her pained expression, and the suspicion of a tear in her eye, led me to wonder whether even someone as redoubtable as Matron Harries would ever truly recover from such an experience. I knew that, were I in her shoes, I might well be haunted by the memory of that dismal drowned youngster until my dying day.

Chapter Eight

THE SCENE OF THE CRIME

As we left Mrs Harries's surgery, I noted that Holmes's attitude had gone from brisk and business-like to pensive. Not only that but a familiar glint had entered his keen grey eyes. I understood, from this alteration in demeanour, that the case had suddenly become more complex and intriguing than he had first thought.

"Well?" I said. "Speak up, Holmes. This is no longer suicide, is it? Nor death by misadventure. Wragge's intuition is correct. Foul play is involved."

"Watson, I should have thought that self-evident. Of course Hector Robinson did not go willingly into the water. The broken fingernails attest to that. They clearly imply that some form of violence was used against him, and that he resisted."

"Yet there was no bruising visible on him, as far as Mrs Harries could see."

"Which, I admit, does not jibe with the notion that he was manhandled by an assailant or assailants. It is rare that rough treatment does not leave its mark upon the recipient. Yet one does not come by splintered and missing fingernails without good cause. As for the notion that it was all an accident... I put it to you that even if a person gets it into his head to go for a swim, he does not enter the water clothed. Either he changes into a bathing costume or, as is the practice among university dons and certain physical culture fraternities, he eschews raiment altogether. Not only that but he brings a bathing towel with which to dry himself off afterwards. And this is assuming he is the kind who relishes immersion in water in early December, when the temperature is nothing short of frigid. I was already finding it hard to accept that Robinson might have been that sort, having been told by you, Wragge, that his mother said he was a poor swimmer. It is impossible to countenance now, given what we have just learned about the condition of the body."

"So it would appear that Robinson was dragged from his bed, hauled downstairs struggling, and thrust into the lake," said Wragge. "And I'd wager good money that Pugh and Wyatt did it, the fiends." He clenched a fist. "Those arrogant bullies. I despise them and all they stand for. I've half a mind to seek out them right now and pummel a confession out of them. Hardly decent schoolmasterly behaviour, I realise, but what's the worst that could happen? My career is forfeit anyway, it would seem."

"Pray restrain your fiercer impulses for the time being, Mr Wragge," said Holmes. "Let us visit the lake instead, the scene of the crime."

We exited the building via the library, a large, oak-panelled room where I used to while many a spare hour reading, especially on those long Sunday afternoons that seemed to stretch out endlessly. A pair of glassed double doors gave onto the rear terrace, which overlooked the playing fields. These at present consisted of two rugby pitches, it being the winter term; in spring they would be reconfigured for hockey, while summer would see them amalgamated into a single cricket pitch. The lake lay beyond, and we crossed over to it, taking care where we trod because the going was treacherous. The passage of countless rugby boots had churned up the ground, leaving it a mass of torn-up divots and small muddy craters, like a battlefield in miniature. By now the sun was very low, touching the horizon, and the daylight was growing dim. It was not quite 4PM, and evening was coming on fast.

"That's new," I said to Wragge, pointing to a handsome brick sports pavilion that stood sentinel to the south of the playing fields.

"Nice, isn't it?" Wragge said.

"Beats that rickety clapboard shed we had."

"Bought with a donation by Lord Gilhampton, no less," said Wragge. "Hosea Wyatt's father. His lordship also paid for a full set of new sports equipment – balls, nets, wickets, batting pads, hockey sticks, the lot. Most generous of him. You can see why Mr Gormley turns a blind eye to his son's shortcomings."

"But the old boathouse is much as it was," I said, gesturing in the opposite direction towards said structure. Perched at the northernmost tip of the school grounds, it leaned out drunkenly on wooden pilings over one of the broader channels in the marshes. "Barely standing up. I'm surprised it hasn't been demolished and replaced too."

"It isn't in use any more. The school rowing dinghy rotted through and sank – nobody had gone out in it in years – and the decision was made not to get another. Unless Lord Gilhampton or someone of that ilk stumps up the money, the boathouse is probably just going to be left like that until it falls down of its own accord."

Arriving at the lake, Wragge and I stood back while Holmes proceeded to the water's edge. There, he crouched down on his haunches to take in the prospect. The lake was perhaps fifty yards in diameter at its widest, and its banks were fringed with brittle, winter-brown bulrushes. The breeze sent ripples across its murky surface like a host of tiny, writhing white serpents.

Abruptly, Holmes rolled up one sleeve and, bending forward, delved an arm into the water, all the way up to the elbow. He rummaged around on the lake bed a while, stirring up a cloud of silt, before withdrawing the arm and shaking off the weeds that had become entangled about his hand. He wiped a few thin smears of mud off on the grass. Then he put hand to mouth and sucked the tip of one finger. He smacked his lips, frowning as a wine connoisseur might when sampling a complex Burgundy.

Wragge shot me a curious look. "Did he just…?"

I responded with a nonchalant sigh. "That's nothing. I have seen him taste dirt granules. He also has a fondness for trace amounts of poisons." To Holmes I said, "What are your thoughts?"

"There are one or two anomalies here which I am hard put to reconcile," came the reply. "The most glaring is that, if Robinson was forced into the water and held under, he would surely have panicked. He would have thrashed and writhed, and in the process, weeds from the lake bed would have become wrapped around his limbs and mud would have adhered to him plentifully. Yet if Mrs Harries has furnished us with accurate testimony – and there is no reason to suppose that she has not – the body was clean. Scarcely any weed clinging to it, and precious few mud stains. Then there is the question of—"

He was interrupted by a loud, coarse voice that bellowed, "Hoy, you! Get away from there!"

The source of the injunction came lurching towards us across the playing fields: a scarecrow of a man with a ruddy face and a lumbering, effortful gait. He was making a beeline for us, shaking his fist.

It was God, and he was angry.

Chapter Nine

THE WRATH OF GOD

God Talbot, old when I was a boy, looked positively ancient now. His cheeks were gaunt and grey, and a mop of unruly white hair protruded out from under the brim of a battered brown felt hat. His sideburns were prominent and unkempt, as were the silvery whiskers that hung haggardly from his chin. The large bunch of keys attached to his belt by a ring jangled noisily at every step. I had always associated Talbot with the sound of those keys. There were dozens of them, one for every lock in the school, it seemed, and several to spare.

His limp was even more pronounced than it had been, I was sure. As ever, his right leg did most of the work, the left managing little more than a kind of tentative half-skip, so that his entire body had to go through a tortuous corkscrewing motion with every step. Yet I noted that his left foot barely touched down at all any more, and he winced slightly whenever it did.

From my vantage point as a trained medical practitioner, I was able to diagnose a malformed hip. The abnormality had doubtless occurred *in utero*, resulting in Talbot being born with one leg shorter than the other. Through relative lack of use, that leg would have become progressively weaker as he grew to manhood, and now in his dotage it could bear almost no weight at all. The hip itself was also, I thought, afflicted with arthritis, judging by the discomfort that walking evidently caused him.

Undiminished by age, however, was the groundskeeper's irascibility. As he approached, he subjected Holmes to a blistering, fist-shaking tirade. Who was he? What was he doing there? What business had he dipping an arm into the lake? Did he not know what had happened here lately?

It wasn't until he came closer that his temper abated somewhat. "Oh, Mr Wragge," said he in marginally softer tones. "I didn't see you there. My focus was on this fellow, and I wasn't minding much else."

"Yes, both of these gentlemen are with me, Talbot," Wragge said.

"Ah, so *you* are Talbot," said Holmes.

"That's me," said the other. "What of it?"

Holmes introduced himself. "I have been granted permission by your headmaster to enquire into the matter of young Hector Robinson's death. Mr Wragge will confirm it."

"Indeed I can, Talbot," said Wragge. "Everything here is above board."

"Well, that's as may be," Talbot said to Holmes, regaining some of his previous ire, "but I can't have you loitering beside the lake. That there water's dangerous. It's claimed a boy's life, and I won't have it claiming anyone else's. I've been a-yelling at any lad what I sees going near it, telling 'em to clear off. Suppose one of 'em happens to look out of a window now and spies you, shirtsleeve all pulled up, like as you're meaning to strip off and dive in. He might get the notion it's all right for him to have a try too, and if there's no one else around, no one what could rescue him, who's to say he mightn't get 'isself into trouble and wind up drownded just like Robinson was."

"Your solicitude is perfectly understandable, Mr Talbot."

"My solici-whatnot is none of your business, mister," Talbot retorted.

"All I mean is that, as the one who had the misfortune to discover Robinson's body, you are naturally sensitive on this subject and have no wish to see the incident repeated."

"Aye, well, that is true enough."

"You found the body first thing in the morning, is that so?"

"I did. And?"

"And are you commonly up and about so early in the day?"

"Every day, sir." Talbot tilted his head, scratching one of his voluminous sideburns. "What do you mean by all these questions?"

"I am simply seeking enlightenment, my good man. You are under no compunction to answer me, but I would regard it as a great courtesy if you did. It was still dark at that hour, I should imagine."

"Sun weren't up yet but there was a chink of light to the east. I'm an early riser, and I like to be about my business as soon as I can."

"There's a lot to be done, I should suppose," said Holmes. "No end of toil. The school grounds are extensive, and their maintenance, as your sole responsibility, places great demands upon your time."

"Now, there's no arguing with that."

"I have often thought that one may judge a man's level of obligation to others by the number of keys he has upon his person. Someone with as many as you have plainly must find his services in great demand."

Holmes's mixture of cajoling and calm dominance, not to mention his judicious use of blandishment, was working wonders on Talbot. The groundskeeper appeared to some degree placated, although he remained discernibly wary nonetheless. I thought of a lion, gradually acceding to the lion tamer's will, yet still unpredictable and apt to lash out.

"Nobody does more around Saltings House than me," he asserted. "All year round, I'm hard at it."

"You have a profound sense of duty," Holmes said. "Hence, having pulled the body out of the water, you went directly to fetch Mrs Harries."

"Seemed like the right thing to do. If anybody could have helped, it was Matron. Alas, she could not. But you can't say we didn't try, sir, either of us. Try to make things right."

Talbot choked back a sob and thumbed one of his rheumy eyes, and all at once he looked frail and every inch the elderly cripple. I found myself feeling a pang of compassion for him, something my much younger self, who had routinely regarded him with awe-filled terror, would have found almost incomprehensible.

"This is a freshwater lake, is it not?" said Holmes.

"That it is."

"I'm surprised. I would have assumed it was saltwater."

"Then you'd be wrong, sir."

"But the marshes lie over yonder, not two hundred yards away, and are sluiced by seawater. Are you saying the lake isn't an offshoot of them?"

The aged rustic looked sly, pleased to have knowledge that the gentleman from London did not. "The lake is fed by an underground stream. The school gets its drinking water from the same source. Nothing salty about it."

I could have told Holmes this myself, had he asked, and so could have Wragge. More to the point, I was sure Holmes had already worked it out from tasting the lake water.

"Well, at any rate, that is all I need from you, Mr Talbot," Holmes said. "You are a busy fellow, and I shan't detain you a moment longer."

"Just steer clear of the lake," Talbot said, with some of his former surliness. "I've delivered my warning."

"And I shall heed it," said Holmes.

"Then I'll be on my way." Talbot touched a finger to forehead. "Good morning to you, Mr Wragge. To both you gents too."

With that, he turned and shambled away from us, at a considerably less vigorous rate than he had come, but those keys of his still jangling, ever jangling.

Chapter Ten

BRAWL IN THE DINING HALL

"**W**hat a charming sort," Holmes said when Talbot was out of earshot. "The Kentish son of the soil in all his glory. You caught the strong whiff of alcohol emanating from him, did you not? No? Neither of you? Well, I was much closer to him, and it was quite pungent. But then you yourself, Wragge, said that Talbot was 'fond of a drink'. The broken capillaries on his nose and in the whites of his eyes are further testament to that. Quick-tempered and a dipsomaniac – not a happy combination, I would say. And usually a recipe for an abbreviated life, although not in this instance. Does it not seem to you that he is a man with something to hide?"

"You mean his alcoholism?" Wragge said. "That is hardly a secret. Everyone from the headmaster down knows about it. The feeling is that as long as it doesn't hinder him from doing his job, there is no reason for him not to remain employed."

"Principally I mean his use of the phrase 'try to make things right'. It is as though he personally had something to atone for."

"Or," I countered, "he could simply have been expressing his wish that the boy should be brought back to life. That would be making things right, wouldn't it?"

"I am reading too much into it, am I?"

"It is open to such an interpretation. Talbot's vernacular English lacks a certain finesse."

"That it does. 'Who's to say he mightn't get 'isself into trouble and wind up drownded.'" Holmes's mimicry of Talbot's rural burr was pitch perfect. He even lifted his left foot just off the ground and twisted his torso slightly, to make the imitation complete. He was not mocking the fellow as such, merely demonstrating his remarkable facility for impersonating others. "Now then," he said, reverting to his normal self, "time is getting on, and I can't speak for either of you, but having had just a sandwich to eat since breakfast, I am famished. Sometimes an empty stomach refines the brain and sometimes it stultifies it. This is one of the latter occasions. Wragge, what time is supper?"

Wragge consulted his fob watch. "In about an hour. We eat early."

"And the fare at the school dining hall is acceptable?"

"If you call a step above inedible acceptable."

"A step above inedible may not be acceptable but it is tolerable."

We made our way back across the playing fields, Holmes buttoning up his shirtcuff as we went, and re-entered the school. It was a relief to be indoors again. The northerly wind carried something of a Scandinavian chill, insinuating itself through one's layers of clothing into one's bones, and with the sun gone, there was not even its weak rays as mitigation.

We whiled the time in the library, until at last a bell clanged, whereupon we made our way towards the dining hall, which lay in the west wing. Around us, the entire building had begun thrumming with bustle and activity. Desk lids slammed shut, chairs scraped back, doors were flung open, and footsteps thundered. Then, all at once, the corridor we were in became a torrent of moving bodies and raised voices. Boys surrounded us, all dressed alike in knickerbockers, knee-high woollen stockings and dark blue blazers with the school crest embroidered on the breast pocket. They streamed buffetingly by, some of them shoving past us as though we were not people but mere obstacles. The insolence and lack of decorum were startling. Even when Wragge called for everyone to slow down and show some respect, his plaintive demands went unheeded. Mealtimes and hungry boys were always a recipe for chaos, it must be said, but this stampede far exceeded the usual.

To me, it was yet more proof that the pupils at Saltings House were out of control. In their state of extreme perturbation and unease, they were surrendering to their baser instincts, turning feral. Outright anarchy seemed not far off.

The well-lit dining hall was thronged with hungry, jostling boys by the time we arrived there. Kitchen staff were ferrying dishes of soup to the tables and seeing them snatched out of their hands before they could even lay them down. The clamour echoed to the rafters. At the high table, reserved for teachers, a handful of adults sat hunched in misery. It would appear they had long ago abandoned any effort to maintain order and were just trying to get through the half-hour as best they could. If none of them were able to control a single classroom's worth of pupils, what hope had they, even in numbers, of managing the entire school complement?

Holmes, Wragge and I joined them, and soon we were tucking into soup ourselves. It was a dun-coloured, beefy concoction which might have been oxtail and might equally have been Brown Windsor, but either way managed to be glutinous and at the same time insipid. Wragge offered to introduce us to his colleagues, but the racket being set up by the boys made this, and indeed normal conversation, nigh on impossible. I noticed that Mr Gormley had not graced the dining hall with his presence. I could only infer that he found it shameful to be amid so much chaos and yet powerless to avert it; and when I suggested as much to Wragge, he confirmed it. Gormley, he said, had not attended a meal for the past three days.

"He takes his food alone in his study. It's obvious he can't abide the noise and what it signifies."

Then a fight broke out.

All at once the tenor of the hubbub changed, going from rambunctious to savage. In a corner of the room, three of the senior boys were on their feet, engaged in a scuffle. Two of them were belabouring the third. He in return was giving a fairly good account of himself, doling out as many blows as he received. He even elicited a sharp yelp of pain from one of his assailants by means of a kick to the knee. Generally, however, because they were two and he one, he was coming off worse. The rest of the boys looked on in glee, some jeering, some cheering.

Wragge leapt to his feet. "That's Pugh and Wyatt. Those ruffians. Picking on someone else now, eh? Well, we shall soon see about *that*."

I seized him by the arm to waylay him. "Wragge, don't. You are not reasonable when it comes to that pair. You may end up doing something you regret."

"Kindly remove your hand, Watson. This is my business."

"I cannot, in all conscience."

"You don't know Pugh and Wyatt. Someone could be seriously hurt."

"Well, allow me to handle the matter instead. Or another adult. Just not you."

Wragge tried to pull away. I held grimly on. I don't know what the outcome of our tussle might have been, but I did not have to find out, for at that moment another schoolmaster sprang from his seat at the top table and went to intercede.

This fellow was a brawny, barrel-chested giant who swept across the room with his gown billowing behind him like the sails of a galleon in a strong following wind. His sights were set firmly on the brawling trio.

"Yeowell," Wragge said, lip curling.

"The games master?"

"None other."

"Well, the size of him, he should be able to handle things, shouldn't he?"

"He should, but it's Yeowell. That boy, the one fending off Pugh and Wyatt? That's Vernon Agius. Yeowell hates him."

"Nevertheless, he will deal with the three of them even-handedly, surely." I did not add that the same might not have been said for Wragge.

"I wouldn't be so certain."

Yeowell grabbed the boy called Vernon Agius by the collar and wrested him away from the clutches of the other two. Notwithstanding Wragge's assertion, I anticipated that the games master would shield the lad from Pugh and Wyatt, favouring him because he was outnumbered, and perhaps castigate his opponents into the bargain.

Not so. Instead, Yeowell began to slap Agius. "You wretched creature!" he berated the boy. "This is typical. Causing trouble wherever you go. Well, I've had enough of it. Enough, d'you hear? Arrogant pups like you need taking down a peg or two."

Pugh and Wyatt nudged each other in the ribs, delighted at the turn of events. Yeowell, meanwhile, kept up the onslaught of open-handed blows, eliciting louder and louder yelps of pain and protest from his victim, until I myself was ready to step in. What I was seeing was not an act of pardonable, necessary corrective; it was a vindictive attack, nothing short of sadistic.

Holmes seemed to feel the same way as I. He, however, was quicker off the mark. Bounding away from the table, he darted over in a few swift strides towards the affray.

Relinquishing my hold on Wragge, I fixed him with a wry look. "Watch this," I said. "You'll enjoy it."

Chapter Eleven

A PURVEYOR OF
DUNDERHEADED INANITIES

Baritsu was a Japanese form of wrestling. As practised by Sherlock Holmes, however, it often seemed more like a dance, with my friend leading and his "partner" following, albeit unwillingly.

So it was in this instance, as Holmes set upon Yeowell, employing the techniques of that martial art. First, he caught hold of the hand with which the games master was hitting Agius, arresting its progress in mid-air. At the same time, he slipped a leg around the man's ankle. Then he twisted the hand round, turning the fingers back inward upon the wrist.

All of this took place in less than a second, too swiftly for Yeowell to react. Now the games master was helplessly in Holmes's power, even if he did not realise it yet. He let go of Agius and started clawing at my friend's fingers with his free hand, trying to unpick their grasp. Holmes merely twisted the other hand further round. Yeowell had no choice but to bend

over backwards in an effort to alleviate the pressure on his wrist.
At this point, Holmes hooked his leg out from under him, and
Yeowell, already off-balance, crashed to the floor.

At that, a stunned silence fell over the dining hall. The
assembled pupils looked on, agog. Sights such as their fellow
pupils fighting or a schoolmaster walloping a boy were evidently
nothing new to them. To see an adult stranger grapple with a
schoolmaster, however, was a novelty. It was even more of one to
see that schoolmaster incapacitated and humiliated, and so easily,
too. They did not know what to make of it.

Yeowell lay supine, writhing and gasping. Every time he tried
to rise, Holmes bent the hand back harder and, commensurately,
increased the amount of pain he was inflicting. Under restraint,
belly up like a submissive dog, the games master had no choice
but to beg to be released.

"Not until you promise me you will never again mistreat a
pupil so viciously," Holmes said.

"How dare you make such demands!" panted an obstinate
Yeowell. "Anyway, the boy has had it coming for a while."

Holmes pushed the man's hand so far back, the wrist was in
imminent danger of snapping. Yeowell shrieked in an altogether
unmanly fashion.

"All right, all right," he relented. "You have my word."

"Good," said Holmes. "And I shall hold you to it. Believe me
when I say that I am someone who has made it his life's work to
monitor and curtail the activities of miscreants. In that category
I include you. Should I learn that you have broken your vow, I
shall seek you out and break your wrist. Nor will it stop there.

I shall dislocate the elbow and perhaps the shoulder too. Do I make myself clear?"

"Yes. Yes, quite clear."

"Very well."

Holmes released Yeowell's hand. The games master clambered awkwardly to his feet, using his other hand to help himself up off the floor.

"Who the devil are you, anyway?" Yeowell demanded, red-faced both from exertion and chagrin. He had suffered a severe wrist sprain, to judge by the way he was now favouring the hand Holmes had been gripping, and the injury would be a source of discomfort for, I reckoned, a fair few days to come. "You aren't any school parent I recognise."

"All you need know about me is that I am well-connected and have eyes everywhere."

Yeowell glared at my friend, as if trying to gauge how much truth there was to this statement. Nothing in Holmes's stern, implacable expression suggested grounds for doubt.

Rounding on Agius, Yeowell said, "And as for you. You had better watch your step, my boy, that's all I can say."

"I am not scared of you," Agius retorted. Welts were already forming on his face, and blood trickled from one nostril; yet, despite the drubbing he had just taken from both Yeowell and his two peers, he seemed unbowed. This, I thought, was a lad of strong character.

"Address me as 'sir' when you're speaking to me."

"I am not scared of you, *sir*," Agius said, with just a trace of a smirk. "I have been struck by better men than you, and with far greater force. Actually, *sir*, were you hitting me at all, or was it actually a butterfly brushing me with its wings?"

Yeowell's eyes bulged, his jaw jutted, and he looked set to resume his assault on Agius. A soft, reproving cough from Holmes brought him to his senses. Growling, the games master turned on his heel and strode out of the dining hall.

Whereupon, like the release of a pent-up breath, incredulous laughter burst out among the boys. There was a note of derision to the sound, too, and it was clear to me that Yeowell was not at all popular and that, in the boys' view, his comeuppance had been long overdue.

The main course arrived, and with it some semblance of calm to the proceedings. Holmes engaged privately in conversation with Agius for a minute or so, before returning to the high table where we were presented with a lamb and kidney suet pudding of a particularly doughy consistency, accompanied by potatoes and cauliflower so soggy that they disintegrated at the touch of a fork.

"Well done on defusing the situation, Holmes," I said. "What were you saying to young Agius just now? You were questioning him, I assume."

"I asked him about his antagonists, all three of them. That and the reasons for their hostility towards him, and vice versa. In the event, Agius was hardly forthcoming. He did not vouchsafe much beyond telling me that he heard Pugh and Wyatt refer to the late Hector Robinson in a very insulting manner, and he threatened to, in his words, 'give them a good duffing-up' if they did not recant."

"After which Pugh and Wyatt no doubt invited him to suit deed to word," said Wragge, "and he rose to the challenge."

"That would be a correct interpretation of events."

"It certainly sounds like Agius. I have a lot of time for the lad, myself, and what has just occurred serves only to reinforce my impression. He will always stand up for what's right and is ready to defend the weak, even at cost to himself. His home life is troubled, so I understand, but we see none of that here. We see only a bright, able child who, were there any justice in this world, would be Head Boy rather than Jeremy Pugh, in so far as he sets a good moral example to the others."

"In that case, why does Yeowell dislike him so?" I said.

Before Wragge could answer, Holmes invited us, with a gesture, to draw our heads closer together. Through this precaution we might continue our discussion without being overheard by anyone else at the high table.

"There is a simple enough explanation for that," said Wragge. "Agius has had several run-ins with Yeowell. Our games master drives the boys hard on the playing field. He is known to compel the more reluctant participant with fist and boot, and his cruelty towards those not gifted in sports is boundless. The weaker and more maladroit you are, the greater the demands Yeowell places on you. Where the average boy might be required to do ten press-ups or jumping jacks, he will make the physically incompetent boy do twice as many."

"All part of some sort of tempering process, I imagine," said Holmes. "Hardening children in the furnace of exercise."

"Yes, yes, that is very much Yeowell's philosophy. 'The only cure for a puny physique is hard work and pain.' That's one of his maxims. Another is: 'Suffering is the stepping stone to glory.' He trots out these phrases during games practice as though they were epigrams by Martial, rather than the dunderheaded inanities they are. He has only been here one term, but already he is universally loathed, by boys and teachers alike. Mr Gormley, perhaps predictably, is the exception. He admires Yeowell's disciplinarian attitude, which exceeds even his own."

"And Agius has chafed against that, has he?" I said.

"The two of them, Yeowell and Agius, have repeatedly butted heads, to the latter's cost. Only last week he, along with Hector Robinson, earned Yeowell's particular enmity. It so happens that the rugby First Fifteen, of which Agius is a member, were having a practice match against the Second Fifteen. The Second Fifteen consists, essentially, of those senior boys lacking sufficient fitness and skill at the game to make the First team. They're a motley, shambolic lot. Hardly even a team, more a set of punching bags for their more adept peers. So it was that Hector Robinson found himself on the pitch, as scrum half for the Second Fifteen. Not a boy, we have established, who excelled at anything much, and rugby was yet another of his fields of inadequacy."

"The scrum half serves a pivotal role," I said. "He provides a crucial link between the forwards and the backs."

"There speaks the ardent rugby enthusiast," said Holmes.

"I remember you yourself being a fiendishly good Number Eight, Watson," said Wragge. "Do you still play?"

"Now and then. I'm a lot slower these days, though, and my knees aren't what they were."

"Age comes to us all," said Wragge. "At any rate, I happened to be present for the practice match, on the sidelines, serving as a touch judge. Yeowell was refereeing. It was an unusually bruising ordeal for the Seconds. Added to that, it rained hard all day and the pitch had become a quagmire. At one point, Robinson fumbled the ball as it emerged from a ruck and got overrun by practically the entire First Fifteen scrum. He was trampled underfoot and left face down in the mud, dazed. Agius, instead of following his teammates to the try line, went back to check on him and helped him to his feet."

"Decent of him," I said.

"And, to Yeowell, an unforgivable sin. He blew his whistle to halt the game and subjected both boys to a severe tongue-lashing. Agius objected, saying that he feared Robinson had been badly hurt and there was nothing wrong in showing concern for a fellow human being. At this, as you can imagine, Yeowell fairly exploded. I'm told they could hear the bellowing all the way over in the Common Room. He ordered the other boys on the pitch to go indoors and get washed and changed. I went with them. He then made Robinson and Agius run laps of the playing fields."

"That doesn't sound too bad."

"Maybe not, but he kept them at it until both were beyond exhausted and scarcely able to continue. All of this took place in the pouring rain, remember, so they had the cold and wet to contend with as well as fatigue. I happened to glance out of a window – this was perhaps an hour after I went inside – and was astonished to see them still going. Robinson could hardly put one foot in front of the other, and Agius seemed on his last legs too. I was about to head outside and protest, but even as I watched, Yeowell finally called a halt to the proceedings. I opened a door to usher the boys inside, and as I did so I heard him warn them that he was far from done with them. Any further infringement of the rules would be met with similar, and harsher, treatment. 'It's for your own good,' Yeowell said. 'Yours especially, Robinson. You disgust me. You're such an insipid weakling, limp as a lettuce leaf. I intend to toughen you up and make a man out of you even if it kills me – or, come to that, kills you.'"

"Good heavens. Really?"

"His exact words."

"And allow me to postulate the sequel," said Holmes. "Not long afterwards, Robinson was found dead."

Wragge nodded. "Not long at all. The very next morning, in fact."

"Well I never," I declared. "It sets me to wondering, what if Pugh and Wyatt are not the guilty parties after all? What if it is the contemptible Yeowell who drowned Robinson?"

"First you suggested it might be Mr Gormley," said Wragge. "Now Yeowell. Schoolmasters killing pupils – it's unthinkable, isn't it?"

"Unthinkable but not impossible," said I. "Eh, Holmes? Just suppose Yeowell decided to make good on his threat. He wished to 'toughen up' Robinson, and what better way of doing that, for a man with such extreme views on physical culture, than forcing the lad to undertake an early-morning swim in a freezing lake?

Given how he pushed Robinson and Agius to the limit during their laps around the playing fields, it would not surprise me if he did the same as Robinson swam. He made the lad keep going until he could not manage another stroke. He even obliged him to do it in his pyjamas, which would have become waterlogged and weighed him down, making things even more difficult for someone who was already a poor swimmer. The perhaps inevitable outcome was that Robinson went under and drowned, and Yeowell either was unable to, or chose not to, save him. Instead, in fright, he fled the scene."

"It is a plausible scenario, Watson," Holmes said, "and my thoughts have turned in that direction too. Wragge, where might we find Yeowell now?"

"Wouldn't he have gone to the matron's surgery, to have his wrist seen to?" I said.

"Not likely, knowing Yeowell," said Wragge. "That would be an admission of frailty. No, I suspect he will be in the Common Room, administering treatment to himself in the form of alcohol."

"Then that," said Holmes, "is where we must repair to."

Helpings of spotted dick, enveloped in a sludge of custard, had just been laid in front of us. It was no great hardship to abandon this last course of a generally unappetising meal, of which I had eaten very little. We quit the din of the dining hall and made for the Common Room.

Chapter Twelve

HALLOWED GROUND

Yeowell was alone when we entered.

"You again," he snapped. His gaze had gone straight to Holmes. "What do you want now?" He was posturing, trying to seem aggressive, but there was panic in his eyes. Doubtless he was wondering if my friend had come to dispense more of the same treatment he had dished out in the dining hall.

As for me, I was finding it a somewhat bewildering experience to be in the Common Room. The place had been strictly off-limits to us boys, a secret realm for schoolmasters only, of which we caught occasional brief glimpses through the door as it opened and closed. The teachers gathered there to mark work, to smoke and drink, and no doubt to compare notes on pupils. Now, twenty years on, I was able to tread this hallowed ground with impunity, no longer forbidden. For all that, it still felt like trespassing.

"I simply wish to talk this time, Mr Yeowell," Holmes said. "I have no desire to lay you low again. Not unless I have to."

Yeowell pulled on a cigarette, hand unsteady. A large glass of whisky sat on the side table next to him. Wragge had been right on that front.

"Talk?" the games master said. "About what?"

"You and Hector Robinson. To be precise, your possible involvement in his demise."

"My…? Robinson? Demise?" Yeowell spluttered. "What earthly reason are you asking me about that for? What gives you the right?"

"We have not been formally introduced, have we? I am Sherlock Holmes, and I have a mandate from your headmaster to investigate the boy's tragic death. That means I may discuss it with whomever I choose, in whatever manner I choose."

"You are accusing me of killing Robinson."

"Am I? I simply mentioned your possible involvement in his demise. I said nothing about killing."

"But that is the implication."

"To your ears, maybe. I gather you were not fond of him."

"Robinson? No one at Saltings House was particularly keen on the boy. Ask Wragge there. He'll tell you the same."

"But the afternoon before Robinson died, you punished him and Vernon Agius for what you regarded as an infraction on the rugby pitch. You made them run innumerable laps of the playing fields."

"In the rain, moreover," Wragge chimed in. "They were soaked through when they came in. In fact, Agius's rugby kit was still damp the following day. I found it hanging over the end of his bed, still not dry, when I went to the dormitory to gather up

Robinson's things, shortly after the body was found. Agius was one of the dozen boys Robinson shared a dormitory with. I made him take the kit to the laundry."

"So they got wet," said Yeowell. "What of it?"

"They could have caught their death of cold."

"Bosh! Rain or not, there's no law against penalising pupils when they err."

"None whatsoever," said Holmes. "But did it stop at that, Mr Yeowell? Or did you, before dawn the next day, fetch Robinson from his bed and make him go swimming in the lake in his pyjamas?"

"No," said the other, adamantly. "I most certainly did not. Why would I do such a thing?"

"Because you are a thug and a bully," Wragge said. "Because you derive a perverse satisfaction from subjecting defenceless youngsters to barbaric abuse."

"Don't you speak to me like that!" Yeowell retorted.

"I should have spoken to you like that long before, but have been hindered by my own pusillanimity."

"Your own what?"

"It's a long word, I realise. Too long for a games master's brain to cope with."

"Oh, you vile, condescending little pipsqueak," snarled Yeowell. "How very like you it is, to find your courage at last but only when you know it is safe to do so. I invite you, Wragge, to insult me some time when this Mr Shirley Holmes is not around and you don't have his skirts to hide behind."

"It is *Sherlock* Holmes," said Holmes, "and I would be grateful if you would focus upon my line of questioning, Yeowell, rather than indulging in base intimidation tactics. You are quite firm in your contention that you did not force Hector Robinson to swim in the lake?"

"Absolutely. I'd be willing to swear to it on a Bible. For your information," Yeowell added, "I was not even at the school on the night in question."

"You are not resident on the premises, then?"

"Oh, yes, usually I am. My room is a couple of doors down from Wragge's. Isn't it, Wragge?"

Wragge nodded.

"That evening, however," Yeowell continued, "I went to the pub in Trothe. That's the village nearest here, about two miles down the road. I'd had enough of the school and felt like a change of scene. The business with Agius and Robinson had put me in a foul mood. Do you think I enjoyed giving up an hour of my time just to teach those two a lesson? I took no delight in it at all. But anyway, as I said, I went to the pub – The Gurnard Inn – and spent an hour or so there drowning my sorrows. No pun intended."

"What time did you return?" Holmes asked.

"Ah, well, that's just it, you see." There was a hint of triumph in Yeowell's voice. "I didn't. Not until the following morning. I tried heading back to the school shortly before closing time, only to find that the road between Trothe and here had flooded. It's not even a road really, more a track atop a causeway that runs through the marshes, and the combination of heavy rainfall and high tide meant that water had come spilling over the top. I couldn't make it safely across – only patches of the road surface were visible – so I turned around and went back. I took a room for the night at The Gurnard, and sallied forth the next morning, bright and early. The tide had receded and the road was passable. I was at Saltings House in good time for breakfast. No one was even aware I had gone."

"I, for one, wasn't," said Wragge.

"There you go. Wragge had no idea where I'd spent the night. Nobody did. But you can go ahead and ask at The Gurnard, Mr Holmes. You can ask Quimp, the landlord – I was there all night. You can ask his wife, too. She was up when I rose and waved me off as I left. She'll tell you."

"You say you got back here 'in good time for breakfast'," said Holmes. "At what hour precisely?"

"I can't say, precisely, but the sun was up."

"Ah." My friend looked pensive. "Talbot tells us he discovered Robinson's body just as the sun was rising."

"Well, then, there you have it." Yeowell stubbed out his cigarette in the ashtray triumphantly. "Clearly I wasn't at the school when Robinson perished. Therefore I cannot have been responsible. Seems cut and dried to me. Does it not to you?"

Holmes tapped forefinger against lips, musing. Presently he said, "Cut and dried indeed. I am sorry to have bothered you, Mr Yeowell."

We left the games master lighting a fresh cigarette. With just the one fully functioning hand, he had to strike the match by holding it in his fist and flicking his thumb across the head, then lifting the flame to the cigarette in his mouth. As he shook out the match, he looked disgruntled but also somewhat pleased with himself, and I felt he had the right to be both. He had been falsely accused of a heinous crime and had supplied an alibi that convincingly exonerated him.

"So we are back to thinking it must have been Pugh and Wyatt, are we?" I said to Holmes as Wragge pulled the Common Room door shut behind us. "Or was it perhaps Gormley?"

"We are not thinking, with surety, that any of them is the guilty party," Holmes replied. "We are not thinking, with surety, *anything*. Much remains to be unearthed about this affair, and much remains to be pieced together – the presence of blood in Robinson's lungs, for example, along with comparatively little water. But I must confess, I am beginning to flag. I didn't sleep at all last night, and it is catching up with me." As if in illustration, he gave vent to an extravagant yawn. "Wragge, the pub Yeowell spoke of, The Gurnard Inn – is it congenial?"

"I have been there once or twice. It's small but well appointed."

"What about the lodgings therein?"

"Much the same, I would imagine. I've not had to use them myself."

"And you know the way to Trothe, Watson, I assume?"

"I believe so."

"Then that is where you and I shall go," said Holmes. "Wragge, we will return in the morning. Until then, try not to upset Yeowell any further."

"Have no fear on that front," said Wragge, with feeling. "I shall be giving Mr Yeowell a very wide berth from now on."

Chapter Thirteen

A NIGHT AT THE GURNARD INN

The causeway meandered through the marshes, a narrow earthwork built in bygone times, its rutted summit rising just a foot or so above sea level. On either side, reeds rustled in the night breezes, and from a distance there came the distinctive rising cry of a curlew, and now and then the harsh croak of a corncrake. We had borrowed a dark-lantern from the school, and I held it before me to light our way. Holmes, at my side, was in a silent, ruminative mood that I knew better than to intrude upon.

The Gurnard Inn formed the centrepiece of the tiny hamlet – a score of mean little dwellings – that was Trothe. Perched atop a rise in the landscape, effectively an island, Trothe had long been a tight-knit, self-contained fishing community. Outside each house, nets hung between poles to dry, alongside scraps of laundry, while boats tethered to mooring posts lined the wayward channel nearby that led to the open sea. The tide was out, so these small, black-painted vessels currently rested on the mud, canted at an angle in the moonlight, like sleepers waiting to be awoken.

Quimp, landlord of The Gurnard, was tall, spare and taciturn, and sported a beard so magisterially long and white he looked like a wizard in a storybook. His wife, by contrast, was a short, plump, rosy-cheeked creature who chortled at everything and nothing. They had two rooms to let, which Holmes and I took. Each was tucked up under the eaves, the ceiling so low that one could barely stand upright, with enough floorspace for a bed and not much else.

I found myself wondering what Mary would have made of the accommodation. Doubtless she would have called it cosy or quaint, and would have set about neatening it and prettifying it with little womanly touches. My wife was always one for making the best of things. I imagined her now, at home. Before I left that morning she had told me she was set to begin decorating the house for Christmas, and I pictured her now doing just that, perhaps with the maid's help. Up went the paper chains, and the wreaths of ivy around the fireplace, and the mistletoe in the hall, and the baubles on the tree. How I missed her, even after just a few hours' absence. I hoped that Holmes and I would be returning to London soon.

When I went back downstairs, I found Holmes ensconced in one of the snugs, in prime position close by the roaring hearth, with a pint of ale before him. At present there were only a couple of other patrons on the premises. I purchased a drink for myself from the landlord Quimp and joined my friend.

Holmes was in conversation with Mrs Quimp, who stood by

the table. As I sat down beside him, I heard her tell him about the causeway flooding.

"It happens from time to time round these parts," said she. "A spring tide and excessive rain – it's a terrible combination."

"And the causeway becomes completely impassable?"

"That it does, sir. It's the only road in and out of Trothe, and when it's flooded, the village can be cut off from the rest of the world for anything up to twelve hours. We're used to it and don't think much of it."

"One of the pitfalls of living cheek by jowl with tidal marshland, eh?"

"Indeed so, sir. Mr Yeowell, though – he was rather agitated by it all, he was."

"So Yeowell did stay here on the night of the flood, then?" I said.

"Oh aye," said Mrs Quimp. "Your friend was just asking about that before you came down, sir, and I was just telling him that yes, schoolmaster Yeowell was indeed our guest that night. In a right state he was, too, when he found out he couldn't get back to Saltings House. Very frustrated. He even asked if anyone might be able to take him there by boat, but nobody would. When the marshes flood, it's difficult to know where the channels are, see, and you could ground your keel on a mud bank and be stranded. Also, on an overcast night like that one was, there en't nearly enough light to navigate by. The rain were still bucketing down, too, making matters worse. So Mr Yeowell had no choice but to take advantage of our hospitality."

"And he left promptly in the morning, I gather," said Holmes.

"Oh yes. He was gone before dawn. I heard him get up – the floorboards in this building creak something terrible, you gents will need to be mindful of that – and rose myself to see him off. That's dedication to your job, en't it? I don't mean me. Him. Eager to be back at work, eddicating them littl'uns." The woman chuckled to herself. "So eager, he all but ran as he left, and he wouldn't have paid up for the room, neither, if I hadn't called him back and reminded him what he owed us."

"I'm sure you've told my friend this already, Mrs Quimp," I said, "but it was quite definitely the same night that there was the tragedy at the school?"

"The poor lad who died? Yes, sir, the very same. What a thing. It's been the talk of the village. And that's something, since we don't much care to discuss drownings around these here parts." She lowered her voice to near inaudibility for the word "drownings".

"I presume that's a tradition amongst fisherfolk."

Mrs Quimp's cheery manner darkened. "Yes. A superstition, you might say. Don't mention it and it won't happen to you. But we're chary of it even more so in the Saltings area, on account of the witches. You know about the witches, I suppose?"

From our nods, she had her answer.

"It may have been a long time ago," said she, "but legends linger. Old Sarah's bones rest uneasy in the marsh, and her curse hangs heavy over us still. All of us. Everyone remembers William Chapman the witch-finder, and Admiral Hatherthwaite, and the privateer, Markby, and what became of them three. Chapman met his end not half a mile from this spot, and it were Trothe fishermen who pulled his wife and sons out of the water to safety. What's less well remembered is the villagers who've also drowned." Again, she dropped her voice to a whisper for the last word. "*Their* names don't get recorded by history. Nobody considers *them* when it comes to Old Sarah's curse. But every generation at Trothe, we lose at least one of our number to the sea, and the same holds for all the other villages along this part of the coast."

"It is an occupational hazard among fishermen, surely," I said. "The sea is a notoriously cruel mistress."

"Quite so, sir. Still, for us in Saltings the curse is real. And now it has returned to its very point of origin and taken that little boy's life. It's a blight on the region. Always has been and always will be." All at once, Mrs Quimp brightened. Her innate joviality could not be suppressed for long, it seemed. "Well anyway, that's quite enough of that," she said, rubbing her hands briskly together. "Another pint, either of you? And would you be thinking about supper too? We have some excellent lemon sole. Caught hereabouts, of course, just today."

I was about to mention that we had already eaten, but then recalled the deficiency of the school meal and how little of it I had actually consumed.

"As a matter of fact, some lemon sole would be lovely," said I. "Holmes?"

My companion nodded assent, and presently we were tucking into some marvellously fresh and delicate fish, a perfect antidote to the bland stodge that had been served to us at Saltings House.

Over the next hour, various of the locals traipsed into The Gurnard, and Holmes and I enjoyed a companionable evening in their company. They regaled us with fisherfolk stories which, characteristically for that breed of men, vied to be the most outlandish and exaggerated. The catch that was larger than any catch there had ever been, the weight of it reducing freeboard until the tale-teller's boat started shipping water and was in danger of sinking and he had to offload half of it. The sighting of a mermaid off Canvey Island, who'd sung a song so haunting that the listener felt his nape hairs prickle even just thinking about it today. The day a seal leapt from the sea straight into the boat and started eating the morning's haul, before being beaten off with an oar. The ghostly lights which haunted the marshes and whose bobbing, evanescent glow was said to lead the unwary traveller to his doom. Later still, a fiddle and a penny whistle appeared, as if from nowhere, and an hour of raucous sea shanties ensued. Holmes and I retired to bed enlivened, merry and entertained, and we both slept soundly.

The next morning, after a hearty breakfast, we walked back to Saltings House, only to discover that something hellish had happened there during the night.

Chapter Fourteen

DECORATING OR, AS THE CASE MAY BE, DESECRATING

The first intimation we had that anything was amiss came as we were wending our way down the drive. Sobs and wails rent the air, redolent of shock and horror.

As the school itself hoved into view, we spied dozens of pupils milling around outside. Some of the smaller children were clutching one another, many in tears. Older boys were huddled in knots, frowning and frantically gesticulating. Masters stood in poses of stunned disbelief, while Mrs Harries was making herself somewhat more useful, going from one group of youngsters to the next and offering consolation. This was not the same atmosphere as yesterday, that wild, hedonistic abandon. This was darker, more fretful, palpably laden with fear.

"What on earth is going on?" I said to Holmes.

"I have no idea, Watson, but it is evident some calamity has taken place."

"Another death? A drowning again, maybe?"

"Let us hope not."

Holmes caught the attention of Mrs Harries and beckoned her over.

"Do tell, my good lady," said he as she bustled towards us. "What is the cause of all this alarm?"

"You had best see for yourself, Mr Holmes," the school matron replied. "I can hardly bear to talk about it. Disgusting is what it is. Disgusting and… and *evil*."

"And where might one find this evil thing?"

"Old Sarah's Needle."

Holmes glanced at me, and I indicated, with a gesture, which way we should go.

Old Sarah's Needle lay in a dense stand of shrubbery due west of the school building. Whether the greenery had been planted deliberately in order to screen the monument from view, or had just grown up around it of its own accord, I cannot say. Regardless, it contributed to the mystique of the thing. Whether by design or neglect, the obelisk erected by Obadiah Jackson to ward off the dead witch's curse was consigned to a shaded, hidden spot, as though it were an awful secret, something to be ashamed of, something to be shunned.

Indeed, I had always felt there was a pagan aspect to Old Sarah's Needle, nestled in its untamed grove like some ancient shrine to Pan or Dionysus. Seven feet of weathered granite, rising to a pyramidal apex and encrusted with lichen, it bore no inscription. The purpose of its existence was kept alive orally, as with many an occult tradition sacred to heathens, and only ever mentioned in hushed tones.

In addition, it was the site to which Old Sarah's ghost was reputed to gravitate, the destination of her unquiet spirit's habitual journey every Halloween night.

All told, then, the obelisk was to be approached with caution and perhaps a measure of reverence. You did not take it lightly, nor did you show contempt or disrespect for it, for fear of dire repercussions.

Someone, however, had done just that.

We came across Mr Gormley kneeling in front of the obelisk. The headmaster was bent with his brow almost to the ground. His back trembled and his cheeks were ashen.

Old Sarah's Needle itself had been daubed with a tarry, dark red substance that was all too readily identifiable as blood. The source of the blood lay at its base, in the form of Thomas Aquinas. Gormley's tabby cat had been eviscerated, its belly carved open longitudinally, with various internal organs pulled out and on display. The poor creature's eyes stared vacantly and its mouth yawned wide, as if giving voice to a final, silent, pitiful yowl.

Gormley could only gaze at his dead pet, dumbfounded. How long the headmaster had been there like this, I could not tell, although to judge by the knees of his trousers, damp from the dewy grass, it was some while.

This was all bad enough, but there was worse. Most of the cat's blood had merely been smeared onto the obelisk in haphazard fashion, without any obvious pattern. Some, though, had been used to write a message upon the stone:

I HAVE RETURNED
NOBODY IS SAFE

The words had been put there using the tip of a finger. Some of the letters had merged together as the blood had dribbled down the obelisk's angled face, but the text was still clearly legible, and I will confess to feeling a thrill of terror as I read it.

At last Gormley became aware of our presence. He looked up and round at us, his eyes bloodshot and abrim with tears.

"My cat," he said numbly. "My Thomas. He was a harmless little thing. The sweetest of natures, and he asked nothing of me save feeding and petting. Who would do this?" He gestured at the mutilated remains. "Who could be so malicious? So... so *bestial*?"

"That is a good question," said Holmes. "An equally good question is, why append a message to the monument purporting to be from Old Sarah herself? For I can construe the sentences we see here in no other way. Someone would have us believe that the witch is at large and threatening further havoc. Tell me, Mr Gormley, your cat – did it have the run of the school?"

"Yes. He goes where he pleases." The headmaster heaved a bitter sigh. "Went. I mean went."

"At night?"

"Yes. He especially liked to roam outdoors after dark. The hunting is good around here, if you are a cat. Water voles, dormice, the odd rat or two..."

"Who found the creature's body? Was it Talbot, by any chance?"

"No. It was one of the boys. Normally I would wake up around seven to find Thomas Aquinas outside my room, very vocally demanding his breakfast. He was better than any alarm clock. This morning he wasn't there, and I despatched three of the junior boys to go and look for him."

"You didn't do so yourself?"

"I am a busy man, Mr Holmes, and why perform a job that boys can carry out perfectly well on your behalf? Thomas knew his name, and all that was needed was for them to call for him and he would inevitably appear. One of the boys – Ordway, it was – searched this spot, on my recommendation. The undergrowth yields plenty of potential prey, and Thomas always favoured it. Ordway came back screaming his head off. When he finally stopped gibbering with terror and I was able to get some sense out of him, I hurried straight here."

"And has anyone else visited the site other than you and Ordway?"

"No. I have seen to it that none of the other boys is permitted near here, on pain of punishment."

"That is advantageous for our purposes," said Holmes. "Mr Gormley, might I ask you to stand and take a step back?"

"I… I would like to gather Thomas up and take him somewhere to bury him. Would that be allowed?"

"It would be more than allowed. It would be preferred." Holmes's attitude towards the headmaster was very gentle, as was only right and proper. Thomas Aquinas had been just a cat, but Gormley was grief-stricken as though for a person.

He scooped up the limp bundle of fur and made to leave. At

the last moment, he turned. "You'll find whoever did this, won't you, Mr Holmes?"

"You can count on me."

"Thank you," Gormley said, and off he went, cradling the pathetic little body in his arms. He looked quite broken.

"Holmes," I said, "you would never tell someone he can count on you unless you were already confident of success."

"You know me so well, Watson. Look before you. The soil around the monument is well trodden. The footprints are fresh. Here we see a set of small ones, entering the grove and leaving. Those have been left by a child of perhaps nine or ten, and therefore, I feel safe in hazarding, belong to Ordway. A junior boy, remember? The trail tells its story. He came, he saw, he ran. Now, these size ten footprints here are Gormley's. The pattern of stitching they reveal corresponds with the pattern of stitching on the soles of Gormley's brogues, which were clearly evident to us as he knelt. There remain, however, two further sets of footprints as yet unaccounted for. You see them here, here and here? Yes? What do you remark about them?"

I bent to peer where Holmes was indicating. "I would judge that they belong to adults."

"Or, alternatively, to thirteen-year-olds. Boys of that age can often be as large as adults. More importantly, you see that two specific pairs of footprints are somewhat deeper than the rest and show greater definition: these ones that lie here, side by side, just before the obelisk. From them we may infer that their owners were stationary for a while."

"Those prints show where they stood as they were, for want of a better word, decorating the obelisk."

"Exactly. Decorating or, as the case may be, desecrating."

"So they are, without question, the footprints of the culprits."

"You are following my reasoning. Good. Do you note anything else about them? Your face is a blank. Look. The distribution of weight on the right foot of one of the pairs is uneven. More pressure is being put on the toes than on the heel. The same is true of many of the other prints. It is suggestive of someone with a limp."

"A limp," I said. "My goodness! Talbot! Talbot is one of the two malefactors!"

"Dear me, Watson," Holmes chided. "So close, and then, at the last minute, your powers of analysis desert you. It isn't Talbot's right leg that is lame; it is his left."

"Oh yes. Of course. Then who? Who else at the school has a limp?"

"Until yesterday, I imagine the groundskeeper was unique in that regard."

"What changed yesterday?"

"You don't recall? You didn't see? And yet you were right there when it happened, Watson."

"When what happened?"

"When an injury was inflicted that caused significant harm to the recipient's knee, rendering him incapable of walking properly thereafter. I know, beyond a shadow of a doubt, who is responsible for the death of Thomas Aquinas and this grisly act of vandalism." He motioned to Old Sarah's Needle. "Objectionable though it may be, it is, however, a matter of far less consequence than the death of Hector Robinson, and so I shall deal with it in due course. Robinson is the priority, and there are one or two more things I must establish before I can pronounce definitively on that matter. Come, Watson!"

Holmes strode out from the grove with a forthright air, and I followed unresistingly in his wake, much like a coal tender trailing behind a powerful locomotive.

Chapter Fifteen

THE MERCY OF OBLIVION

For the next half an hour, Holmes crossed the school grounds back and forth at a lively pace, I accompanying him yet none the wiser about what he hoped to accomplish. As far as I could tell, he was surveying the land. Every so often, he would pause, squat down on his haunches or else go up on tiptoe, and would gaze around, sometimes shading his eyes against the weak December sun.

He concluded the process by saying, "Yes, I am satisfied."

"With what?" I asked.

"Saltings House," said he, "sits on high ground. High, that is, relative to the marshes. Would you not agree?"

"I would. Even when the tide is at its peak, there remains a good two or three feet of clearance between the edge of the grounds and the water level."

"And last week, when marshes were flooded so severely that the causeway to Trothe was submerged, the school was unaffected. Had it been, the playing fields would still be saturated even now.

More to the point, the school building itself would have been inundated, of which we have had neither visual nor anecdotal evidence. Indeed, why would anyone have built a house here at all if there was any decent likelihood of flooding? The location, we may deduce, is immune to such a danger, even in extreme weather conditions."

"All of this is true, but I don't see your point. What are you driving at?"

"There is one exception to the statement I have just made, Watson. One part of the school that is lower-lying than the rest."

"Which part do you mean?"

"That one." Holmes pointed in the direction of the old, disused boathouse.

"Well, obviously the boathouse is lower-lying," I said. "By its very nature, it sits practically in the water."

"For that reason, it is notable, and worthy of closer study."

Within moments we were at the rickety structure. A set of three wooden steps led down the bank to a short jetty, which in turn led to the boathouse door. This was secured by a padlock whose rustiness matched the weathered decrepitude of the boards from which the boathouse as a whole was constituted. The tide was coming in, water lapping around the building's support posts as it rose. Incrementally, the muddy bed of the channel was becoming covered.

Holmes examined the padlock, its hasp and the door in minute detail. Then, producing a penknife, he began undoing the screws that held the hasp in place, using the tip of the blade.

"It is simpler than picking the lock," he said. "And see how easily the screws emerge. The wood is so damp and aged, it barely retains them. One of them, in fact, is missing."

"Having presumably fallen out," I said.

Holmes paused from his endeavours, scanning the jetty around him. His eye alighted on something tiny wedged between two of the boards. With his fingertips he prised out a screw.

"You are right. And here it is. A match for its comrades, down to the condition of the thread, which has worn away almost entirely through corrosion. Even if so poorly rooted, though, would this screw have come free without some significant impetus?"

Having posed this question, which I presumed to be rhetorical, Holmes returned to working on the still-fixed screws, until he had extracted the last one.

The hasp clattered to the jetty, both portions of it still linked by the padlock's shackle. The door swung a little way inward. Holmes thrust it open fully and we entered the boathouse.

Just inside lay the narrow landing stage with its mooring post to which, in my time here, the school dinghy had been tethered. On a couple of occasions I had gone for an outing in that little rowing boat with friends, paddling merrily up and down the channel for an hour on a summer evening. I remembered Wragge telling us that it had since rotted and sunk.

The interior of the boathouse was dim, but enough daylight filtered in through chinks between the boards that I could make out the twin doors at the opposite end. Their bases stood just above the water's surface and were hung with a fringe of slimy green weed. Between us and them there was nothing but turbid liquid murk. From the ceiling, dozens of matted old cobwebs dangled.

Holmes and I stood on the landing stage, breathing in the dank air. Then my companion set about inspecting the boards beneath our feet, the walls immediately adjacent, and finally the door.

Now his expression turned grim and he nodded to himself in the manner of one whose worst expectations had been confirmed.

"Behold," he said, showing me certain marks on the inside of the door. They were a series of faint parallel lines, criss-crossing one another, pale against the dark of the wood. "What do those look like to you, Watson?"

"Scratches," I said. "Such as might have been scored by a hand."

"Precisely. And as if to confirm the hypothesis, here we find a fingernail in one of them." Carefully, using the penknife again, he teased out the little disc of human keratin from the shallow groove in which it was embedded. He held it up so that we could both examine it.

"Hector Robinson's," I breathed, remembering Mrs Harries's description of the state of the boy's hands. "It must be."

"The nail is the correct size for a child his age, assuming it came from his little finger, which I believe it does, judging by its proportions."

I looked around the interior of the boathouse with fresh eyes, a knot forming in my stomach. All at once the place seemed confining and oppressive, the scene of something horrendous.

"He was here," I said, "on the night of his death."

"Held captive," said Holmes, with a confirmatory nod of the head. "Someone locked him in."

"Hideous."

"That is not the end of it, either. We may readily envisage the sequence of events. It is night-time. Everyone at the school is abed. Robinson is woken up, led from his dormitory and forced into the boathouse, clad only in his pyjamas. The door is closed on him and fastened, and his captor departs. Robinson stands where we are, shivering. The air is bitterly cold, and he is frightened. He does not know how long his imprisonment is to last. Perhaps it will be an hour, perhaps until morning. He resolves to wait it out stoically. It is all he can do. He could call for help, but the boathouse stands a goodly distance from the school. Who will hear? Besides, it is raining hard. 'Bucketing down', in the words of Mrs Quimp. The sound will muffle his cries."

I could picture Robinson's plight all too vividly.

"It gets worse," Holmes continued. "The tide rolls in. The water rises. It would not normally lap over this landing stage, which has been erected so as to remain above water level; but, swelled by rainfall, it does. Nor does it stop there. It creeps upward, ever upward. It is around Robinson's ankles, then his shins. Fear grips him as the icy water advances inexorably higher. He has his first inkling that he is in mortal danger."

"He would also be starting to feel the effects of hypothermia."

"Exactly, the chill of the water adding to the chill of the air. His teeth chatter. His body shakes uncontrollably. Now, at last, he does cry for help, but of course, it goes unheeded. He hammers on the door, begging to be let out, or else for some kind of miracle to save him. This is when one of the screws securing the hasp fell out. The force of his blows propels it from its hole."

"If only more of the screws had gone the same way, the hasp might have slipped off and Robinson could have pushed the door open and escaped."

"Alas, he was not so lucky. But to resume my speculative narrative… Soon, the water is swirling around the boy's knees, inching towards his thighs. It sucks at his legs, and he is finding it hard to stay upright. In desperation he claws at the door, hoping he might somehow be able to burrow his way through the woodwork, but all he gets for his pains is splintered fingernails. At what point, I wonder, did he realise that it was futile? That he was going to die in this forsaken place?"

I shuddered. "One consolation is that, in time, his body temperature would have dropped so low that his heart rate decreased and his blood pressure plummeted precipitately. Unconsciousness would rapidly have followed."

"The mercy of oblivion," said Holmes. "And that is when he drowns. He falls face first into the water, insensible, and thus his life ends."

"It didn't happen in the lake at all," I said. "It was here."

"I already suspected that Robinson did not drown in the lake, given what Mrs Harries told us about the blood and the paucity of water in his lungs. It has been observed that in cases of drowning in salt water, not as much liquid needs be inhaled in order to cause a fatality, compared with fresh water. The density and the saline content incite pulmonary oedema, bringing about a swifter demise than simple suffocation. Not all drownings in salt water result in pulmonary oedema, but it is commoner than with drownings in fresh water. Hence, from that evidence alone, I was minded to think that Robinson died elsewhere than the lake."

"But if he drowned here, why was his body subsequently moved to the lake?"

"Is it not obvious? The perpetrator of this atrocity wished to cover up his involvement. He thought that placing Robinson in the lake would make it look like a swimming accident."

"I realise that, but what I mean is, he could have moved the body from the boathouse to the channel, not all the way over to the lake. Then he would have avoided someone such as you noting the discrepancy between the signs of drowning in salt water as opposed to fresh water."

"I doubt our man is aware any such discrepancy exists. More to the point, everyone was supposed to think that Robinson went swimming in the pre-dawn hours. He would not have ventured into the marshes at that time, by simple virtue of the fact that the tide had gone back out by then and the water level was too low."

"Of course," I said, feeling foolish. "That didn't occur to me."

"It's all right, Watson. It occurred to me, and that is what counts."

"But who did this? What did they hope to gain?"

"The 'who' part is easy," said Holmes. "Who else could have got a slumbering boy out of bed and made him walk all the way out to the boathouse without objection or demur? Who but an authority figure?"

"A schoolmaster!"

"Quite so. If it had been a fellow pupil, Robinson might not have gone quietly. Once he realised what was up, he might have caused a fuss."

"If I were he, I'd have screamed blue murder."

"And therefore awoken anyone in the immediate vicinity and quite possibly the entire school. That is why this deed could scarcely have been the handiwork of, say, Jeremy Pugh and Hosea Wyatt. However menacing those two might be, they could never have been assured of Robinson's full, silent compliance."

"Perhaps they gagged him."

"Robinson would still have put up a fight as they did so, thus causing a disturbance. Besides, a gag is no guarantee of silence. One can still bellow through it, loud enough to make oneself heard. A schoolmaster, on the other hand, could easily intimidate a pupil into doing his bidding. 'Hush, boy. Not a peep out of you, or you will make this worse for yourself,' or something to that effect."

"So it was Gormley after all."

"Gormley? But why?"

"I don't know," I admitted.

"Gormley lacks a motive. He seems to have borne Robinson no particular ill will. No, this was the work of another."

"Who, then?" I demanded. A fury was growing within me. "Which schoolmaster? I should like to meet this individual, whoever he is, and give him a piece of my mind. If only it was Yeowell. I would be even less merciful with him than you were yesterday."

"Oh, but that's just it, old fellow. It *is* Yeowell."

Chapter Sixteen

TWO INDULGENCES

I gaped at Holmes. "How can it be Yeowell? He was at The Gurnard Inn all night. We have indisputable proof of it."

"He was at The Gurnard Inn overnight," Holmes said, "but initially he spent, by his own account, only an hour or so there. He left just before closing time, eleven o'clock, only to have to turn back because the causeway was flooded. From this, if we extrapolate backwards, we can see that he must have arrived at the pub around ten, having left Saltings House perhaps half an hour beforehand. By that time, half past nine, the boys at the school had already gone to bed and would have been fast asleep."

"In other words, he roused Robinson not long after lights out, quietly so as not to disturb anyone else in the dormitory. He locked him here in the boathouse, and then went to The Gurnard."

"Went there with, I believe, the express intention of returning to the school after closing time and releasing Robinson from his confinement. Yeowell's objective was to improve Robinson. He wanted to, in his own parlance, toughen him up and make a man of him.'"

"By trapping him in a cold, draughty boathouse on a winter's night," I said acerbically.

"According to his lights, it is just the kind of treatment that promotes stamina and wellbeing. This, let's not forget, is a man who maintains that 'suffering is the stepping stone to glory'. Unfortunately for him, what was meant to be a remedy turned into a dire predicament, one he could do nothing about. Yeowell was stuck at The Gurnard, just as Hector Robinson was stuck in the boathouse, both of them the victims of an unforeseen phenomenon, an unnaturally high tide. All Yeowell could do was leave the pub as early as possible in the morning and rush back to the school, hoping that Robinson had survived. In this aspiration, he was to be gravely disappointed."

"Mrs Quimp said he fled in such haste, he forgot to pay his bill and she had to call him back. He must have been beside himself with anxiety."

"I imagine he ran every step of the way from Trothe to Saltings House, only to discover, to his horror, that the worst had happened. Then all he could think to do was deposit Robinson's body in the lake and lock up the boathouse again. He managed all this before first light, then lay low until breakfast, by which time Talbot had discovered the body. Thereafter, Yeowell simply pretended the death had had nothing to do with him."

"The absolute, unutterable fiend. All this time, he has been brazenly lying to us."

"Not lying, Watson. Merely omitting the truth. Would you not do the same in his position?"

"He could have come clean. He has an innocent boy's blood on his hands."

"And yet he is not a murderer. At best, he is guilty of causing death by misadventure, although a halfway decent lawyer might argue it down to criminal negligence."

"You sound like you are defending his actions."

"Robinson's death was largely the product of a cruel twist of fate. In that respect, Yeowell may be pardoned for it, just about. What is indefensible is not owning up to it, and for that, he must certainly be punished."

"Then let us go and confront him," I said. "This instant."

"Before we do so – and I am as eager to see Yeowell in custody as you are – would you mind granting me two indulgences?"

I seethed, but relented. "Very well. Yeowell will keep for a little longer. What do you want?"

The first indulgence was allowing myself to be locked in the boathouse. I stayed put while Holmes went outside. He closed the door and reattached the hasp, screwing it back into place. Then he asked me to push against the door and beat on it from within, much as Hector Robinson must have done.

"Put your back into it, Watson," Holmes advised from the other side. "Really give it your all."

I strained and pummelled, until I felt the door start to give. This spurred me to greater exertions, and all at once the hasp burst free. All I then had to do was tug the door open and step out.

"Well?" I said. "What does that prove?"

"It tests a theory of mine," Holmes replied, "but whether conclusively or not, I cannot say. I was wondering whether Robinson could have liberated himself if he had devoted sufficient effort to the task. On the balance of probabilities, it is unlikely. It took you how long? A little under two minutes."

"But I am a grown man," I pointed out.

"And a strapping specimen, too. Whereas Hector Robinson was a mere stripling, and a sickly one at that. Moreover, this time around, the screws in the hasp were almost certainly looser than when he was a prisoner. My removing and returning them to their holes would have left them less tightly seated."

"In addition, you mustn't forget that Robinson was wading in water. His footing would not have been anywhere near as firm as mine."

"Quite so. All in all, this may have been a fruitless experiment. I still think it was worth conducting, if only because… No." Holmes shook his head. "It was a tenuous idea, and I must eliminate it from my considerations. Robinson was doomed from the outset. Nothing and no one could have helped him."

"What is this second indulgence of yours, then?" I said.

"Oh, as to that, it should not be too difficult to corroborate Yeowell's culpability. The padlock points the way."

"How so?"

"It is all a matter of keys, Watson."

"Keys?"

"The padlock tells us that Yeowell did not act entirely alone."

"He had an accomplice?"

"In a manner of speaking," said Holmes. "Who has the power to unlock any door at Saltings House School? Who is potentially as omnipresent here as the deity that gives him his nickname?"

Chapter Seventeen

BLOOD MONEY

We found God Talbot at work, scrubbing the cat blood off Old Sarah's Needle with a wire brush and soapy water. The groundskeeper did not seem best pleased to see us, and I would have ascribed this to his generally unfriendly disposition had I not known that he was connected in some way to Hector Robinson's death. Now, behind his animosity, I was sure I detected a certain evasiveness.

"What now?" Talbot snapped. "I'm busy."

"A disagreeable task," Holmes commented. "I don't envy you."

"I do what I have to," said the other with a scowl. "If there's a dirty job needs sorting out around the school, it's me they call."

"Does that extend to lending Mr Yeowell a key?"

Talbot paused in his scrubbing. Pink foam slithered down the side of the obelisk.

"The key," Holmes elaborated, "to the boathouse."

"I don't know nothing about any of that," Talbot muttered.

"A dirty job indeed, being complicit in young Robinson's drowning."

Talbot rounded on us. "You have some nerve, sir, making accusations like that. It weren't nothing to do with me."

"Not directly, no. But how else did Yeowell gain access to the boathouse? I see at least five keys on the ring hanging from your belt that would fit the padlock on the boathouse door. Given the opportunity, I'm certain I could establish which exact one, just by close inspection. It will be tarnished from a long period of disuse and bear minuscule scratch marks indicating it has been employed recently. Now, I am not suggesting for a moment that you knew in advance what Yeowell intended. I doubt he told you. He asked for the key, perhaps offering some pretext or other, and you obligingly gave it to him. He has since returned it to you, and you are shrewd enough to have worked out that there is a clear association between his borrowing the key and the death of Robinson. I believe you even suspected it the moment you discovered the body. You spoke of 'making things right', with reference to that fateful morning. This, I submit, applied not just to Mrs Harries but to you yourself as well. By fetching the woman who might just know how to revive the boy, you were hoping to make up for the part, however tangential, that you played in the tragedy. A vain hope, as it transpired. Come now, man, you know I am right. You may as well confess."

Talbot stared at Holmes, and then at the bloodstained brush in his hand, and suddenly his shoulders slumped and all the stiffness and anger seemed to drain from him.

"It weren't my fault," he said softly.

"We know that."

"He's my superior, Yeowell is. Him and all the school staff. Any of them asks for a thing, I give it them, no questions. He didn't even lie about what he wanted the key for. I was curious to know, and he just came right out and said it. 'I have a lad – Robinson – who needs straightening out. An hour or so locked in the boathouse will do him a power of good.'"

"When was this?"

"Evening, it were. Around suppertime, just as I was finishing work for the day. Then, overnight, the marsh flooded. Of course, I was abed at the time. I didn't know a flood was coming, and even if I had woken up for some reason and realised what was happening, I had no reason to think Yeowell hadn't already removed Robinson from the boathouse well before."

"Otherwise you would surely have gone to his rescue."

"Of course I would have," Talbot declared. "Next morning, though, what do I find but a drownded body in the lake? I knew immediately who it was and what had befallen the lad. Didn't take much to put two and two together, did it now?"

"Quite."

"But then I'm all of a pother. I know what's gone on, more or less. Do I tell the headmaster? I ought to. I've a mind to. But just as I'm still trying to decide, Yeowell comes along and finds me and hands back the key. I tell him I have a good idea what he did, and he gets all puffed up and mighty, and he starts shaking a fist and making all kinds of threats, calling me names I don't care to repeat. I'm having none of that, though.

I'm not the sort to be browbeaten, not by the likes of anyone, and I stand up to him. I say, 'If you don't make a clean breast of it, Mr Yeowell, I damn well will.' At that he says to me, 'You shan't breathe a word to a soul. You peach on me, Talbot,' he says, 'and I'll drag you down with me. I'll say you lent me the boathouse key knowing full well what was going to happen to Robinson, and knowing full well it was going to flood, too. A groundskeeper knows about the weather. You could have warned me and you didn't.'"

"Blackmail, of a kind."

"That's right, sir. Anyway, I tell him what I just told you, that I had no idea there was a flood due. I'm not some kind of soothsayer, am I? But that cuts no ice with Yeowell. 'You can try to deny it,' says he, 'but it won't help you. They'll believe me over you. I'm a schoolmaster, whereas you are a lowly menial, and one with a drink habit, what's more. You'll lose your job, your livelihood, your good name, such as it is – you'll lose everything.' I can see the truth in this, but still I hold firm. That's when Yeowell changes tack. He gets all wheedly and nice-sounding. 'We can both get away with this, Talbot,' he says. 'All we have to do is keep quiet. You and me, we can look after each other.' And then he reaches into his pocket."

"Money," said Holmes.

Talbot bowed his head. "Money, sir, that's right. 'How about this?' says Yeowell, and he hands me a half-sovereign. 'A sign of my good faith. And that's just for starters. There's more where that came from. Think what you could buy with it. A drink. Several drinks. Some good whisky.' Well now, sir, I am not a strong man when it comes to drink. I am in pain, constant-like. My gammy leg has always ached, all my life, and in recent years it has got worse. The drink helps soothe it. Yeowell, he hit upon my weakness. My – what do you call it? My Achilles heel."

It was almost literally an Achilles heel, I thought; but I did not voice the thought.

"He promised me a half-sovereign a week from then on," Talbot said. "I haggled and got him up to a full sovereign. I am not a rich man. A whole sov, to spend as I saw fit, and all just for saying nothing. We shook on it, he and I, and I considered it a good deal. Not only was I protecting myself, I was profiting. It shames me to think of it now. Talk about blood money. But that is as far as it goes," he concluded. "That is all I did. I made a pact with Yeowell."

"In the eyes of the law," said Holmes, "you are an accessory after the fact, Talbot. You knowingly aided in covering up a criminal act and, for that matter, took payment for it. That carries a hefty sentence."

Pale and trembling, Talbot nodded.

"However," Holmes said, "there are extenuating circumstances, and I am willing to overlook what you have done, safe in the knowledge that this is going to weigh on your conscience for the rest of your life."

"That it is," Talbot said. "That it is."

With miserable solemnity, the groundskeeper turned back to Old Sarah's Needle and began scrubbing once more. I imagined he was thinking what I was thinking, namely that some dishonourable deeds could be erased, and some could not.

Chapter Eighteen

NOT AT LARGE FOR LONG

Holmes and I left Talbot to his labours.

"Next on the agenda," my companion said, "detaining Yeowell."

In that enterprise, however, we were destined to fail. The games master, we soon ascertained, was nowhere to be found. We searched high and low for him, with Wragge joining us on the hunt. Final confirmation of Yeowell's absence came when we tried his room, where the bed appeared not to have been slept in and the wardrobe had been cleared out. It was plain that the fellow had packed his bags and quit the premises, very likely late the night before.

"Yeowell knew you were on to him," I said to Holmes, "and saw no alternative but to flee."

Holmes did not respond. His lips were pursed with chagrin, and I could see he was fuming inwardly.

"There, there, old fellow," I soothed. "Look at it this way. You have been proved right. Yeowell's absconding is tantamount to an admission of guilt. All we need do now is wire Scotland Yard and furnish them with a description of the fellow. The police will pick him up in no time. He won't stay at large for long."

"Yes," Holmes sighed. "I suppose so. I would far rather have had the satisfaction of apprehending him myself, but as a second best, it will do."

"For my own part, I cannot believe it," said Wragge. "Yeowell was an awful person, but to have done *this*? And then to carry on as though everything was normal? The depths of that man's cold-heartedness!"

"There does remain another mystery for you to clear up, Holmes," I said cajolingly. "To wit, who killed Thomas Aquinas and besmirched Old Sarah's Needle."

"Yes, that," Holmes said curtly. "We can attend to it easily enough. Wragge, would you be so good as to fetch Messrs Pugh and Wyatt? Bring them to us separately if you can."

"They are in the same form for every subject, and at this hour they will be in lessons. I can call them out one at a time, I suppose."

"No, it's of no matter. They can come together, but regardless we are going to place them in separate rooms. May we employ your bedroom and Yeowell's for that purpose?"

"Mine is at your disposal, and Yeowell's – well, he isn't using it any more, is he?"

So it was that Jeremy Pugh and the Honourable Hosea Wyatt were brought to us, and never had I seen such a smug, complacent pair of young reprobates. They swaggered up, not an inch of remorse or concern to be seen on their faces. I now noted that

Wyatt did walk with a discernible limp, his left knee stiff, the result of that kick from Vernon Agius at supper the previous day. I felt little compassion for him, and mentally commended Agius on the accuracy and force of the blow.

Even after each boy had been sequestered in a different room, both maintained their obdurate air. They thought themselves untouchable, and perhaps, until Sherlock Holmes came along, they had been. He, however, soon set them straight on that.

First to Pugh, then to Wyatt, he said the same thing. "Own up to your misdeed now, and I will exculpate you and lay the blame fully on your partner in crime."

Neither took the bait, but then Holmes had not expected them to. "This is the first stage of the process," he confided to Wragge and me in the corridor outside. "The cogs are starting to turn in their brains. Each is seeing the possibility of a way out. It is all a question of how deep each's self-interest runs."

He left them stewing for twenty minutes, after which he went in to talk to Pugh. "Your accomplice has forsaken you, Pugh. He has surrendered you up. The blame for killing Mr Gormley's cat lies solely with you. What do you have to say about that?"

Pugh replied, "I don't believe you. Hosea's no squealer." Almost to himself, he added, "Is he?"

Holmes went to Wyatt and announced that Pugh had just named him as the guilty party. Wyatt was visibly shocked. "But Jeremy… It was all his idea. I just went along with it. It seemed like a lark. We sneaked outdoors after lights out and called for the cat. He came, and Jeremy had a knife, and then… It was just for fun. Everyone is in such a lather about the witch's curse.

We just thought we would stir the pot a little more. It's hilarious to see old Gormley losing control. He hates it so much."

Holmes revisited Pugh, who in the interim had decided that honesty was the best policy. "Listen, Mr Holmes, I did it. You'll put in a good word for me with Mr Gormley, won't you?"

Wyatt, on the other hand, craved no such intercession. "All said and done, Gormley won't do a thing about it. He grovels before my father all the time. Pater gives a lot of money to this school. At worst, Jeremy and I will receive a dressing-down, maybe a detention."

Wyatt was wrong about that. It seemed that Gormley's forbearance had its limits, and the massacre of his beloved Thomas Aquinas pushed him past them.

"I cannot forgive what those two have done," he said to us, "nor can I overlook it. I would appreciate it if you would leave this to me to resolve, Mr Holmes. Rest assured, Pugh and Wyatt will get everything they deserve, and to hell with the consequences. As for Vincent Yeowell, he has forever sullied the reputation of Saltings House. I pray for his swift arrest and the severe penalty that will be coming his way."

I later learned, courtesy of a letter from Wragge, that Pugh and Wyatt were subjected to a sound thrashing by Mr Gormley, such that neither boy could walk properly or sit down in comfort for some time afterward. Moreover, they were summarily expelled from the school and would carry that black mark for the remainder of their academic lives. This did not appear to have an adverse effect on their prospects in adulthood, however, since each went on to have a flourishing career. Pugh became a journalist at one of the country's most prominent newspapers and rose quickly to the position of editor at a relatively young age, while Wyatt followed his father into politics, becoming Member of Parliament in a safe Conservative seat and soon gaining a cabinet position, with a fair hope of eventually becoming Prime Minister. Then the Spanish 'flu, being no respecter of status or future prospects, took the lives of both.

As for Gormley, he retired at the end of that term, and a replacement headmaster was installed. A fair few parents did remove their children immediately after the events related here, and for a while my alma mater bore the taint of scandal, but the new head worked tirelessly to restore its reputation and, in time, succeeded. I gather that these days Saltings House is considered one of the premier prep schools in the Home Counties. Wragge remains on the teaching staff, well into venerable middle age, and there has, by all accounts, been no recurrence of Old Sarah's curse. The witch's malediction seems at last to have lost its potency, assuming it ever had any.

On that front, I shall offer this brief postscript to the tale, which readers may make of what they will. It was Holmes who drew my attention to the headline in *The Times*, not two days after we returned to London from Kent:

PASSENGER LOST OVERBOARD
ON CHANNEL FERRY

It seems that a man was swept from the foredeck of a Dover-to-Calais ferry by an unusually large wave. His description matched, in every respect, that of Yeowell the games master, and Holmes was in no doubt that the felon had been attempting to evade justice by fleeing to France and had fallen prey to rough seas.

"Or," my friend noted slyly, "can it be that Old Sarah has added yet one more victim to her tally?"

The Second Terror

THE COTTON MILL GHOST

1890

Chapter One

THE WHISTLE OF A MASTER
SUMMONING HIS DOG

The yuletide period of 1890 was an exceptionally busy one for
Sherlock Holmes, not least because, in the week leading up to
Christmas Day, he was called upon to investigate eerie goings-on
at Fellscar Keep, a castle in Yorkshire, where it appeared that a
sinister entity from the region's folklore was on the prowl. This
adventure, which tested Holmes's wits and my courage to the
limit, I have chronicled under the title *The Christmas Demon*.

Then, during the interval between Christmas and on into
the early part of the new year – that empty stretch when the
weather seems at its dreariest and most people have little to do
save sit at home and wait for normal workaday life to resume –
Holmes was hired to look into the matter of a ghost haunting
the London home of a wealthy industrialist. This is the case that
I now recount here.

The first intimation I had that Holmes's prowess as a detective
was yet again required came one lunchtime as I mounted the

seventeen steps from the hallway at 221B Baker Street to his rooms. From above I heard a cry that was half incredulity, half indignation.

"Commands! *Commands* me!"

I entered Holmes's lodgings to find him furiously scribbling an answer to a telegram. Such was the intensity with which he wrote, the pencil scored through the paper several times. He thrust the reply slip at the waiting messenger, along with a coin, and the boy snatched both from him, mumbled a farewell and scurried from the room, almost colliding with me in his haste.

"Holmes," I reproached him. "You terrified that poor lad with your bellowing. He ran out of here like a scalded cat."

"Commands..." my friend grumbled.

"Evidently something in that telegram has upset you, but there is no justification for so intemperate an outburst."

"I will not be commanded to do anything, Watson. I am no man's lackey, no matter how rich or respectable he may be."

"Pray, have a drink." I poured him a glass of sherry, which he knocked back at a single gulp. "Your nerves seem under strain. You have had a hectic time of it lately. Might I propose a holiday? The Scottish scenery is remarkable at this time of year. Snow-capped Munros, majestic frost-whitened glens..."

"Surly locals, inedible food..."

"I hardly think that fair."

"The two things are inextricably linked. If haggis, crappit heid and Cullen skink formed a regular part of your diet, you, too, would be surly."

"You could hire a ghillie and go deerstalking with him."

"I'm not sure I have the appropriate headgear," he replied in a droll manner.

"Switzerland, then. You've expressed an interest in skiing. Now's the time to give it a try."

"Watson, just because I once made a comment to the effect that skiing appears a healthful and invigorating pastime, it does not automatically mean I wish to strap a pair of planks to my feet and hurtle down a mountainside, most likely colliding headlong with a pine tree."

I gave it one more attempt. "How about the south coast? You are particularly fond of Sussex, and it's just a short hop away. You could rent a cosy little cottage somewhere on the Downs, perhaps with a view of the sea. Read, go for walks…"

"I would be bored to tears within a day."

"There is just no helping you sometimes," I said with a touch of vexation. "Well, seeing as you are so little inclined towards hospitability this afternoon, I shall take my leave, in the hope that when I next visit, you will be more amenable to company. Good day."

I had not removed my coat, scarf and gloves yet, so it was a simple matter to turn on my heel and make for the door.

"Watson, stop," Holmes said. "From the bottom of my heart, I apologise. I should not have spoken to you as I did, nor given the messenger boy such a scare." He sounded genuinely contrite. "You are right, I'm not in the most congenial frame of mind at present. I have been working hard, without scarcely a break, and I am at a low ebb. That telegram was simply the final straw. Do you forgive me?"

I could never stay angry with Holmes for long. "I forgive you."

"Capital. Help yourself to a drink and some tobacco then, while I stoke the fire. Mrs Hudson knows you are here, I take it? Then doubtless she is even now preparing an extra serving of lunch to bring up along with mine. That woman is an incomparable hostess, never failing to take into account the needs of everyone under her roof. I believe curried turkey is on the menu today."

As I made myself comfortable, I asked about the telegram. "Why has it irked you so?"

"See for yourself." He handed it to me. "No name, no greeting, not so much as a please or thank you, just the whistle of a master summoning his dog."

A GENTLEMAN OF MEANS COMMANDS YOU TO
ATTEND HIM AT HIS HOME. ADDRESS AND TIME
WILL BE SUPPLIED UPON YOUR CONFIRMATION.
IMMEDIATE REPLY EXPECTED.

"It is certainly peremptory," I said.

"It is downright rude," said Holmes. "The sender belongs to the mercantile class, I'll wager, someone who habitually regards people as commodities. To him, engaging Sherlock Holmes is like placing an order. He demands; I am purchased. Well, I won't have it."

"What did you say in your reply?"

"I told him that I too am a gentleman of means and that it is the custom that clients attend me at *my* home, not theirs. I may also," he added, arching one eyebrow, "have remarked upon his lack of manners and said that neither wealth nor anonymity confers exemption from common politeness."

I chuckled. "That's the last we'll hear from him, I imagine. The dog has turned round and nipped his fingers."

We engaged in pleasant conversation for a while, and when the curried turkey arrived we set to eating it with relish. Holmes seemed to have shaken off his splenetic mood and was his usual self again, and I was glad to see it. I flattered myself it was my presence that had had this beneficial effect. My companion, though he might never admit it, needed me. Like many who live alone, he was too much in his own head and required someone to draw him out of his thoughts and remind him of the value to be derived from the society of others. Often Holmes seemed to treat his fellow human beings purely as puzzles that had to be unravelled. He ceased to see us as people, and correcting this defect was one of the functions I fulfilled in his life.

Just as we cleared our plates, the doorbell rang downstairs, and shortly afterwards a sleekly dressed but very portly man entered the room.

"Which of you is Mr Sherlock Holmes?" the new arrival demanded, flapping a pudgy hand at each of us in turn.

"I have that honour," said Holmes.

"You arrant knave, sir!" roared the other. "Turning down my invitation like that. Forcing *me* to come to *you*. Nobody does that to me. Nobody!"

"I take it you are the one responsible for the somewhat discourteous telegram earlier."

"Your reply was no less discourteous."

"And I regret the tone I took and crave your pardon for it. An hour in the company of my friend Dr Watson here has restored my equilibrium. He is my conscience made manifest, and once again he has demonstrated to me, by his example, that one should always meet incivility with civility. In that spirit, I would be grateful, sir, if you took a seat and shared with us whatever dilemma you are currently facing, on the understanding that I will, if it is in my power to do so, resolve it."

There was a touch of glibness in the way Holmes spoke, and our guest could not have been oblivious to it, but he was appeased nonetheless.

"Indeed. Yes. Very well. I shall do just that."

He flopped down into the chair indicated by Holmes and, producing a silk handkerchief, began mopping his brow. He had been perspiring freely when he came in, in spite of the temperature outside being close to zero; this and his ruddy complexion, not to mention a visible shortness of breath, led me to diagnose chronic high pressure diathesis. A further, subtler symptom was the blood spot in the white of his left eye, a blemish known as a subconjunctival haemorrhage, a common feature among those whose blood pressure is constantly and excessively elevated. I did not know whether the cause of the ailment was his excessive weight, his profound irritability, a combination of the two, or some other hidden factor. Had I been his doctor, however, I would have recommended a less rich diet, a reduction in the intake of alcohol, a gentle fitness regime, and a lengthy rest cure, in line with the advice of Dr Mahomed of

Brighton, the late expert in this field, who was the first to give high pressure diathesis its name. Otherwise the gentleman's condition, left unaddressed, might soon prove the death of him.

"My life is a nightmare, gentlemen," the man said. "A living nightmare. I am being haunted, you see. Haunted by a vengeful ghost!"

Chapter Two

SOOTY PRINTS

"**B**ut first, I suppose I should introduce myself," the visitor said. "I am Eustace Agius."

"The industrialist," said Holmes. "Owner of several cotton mills in the North."

"The same."

"Agius," I said, frowning. "I know that surname."

"I am rather eminent," said Agius, with no show of modesty to mitigate the remark. "I have not been a stranger to the society columns, nor the financial pages."

"No, I recognise it from elsewhere. Agius, Agius… Yes!" I snapped my fingers. "That's it. We met a boy, this time last year, at Saltings House School. His name was Agius, and his Christian name was… Virgil? Victor?"

"Vernon."

"Any relation?"

"Of course he is a relation, Watson," Holmes rebuked me. "How else would Mr Agius know the boy's Christian name?"

My face grew warm. "Oh yes. How foolish of me."

"Vernon is my son," Agius confirmed.

"I can see the family resemblance," I said. Indeed, the older Agius and the younger shared many distinctive features, from pale blue eyes to a very forthright nose. The father, however, was bulbous in body where Vernon Agius was slim, balding where the lad had a full head of hair, and above all hot-tempered where his son, as I recalled, was possessed of steady nerves. "How is the young fellow? He made quite an impression on me, even after only a short acquaintance. I liked the cut of his jib."

"Vernon is well. He has just embarked on his first year at Harrow and is already making his mark there. But I am not here to talk about him. Or rather, I am, in a roundabout way. The fact is, Mr Holmes, you in turn seem to have made quite an impression on my Vernon."

"I did help unpick that rather knotty problem at Saltings House. I also defended your son against an assault by a schoolmaster. That may well have endeared me to him."

"Quite, and what an outrage that whole business was. A schoolmaster killing one of the pupils in his charge. My wife was all in favour of sending Vernon to a different school, but we elected to leave him at Saltings as he had only two terms remaining and he appeared to like the place well enough, in spite of everything. He was appointed Head Boy, what's more, for those last two terms, and left with the highest of commendations from the headmaster."

"It is good when one's child's virtues are recognised."

"Well, yes," said Agius, as if this didn't much matter to him.

"At any rate, he owns both of your books, Doctor, you'll be pleased to hear. The first one and the latest. I often see him with his nose in one or other of them."

I responded with a gracious nod.

"That is how I know he is an admirer of yours, Mr Holmes," Agius went on. "That and his mentions of your name. We don't talk much, Vernon and I, but he has spoken about you in my hearing more than once, and never without clear approbation. Likewise, others in my circle habitually refer to you in reverent whispers. Hence, I am consulting you now. If you are half the genius everyone seems to think you are…"

"I would never dub myself a genius," said Holmes. "I am merely a man who has trained himself to observe and analyse with a high degree of acuity."

"Well, be that as it may, but you seem the best-equipped person to help me, and therefore you must."

"Best equipped to tackle a ghostly manifestation? That remains to be seen. Tell me about this phantom of yours."

Eustace Agius rubbed his forehead hard, then commenced. "Not long ago, I began to notice strange footprints and handprints about the house. They were formed of soot and kept cropping up in different places – on the door to my study, for instance, or on the carpet outside my dressing room. Naturally my first thought was that it must be the fault of one of the servants. We have an especially silly girl who works as our housemaid. Peggy is her name. She does not seem to understand even the basic requirements of the job and, when it comes to cleaning, often leaves things dirtier than when she started. My wife is forever having to correct her. I accused Peggy of being responsible for the marks. She swore blind she was not. I pressed her hard on it, and she burst into tears. 'I swear on my mother's life, sir,' said she, 'I would not leave such a mess.' I still did not believe her, but I hoped that challenging her on the matter would get her to buck up her ideas and be more careful in future."

"And did it work?"

"No. The handprints and footprints continued to appear. The next occasion, as it happened, was the day after I upbraided Peggy. There was a handprint on a letter, which I found as I was going through my correspondence. It is my habit to open my post and divide it into two piles, urgent and non-urgent. The former I tackle straight away, the latter I leave for a day or two until the letters number a dozen or more, and then I go through them in one fell swoop. That morning I was doing just that, and I picked up the next letter in the stack, and that was when I saw it: the black shape of a hand, clear as day, covering the letter below."

"So the letter in question was not top of the stack."

"No, it was the third or fourth down."

"And the letter had been perfectly normal when you first opened it?"

"Nothing on it save handwriting, I assure you."

"And were any of the other letters in the stack similarly sullied?"

"Only the one that had been lying on top of the one with the handprint. A little of the soot had rubbed off on its reverse. Why do you ask?"

"I simply wished to clarify the picture. Go on."

"The same day as that incident occurred, I discovered a pair of sooty footprints right by my bedside, just as I was about to turn in for the night," said Agius.

"Prints of a bare foot, or of the sole of a shoe?"

"Why do you ask?"

"It may or may not be germane."

"The sole of a shoe, as it happens."

"That is good to know. Continue."

"Now then, as you might imagine, I raised hell," Agius said. "I summoned every member of the household staff, I showed them the footprints – shoeprints, whatever you want to call them – and demanded to know who had left them there. Each proclaimed his or her innocence. I levelled my accusations at all of them but in particular at Sturridge, my valet. He is the one who would have been in the bedroom most recently, discharging his evening duty of turning down the covers and laying out my nightwear. Sturridge is a dependable sort, not prone to flights of emotion. Nor is he a liar. I trust him implicitly. He told me categorically that he could not have been the culprit. His shoes were clean, he said; and he showed me the soles to prove it. Moreover, as he pointed out, the footprints did not match his in size, whereupon I had him stand beside them to test the truth of it. He was right. I proceeded to do the same with every other member of staff, including Peggy, with the same result. None was a precise match."

"That was thorough of you."

"You don't get to my position in life without being thorough, sir."

"I presume you did something similar with the handprints."

"I could not, since they had all been cleaned up more or less as soon as they appeared, at my instruction."

"What about the one on the letter?"

"I burned that letter," said Agius.

"Why?"

"The content was of no importance to me, and I just didn't want the thing in the house any more, with that horrid, nasty mark on it, so I disposed of it."

"A pity. It might have been useful to you in your enquiries, more so than the shoeprint."

"In hindsight, I see that. Anyway, back to my account of events. Just as I was dismissing all of the other staff members from the bedroom, Sturridge piped up with another valid point. Had he or any of the other servants been guilty of walking into the room with dirty feet, he said, there would surely have been a line of marks leading in from the door and out again. Gentlemen, I could not gainsay the logic of the statement. The prints by the bed were discrete. There were just the two of them in that spot, and none evident anywhere else in the room."

"That is certainly singular," Holmes remarked.

"I should say so," Agius agreed. "It wasn't until Sturridge made his observation that I realised what was so damnably queer about the whole situation, and I could have kicked myself for not seeing it sooner. Each mark that had appeared was a solitary thing, one here, another there, isolated. If somebody with a soot-stained hand had been going through my correspondence, for example, would they not have left smudges on several of the letters?"

"Instead of a handprint on just a single one? Yes, that struck me as odd, which is why I posed my question about the other letters in the stack."

"The same goes for the rest of the marks. It is as though whoever put them there abruptly shimmered into existence, and then, just as abruptly, out of it. I found the idea somewhat unnerving, I can tell you, but I am a hard-headed, rational man and was able to dismiss it."

"You are sure the prints were made of soot?"

"Quite sure, Mr Holmes. I rubbed some onto my finger and smelled it. Household soot, I'll stake my fortune on it."

"Very good."

"And if it had begun and ended with the prints," said Agius, "that would have been that. A mystery perhaps, but a none too troubling one. Worse was to come, however."

Chapter Three

A SUPRAMUNDANE INFLUENCE

Eustace Agius looked gravely at Holmes. "The night before last – it must have been around three in the morning – I awoke to an eerie sight. A weird, flickering orange light filled the room. At first I supposed it to be the fire in the hearth. The embers had caught alight again and were issuing flame, that was what I thought. However, the fire had burned low by then and was offering no more than a feeble glow. Besides, the light was brighter than that of any fireplace, and it was coming from outside. I could see it around the edges of the curtains, pulsing and shifting. It dawned on me that a nearby property must be ablaze, and so I leapt out of bed and hastened to the window. Can you guess what happened next?"

Holmes shook his head. "It is not my habit to guess *anything*. Baseless speculation is a practice best left to gypsy fortune tellers and gossiping housewives."

I masked a smile. If ever a statement summarised Sherlock Holmes's temperament and philosophy, this was it.

"I whisked open the curtains," Agius said, "and in that same instant, the light vanished."

"Vanished?"

The industrialist spread out his hands. "Vanished, as though it had never been. I peered out. I could distinguish the shapes of the houses behind mine, silhouetted against the night sky. Lights glimmered faintly in a couple of windows. Aside from that, all was darkness. Certainly there was no great blaze casting its illumination on the scene. I stood there at the window for what must have been ten minutes, trying to puzzle it out. What could have caused that mighty flickering brilliance? Eventually I closed the curtains and returned to bed, but sleep did not come easily. I wondered if perhaps I had dreamed the whole thing, but I was sure I had not, and I remain firm in that conviction even now. There *had* been a fiery light outside, and it disappeared as soon as I looked for it."

"Might I ask, Mr Agius," said Holmes, "if anyone else saw this alleged blaze? You are a married man. You mentioned a wife a moment ago. Besides, the society columns often celebrate your exploits, and just last week, if I recall rightly, Mr and Mrs Eustace Agius are recorded as having attended a grand Christmas ball thrown by the Duchess of Holmthorpe at her house on Park Lane."

"You mean did my wife witness the phenomenon too? No, she did not, for the simple reason that she sleeps in another room."

"That is what I was getting at. I was trying to be delicate."

"We have slept apart for many a year. It is not that unusual an arrangement among married couples."

"Indeed not."

"Among other things, I am a heavy snorer and Faye – that is my wife's name – is a light sleeper. It is not a favourable combination."

"I did not mean to pry. I simply wished to establish whether there is a corroborating witness."

"There is none. I quizzed the household about it the next morning, Faye and Vernon included. Nobody had seen any such light in the night. My mystification was great, you won't be surprised to hear, and it was compounded by what came next."

"And what did come next?" Holmes asked.

"Smoke," said Agius. "That afternoon, I was in my study, going over some papers, and all at once smoke began issuing forth from beneath a cupboard door. A great white cloud of it billowed up, dispersing throughout the room and bringing with it a sharp, acrid smell. Soon my study was filled with haze and I had to throw open a window. Once the air had cleared, I checked inside the cupboard. There was nothing there."

"Nothing at all?"

"Nothing that should not have been there – ledgers, folders filled with documents, stationery and the like. Nothing untoward. No ashes, for instance. Not even a scorch mark."

"Well, well, well," said Holmes. "That is intriguing. What are we supposed to make of it all?"

"It may sound absurd," said Agius, "but I can only ascribe these incidents to some supernatural source. And from one such as me, that is quite an admission. I have racked my brains to come up with an alternative explanation and I cannot. Nor am

I alone in thinking that an otherworldly agency is involved. Among the servants, the prevailing opinion now is that the house is haunted. The scullery maid has handed in her notice for that very reason. She is a young Irishwoman, a devout Catholic and somewhat highly strung. She said she cannot stay a moment longer in a building where – and I quote – 'the very Divvil himself is abroad'. You know how these below-stairs folk are, prone to fancy and superstition, and yet I myself feel much the same as they do. For some reason, a spectral entity has taken up residence within my walls and is committing disruptive acts. Acts which all seem aimed at me."

"Or at any rate, you are the one who observes them."

"Amounts to the same thing. It is putting me under great strain, Mr Holmes, as you may well imagine. I barely slept a wink last night, worrying what inexplicable event would next be visiting itself upon me. I have brooded on the matter, and this morning I decided I would consult you, to see if you might shed light on it. Faye is quite convinced I am deluded. She says I am reading far too much into things which are, on the face of it, inconsequential. Vernon, meanwhile, gazes at me pityingly in that way that boys of his age often will with their fathers, as though 'the dad' is a doddering old ninny. He does it when he thinks I am not looking, but I have seen it. The truth is, I am scared." Agius wrung his hands. "So far, nothing has occurred that has caused direct harm or lasting damage, but what if that changes? What if these – let us call them materialisations – what if these materialisations are a mere prelude? What if there is worse to come?"

Holmes eyed the fellow evenly. "Given all you have just said, Mr Agius, I see two possibilities. One is that you are indeed being haunted by a discarnate entity from beyond the veil and it is taking a peculiar delight in disturbing you with weird, random materialisations, to use your word. The other possibility is that you are simply the butt of a series of practical jokes. Some prankster is amusing himself by playing tricks on you, and in light of the fact that there is a fourteen-year-old boy in your house, I would look no further than him."

"Vernon? You think Vernon is behind it all? Never. Not my son."

"You yourself just said that he gazes at you pityingly."

"He does, but he is hardly likely to launch a campaign of harassment against me. He would not dare. If I found out it was him, I would tan his hide, and he knows it. Besides, the first handprint appeared over a month ago, when Vernon was still at school. Term only ended a week before Christmas."

Holmes conceded the point. "When you said the affair started 'not long ago', I took you to mean more recently than a month. Therefore your son, quite clearly, is absolved. That still leaves plenty of suspects, though. Your household staff numbers how many?"

"All told, a dozen. You think it is one of them?"

"I think that only someone resident on the premises could consistently contrive such feats. Anyone from outside the house would not have ready access to your study, say, or your bedroom."

"But the prints that appear as if from nowhere. And the fire that was no fire... The smoke... We are not talking about everyday events, Mr Holmes. They are, without doubt, indicative of a supramundane influence."

"In which case," said Holmes, "I advise you to seek the help of a priest or a psychic medium, rather than a consulting detective."

"You will not investigate, then?" Agius managed to sound both aggrieved and forlorn.

"No, sir. Unless you are not telling me the whole story, I see no reason to become involved."

"I have told you everything."

To my eyes, Agius seemed to be blustering, and I wondered whether he did have something to hide.

Holmes did not press him on it, however. "Then that is that. I am sorry you have wasted your time coming over here."

Agius delved into an inner pocket to produce a chequebook and pen. He dashed off a cheque and handed it to Holmes. I glimpsed the figure written on it, and it was all I could do not to let out a whistle of astonishment. He was giving Holmes £400, more than a year's salary for a general practitioner like me.

"There," said Agius. "Does that change your mind?"

Holmes held the cheque out to him. "Take it back. I neither want nor need your money."

"Keep it," said the industrialist, rising. "It's yours. You'll take my case."

"I shall not."

"I'll see you at my house tomorrow, nine AM sharp. Tarleton Crescent, Knightsbridge. Number 23."

Without any further ado, Eustace Agius took his leave.

Chapter Four

THE WORST POSSIBLE
BEST FRIEND

"Holmes," I said, after the industrialist had gone, "that is a fantastic sum of money."

"I have been paid larger," my friend replied airily, eyeing the cheque.

"Could you not see your way to giving the case a cursory examination? At the very least you could go to Agius's house tomorrow and pretend to look around."

"And then feel justified in cashing this cheque?"

"Why not?"

"It would be fraud."

"Not if, by feigning involvement, you were able to put Agius's mind at ease. Just the fact that Sherlock Holmes was treating his problem with a modicum of seriousness might help lower his heightened state of anxiety, whether or not you are actually able to fathom what is going on. Then, if you still don't want his money, you could always donate it in full to an orphanage or the Salvation Army. That way, you will have done two good turns, with very little effort on your part."

"I see that the Christmas spirit still lingers within you, Watson. Goodwill to all men, charitable giving, altruism and so forth. You are clearly far more virtuous than I. The trouble is that our friend Agius was not being wholly honest with us."

"He has lied? How so?"

"It isn't that he has lied," said Holmes, "more that he has withheld a salient fact or two. Would you do me a favour and reach for that commonplace book on the shelf by your elbow? The one with 'Spring 1889' on the spine. No, that's '1888'. I grant you, my penmanship has room for improvement. There's the one, yes. '89. Now pass it here. Thank you."

Holmes leafed through the book, one among his many collections of newspaper clippings. Any press item that caught his eye, especially if its content was unusual or connected with criminal activity, he would cut out and paste into these books, which, together, formed a reference library of the extraordinary and the nefarious going back to the beginning of his career as a detective.

"Yes, here we are," he said presently. "From *The Times*, dated the eighteenth of May. 'Fire at Cotton Mill. Ninety-six Currently Thought Dead. Terrible Scenes. Victims Trampled in Stampede to Escape.' I shan't bother to read you the entire article, which is lengthy and couched in no less florid a style than the headlines. I shall give you the edited highlights. 'Yesterday a fierce and uncontrollable conflagration broke out at a Rochdale cotton mill belonging to the distinguished industrialist Eustace

Agius. The inferno is believed to have started when a spark from an electric light ignited cotton fibres in the air. The flames spread quickly through the building, soon consuming it entire.' There follows a paragraph relating the mill's statistics. It was one of the largest in the land, built by Agius himself to his own specifications. 'Housing over a thousand steam-driven spindle mules and a similar quantity of power looms…' 'Affording employment to hundreds of locals…' 'Not constructed using the latest fireproof materials such as cast-iron columns and wrought-iron roof trusses…' Now we get to the nub of it, the deaths themselves. 'No sooner did the fire take hold than panic ensued and mill workers rushed for the exits in their droves. Alas, the great and abiding pity of it is that not all were able to make it to safety.'"

"What a ghastly business," I said.

"The prose or what it is describing?"

"That is rather flippant of you, Holmes," I chided.

"Yes. I apologise." He read on. "'The death toll is reckoned to be in the mid-nineties, but not all the workforce has yet been accounted for. The fire brigade have extinguished the flames but the ruins remain too radiantly hot still to be entered. When it is safe to do so, the victims' bodies can be recovered and the full tally established.'"

"Those poor men."

"But that's it, Watson," said Holmes. "It wasn't only men. 'Counted amongst the departed are a significant number of women and children. According to reports they were trampled underfoot during the rush to escape, being weaker in body and smaller in frame than their adult male colleagues, who left them in their battered, semiconscious condition to burn to death.'"

"Agius employed women and children?" I said.

"It is not unheard of."

"But aren't there laws against such things nowadays? Especially regarding children?"

"There are laws governing the working hours and moral welfare of children employed in heavy industry. They have to be older than ten, to begin with, and must possess a school leaving certificate before they are permitted to enter gainful employment. More generally, there are laws ameliorating the conditions under which all factory workers operate, from decent ventilation and sanitation to necessary safeguards placed on the machinery they toil at. The Factories Act of 1833 is the principal piece of legislation in that respect, obliging factory proprietors to have their premises inspected by the relevant officials on a regular basis. It seems, however, that Eustace Agius may not have complied wholly with the Act's strictures."

Holmes scanned the article.

"Where is it mentioned?" he said. "Ah yes, here. The final paragraph. 'Questions have been raised with regard to the comparative lack of exits at Mr Agius's establishment. It seems there was an insufficient number of these for the size of the workforce, and employees had frequently voiced concerns on the issue since the cotton mill first opened its doors. This leads one to speculate whether the deaths during the fire may have been reduced in number considerably, if not eliminated altogether, had there been less of a crush of people trying vainly to evacuate via limited points of egress. However, since the mill repeatedly passed muster with the Factory Inspectorate, the value of such criticism is moot. Mr Agius, who is believed to be singlehandedly the producer of one fifth of Britain's cotton, could not be reached at this time to offer comment.'"

"Reading between the lines," I said, "the reporter is suggesting that the Factory Inspectorate were negligent in their responsibilities."

"That or Agius bribed them," said Holmes. "Such 'visitors', as they are known, traditionally work in pairs and consist of a clergyman and a Justice of the Peace."

"Unimpeachable figures, surely."

"Unimpeachable, yes, but unbribable? Perhaps not. It is quite possible that Agius waved large sums of money under their noses. Sums like this." He brandished the £400 cheque. "That could easily turn a man's head, however much of a paragon of probity he is meant to be."

"Turn his head in such a way that he turns a blind eye."

"Indeed."

"But why skimp on the number of exits in a factory?" I mused.

"Corner-cutting. Lowering overheads. A means of restricting the arrival and departure of workers so that they may be more easily monitored. I don't know the answer. I am not an industrialist. What I do know is that this is far from being the only occasion on which Eustace Agius has been found deficient as an employer. He has a track record stretching back to the early days of his career. Complaints have been routinely levied against him with respect to malpractice and violations of workers' rights. Yet not once has he been called to account for his misconduct, not even for this fire at Rochdale."

"There were no legal repercussions? No inquiry?"

"None. Since the Factory Inspectorate had determined that everything was above board at the mill, then technically speaking Agius did no wrong. Nevertheless, responsibility for ninety-six deaths, or whatever the final total was, is no easy thing to bear. Could you, Watson, sleep well at night knowing that your miserliness was to blame for so great a loss of life?"

"I sleep badly when I lose even a single patient."

"Thus speaks a man of enormous sensitivity and integrity. And it is not as if it's your fault when a patient in your care dies. It is merely disease overcoming your wherewithal to treat it. Agius, by contrast, could have prevented those ninety-six deaths by the simple expedient of including more doorways in his mill. That he failed to do so must surely prey on his mind."

"Must it? When he is, by his own admission, hard-headed?"

"Even the hardest-headed know guilt," said Holmes. "They are just not prepared to admit it, to themselves least of all."

"So these ghostly goings-on at his house…"

"It is telling, is it not, that the mysterious 'materialisations' Agius described are all linked to fire in some way or other. Soot, flames, smoke – the theme is consistent."

"You're suggesting that he *is* being haunted after all?" I said. "That the ghost of one of the ninety-six who perished in the cotton mill blaze is now plaguing him, manifesting in ways that point directly to its origin and cause of death?"

Holmes chuckled. "Watson, if I were sincerely suggesting that, I'd hope you would consign me to a sanatorium long enough for the brain-fever to abate and sanity to reassert itself. The point I am trying to put across is that if you wished to disturb the mental balance of a man who has almost a hundred needless deaths to his name, you could hardly do it better than by assailing him with tangible reminders of his offence."

"Then someone is trying to drive Agius mad."

"And, by the looks of it, succeeding. The man's state of agitation is extreme. He is a whisker away from full nervous collapse."

"Then for that reason, surely, the case merits looking into," I said. "You cannot allow someone to be hounded into debility, however disagreeable you may personally find him. Not if it lies within your power to prevent it."

Holmes fixed me with a steady gaze for several moments, then heaved a deep, resigned sigh. "Watson, you really are the worst possible best friend. It is quite exasperating how you consistently appeal to my better nature and convince me to do right when the imp on my shoulder is whispering to the contrary. Without you, I would lead a quieter and far more ethically compromised life."

I took these comments in the ironical, jocular spirit in which they were intended, and responded in kind. "I am sorry to be such a burden to you, Holmes."

"You can scarcely comprehend how my back aches and my knees buckle with the weight of carrying your rightness. All right then, old fellow, you win. I shall wire the arrogant Agius to tell him that I will, after all, be keeping our nine o'clock appointment tomorrow at 23 Tarleton Crescent, Knightsbridge. As your punishment for spurring me into reluctant action, however, I insist that you accompany me."

"Accompany you? On an investigation?" I said with a grin. "Well, if I *must*."

Chapter Five

THE INDUSTRIALIST'S WIDOW

Neither of us could have foreseen – not even Sherlock Holmes, whose powers of perception were such that they sometimes verged on precognition – the next development in the case.

We arrived at the Agius residence at the appointed hour the next morning. It was one among a sweeping arc of tall, cream-coloured Georgian townhouses overlooking a semi-circular private park that would have been, in summer, leafy and charming. This street was one of the smartest in town, if not *the* smartest, home to aristocracy, politicians and paragons of the professional class. Many of the residences still had their Christmas decorations up, from holly wreaths upon the front door to bauble-bedecked trees visible in a ground-floor window.

Holmes's knock was not answered immediately, which surprised me somewhat. We waited fully three minutes before at last the door opened. Out peered the solemn face of what could only be the Agius family's butler.

"Yes?"

Holmes presented his card. "I have an appointment."

The butler studied the card. "Might I ask with whom, sir?"

"With Mr Eustace Agius, of course. He is expecting us at this very minute."

"Ah." The servant seemed discomfited, even embarrassed. "Sir is unaware, then, of the recent misfortune."

"Misfortune?"

"Please, if you wouldn't mind waiting a moment…"

The butler withdrew, closing the door, and Holmes and I had no choice but to stand on the front doorstep, clapping our hands and stamping our feet to ward off the cold.

"What on earth do you think is going on?" I asked my companion.

"I am not sure, Watson," came the reply. "The data are insufficient, but I fear the worst."

Presently the door reopened, and now it was young Vernon Agius, no less, who looked out. The lad had gained a good three or four inches in height since our last encounter, and his features had lost much of their childish roundedness, with adult angularity beginning to assert itself. He also looked somewhat wan.

"Mr Holmes," he said. "And Dr Watson. It is an honour to make your acquaintance again."

"The feeling is mutual," I said.

"Might I enquire why you are here?"

"We have come at the behest of your father," said Holmes.

"My father…" Vernon's tone was both puzzled and perturbed.

"Pray tell, young man, what has happened?"

"I regret to say, Mr Holmes, that my father is…" Vernon faltered. "Well, not to put too fine a point on it, he is dead."

"Dead?" I declared. "Good heavens."

"Yes, Doctor. It occurred late last night."

"My condolences."

"Thank you."

"How?" Holmes demanded. "What was the cause of this terrible event?"

"Holmes," I said, "a little consideration, perhaps. There's no need to interrogate the boy quite so forcefully. He has just lost his father."

"I appreciate that, Watson. Still, there is no harm in asking, surely."

"It is fine," said Vernon. "I don't mind. My father suffered a heart attack, Mr Holmes. It was sudden and quite devastating. Little could be done for him. He expired right here, in the house. The body has been taken to the morgue, and funeral plans are already in hand. As you can imagine, the whole household is reeling."

"Naturally," I said. "We shan't trouble you any further, my boy. Again, condolences. Come along, Holmes." I plucked at my friend's sleeve.

He, however, remained put. "Might we be permitted to enter, Vernon?"

"What for?"

"If nothing else, it would be remiss of us not to pay our respects to the lady of the house and offer her commiseration.

As gentlemen, and as acquaintances of her late husband, we can do no less."

"I must say, until now I was unaware you even knew my father, Mr Holmes."

"He and I have conducted business together."

I darted a sidelong glance at Holmes, which he studiously ignored. His characterisation of his relationship with Eustace Agius was an overstatement, to say the least. Some might even call it a blatant distortion of the truth.

"Let me see if Mama is up to receiving visitors," Vernon Agius said. "In the meantime, you should come in. I can't have you standing out there in such chilly weather."

The hallway was large, richly decorated and, above all, blessedly warm. A fire blazed in the hearth, and I stationed myself beside it and basked in its radiance. Now that we were indoors, many of the traditional signifiers of a household in mourning were apparent. Pictures on a sideboard had been laid face down, and paintings on the walls had been turned round so that their backs showed. The longcase clock in the hallway was stopped, as was the one on the mantel, and curtains everywhere were half drawn.

I felt moved to enquire of Holmes why he was so keen to meet Eustace Agius's widow but, in the event, I refrained from voicing the question. I presumed that he had his reasons, beyond those he had vouchsafed to Vernon, and that his true motive would become apparent soon enough. In fact, if I knew Holmes, his hackles were up. He sensed something amiss here and would not be satisfied until he had established whether or not his suspicions were warranted. The game, in other words, was afoot.

Shortly, Vernon returned and invited us to follow him.

"Mama is in the conservatory," he said. "She is very tired, as you can understand. We have had a disturbed night, all of us, and I would prefer it if you did not outstay your welcome."

"We shall trouble her no longer than is necessary," said Holmes.

"Frankly," the boy confided, "if it wasn't you, Mr Holmes, I would have turned you away. But who can say no to a great man such as yourself? And you too, Doctor. I must admit, I am an admirer of your writing."

"Thank you. Your father implied as much, telling me you have read and reread both of my books extensively."

"He noticed that, did he? Well, I suppose it is obvious, for the pages have started to fall out of my copies through use. May we expect more from you?"

"I am working on some shorter pieces which I hope to publish soon. There is a publisher called George Newnes who is setting up a new periodical mixing fiction and factual articles – I believe it will be called *The Strand* – and he is very interested."

"Pieces relating more of Mr Holmes's exploits?"

"What else?"

"I am glad. When this *Strand* magazine appears, I will be sure to take it, purely so that I can enjoy these further tales of yours."

"You are too kind."

The conservatory was well heated, a wood-burning stove issuing warm air in such profusion that the windowpanes were clouded with condensation and the atmosphere felt almost oppressively humid. Amid a bountiful array of tropical plants sat Mrs Agius, perched in a wicker chair with her chin on one fist, gazing out through the misty glass at a winter-sparse rear garden. She rose to greet us, thus revealing a tall, statuesque frame, which was draped in black silk as befitted her new station in life. Her face had a certain hauteur about it but was handsome nonetheless, with eyes of a luminous jade green and a mouth that bespoke intelligence and forthrightness. She extended a gloved hand, which we each clasped in turn, then ushered us to a pair of wicker chairs that were positioned opposite hers.

"If you need me, Mama," Vernon said, stroking her shoulder, "just call." She, in turn, patted her son's hand absently.

With a nod of farewell towards Holmes and me, Vernon retired, leaving the three of us alone.

"Madam," said Holmes, "may I first tender my deepest sympathies."

"I likewise," I chimed in.

"Kind of you, gentlemen," said Mrs Agius. Her voice was husky, and whether this was its natural timbre or a state brought on by a surfeit of emotion, I found it rather appealing. "Eustace's death has come as a great shock. And yet…"

"And yet?" Holmes prompted.

"I cannot say it was wholly unexpected. Vernon informs me that you knew my husband."

"If I am honest, Mrs Agius, that was a slight exaggeration on my part. Our acquaintance stems back no further than yesterday, when he came to call on me regarding a certain matter. You did not know about this? He did not tell you?"

"Eustace and I…" The industrialist's widow groped for words. "We did not share everything with each other. That is not to say that we kept secrets, simply that he had his path and I had mine, and not often did the two intersect. I was seldom privy to his business affairs, for instance. He rarely consulted me about any of that. Similarly, his personal dealings were not always known to me. If he were to go out of the house without me, I knew better than to enquire the destination, even though it was likely to be one of his clubs; he had memberships at all the important ones. I learned, long ago, that to pose such a question was to invite a sharp response, and sometimes a vicious one. I don't think it indiscreet to tell you that ours was not a close marriage. So if Eustace went to see you yesterday, Mr Holmes, I do not doubt that he did, but by the same token you should not be surprised that he did not divulge the fact to me."

At that moment, a small dog waddled into the conservatory. Vernon had left the door to the main part of the house slightly ajar, in such a way that the dog was able to nudge it open with its muzzle. It was a fawn-coloured pug with a black face, and it went straight to Mrs Agius, claws clacking on the terracotta floor tiles.

"Otto, my darling," said the lady, leaning down and gently kneading the rolls of skin around its neck. The pug preened. "Otto is royalty, you know," Mrs Agius told us. "By association, at any rate. Our queen herself bred him and gave him to me as a gift."

Her Majesty's fondness for pugs is well documented, and I have to admit I was somewhat impressed that this particular little beast bore such a noble provenance. On the other hand, and at the risk of sounding treasonous, I have never had any great liking for the breed. The squashed features and bulging eyes of pugs, to me, lend them an air of utter vapidity.

Mrs Agius ceased her ministrations, and the pug settled down on the floor by the stove and began licking one hindleg.

"If you knew Eustace at all," Otto's mistress resumed, "you would know that he was not a well man."

"I am not a certified medical professional like my colleague," said Holmes, "but it was apparent even to me that your husband was not in the best of health."

"I noted signs of elevated blood pressure," I said. "Was there more to it than that?"

"Angina pectoris," said Mrs Agius. "Eustace had suffered from it for years. He visited doctors, and they all said the same. He should lighten his workload, for the stress of conducting business at such a high level was enormous. He should lose some weight. He should drink less, eat better, take up golf, go for gentle walks – anything to ease the strain on his heart and improve blood flow to it. Eustace, however, was unwilling to alter his lifestyle in any way, and moreover refused to delegate responsibility for his cotton mills to subordinates. He was stubborn to a fault. Instead, he sought the most convenient means of alleviating his condition, namely medication."

"Amyl nitrite?"

"Just that, Doctor. He was prescribed amyl nitrite 'pearls' and would use one whenever the chest pains struck."

"I take it that, on this unfortunate occasion, the remedy was ineffective," said Holmes. "Or did he not have the opportunity to resort to it?"

Mrs Agius scratched her pug's ears, debating inwardly. "I will share with you the details of his death," she said at last, having made up her mind. "They are, for want of a better word, unusual. I would not normally be so forthcoming. The two of you are, after all, strangers. Yet I am not unaware of your reputation, Mr Holmes. The talk in London society often turns to you. Just the day before yesterday, in fact, the Countess of Morcar was singing your praises to me, regarding that business with her blue carbuncle last year. Then there is Vernon, of course. You have, in him, an ardent devotee, and if my son is convinced of your *bona fides*, that is good enough for me. I feel you are to be trusted. Bear in mind, however, that much of what I am about to tell you is second-hand. I was not present at the incident which precipitated Eustace's demise. I only came in in the immediate aftermath. Everything that led up to it is fantastical and you can be forgiven for discrediting much of what you are about to hear."

Chapter Six

THE FINGER OF BLAME

As Mrs Agius began her narrative, I marvelled at her composure. Many a woman in her situation would have been rendered incoherent with grief, barely capable of speech, let alone of recounting in such measured tones the death of her husband. There was in her that steeliness that one often finds in an Englishwoman of good breeding, a determined resolve not to allow feelings to overwhelm her sense of propriety. At the same time, given how she spoke about Eustace Agius with so little affection, and sometimes even contempt, his removal from her life can hardly have been a great wrench. It was clear that she and he had been as estranged as a husband and wife can be while still remaining married.

"Unless I am greatly mistaken, Mr Holmes," Mrs Agius said, "Eustace went to see you yesterday regarding the somewhat queer set of incidents that have taken place in this house lately. Am I correct?"

"You are, madam."

"I thought so. I cannot imagine what other reason there might have been. Whenever your name crops up at dinner parties and the like, it is commonly in association with episodes that might be termed bizarre, even outrageous. So you are aware of the alleged haunting, then."

"Your late husband went to some lengths to apprise me of it and all its various aspects."

"Last night, the so-called ghost again made its presence known, this time in a manner more emphatic and startling than any previous."

Holmes leaned forward slightly in his chair. "Go on."

"Remember, I was not there at the time," said Mrs Agius. "I did not see the ghost myself. I am only reporting what I have been told, which is this. Around midnight, Eustace was awoken by the sound of glass breaking. It came from downstairs and, thinking it might be a burglar gaining entry via a window, he felt the urge to investigate. We do not share a bed, Mr Holmes, before you ask, nor even a bedroom."

"Your husband said something to that effect. He said also that you are a light sleeper. But you did not hear this sound yourself?"

"I did not. Eustace's room is on the first floor. Mine is on the second. Perhaps that would account for it. At any rate, he lit a lamp and ventured out, but did not go downstairs straight away. Rather, he went up to the topmost floor, where the servants' quarters are, and roused Sturridge, his valet. It is thanks to him – Sturridge – that I have knowledge of this chain of events.

"Sturridge and my husband then stole down to the hallway together. If there was a burglar on the premises, Eustace had no wish to confront the felon alone. He also wanted to catch him in the act. That was why he had gone up to Sturridge's room rather than simply rung for him. The sound of the bell might have alerted an interloper and sent him running. So he said to Sturridge, at any rate.

"Eustace gave Sturridge the lamp and made him go ahead, himself following close behind. Sturridge is of stout yeoman stock, solidly built and quite unflappable. A good man in a crisis, and a good man to shelter behind, too.

"Even he, however, was taken aback by the sight that greeted them as they reached the hallway. It was no burglar. It was... well, it was a figure. An apparition. A thing composed entirely of blackness; tattered, horrible."

Mrs Agius paused a moment, then continued.

"'I never saw nothing like it, ma'am.' That is what Sturridge said to me later, after it was all over. 'Never saw nothing like it, nor ever want to again.' To hear so level-headed a fellow say these words, and with a blanched face and a quiver in his voice, too – if you knew him, gentlemen, you would know how remarkable that is.

"This apparition, according to Sturridge, arose from the floor as if passing up through it from below. It took shape, adopting a human-like form, and for a while it simply hovered there. It had no features that Sturridge could make out. It was just an outline, he said, 'a hollow, blackened mockery of a man'.

"As if this was not bad enough, the figure then abruptly raised an arm. Clearly it was pointing, and just as clearly it was pointing at Eustace. Sturridge is in no doubt about that, nor about the nature of the gesture.

"'It was accusation, ma'am,' he said. 'That's the only word for it. As when a witness is asked in court to confirm that the suspect in the dock is the person he saw committing the crime. The finger of blame.'

"Next instant, the apparition shot towards the ceiling, vanishing from view. Thereupon, my husband let out a shriek of horror and collapsed to the floor, clutching his chest.

"Sturridge had the presence of mind to know what to do. He had seen Eustace suffer one of his angina attacks before. This one was plainly more acute than any hitherto, but he knew nonetheless that application of an amyl nitrite pearl was the necessary recourse. He ran upstairs to my husband's room and fetched the little pillbox in which Eustace kept the medication. As he emerged, he encountered me. I had come down from my own room, having been disturbed by Eustace's loud, piercing cry. Sturridge hurriedly filled me in on what had happened. I asked him for the pillbox and hastened down to the hallway.

"There lay my husband, writhing on the floor, gasping for breath. By the lamp's light I could see that his face had gone purple. There was no time to waste. I took out one of the pearls and broke it in half under his nose.

"'Breathe it in, Eustace,' I said. 'Breathe deeply. This will help.'

"He inhaled the amyl nitrite fumes, and I fully anticipated that within moments his pain would ease and his face resume its natural hue. Not so. Rather, his writhing grew more intense, and his eyes began to bulge. There was nothing for it but to try another pearl. Even then, I sensed that it was futile. The amyl nitrite was not taking effect. A third pearl was similarly ineffective, and by that point I realised all I could do was cradle Eustace's head in my lap and hope against hope that he would recover of his own accord. He did not.

"The last thing he said to me was simply my name. He uttered it, and all at once his body stiffened, then relaxed, and he was gone.

"That is my sorry tale, gentlemen. Sturridge will endorse every word of it. I did everything in my power to keep Eustace alive." Mrs Agius shrugged her shoulders. "It was not enough."

"It is clear to me, Mrs Agius," I said, "that the angina attack was a severe one. The amyl nitrite might have worked, inducing the vasodilation that would have eased the constriction of the blood vessels to your husband's heart. However, in extreme cases this is not always guaranteed, with the result that a full-blown heart seizure ensues. I know it must seem cold comfort, but your actions cannot be faulted. I myself would have done just the same as you, and it would not have changed the outcome one iota. Your husband's fate was in the hands of a higher power."

"Doctor, I appreciate what you are trying to do, but your reassurance is unnecessary," said Mrs Agius. "You must understand that I feel very little sorrow over Eustace's death. Much though I would like to present the image of mourning,

I cannot. These widow's weeds I am wearing are purely for show. It is what is expected. Eustace was – there is no other word for it – a monster. He terrorised me. He terrorised Vernon. He terrorised everyone he met. Am I happy that he is no longer with us? No, I am not. Happy suggests glee, and glee is petty. But I am relieved. A weight has been lifted from this household. For the first time in a long while, I look to the future with optimism, whereas before all I could see was a continuation of the dull, relentless misery that seemed my lot in life."

"That is refreshingly frank of you, madam," Holmes said. "Many in your position would feel moved to gnash their teeth and wail, so as not to look callous."

"I prefer candour in all things, Mr Holmes."

"In that spirit, then, might I ask a question or two?"

"I assumed, you being the great detective that you are, you would not be able to leave without doing so."

This wry rejoinder brought a small smile to Holmes's lips, and also to mine.

"Firstly," said he, "you have been at pains to prefix any reference to supernatural occurrences in the house with a qualifying adjective: 'so-called ghost', 'alleged haunting'."

"I have. Is that a question?"

"You do not believe that some malign, unearthly entity had begun to terrorise your husband, just as he was wont to terrorise others?"

"I have no patience with any of that sort of nonsense. It is all bunkum."

In that respect, Mrs Agius was, I thought, a woman after Holmes's own heart.

"Did you yourself see any of the weird manifestations your husband experienced?" my friend said.

"I saw a few of the sooty handprints and footprints that appeared around the house. I saw neither the fire in the night nor the burst of smoke in Eustace's study, and likewise, as you know, I did not see the black figure in the hallway."

"What did you make of the prints?"

"I made of them precisely nothing," said Mrs Agius firmly. "The obvious assumption is that one or other of the servants caused them. It is winter and the fireplaces need constant tending. Soot gets everywhere. It is just a fact of life at this time of year."

"Your husband claims the shoeprints in his bedroom matched none of the servants'."

"My husband was clearly in error."

"We are told, too, that they were a discrete pair by his bedside, rather than a trail. What is your view on that?"

"I have none, other than that perhaps the servant responsible for the mess tried to remedy it, cleaning up the other shoeprints but carelessly missing out those two."

"Then may I turn to the subject of your husband's business affairs?"

"I have told you, not an area in which I had much involvement."

"You cannot be unaware, though, of the mishap at his cotton mill in Rochdale the year before last."

The widow gave a hollow laugh. "'Mishap' is putting it mildly."

"Eustace Agius had a reputation as a canny dealer."

"Another euphemism. You are quite the diplomat, Mr Holmes. My husband was a notorious shark. That much about his professional life was common knowledge, and I, for one, was not ignorant of it. Scruples were alien to him. If he could penny-pinch, he would. If he could do a rival down, he would. If he could wring another ounce of effort out of his already overtaxed workers and not pay for it, he would. Few get to be millionaires without trampling others underfoot. It is just the way of the world."

"Few get to be millionaires without making enemies, either," said Holmes.

"Ah, so that is where you are going with this line of enquiry. Did Eustace have enemies? He undoubtedly did. Might they have wished him harm? No question. Could one of them have cooked up an elaborate scheme to scare him to death by means of a fake haunting? It is quite preposterous."

"You say that with great certainty."

"Do you not think so yourself? There are far easier ways to kill a man than to stage a series of paranormal-seeming incidents at his home, in the hope that this will bring on a fatal heart attack. A knife in the dark, a gun in the street, poison in his drink – so much simpler and more reliable. Can it be, Mr Holmes, that with your penchant for the out-of-the-ordinary, you look for convoluted conspiracies and dark stratagems where none exist?"

"On the contrary, madam. One of my abiding principles is that the most straightforward explanation is the likeliest. Whenever I am confronted with a complex-seeming problem, that is invariably the approach I adopt."

"Even so, it seems as though you are not discounting the possibility that a plot was devised against Eustace by someone he wronged, and his death was its culmination."

"It is an avenue of investigation worth pursuing," said Holmes, "if only to rule it out."

"In that case," said Mrs Agius, "if you will excuse me for a moment, I have something to show you."

Chapter Seven

ANONYMOUS SCREEDS OF RAGE

Mrs Agius was gone for several minutes, during which time Holmes and I sat in silence in that sweltering conservatory. Otto the pug got up and snuffled around my ankles, perhaps hoping for attention or a titbit. When none came, back to the stove-side the dog went, lying down on its belly and resting its head on its forepaws with a wheezy sigh.

When she returned, Mrs Agius was carrying a sheaf of letters.

"Cast an eye over these," she said, giving them to Holmes. "The handiwork of someone making no bones about the fact that he wanted Eustace dead."

Holmes perused the letters, I leaning over his shoulder to look. There were a dozen of them in all, and each was written in the same hand, a jagged, angry scrawl that was sometimes hard to decipher. Each, too, expressed sentiments to match the handwriting.

One said, "Mr Ageus you are an evil fellow what needs just retribution for his misdemeanours." Another said, "'Ow's yersen?

Me, I'm still greeting for my missus who is dead now these nine month all thanks to you, trampled to the ground and burned. If I ever see you, yer great bowd brosen, you'll receive such a larruping from me as will make the trials of Job seem nothing by comparison." Yet another said, "You should be feart of me, Ageus, for I am vengefull and thirsting to see you brought to book. My wife were a good and honist lady who oughtnt not to have died by fire as she did, leaving our babbies motherless, and the fault is yours and you shall surely have your just deserts, do not moither yourself on that front."

The author of the letters accused Agius of paying off Factory Inspectorate visitors. "They wouldnter let you build the mill as you did, save for you greesing their palms with a wad of money thick enough to choke a donkey. Them I condemn for taking your brass, you I condemn the more for giving it them. Yet you shall pay not in money but in other ways for 'ow you have tret us wrong."

The final letter was a capitalised howl of anguish and despair: "YOU SHALL SCREEM AS YOU PERISH AND YOUR SKRIKING WILL ECHO DOWN TO PERDITION WHERE THE DULE AWAITS YER AND YOU SHALL BURN IN FLAME AS MY WIFE DID AND SO MANY OTHERS."

None of them bore the sender's address, a salutation, or a signature. They were anonymous screeds of rage, rife with misspellings and couched in a dialect that I reckoned to be northern, possibly from the Manchester area.

Holmes spent some time examining them. He held the paper up to the light. He sniffed it. He peered at the words so closely and minutely, he went almost cross-eyed.

At length he said, "You do not have the envelopes these came in by any chance, Mrs Agius?"

"I do not. Eustace threw them away."

"That is a pity. They could have told us much. The letters themselves are instructive, but postmarks and stamps might have filled in a few blanks. I don't suppose your husband had any idea who they were from?"

"None whatsoever, but one may hazard a guess. The husband of one of his employees."

"The widower of one of his employees, you mean."

"If you wish to be pedantic, yes," said Mrs Agius. "The unnamed woman must have been among those poor souls who perished in the blaze at the Rochdale mill. That would make her widower one out of many such bereaved men."

"When did the letters start coming?"

"Earlier this year, in springtime."

"Around the first anniversary of the fire, in other words."

"It could have been."

"At what intervals did they arrive?"

"Once a fortnight, more or less. Eustace read the first one aloud over the breakfast table and dismissed it with a snort and a scornful laugh, although a slight pallor had come to his face, I could see, and his hand trembled somewhat. As further letters arrived, and their content grew increasingly ugly and threatening, he found them less amusing and less easy to discount. When eventually they stopped, he was relieved, I could tell."

"Why did he keep them?" Holmes asked. "At first they meant little to him. Cumulatively, he found them upsetting. In either case, surely he would have got rid of them, by burning them, perhaps, or else tearing them to shreds, in order to dispose of a source of nuisance. I understand he did just that with the letter upon which the sooty handprint appeared."

"Eustace was not a man to discard anything that could be of use to him at a later date," Mrs Agius replied. "He said that if ever the sender turned up at our door in person, or committed violence on him, the letters would be evidence of malice aforethought. They could be presented to the jury at trial and would ensure that the perpetrator was locked away for a very long time."

"They could indeed." Holmes passed the letters back to Mrs Agius. "Madam, before we go, might I prevail upon you to show me the pillbox containing your late husband's amyl nitrite pearls?"

"Whatever for?"

"Merely to assure myself that there is nothing wrong with it or them."

"You think the pearls might have been tampered with?"

"I think nothing until I have seen evidence," said my friend archly.

"Well, I'm unsure where the pillbox has got to. The maid might know." She rang a small bell from the table beside her. A maid appeared, curtseying, and was given her instructions.

Presently she returned, bearing the pillbox. "It was in your room, ma'am. You left it there after… after last night."

Mrs Agius dismissed the girl and passed the pillbox to Holmes. It was a plain, oval thing made of silver, with a hinged lid. He studied its exterior from all angles, then opened it and inspected the pearls within, of which there remained three. Each little capsule of inhalant sat snug in its sleeve of cotton mesh, the ends of which were crimped off much in the manner of a sausage. He gave the box to me to look at as well.

"Your professional opinion, my friend?" said he.

"To my eye, the pearls look to be the genuine article," I said. "There is the manufacturer's name, printed on the sleeves. As for the pillbox, it appears unremarkable. I have seen dozens like it. In short, everything seems in order."

"I concur. Nevertheless, might I, Mrs Agius, be permitted to crack one of the pearls, in order to check its contents?"

The widow flapped a hand, indicating that she cared little whether he did so or not.

"Be careful, Holmes," I said. "If, as you suggest, the pearls may have been tampered with, there could be *anything* inside those phials. Some liquid poison, for instance, whose vapours are deadly."

"I shall take the merest of sniffs," he assured me. He crushed the pearl between his fingers, the capsule breaking with a muffled *crunch*, and held it a few inches from his nose. "It certainly smells like amyl nitrite and nothing more sinister."

He cut open the sleeve off another of the pearls with his pocketknife and slid out the little glass cylinder from within. He studied this, and the clear, yellowish liquid it contained, thoroughly.

"The glass is intact," he averred. "The capsule has not been interfered with in any way. It would be fair to say that these pearls are nothing other than they seem."

He returned the pillbox to Mrs Agius, then rose to his feet, motioning that I should follow suit.

"I am grateful for your indulgence, madam," he said. "Watson and I have now imposed on you far too long. You have been more than generous with your time. Again, for what it's worth, you have my sympathies."

"Mine too," I said, and followed Holmes out of the conservatory.

Back in the hallway, my companion halted and cast his gaze about, with the avid eye of a bird scanning for seed. The chessboard-patterned floor, the walls which were hung with landscapes and portraits, the dark rug, the chandelier above with its brass branches, the staircase which rose steeply to the first-floor landing and spiralled onward to the floors above, the banister rail, the coatrack, the sideboard, the solitary bookcase, the stopped clocks – all these were subjected to scrutiny.

While Holmes was in the throes of this survey, Vernon Agius appeared from a doorway that led to a drawing room.

I greeted him. "Your mother seems to be bearing up well."

"Mama is a strong woman," Vernon said. "She has endured much in her life."

Holmes pivoted round to address the lad. "She spoke just now of your father terrorising her, and indeed you. Is it this that you're referring to?"

"Among other things. Mr Holmes, I am not going to eulogise

my father, nor am I going to pretend I am sorry that he is no longer with us. He was a tyrant, plain and simple. He was quick to anger, and…" Vernon hesitated, then continued. "And he could be free with his fists, too, when the temper was upon him. My mother took the brunt of it, but I myself was not immune. It wasn't until I was twelve that I started to fight back. That was when I had grown large enough to be a match for him, or at any rate look him in the eye and try to give as good as I got. It didn't serve me well, defying him. On the contrary, it made the beatings I received that much fiercer. But at least I felt I had done *something*. I was no longer just a meek, passive victim."

I recalled Wragge telling us, at Saltings House a year earlier, that Vernon Agius had "a troubled home life". Only now did I appreciate *how* troubled. In light of what the boy was saying, it made sense to me that he had stood up to the martinet games master Yeowell and confronted his bullying peers Jeremy Pugh and Hosea Wyatt, in the former instance defending Hector Robinson while he was still alive, in the latter instance after Robinson was dead. In Robinson, Vernon had seen himself. He had seen someone helpless, at the mercy of those more powerful and more aggressive. It had struck a chord, and his reaction had been heartfelt and visceral.

"I am sorry to hear it," I said to him. "You are brave, not only in your actions but in confessing to us what you have suffered. Your mother feels that an oppression has been lifted from her now that your father is gone, and you must feel the same way. I trust that, henceforth, life will be lighter and brighter for you."

"You are kind, Doctor." Vernon looked genuinely moved. "Your words mean a great deal to me. May I shake you by the hand?"

"Most certainly."

The boy engaged in a hearty handshake with me, and also with Holmes. In that moment, or so it seemed to me, young Vernon Agius was well on his way to becoming a man.

Chapter Eight

FROM THE EPISTOLARY
TO THE PRACTICAL

olmes elected that we should walk back to Baker Street from Knightsbridge, rather than take a cab. The exercise, he said, would do us good, and he set off at a forthright pace, his steps so rapid that he seemed constantly about to break into a jog. I did my best to keep up.

As we threaded our way through Hyde Park, he said, "Your thoughts, Watson?"

"On the case?"

"What else?"

"Well, for a start, *is* there even one?"

"What do you mean?"

"Mrs Agius has not indicated that she wishes you to look into her husband's death for her," I said. "Neither, for that matter, has young Vernon. And as for any obligation you had towards Eustace Agius, that has surely expired, along with him."

"On the contrary, Watson. I still have a cheque for four hundred pounds, made out in my name, signed by the man himself."

"But you were reluctant to earn the fee in the first place. Now you have every excuse not to do so. If keeping the money unwarrantedly goes against your conscience, donate it to a charity instead, as I proposed yesterday."

"I certainly could do that," Holmes allowed. "Nevertheless I am convinced that there is something awry in this whole business, and regardless of whether I have been officially engaged to make enquiries, I am going to pursue the matter. I shall do it for my own satisfaction, if nothing else, although of course I can hope to justify the handsome sum Agius tendered me. So, to repeat, Watson: your thoughts?"

"Very well," I said with a resigned sigh. "If past experience is anything to go by, you are inviting me to draw conclusions which you will then, as is your habit, deride and overturn."

"Only if they are hopelessly muddleheaded."

"Which they usually are."

"Can I help that?"

I braced myself for the belittling that seemed the almost inevitable outcome of anything I was about to say. "It does appear as though a beneficent providence has intervened in the lives of both Mrs Agius and her son."

"In the form of a ghost?"

"In the form of a death. They have been liberated from Eustace Agius's despotic influence. I cannot help but feel that, all in all, the world is a better place without him. Harsh as it may sound, the man was undeserving of his wealth and status, and indeed of breath. I try to see the best in people, but where Agius is concerned, I rather hope he is even now, as the anonymous letter writer said, burning in flame."

"Yes, the letters," said Holmes. "I am more interested in discussing those than questions of morality and divine judgement. They were unusual, were they not?"

"Unusual? I found them rather straightforward. Their origin is obvious, as is their intent."

We were circumventing the Serpentine as I said this, passing a group of ducks that were huddled together on the frosty riverbank, their beaks buried beneath their wings. In answer to my remark, Holmes let out a loud, high-pitched "Hah!" which startled the birds, causing them to flap and quack in alarm.

"Obvious?" he said. "The only thing obvious about their origin and intent, Watson, is that the former was designed to obscure the latter."

"How do you mean?"

"The letters were from a working man, a man of common Mancunian stock, poorly educated, whose wife died in the cotton mill fire. Yes?"

"Well, yes. No?"

"No. They were not. That was only what they purported to be. The notepaper, to start with, was of high quality. Good, thick stock, watermarked, well milled, in a fashionable cream colour. Not the sort of paper a working man might easily afford. One or two of the sheets bore very faint traces of a scent, too. I was able to identify it as a gentleman's cologne which doubtless had rubbed off onto the paper from the author's sleeve or hand. Cologne, again, is not an item a working man might easily afford. True?"

"True."

"Then there was the handwriting. Although it looked as though the letters had been penned in a hurry, dripping with the righteous anger of the unjustly bereaved, the handwriting nonetheless bore signs of cultivation. By and large, the letter forms were those of someone who has been taught italic calligraphy. The serif of the descender of the 'g', for instance. The 'l' consisting of a single downstroke. The final flick on the lower-case 'm' and 'n'. Tell me, would a working man utilise, or even be familiar with, italic calligraphy?"

"Unlikely," I said.

"Highly," said Holmes. "As to the language, there was plenty of slang in it, enough for it to pass as the handiwork of a Mancunian native: 'feart', 'moither', 'larruping', 'skriking', and so on. Likewise that talk of 'the Dule' – the Devil – and calling Agius a 'bowd brosen', which I believe means 'bald fatty'. Yet in amongst these and the many misspellings there were also instances of high-flown phrasing. 'As will make the trials of Job seem nothing by comparison' was one; 'thirsting to see you brought to book' another. The disjuncture between the two styles was quite jarring. It is almost as though someone from a well-born, well-heeled background was attempting, and failing, to sound authentically low-class. Try as he might, his natural refinement could not help but show through."

"If you say so, Holmes. None of this was apparent to me."

"And what about the dropped aitches? ''Ow's yersen?' 'For 'ow you have tret us wrong'. I put it to you that a man may speak like that but will not write like that, phonetically, using apostrophes to denote the missing aspirated consonants. Rather, he will write the words as he sees them written everywhere else, correctly and in full. Only a novelist wishing to evoke a regional accent in dialogue will resort to such techniques. The same is true of the letters' vernacular usages. All in all, I was led inescapably to the conclusion that the letter writer was a person striving very hard to conceal his true identity. Yet, if I have learned anything from my frequent use of disguises, the art of impersonation lies in subtlety – just the right amount of makeup, a judicious turn of phrase here, a nuanced gesture there. Lay it on too thick and you give the game away. A light touch is required to make the ruse convincing, and our letter writer signally lacked it."

"Then if the letters did not come from this supposed Mancunian widower," I said, "who did they come from?"

"The salient question is not so much 'who?' as 'why?'. Why direct such venom at Eustace Agius? Why do it by pretending to be some generic, non-existent individual?"

"The pretence, surely, was born out of fear of reprisal."

"Granted, but why go to such lengths?" said Holmes. "A series of brief, pithy missives casting aspersions on Agius's character and integrity would do just as well. That is how the majority of poison pen letters are. None of this playacting rigmarole."

"Do you think there is a connection between the letters and

the hauntings? If there were a dozen letters in all and they arrived fortnightly, then by my reckoning they ceased coming in late autumn. It was not long after, in November, that Agius discovered the first sooty handprint."

"From which we are to infer that the ghost at 23 Tarleton Crescent is the unquiet spirit of the letter writer's late wife?" said Holmes.

"No, you seem adamant that the ghost is bogus, some sort of hoax. However, could the letter writer have decided to change his angle of attack?"

"Graduated from the epistolary to the practical, you mean?" My companion cocked his head to one side, nodding. "That has occurred to me, and as conjectures go, it is not implausible. Certainly the timing supports the idea, as you have pointed out, and there is a thematic consistency between the one and the other, in as much as the shade of a woman might well seek revenge from beyond the grave against the man whose disregard for safety was a contributing factor in her death. One could argue that the letters were sent in order to prepare the ground, planting the seeds of what was to come, suggesting the idea of a ghost in Agius's mind – an idea that was then given flesh, as it were, by subsequent events. And yet the link remains fragile, and perhaps is nothing more than coincidence…"

Holmes's voice trailed off. Then, clapping me on the back, he said, "The letter writer is an impostor, that much I am sure of. I think what's called for now is some imposture of my own."

"You are going to resort to one of your aforementioned disguises?" I said.

"Absolutely correct, old fellow. The person I need to speak to, without his knowing who I really am, is Sturridge."

"Agius's valet."

"The very same. After all, if you want to find out everything there is to know about a man – his truths, his motivations, his secrets – who better to ask than his valet?"

Chapter Nine

A RAT CATCHER CALLS

The following evening, Mary and I were sitting by the fire – I perusing the latest *Lancet*, she busy with her cross stitch – when there came a ring at the door. The maid, Enid, went to answer it and returned shortly to announce that the caller was a rat catcher.

"Says he's come to set his traps," Enid said.

"At this hour?" said Mary, eyeing the clock, whose hands stood at shortly before nine. "It's rather late for a tradesman to come by, is it not?"

"I told him that, ma'am. He says there's an infestation of them in Paddington at present. Rats, that is. Him and the other rat catchers are working all the hours God sends to keep on top of it."

"Very well then." Mary's voice carried a note of bemusement. "Show him in."

The rat catcher entered the dining room, clutching his flat cap in both hands and bowing humbly. His overcoat hung open to reveal a shabby, many-pocketed waistcoat and trousers that were tied below the knee with leather gaiters. His hair was an unruly greying mop and his knuckles were gnarled, coarsened by years of manual labour.

"Beg pardon for disturbing you, sir and madam," said he. "Only, like I just told this young lady of yours, there's rats running loose all over this 'ere corner of London. Comin' up from the sewers in their hundreds, they are, in search of grub. You'd do well to 'ave me visit your basement and your larder and lay down traps and poison."

"Alternatively, Mr Holmes," said Mary, "you could join us by the fireside, and perhaps have a drink. Enid, would you fetch a glass of wine for our unexpected guest? There is still some of the claret left over from supper."

The rat catcher stopped stooping and straightened up, his expression going from importunate to good-humouredly rueful.

"Really, Mrs Watson," he said in those sharp, clear tones I knew so well, "your perspicacity is second to none. Watson? Did *you* know it was me?"

"Of course," I said.

"Don't lie. You were taken in."

"All right. Yes. I was."

"I could see you puffing yourself up, becoming indignant at the intrusion of this grubby manual labourer on your pleasant evening meal."

"I was about to tell you to come back tomorrow during the daytime."

"Whereas your dear wife saw through me in an instant."

Holmes peeled off his wig and smoothed out his real hair, before taking a seat. "What gave me away, Mrs Watson?"

"Three things, Mr Holmes," said Mary. "First, our usual rat catcher came by only last week. You could not have known that; neither did John, as he was out on his rounds at the time. The fellow would not have returned so soon after the last time. Nor would another rat catcher dare encroach upon his 'turf'. They are a highly territorial breed, these men, and to poach a rival's clients is considered an unforgivable transgression. Therefore it was likely that whoever was calling was not what he claimed to be."

"I see. Your reasoning is impeccable. And the second thing?"

"Rare is the rat catcher who goes anywhere without his terrier. Our regular man has a Yorkie constantly at his heels. That dog is the sweetest-natured little thing until she spies a rat, whereupon she becomes a lethal living missile."

"I shall bear that in mind if I adopt this role again in future. Perhaps Mr Sherman of Pinchin Lane will be able to rent me a terrier. And the third and final thing?"

"Your eyes, Mr Holmes," Mary said. "That is what clinched it for me. You cannot change your eyes. You can squint, you can don spectacles, but in their vivacity and their flinty greyness they remain quite distinctive. A woman always pays attention to a man's eyes, and no man has eyes quite like yours. They are unique."

"Capital!" Holmes declared, clapping his hands. "Watson, you could learn a trick or two from your wife. Her powers of observation are so great, they rival mine. It's a wonder you can get away with *anything*, having so vigilant a spouse."

"I would be foolish even to try to hoodwink my Mary," I said, leaning across to pat her arm.

We passed a while in idle, enjoyable chitchat until, in the end, Mary withdrew. "I shall leave you two men to talk alone," said she. "Mr Holmes would not have come here, hotfoot from some covert investigation, if he did not have something of import to relay. Goodnight, Mr Holmes."

"Goodnight, my dear lady," Holmes said, courteously half-rising from his chair. "Your company has been an adornment to the evening and your absence will leave a gaping void."

"Not too late to bed, John," my wife warned me.

"I shan't keep him up," Holmes said.

"I shall hold you to that promise, sir."

"An excellent woman," my friend said after Mary had gone. "You could not have chosen better."

"I'm not sure it was actually my choice at all," I said, fetching the humidor and offering Holmes a selection of cigars. "I like to think that I wooed Miss Mary Morstan, but in hindsight it was she who, through little signs and hints, did the wooing. I merely, without realising it, followed where she led."

"Yes, the wiles of the fairer sex. Wondrous creatures though women are, I cannot see myself ever becoming enmeshed in the nets of one. What a distraction it would be, to surrender my independence to a being of pure emotion! What a threat to the stability of a mind that prizes logic above all else!"

"Surely Mary displayed a sound grasp of logic earlier, when she penetrated your disguise almost before she even saw you."

"Her deductive analysis cannot be faulted," Holmes allowed,

"but what was it that settled the matter for her? My eyes. Her womanly fascination with my eyes."

"Well, be that as it may…" I lit my double corona, and Holmes followed suit with his panatela. "I presume you have interviewed Sturridge the valet, while rigged out like this. What have you gleaned from him?"

"A great deal, Watson. At first, I needed to know what he looked like, and so, dressed as a lowly vagrant, I loitered around Tarleton Crescent yesterday afternoon and evening, watching the comings and goings at number 23. I quickly established that the sturdy fellow in a high-buttoned tailcoat who appeared at the front door a couple of times must be Sturridge. Not only did he fit the description given us by Mrs Agius – 'stout yeoman stock, solidly built' – but I overheard a housemaid address him by his surname. Around seven PM, Sturridge left the property, and I shadowed him. He did not go far, just to a pub a few streets away, The Red Lion, where he passed an hour before returning. This evening, I headed back to Tarleton Crescent, now tricked out as Charlie Jepson, rat catcher by trade. Sure enough, Sturridge ventured out at roughly the same time as before. Once more I dogged his footsteps all the way to The Red Lion, where, after a brief interval to give him a chance to get comfortable, I entered.

"Sturridge was alone at a table, supping a pint. I bought one for myself, then ambled past him with the drink in my hand, only to stumble and – ah, disaster! – spill it on him. Not the whole pint, mind you, but enough to make a mess of his jacket front. I was all apology, swabbing at the beer stain with my handkerchief, begging forgiveness.

"'A thousand pardons, mate,' I said. 'Clumsy old thing I am! You should hear my missus. "Charlie Jepson, you great lumbering oaf," she says. "You can trip over an ant on the floor, you can."'

"Sturridge was irked, and no wonder; but the more I abased myself, the calmer he became, and once I had offered to buy him a pint as recompense, he was entirely willing to let bygones be bygones.

"As is the way of things, you cannot buy a stranger a drink and not fall to talking with him. Soon I was ensconced at Sturridge's table and we were nattering together as amiably as if we had known each other for years. Remarkably, he and Charlie Jepson turned out to have much in common. Both were born and raised in Bermondsey, both played as children among the local wharves and on the mudflats in the shadow of Tower Bridge, and both recalled with nostalgic fondness the noxious smell of the district's tanneries and the pleasanter aroma emanating from the Peek, Frean and Co. bakery on Clements Road, which has led to the borough being known colloquially as Biscuit Town."

"Flagrant bluffing on your part there, Holmes," I said.

My friend shrugged. "Sturridge offered the reminiscences. I merely echoed them, adding a few plausible details of my own, based on my existing knowledge of the area. The part about the Peek, Frean bakery and Biscuit Town, for example – that was my contribution. At any rate, having gained his trust, and cemented it by buying him another beer, I began gently to probe him about his current situation. The fellow was in a dark mood.

"'I fear for my future,' he lamented. 'I am a gentleman's valet, and it looks as though I am going to be out of a job.'

"'I'm right sorry to hear that,' said I. 'I'm sure, though, that a fine, upstanding bloke such as yourself will have no difficulty securing a similar position somewhere else. There must be gentlemen aplenty in London seeking a reliable valet.'

"'But I've been in my master's service for nigh on ten years,' said he, 'and I've grown quite comfortable where I am. I can't say he was an easy man to work for, but I knew how to handle him.'

"'Of course you would,' said I. 'Us Bermondsey boys are nothing if not capable.'

"At that, Sturridge laughed appreciatively. 'So we are. If you've grown up among the crooks and vagabonds you find on Jacob's Island and down the Old Kent Road, there's little in the world that can frighten you. Least of all a posh gent's bad temper. He wasn't kind to anyone, my master wasn't, not even to his own kin. Oh, the way he treated his wife and his son – it wasn't right, Jepson. Not right at all. A man from our old manor might behave like that, but you'd never expect it of a toff, would you? Just goes to show, people are people, whatever their station. Still, I had the measure of him, I could weather his storms, and it was a good living.'

"'What happened?' I said. 'If it ain't rude of me to ask. If it is, just say so. Just say, "You've a right bloomin' cheek, Charlie Jepson," and I'll sling my hook.'

"'How did it all go wrong? Thereby hangs a tale, my friend.'

"'I have time, Sturridge,' I said. 'I also have coin.'

"The valet considered a moment, then held out his empty glass to me. 'Fill her up, and I'll tell you.'"

Chapter Ten

THE PRECARIOUS FOUNDATIONS OF GREAT WEALTH

Sherlock Holmes puffed out a plume of cigar smoke, then scratched at one of his knuckles, peeling off a little of the carefully applied theatrical putty that made them look so callused.

"I shan't regale you with the entire story in Sturridge's voice, Watson," he said. "I shall give you the elements of it that are pertinent. Sturridge first of all identified his master as Eustace Agius. At the name, I looked blank, and he explained about Agius's cotton mills and pre-eminence in that industry. Then he embarked on an account of the hauntings at the house, confirming everything that both Agius and Mrs Agius already told us. He pronounced himself baffled by the sooty prints.

"'When Mr Agius showed us those foot marks on the carpet by his bedside,' he said, 'I was quite flummoxed. "Blow me down," I thought. "Where could those have come from?" I half-wondered whether it might even have been my doing, since I was the last to enter the bedroom before him. Footprints like that don't just appear out of nowhere, do they?'

"He also spoke of the unease that developed among the domestic staff as the weird phenomena continued. The more superstitious among them would go around muttering prayers to themselves and, as we know, the scullery maid became so distressed by it all that she resigned.

"'After a while, Mr Agius grew desperate,' Sturridge said. 'He even went to see the detective fellow – Holmes is his name? This was the day before yesterday. He told me the man had scored some notable successes getting to the truth of some very odd affairs. He came back in high dudgeon. "The fellow is an insufferable prig, Sturridge!" he said. "Accused me of lying! Practically laughed in my face! But I have handed him a substantial cheque all the same. He is supposed to be dropping by tomorrow. He'd better, that's all I can say. He'd damned well better."'

I chortled. "I'm surprised you could keep a straight face, Holmes, hearing yourself referred to in such disparaging terms."

"All Charlie Jepson did was shake his head wearily," Holmes said, "as if he had met many an insufferable prig in his time and was all too familiar with the type.

"Then Sturridge got round to talking about the fateful night. He was hesitant, to begin with. 'You really will think me half-baked if I tell you this,' he said. 'I'm not sure I should. I mean, who, if he wishes to be taken seriously, will admit he's seen a ghost?'

"To this, Charlie Jepson replied that, in his opinion, 'spooks, goblins and whatnot' were real, and he mentioned an occasion when, laying his traps in a workhouse basement down Southwark way, he had come upon one of the legendary rat kings – a half-dozen of the verminous creatures with their tails all knotted together, still alive but unable to separate from one another, squealing and squirming. Of course he killed them, but a rat king is famously an ill omen, and what should happen just a day later but his own mother died. 'Taken sudden, from a stroke, and you tell me the two things ain't connected.'"

"Oh, Holmes," I admonished. "What an appalling fabrication."

"But it served a purpose, Watson. It helped Sturridge overcome his reluctance. He proceeded to recount how he was awoken by his master shortly after midnight and accompanied him down to the hallway to investigate a noise Agius had heard. By this point in our conversation Sturridge was well inebriated, but despite that, or perhaps because of it, his descriptions were vivid and compelling. He told me how, by the light of the lamp, he saw shards of glass glinting on the floor. It was a wineglass, he said, that had somehow been smashed to smithereens. He was able to identify it as such because he was the one who tidied up the debris later. 'That wineglass breaking must have been what woke up the master,' he said. 'But as to how it got there on the hallway floor, I have no idea. It and its kind belong in a cabinet in the dining room.'

"The mystery of the wineglass, however, was the least of his worries, because then all at once the phantom manifested. The apparition was, according to Sturridge, 'all ragged and torn-looking, like a shadow that has suffered a mauling'. He said that, at the sight of it, his breath caught in his throat and his heart temporarily seemed to stop beating.

"'I did a stint in the army before I went into service,' he avowed. 'Infantryman. Private, rising to lance corporal. Saw action in the Zulu War, both at Isandlwana and Rorke's Drift. I reckon myself a man of courage. Well, I'll tell you, Jepson, that *thing* gave me the collywobbles like you wouldn't believe. The way it hung there in the air, swaying from side to side, this… this patch of greater darkness amid the gloom. And then it raised its arm…'

"You should have seen the way the beer in Sturridge's glass slopped as he lifted it to his lips and took a deep draught, Watson. That was how unsteady his hand was.

"The phantom whisked upwards, vanishing, and Agius collapsed with a cry. Sturridge, recognising the symptoms of a severe form of angina attack, roused himself from his horrified stupor and ran to fetch the pillbox containing his master's amyl nitrite pearls. Intercepted by Mrs Agius, he gave her the pillbox as requested and let her administer them to her husband. He watched as she took three of the pearls out of the tin, one after another, and broke them open beneath Agius's nose. In her haste and agitation, he said, she fumbled with the first one and dropped it. The little glass ampoule became lost in the folds of her nightgown, but she recovered it soon enough and applied it. The next two followed, but Sturridge saw, with mounting consternation, how the pearls were failing to take effect.

"'And then my master was gone,' he said. 'His head was in Mrs Agius's lap, and he looked up at her, and he said her name, Faye, and the word became this terrible gargling rattle, like so: "Fayeggghhh". And that was it. Frightened to death. There's no other way to describe it, Jepson. My master was frightened to death by that ghastly black phantasm; and if my own constitution weren't as robust as it is, I might well have gone the same way. Even now, just reliving the moment, my palms are damp and there's a knot in my belly. I don't know as I shall ever get over it.'

"Charlie Jepson was as sympathetic as could be. He said he did not doubt the veracity of Sturridge's tale for a single moment.

"But that was far from the end of it, Watson. Slurring his words now, Sturridge began to betray greater confidences, just as I had hoped he would. It seems that Eustace Agius's cotton mill empire was not the mighty, unshakeable edifice one might have assumed. In the last months of his life, Agius was no longer overseeing its running as diligently as he ought. There were various reasons contributing to this, Sturridge claimed. One was his increasing ill health. Another was the fire at the Rochdale mill and the related deaths.

"'You heard about that?' Sturridge asked me.

"I said I remembered reading something about it in the papers.

"Sturridge said that Agius might have made out that he was unaffected by the catastrophe, but deep down it had unnerved him. Time and again he would refer to it, insisting that he had done no wrong and that accidents could happen in even the best-ordered workplaces. Yet ever since the blaze, he had become withdrawn, a shell of himself, and often Sturridge would find him sitting at his desk, staring into the distance, head in hands, hollow-eyed.

"The upshot was that Agius lost his sure-footedness and began making poor business decisions. He was, for instance, paying over the odds for his raw cotton. Normally he would force his suppliers in India and the Americas to pare their profit margins to the bone. That was no longer the case, and the suppliers eagerly exploited his weakness, inflating their prices. Where he had screwed every last penny out of them, now they were doing the same to him.

"His insurance liabilities had risen steeply, too, as a result of the fire, and there was a lawsuit about the incident which never got to court, but the services of a Chancery Lane lawyer do not come cheap. In short, financial cracks were appearing everywhere, widening into chasms, and in order to fill these holes Agius was having to find money from elsewhere. At first he tried bank loans, but when these proved too costly he resorted to other means. He had savings, the majority of which derived from a large inheritance his wife had received after her father died. He started dipping into this, the inheritance, of course, rightfully belonging to him as her husband. Yet the hunger of his debts was immense and would not be sated."

"How could Sturridge, a mere valet, know so much about his master's business affairs?" I said.

"Through the simple act of eavesdropping," said Holmes. "He overheard arguments between Agius and his wife, and also conversations in Agius's study between the man and various creditors. What he did not know for a fact, he could infer. Sturridge is no fool. In short, he was of the opinion that Eustace Agius was mere weeks away from bankruptcy."

"Heavens!" I said. "And he one of the richest men in all England."

"Often great wealth rests on precarious foundations," Holmes said. "It is a teetering tower of borrowing, leveraging and promissory notes, and all it takes is a few small shocks to bring the whole structure tumbling down."

"The prospect of imminent ruin must have been agony to him."

"In that respect, dying is perhaps the best thing that could have happened to Eustace Agius. Sturridge himself said as much. 'Where my master is now, Jepson, he's better off. He's certainly not any poorer!' he added, as a weak joke.

"'The way his finances were going,' I said, 'it sounds as if you'd have been out of a job anyway, even if he had lived.'

"'That is almost certain,' Sturridge agreed. 'Within a few weeks, a few months at best, I'd have probably been as you find me now. Really, his death only hastened the inevitable.'

"I bought him one last pint and made my excuses. 'I have to be up at the crack of dawn,' I said. 'Them rats don't keep sociable hours. Pleasure meeting you, Sturridge. I hope your life takes a turn for the good soon.'

"'I apologise for bending your ear for so long.'

"'Think nothing of it. If I can't do a fellow Bermondsey boy the favour of listening to him, what use am I?'

"With that, I departed from The Red Lion and came post-haste to Paddington and the home of one Doctor John H. Watson. Upon whose hospitality I have, I see, impinged long enough."

I had just succumbed to an enormous yawn. "I'm sorry, old fellow. Today was long and rather hectic. Winter illnesses, you know."

"That's fine. I did, after all, promise the fragrant Mrs Watson that I would not keep you from bed for too long." As Holmes rose, he said, "This case is far from done with. I am determined to get to the bottom of it, and to that end I have posted several of the Irregulars outside 23 Tarleton Crescent on rotating shifts, in order to watch over the proceedings there and alert me to anything of interest."

"You think the 'ghost' may reappear?" I said.

"I think, my good sir," said Sherlock Holmes, returning the grey wig to his head and readopting Charlie Jepson's south-east London accent, "that there's still rats to catch."

Chapter Eleven

AN IRREGULAR GIRL

Two days later, on the afternoon of New Year's Eve, I wended my way over to 221B Baker Street. I was curious to learn whether any rats had been caught yet.

There, with Holmes in his rooms, I found a girl of perhaps thirteen or fourteen. She was dressed in clothes that were one step up from rags, while her hair was cut in a short, choppy fashion that, coupled with a snub nose and a determined set to the jaw, made her look boyish. I recognised her as a member of the gang of street Arabs known as the Baker Street Irregulars, although her name at that moment escaped me. She was helping herself to one of Holmes's cigarettes, at Holmes's behest. I watched her light the thing with a practised air and exhale a lungful of smoke gratefully.

"That's fine baccy," the girl said with approval. She studied the cigarette packet. "What are they called? Pasha? Is that how you say the word? That's the brand I'd buy, if I had the money. Beats a poxy Woodbine anyway."

"There's a half-dozen left in that packet," said Holmes. "Keep them, they're yours. Ah, Watson. What fortuitous timing. You remember Nell Baxter, do you not? Known among her peers by the sobriquet 'Mousy'."

"Young lady," I said, with a nod.

"Doctor," said the urchin, tucking the cigarette packet away in a pocket. "Nice to see you again. And looking as dashing as ever, may I say."

I was unsure how to respond to a compliment on my appearance from a girl young enough to be my daughter, so I merely coughed and studied the bearskin hearthrug at my feet. This seemed to amuse her.

"Mousy has only just arrived," said Holmes, "but she comes with news."

"A development in the Agius case?" I said.

"I believe so. Mousy?"

"As I was just telling you, Mr Holmes," said the girl, "me and the other Irregulars, we've been doing exactly like you asked. We've been keeping an eye on that house in Tarleton Crescent day and night, in pairs. Wiggins has been organising it all, giving us the times we have to be there and suchlike. He's good like that, and it's him, as well, what suggested that the bit of park out front would make a decent place to hide. Just hop the railings and huddle down behind a tree. Nobody else is going in there, not at this time of year, when the grass is all mud and there's heaps of cold, wet leaves lying everywhere, so you're not likely to be spotted. Doakes, he did come a cropper, mind. A bluebottle doing his rounds caught sight of him and

McGee, and told them to come on out. Well, obviously, Doakes and McGee made a run for it. They weren't kowtowing to no policeman. McGee got away, but Doakes ain't so fast on his feet, on account of his hammer toes, and that copper was one of the ones who's got a bit of oomph. Caught up with Doakes and gave him a proper clobbering before sending him packing. Ragamuffins like us don't belong in snooty old Knightsbridge, now, do we?"

"A tragic tale," said Holmes. "I trust Doakes isn't the worse for wear after his brush with the law."

"Oh, lor' lumme, no," said Mousy with a casual shrug. "Doakes has been roughed up by experts. This weren't more than a light dusting by comparison, and the thick ear he got will calm down in no time."

"Then, to the point, Mousy. We don't have all day."

"Of course, Mr Holmes, of course. Well, it ain't but two hours ago that we was beginning our second turn as lookout. That's me and Davey Walters, doing the midday-to-eight shift. There weren't much to report when we did the same shift yesterday. We saw the coalman making a delivery, and the butcher's boy too, and at one point a maid came out to walk a dog. Little trotty thing with a curly tail like a pig's. The dog, that is, not the maid. It was just the usual to and fro you'll see at a big house like that."

"Yes," said Holmes. "You and the other Irregulars were to come to me only if anything out of the ordinary occurred. That was the instruction I gave you, through Wiggins."

"And it did occur, sir," said Mousy. "I'm just getting to it.

Yesterday, Davey and me, we didn't see hide nor hair of the lady of the house. Her son neither. It was them you told us to watch out for in particular, and they stayed put. None of the others has seen them either, I'm told. Then, around lunchtime today, who should pop her head out the door but this high-class woman. It were Davey who spied her first. She was handsome, like you said, Mr Holmes, and dressed all in black. That's how we knew it must be the missus, the widow of the homeowner. She had a look both ways, as if to check whether the coast was clear, then stepped out sharpish and took off down the street. Naturally, I decided to tail her. I mightn't have, but she was acting so furtive-like, and I thought to myself, 'If this ain't what Mr Holmes means by out of the ordinary, I'm the Queen of Sheba.' She was carrying a big old leather suitcase with her, what's more. A – whatchemacall – a Gladstone bag. Looked heavy, it did, and it clinked a bit as she walked. I wondered why a gentlewoman would be hauling her own suitcase along when there's servants what are supposed to do that sort of thing for her. I also wondered why she was on her own. Ladies like that, they don't tend to go out and about without an escort or a companion, do they?"

"Ah, now all of this *is* interesting," Holmes said. "Your instincts seem sound, Mousy. Go on."

"So anyway, I tailed her, like I said, leaving Davey to carry on watch duty without me. I'm a good tailer, I am. Stealthy as the creature I'm named after, and as hard to notice. The woman walked all the way to Knightsbridge itself – the road, I mean – and I thought she might catch a cab there. But no, she just kept plodding onward, on foot, past Hyde Park Corner, along Piccadilly, then up into Soho, and there she came to a house. It was a boarding house, with a sign in the window saying 'Rooms To Let'. She knocked on the door, and a landlady – must have been – answered. They spoke, the landlady went inside, and then this bloke came out a minute later and greeted the gentlewoman."

"Describe him, this 'bloke'."

"Tall. Not fat but not thin. Kind of pear-shaped. Red hair, parted in the middle. Big, bushy moustache, he had, and a right old droopy one at that. Like a pair of squirrel tails hanging off his top lip. Loud, booming voice, too, only I couldn't make out anything he said to the gentlewoman, or for that matter her to him, on account of I was too far away and there was a lot of traffic and people passing by. His voice carried but his words didn't. In the woman went, anyway, him taking that Gladstone bag off her, and then I waited."

"How long?"

"Weren't more than thirty minutes. The clock bell of St Anne's sounded the quarter-hour twice while I was there. When the lady came out, the bloke was with her and he saw her off with a handshake. She was carrying the suitcase again, although now, I can't swear to it, but it didn't look nearly so heavy. She wasn't having to lug it any more, like before."

"Might it even have been empty?" Holmes asked.

"It might have, I suppose."

"And where did she go next?"

"All the way back home. She was quicker now, on the return journey, maybe because the suitcase didn't weigh so much, or maybe because she was done with her business up west, glad it was over, and keen to be in her house again."

"Yes, let's not speculate on things for which we have no concrete evidence, Mousy."

"I'm just telling you what I saw. There was a spring in her stride, at any rate. That's for definite. And as soon as she closed the door behind her, I checked with Davey Walters that there hadn't been any other arrivals or departures, and he said there hadn't, so off I trotted, straight here to your place."

"You have acquitted yourself admirably, young lady," Holmes said.

"Thank you, sir," the girl said, extinguishing her cigarette, which she had smoked down to a stub.

"One small detail remains unaccounted for. The address the lady visited."

"Not a problem, sir. I made a note of it, up here." She tapped her head. "It was halfway up Frith Street as you head north towards Soho Square, on the right." She gave the house number. "Dark green door, and the sign in the window, of course."

"Excellent. Here you are."

Holmes pitched her a half-crown, which Mousy caught smartly and slipped into a pocket.

"Should we keep up the watch at Tarleton Crescent, Mr Holmes?"

"For the time being, yes. I will inform Wiggins when it is no longer required."

Mousy Baxter skipped out of the room, extracting a fresh Pasha cigarette from the packet as she went.

Chapter Twelve

PUTATIVE PARAMOURS

"It's incredible," I said.

"You think Mousy is lying?" said Holmes.

"Oh no. What would she gain by that? She'd never be so reckless. You would be able to disprove her, and she would lose your trust and with it her place among the Irregulars. That would deprive her of a source of revenue and, indeed, of free cigarettes. I mean it's incredible that Mrs Agius is conducting an affair."

Holmes cocked an eyebrow. "An affair?"

"That's what it is, isn't it? Faye Agius has a lover, over in Soho. I may not like the idea but it clearly is the case. They have been trysting for a while, but this was the first time she has dared visit him after her husband's death. Brazen of her to do so mere days after the event. You'd think she might leave it a little longer before arranging a fresh assignation. Still dressed in mourning, too."

"Perhaps she could not wait to bring him the good news."

"Yes, that must be it. 'Darling, my husband is dead. At last we are free to be together – to marry, even.'"

My friend barked a laugh. "Watson, do you know what you are? An incurable romantic. You have partnered Mrs Agius with this moustachioed, redheaded bravo. Knowing that her marriage was loveless, you have given her passion. Knowing that her husband was a brute, you have given her a Sir Lancelot. It is a marvellous fiction, but it does not stand up to the facts. Think about it. A woman leaves the house to meet up with a lover. Her movements are furtive."

"Just as Mousy described. For the same reason, secrecy, she eschews a cab. She does not want anyone knowing where she has gone. No witnesses whatsoever."

"Yes, but does she take a heavily laden Gladstone bag with her?"

"I don't know. I am no expert on extramarital affairs. She might."

"Well, even so, compare the widow Agius's journey to the boarding house with her journey back. Mousy said that her pace thither was 'plodding' but, on her return, she had a spring in her stride. Let us disregard the emotions Mousy ascribed to her, which she could not have known, and accept the testimony purely at face value. Mrs Agius went there slowly but came back quickly. Surely, if she were going to meet a lover, the variation in pace would be the other way round. On the way out, she would be excited, full of hope and anticipation. She would quicken her steps so as to reach her destination sooner. On the way back, by contrast, she would be slower, in a ruminative mood, suffused with happiness, her thoughts lingering on the liaison just past."

"I suppose so."

"And how did they part, these putative paramours? There was no kiss on the doorstep, no loving caress, only a handshake."

"It could be that they did not want to appear affectionate in public view," I countered. "Their affair must remain clandestine for now."

"And then what about the condition of the Gladstone bag?" Holmes said. "Full when Mrs Agius arrived at the boarding house, empty when she left."

"She was bringing over clothes," I suggested. "She deposited them with the man as part of their plan to elope together at a later date."

"Clothes, Watson, do not clink, and the contents of the Gladstone bag did."

"Oh yes."

"No, put all the elements together, and an affair is the least likely explanation. Rather, I propose that this was some sort of delivery. Mrs Agius was bringing the man something, or returning something to him."

"Then what does that make him? Colleague? Collaborator?"

"His precise function remains to be determined, and that is next on the agenda for me," said Holmes. "I cannot get to work on it just yet, however. I am awaiting a messenger. I have sent a telegram to a certain Mr Danvers Lockforth, and his response will, I hope, be highly instructive."

"And who," I asked, "is Mr Danvers Lockforth?"

"Mr Danvers Lockforth is a cotton mill proprietor, much like the late Eustace Agius. He resides up in St John's Wood, and if what I am told is correct, there was little love lost between the two men."

"A business rival?"

"Not quite," said Holmes. "Lockforth is not in the same league as Agius. Rather, he became the hapless victim of the other's sharp practices. Would you like to hear what happened?"

"Rather."

"Then I shall do my best to condense the whole sorry saga into just a few sentences."

Chapter Thirteen

THE WHOLE SORRY SAGA OF DANVERS LOCKFORTH, IN JUST A FEW SENTENCES

"A year ago, not long after the Rochdale fire, Eustace Agius was looking around for a new cotton mill to buy," said Holmes. "Rather than rebuild the immolated mill, it was cheaper for him to purchase a going concern. His eye alighted on the one owned by Danvers Lockforth. It sits on the banks of the River Spodden, whose flow powers its waterwheels. Now, back in 1847, as part of the Rochdale Waterworks Amendment Bill Enquiry, it was proposed that a reservoir be constructed upstream of all the mills on the Spodden. There are several dozen of them, turning out either cotton or wool. The mill owners objected, saying that damming the river would result in a decrease in current and thus adversely affect their operations, and the proposal was dropped. Agius, however, was cunning. He let it be known that the Rochdale authorities were reconsidering the reservoir plan. He made sure, in particular, that this rumour reached the ear of Danvers Lockforth."

"How on earth do you know all this?" I said.

"Mycroft," Holmes replied simply. "My brother is a font of useful information. He couples that with being remarkably indolent, but if given sufficient impetus – if the pump is primed, so to speak – then he gushes forth. I had him ask around within his elite social circle, probing for details about Eustace Agius's business dealings. In particular I wished to know about the man's enemies. Mrs Agius told us that her husband belonged to all the important clubs, and so does Mycroft. The Diogenes is just one among his many Pall Mall haunts. Mycroft did not have to look far, therefore, to unearth someone who could enlighten him with regard to the ins and outs of Agius's activities."

"I see."

"That is how I know that Agius, via an intermediary, fed Lockforth the falsehood about the reservoir plan. By all accounts, Lockforth is a worrier, prone to bouts of melancholy, and no great commercial brain. He inherited the business from his father and has managed it badly. Fearing that his mill was in jeopardy, and with it his livelihood, he fell into a panic. He did not even seek to ascertain whether there was any truth to the story. He fell for it, as they say, hook, line and sinker. Then, promptly, Agius came to him with an offer for the place. An exceptionally low offer, but Lockforth, seeing little alternative, took it. Agius assured him he was getting a good deal. He even made it seem as though he was doing Lockforth a favour. Nobody else would take the mill off his hands, not with the threat of ruin looming over it."

"How despicable," I said, "taking advantage of a competitor's ineptitude and gullibility like that."

"You will never be a captain of industry, will you, Watson?"

"I should hope not, if that's what it takes."

"The business magnates of our age have much in common with the pirates of yore. They sit in boardrooms rather than sail galleons on the ocean main, but in their cutthroat, backstabbing ways the two breeds are otherwise indistinguishable. Agius certainly plundered Lockforth, and Lockforth soon realised that he had – at the risk of stretching this metaphor to breaking point – been forced to walk the plank. He was not best pleased, as you can imagine. He might not have been ruined, but he had parted with his principal financial asset for a small fraction of its true worth. The realisation sent him into a downward spiral of dejection and gloom. Agius, meanwhile, gloated about his accomplishment to all who would listen. 'I dunned that idiot' was the gist of it."

"This is all very sad to hear, and no mistake," I said.

"It is more than sad, Watson. It is sinister. Think about it. In Danvers Lockforth we have a man with a grievance against Eustace Agius but no legal form of redress. Contracts were signed, after all, and although the methods by which Agius drove down the price for the mill were underhand, there was nothing intrinsically unlawful about what he did. How, then, might Lockforth's resentment manifest itself?"

"In hatred. A grudge."

"And…?"

"And," I said, "he might pen a series of letters in order to vent his spleen."

"There we have it," Holmes said, in a satisfied tone.

"Letters," I went on, "framed so as to come from the widower of a woman killed in the Rochdale mill fire. Lockforth did not feel he could confront Agius openly. Perhaps he was too much of a coward. Perhaps he was embarrassed at the way Agius had defrauded him. So he decided instead to get his own back by trying to prick the other's conscience. At the very least, the letters might make Agius feel some of the self-loathing and remorse that he himself was feeling."

"If there was a chink in Agius's armour as far as Lockforth was concerned, then it surely would be the fire."

"Could Danvers Lockforth be the man Mrs Agius met in Soho?" I said. "Could the two of them be in cahoots somehow?"

"Lockforth lives in St John's Wood, as I said."

"But a boarding house in the West End would serve as a useful rendezvous, somewhere midway between their homes and neutral for them both."

"A fair point," said Holmes. "However, Lockforth is slight in stature, not that you could have known that. I do only because Mycroft was good enough to dig up all the intelligence about him that he could. Lockforth has dark hair, too, and is normally clean-shaven. I do not believe he possesses what Mousy described, so winningly, as 'a pair of squirrel tails attached to his top lip'. Our redheaded fellow is somebody else altogether. But I applaud your efforts to forge a connection there. It shows you are thinking."

"How kind of you to say so," I said drolly. "Heaven forfend that I should fail to think."

Holmes did not seem to notice my little barb. His hide was as thick as mine was thin. "Lockforth's authorship of the letters, or otherwise, will be confirmed shortly," he said, "once my telegram to him has been answered."

"What did you say in it? I don't suppose you asked him outright whether he is responsible."

"Nothing so banal as that, Watson. Rather, I— But wait. I hear rapid footfalls on the pavement outside. They sound very much like those of a messenger boy. And there goes the doorbell."

The messenger appeared a moment later, bearing a telegram. Holmes gave him a coin and he departed.

"Now then, what do we have here?" said Holmes, opening the folded slip of paper. He examined it, then laughed heartily. "Oh, this is perfect. It is not a reply telegram at all, Watson. Just as I hoped, it is my original wire, returned as 'misdelivered'. Take a look."

The telegram, addressed to Danvers Lockforth and sent by one "Dr Ormond Sacker", read:

> YOUR UNCLE ALGERNON GRAVELY ILL.
> MESSAGE BY RETURN IF COMING.

Beneath this was a couple of handwritten lines:

Sent to wrong recipient.
No Uncle Algernon known.

"Who is this Dr Ormond Sacker?" I asked.

"Merely an alias," said Holmes. "The telegram, given its content, would carry greater weight coming from a medical man, and does Ormond Sacker not sound like a stalwart chap? The name may be somewhat baroque and it does not have the ring of, say, John Watson – what could be more down-to-earth and dependably English than 'John Watson'? – but it is a good second best."

"I see."

"But what about the penmanship of Lockforth's reply? That is the point of real interest here."

"It looks dashed-off. He wrote in a hurry."

"Nevertheless it betrays a knowledge of italic calligraphy. I did not choose the name Algernon for this fictitious uncle on a whim. The word contains three of the letters of the alphabet to which I drew your attention when we were discussing the penmanship of the anonymous missives. My hope was that Lockforth would reproduce it in his response, and happily the gamble paid off."

"You were also gambling that he did not actually have an uncle called Algernon," I said.

"That, I grant you, would have been an embarrassing gaffe. Lockforth would have hurried round to his uncle's, only to find that the man was not at death's door after all, which would have been a source of great perplexity to them both. I would then have had to resort to some other method of obtaining a sample of Lockforth's handwriting. Most probably I would have gone to his house, posing as a priest seeking signatures on a petition about the plight of underprivileged children or fallen women, something along those lines. Beside his name Lockforth would have been required to add his address, and that might have given me enough characters to go on. As it is, we now have an 'l', a 'g' and an 'n' to compare with those we found in the letters from the Mancunian widower. The 'l' here is a single downstroke, the descender of the 'g' carries a serif, and the 'n' has a final flick. Overall, the handwriting is a close match to that of the letters. There is one thing that might settle the matter for good, though."

Holmes beckoned for the telegram. I returned it to him, and he raised it to his nose and inhaled.

"Yes," said he. "As I thought. Cologne. The same kind as on the letters. Bay rum, if I'm not mistaken. Notes of neroli oil, oil of cloves, and, of course, rum and bay tree berry extract. Danvers Lockforth is definitely our man when it comes to the Mancunian widower letters. It is beyond doubt."

"Therefore he is also our man when it comes to the spectral shenanigans at Tarleton Crescent."

"That is *not* beyond doubt," said Holmes.

"But they started when the letters stopped."

"There may be many reasons why Lockforth gave up sending the letters. He may simply have grown tired of it. He may have felt that it was not achieving any tangible result. There is, I am certain, a correlation between the letters and that which you have dubbed, with your characteristic flair for language, 'spectral shenanigans'. However, it is not as simple as Lockforth taking a more active approach in his campaign against Eustace Agius. As for the phenomena themselves, I am beginning to formulate a solution which may account for them."

"And?"

"Not yet, Watson."

"It is not fully developed, is it?" I said. "Otherwise you would be prepared to share it with me now. Instead I am simply going to have to wait until it, and you, are ready."

Holmes rewarded me with a sly wink. "Old friend, you know me so well."

Chapter Fourteen

AN EVENING AT THE TIVOLI

A further two days elapsed, a new year had dawned, and then a note arrived from Holmes at breakfast time, requesting that I join him that evening at the Tivoli on the Strand. It was, as was typical of my friend, a summons rather than an invitation. No allowance was made for the fact that I might have a prior engagement or, indeed, might not want to go. I remembered how incensed he had been when Eustace Agius demanded that he call, in that peremptorily worded telegram. Apparently Sherlock Holmes could not see in himself the flaws he deplored in others.

"The Tivoli?" said Mary, when I showed her the note.

"Yes," I said. "The theatre. You know the one. Built on the site of the old Tivoli Beer Garden and Restaurant. They finished it just last year, having lavished a small fortune on it, I hear."

"I'm aware what the Tivoli is, John. I'm also aware what they put on there. Music hall."

"What of it? Do you have something against music hall?"

"No."

"Gilbert and Sullivan, after all, is hardly highbrow. No offence," I added quickly.

"None taken," my wife said, and I knew then that some had been, and that I had blundered. "It's just that music hall," she went on, "isn't a form of entertainment one would normally associate with Sherlock Holmes. His tastes run more to violin concertos and Italian opera, don't they?"

"True. I can only assume he has good reasons for wanting to go, and for asking me to accompany him."

"It's lucky you didn't have anything else planned for this evening."

"I daresay if I had, I'd have been expected to cancel it."

"At any rate, let me go and fetch out your white tie and tails for airing," Mary said. "Oh, and, John?"

"Yes?"

"When I buy tickets for the next Savoy operetta, should I purchase two or just one?"

"Two. Definitely two."

"Good. I should hate to go alone, even if it isn't in any way *highbrow*."

"Mary, I misspoke. I didn't mean… I wasn't saying that…"

Sweetly, impishly, Mary patted my cheek. "John Watson, you are so easy to fluster. It's quite endearing. I know full well that many consider Gilbert and Sullivan's output to be fluff, but we can't help liking what we like. And the fact that you come to see their operettas with me, even though you don't enjoy them, is proof of your love for me. A wife could not ask for more."

Evening came, and I headed out, dressed in tie and tails, with the addition of hat, gloves, scarf and thick overcoat, this outerwear much needed because a heavy snow had begun to fall. Mary saw me off on the front doorstep, making a small adjustment to my bowtie and giving me a peck on the cheek.

"I trust your night of comic sketches and sentimental songs will not be too intellectually taxing," she said with a pert smile.

"You're not going to forget that 'highbrow' remark of mine for some while, are you?" I said.

"Not ever. Now go and have fun with Mr Holmes. And beware of chorus girls. You're looking especially smart and handsome right now, and I know what those ladies are like. You'll be catnip to them."

Blushing somewhat, I climbed into the waiting hansom, and half an hour later disembarked outside the Tivoli, where I was greeted at the entrance by Holmes.

"Come along, old friend," said he, hastening me indoors. "It's curtain-up in five minutes."

"Yes, apologies for the tardiness," I said. "Not my fault. I left in good time, but the traffic was terrible. This snow."

We checked in our hats and coats at the cloakroom. The attendant, recognising Holmes's face, said, "Back again, sir? Didn't we see you just yesterday?"

"It is an excellent show," said Holmes. "I thought I would share it with my friend."

The house lights were starting to dim as we took our seats.

"Holmes," I said, leaning close to him, "why on earth are we here? I've nothing against variety theatre *per se*. I just wonder why you asked me along, and at such short notice, too."

"Hush, Watson. Not now. You'll see soon enough. For the time being, just sit back and be entertained."

The curtain rose, the calcium lights on the proscenium flared into life, and the acting manager, in cravat and elaborately patterned waistcoat, came onstage and began his introduction.

"Ladies, gentlemen, and all points in between," he said, and the quip brought gales of laughter from the audience members in the circle and upper circle and polite smiles from us in the stalls. "Prepare yourselves – brace yourselves – gird your loins and adjacent parts – for a night of riotous pleasure." The "gird your loins" line likewise greatly amused the people in the cheaper seats. "Tonight you are going to witness marvels! Miracles! Majesty! Mystery! Mastery! Mockery! There will be songs. There will be skits. There will be acts the likes of which you have never known before. You will laugh. You will cry. You will thrill. You may even faint. And, gentlemen, if the lady next to you looks as if she is about to swoon, remember to grab her tight so that she does not do herself a mischief. Of course, it may be that she wants *you* to do *her* a mischief, in which case grab her even tighter. Just try not to disturb your neighbours, eh?"

There was plenty more where that came from, and it was unsophisticated stuff, to put it mildly, but all the same I was hard pressed not to chuckle. I was rather relieved, though, that it was Holmes beside me and not, say, Mary. I doubt she would have approved of the acting manager's patter, and I would have felt duty-bound to match her disapproval with my own. Then again, the majority of the smartly dressed women around us were cackling loudly and unashamedly, along with the men. Coarse humour, it seemed, transcended the boundaries not just of class but of gender.

There was an orchestral interlude, and then the first act came on. It was a comedian, Bumpo Rattigan, whose repartee made the acting manager's seem positively genteel by comparison. He paraded up and down the stage in a gaudy checked suit and a brown bowler several sizes too small for his head, prefacing almost every joke with "I say, I say, I say…" and guffawing over the punchline as if the witticism were entirely new to him, something he had come up with on the spur of the moment. The limericks he reeled off were little short of indecent, and one or two of the jibes he aimed at the great and the good of this land were scurrilous and might even be considered slander. He left the stage showered in applause, and also bathed in sweat – but then he had arrived perspiring profusely already, leading one to infer that he had come to the Tivoli hotfoot from a performance elsewhere. Similarly, he doubtless had further engagements lined up tonight, for this was a common practice among variety acts. They careered around between West End theatres like balls on a billiards table, timing their turns so that they could fit as many as four or five into an evening and thereby make as much money as possible.

The next act was twin sisters Florrie and Gracie Smith, who danced and sang in perfect unison, each mirroring the other's movements. Their material was in stark contrast to that of Bumpo Rattigan, consisting of unobjectionable ditties such as "Where Did You Get That Hat?", "Pretty Polly Perkins of Paddington Green", and the Marie Lloyd favourite "The Boy I Love Is Up in the Gallery".

Following them came some Cossack dancers, a troupe of minstrel singers, and a ventriloquist. The last was extremely adept at his art. Not only did his lips stay firmly unmoving as he threw his voice, but the doll in his lap – carved in the likeness of an apple-cheeked schoolboy – seemed a separate entity altogether. Rather than him manipulating it, it appeared to be imbued with an eerie life of its own. It answered him back, scorned him, and at times even left him tongue-tied with its effrontery. I wasn't sure whether to be impressed or worry for the fellow's sanity.

There was a juggler who kept more balls in the air than I thought humanly possible. There was a short play about fairies, during which dancers in form-fitting costumes with gossamer wings flitted to and fro against a woodland backdrop while some sort of romantic narrative involving bewitched lovers and mistaken identities played out in the foreground. There was a dog acrobat act, with a trainer making miniature poodles climb ladders, jump through hoops and walk on their hindlegs, and applying judicious taps of a dressage whip to any canine that failed to perform as desired.

During the interval, I again prevailed upon Holmes to explain why we were there.

"I've no wish to seem ungrateful," I said. "It's splendid of you to treat me to an evening out. All this gaiety just seems a little frivolous, that's all."

"Frivolous, perhaps," said Holmes, "but it will also be enlightening."

"What can be so remarkable about this show that you have attended it two nights in a row?"

"Wait, Watson." His expression was damnably enigmatic. "Just wait. All will become clear soon."

The second half opened with Professor Astronomo, whose claim to his academic title seemed as spurious as his surname. His act was called "Denizens of Other Worlds" and entailed displaying images which, he alleged, had been captured through a telescope. Cast by slide projector onto a large sheet stretched behind him, they showed a range of humanoid alien beings: Venusians whose leathery fireproof skin protected them from the searing temperatures on their planet's surface; armoured Martians looking a little like African tribesmen and engaged in internecine warfare; squat Jovians whose powerfully muscled bodies enabled them to endure the immense gravitational forces on Jupiter; and Neptunians with layers of walrus-like blubber that insulated them against the arctic conditions which prevailed out there at the limits of our solar system. While we in the stalls greeted everything he said with amused scepticism, up in the circles they were enthralled and aghast. It did not seem to matter to them that the pictures were clearly hand-drawn illustrations rather than photographs. Professor Astronomo delivered his lecture in a high-flown style and peppered it with scientific-sounding terminology, and they lapped it up.

An actor recited Shakespearean soliloquies. A mime artist wordlessly evoked agony, ecstasy and a whole spectrum of other emotions. A baritone belted out a succession of bawdy songs that wouldn't have been out of place in an East End pub, and we in the audience were invited to join in.

Then came the penultimate act of the night, a conjuror.

The acting manager, who throughout the evening had proved himself no stranger to exaggeration and embellishment, became positively hyperbolic in his introduction.

"You will never have seen the like of this fellow before," he declared. "You will never see the like again. He is a wonder of the world. He astounds. He astonishes. He takes the breath away. You will not believe your eyes. You will not believe your ears. You will not believe *any* of your five senses. Ladies and gentlemen, magic is real, and you are about to see it wielded by the deft hands of… Kavanagh the Great!"

Out from the wings stepped a man in tailcoat and top hat, and all at once I finally understood why Sherlock Holmes had brought me there.

Chapter Fifteen

KAVANAGH THE GREAT

Kavanagh the Great was tall and somewhat thick around the waist. He had a big red moustache which hung either side of his mouth in luxuriant profusion, the tips extending below his chin. When he removed his hat while bowing hello to us, he showed off a head of hair, neatly centre parted, whose auburn hue matched that of the moustache. When he spoke, his voice resounded across the auditorium, loud and stentorian enough to be clearly heard even up in the gods.

This, I thought, must surely be the man whom Faye Agius had gone to meet at the Soho boarding house.

Kavanagh proceeded to run through a repertoire of conjuring tricks. He made playing cards appear and disappear from his hands. He produced a posy of flowers as if from nowhere, handing this to a woman in the front row with a gallant flourish. He turned a single coin into two, then three, then dozens.

All of it was straightforward enough prestidigitation, albeit of a high standard. I had seen other stage illusionists do the same, or similar, plenty of times before.

This, however, was merely a prelude. Gradually, Kavanagh's tricks became grander, more complicated and more baffling. At one point, he summoned up a wall of fire in the middle of the darkened stage. As the flames crackled and flickered, he walked towards them with a purposeful gait. He warned the audience not to be alarmed, but expressed the hope that there was a doctor in the house, just in case. Then he promptly dived headlong into the blaze. There were gasps and cries all over the auditorium, which turned to hoots of delight as Kavanagh emerged the other side of the wall of fire unhurt and intact, not even the slightest bit singed. Then, turning, he clicked his fingers and the flames were gone in an instant.

After this, Kavanagh moved stage right and gave a short speech about saints who had been able to appear in two places at once. "This ability," he said, "known as bilocation, was deemed proof that such men and women were beloved of God and gifted with divine grace. The seventeenth-century Spanish nun, the Venerable Mary of Ágreda, was one such, as was Saint Martín de Porres, a monk of Peru from the same era. Now, I do not pretend to sainthood, ladies and gentlemen. I am an ordinary, flawed human being, just like any of you. Hence I cannot bilocate, as those pious individuals could. However, I can come close. By that I mean that I am able to stand here…"

So saying, he vanished amid a puff of smoke.

"And, at practically the same moment, here," he said,

reappearing centre stage amid another puff of smoke. "Indeed, arguably I can go one better than a saint…"

Suddenly he was gone again, manifesting stage left amid yet another puff of smoke.

"And be in *three* places more or less at once," he said.

Cheers and wild applause followed, and Kavanagh, beaming broadly, bowed. I have to admit to clapping as hard as anyone. It had been a remarkable feat. Kavanagh really had seemed to transport himself from one spot to the next in a flash, covering a distance of at least twenty feet each time. I could not see how it had been humanly possible, but he had done it nonetheless.

Now an assistant came on, a slip of a girl in tights and corset, whom Kavanagh introduced as Elsie. He announced that he was going to hypnotise her using his mesmeric powers, which had been taught to him by a Tibetan lama.

"Once Elsie is fully under my spell," he said, "I am going to persuade her that she is weightless. That way I shall be able to make her hover in midair, and even rise several yards off the ground. For this act, I shall entreat you to keep the noise to a minimum, so as not to interfere with the hypnotic process."

Elsie closed her eyes and Kavanagh waved a hand in front of her face, muttering incantations, until all at once the girl collapsed in his arms. He carried her to a pair of trestles and laid her supine upon them, before draping a sheet over her. Elsie lay stiff as a board under the sheet, her shoulders on one of the trestles, her calves on the other.

Kavanagh wafted his hands up and down along the contours

of her body, while the lights dimmed and the orchestra played ethereal-sounding music. Then, abruptly, he snatched one of the trestles out from under her. Elsie continued to lie horizontal. He snatched away the other trestle. Elsie floated, unsupported.

The orchestra fell silent, save for the drummer, who rattled a tattoo on his snare. The audience, similarly, were quiet, save for a few excited whispers. The tension in the auditorium was palpable. Everyone was on tenterhooks.

Kavanagh lofted his arms high, and Elsie, still covered by the sheet, began to rise. Up she went until she was level with his head, then further still. Twelve feet, fifteen, twenty… She was drawing level with the base of the proscenium arch, almost gone from view, when the sheet whipped sideways as if of its own volition, hurtling into the wings like a slithering eel.

There was no Elsie.

The audience broke into rapturous applause. The applause intensified as Elsie appeared at the rear of the auditorium and came sauntering down the aisle that bisected the stalls, smiling and nodding in acknowledgement as she went. Kavanagh helped her back up onto the stage, where she curtseyed while he took a bow. The applause continued as the pair strode off hand in hand and the acting manager came on.

"Didn't I tell you, ladies and gentlemen?" he said. "Was it not incredible?" He began to announce the next act, but a firm tap on my arm distracted me.

"Watson," said Holmes, standing.

"We're leaving? But the show isn't over yet."

"But Kavanagh the Great may, like his fellow artistes, have

another engagement lined up imminently. I would like to catch him before he goes."

So we made our way along the row, sowing disgruntlement in our wake among the theatregoers whose view we obstructed and toes we trod on. As the show's grand finale commenced – a famous Parisian songstress, "straight from Montmartre", performing a selection of *chansons réalistes* – we hurried to the foyer, collected our outer garments from the cloakroom, and raced outside. The snow was still coming down in thick flurries as we went round to the stage door.

Holmes knocked, and a burly, bull-necked stagehand opened the door. He eyed us up and down, seeming to find us as interesting as fleas.

"Yes?"

"Has Mr Kavanagh, the illusionist, left yet?"

"Who's asking?"

"An admirer." Holmes brandished a playbill. "I would be honoured if he were to autograph this for me."

"He's on his way out. You'll have to wait."

The stagehand slammed the door in our faces. We remained where we were, snow slowly accumulating on our hats and shoulders, for the next ten minutes.

"I understand, now, why we have attended the show," I said to Holmes. "I'm not sure I understand why you came twice."

"Ah, the first time I went alone, Watson, simply to confirm my suspicions, which were until then only half-formed. This time, I wanted you along so that I might have my loyal accomplice with me when I pounce. You like to be on hand for these moments, don't you? Eyewitness to Sherlock Holmes making one of his grand exposés."

"Well, yes, I do. Of course."

"It makes it easier for you to write about the event if you are present. The drama on the page is all the richer for it."

I masked a smile. In his way, my friend was as much of a performer as any of the stage acts we had just seen. He was as much in need of an audience, too, even if that audience consisted of just one man.

At last the stage door reopened. Kavanagh the Great emerged, leading a small procession. Behind him came Elsie, the assistant, followed by a pair of men carrying a large and clearly very heavy trunk between them.

"Kavanagh the Great!" Holmes declared, clasping his hands together in joy. "It's an enormous honour, sir. May I shake you by the hand?"

"Certainly," said Kavanagh.

"Your performance…" Holmes looked, for all the world, like an awestruck fanatic. "Quite brilliant."

"Thank you."

"May I ask you a couple of questions? Would that be acceptable?"

"I don't have much time," said Kavanagh brusquely. "I have to be at the London Pavilion by nine thirty sharp."

"It won't take long."

"Very well."

"First of all, with the magic lantern you use to project an image of flames, I presume it features a pair of painted glass slides that move on small rails." All at once, Holmes was his usual, brisk self again, no longer playing the starry-eyed enthusiast. "The phantasmagoria shows of the last century employed such a system, and yours is merely a variant of that. As the slides cross back and forth, so the flames appear to flicker. I perceive the influence of Childe's chromatrope in the illusion as well."

Kavanagh glared at him. "What is the point you are making?"

"If I am right," my friend continued, "your 'wall of fire' also incorporates the Pepper's ghost technique. The image from the magic lantern is reflected from below onto an angled pane of glass onstage. You pass behind the pane, but to the audience it seems as though you are passing through. The sound of flames, meanwhile, is replicated by assistants offstage rattling boxes of dried peas and scraping a sheet of canvas."

"I am not willing to discuss the matter," Kavanagh said. "You may theorise to your heart's content how I pull off my illusions."

Holmes was quite unabashed. "As for your version of saintly bilocation, or perhaps it should be 'trilocation', I see that one of these men here is much the same height as you and shares your complexion. I reckon that with the addition of an auburn wig and matching false moustache, he might easily pass for you. Your look is very distinctive, after all. Distractingly so, one might say. The trick, then, simply relies on his participation. By means of clever lighting effects and detonations of flash powder, you seem to disappear. In fact, you move swiftly from stage right to stage left while your accomplice, standing centre stage, suddenly comes into view. You pass behind him, unseen, speaking your line while he mouths the words silently, and pop up stage left as he, in turn, disappears."

Kavanagh bared his teeth. "Out of my way, sir. I have places to be."

"I am not trying to undermine your artistry in any way," Holmes said. "You are as proficient a conjuror as any I have seen."

"And you are as persistent a nuisance as any I have met. Move!"

Holmes stayed firmly put. "Your professional secrets are safe with me. There is, however, another kind of secret that I am prepared to expose: your connection with Faye Agius."

The illusionist blinked. "Who?"

"Widow of the late Eustace Agius."

"Never heard of the woman."

"Come, come," said Holmes. "That will not do. You have aided her, Mr Kavanagh, in the commission of a deception, one which may well have led to her husband losing his life. That, whether you realise it or not, makes you an accessory to murder, and I think it is something you and I should talk about."

Kavanagh was thunderstruck. "I never... I don't..." he stammered. Then, collecting himself, he turned to his colleagues. "You three go ahead to the Pavilion. Get things ready there."

"Is everything all right, Mr Kavanagh?" said Elsie, touching his arm solicitously. "Is what this man is saying true?"

"No, my dear. No, no. A misunderstanding, that's all. Shouldn't take long to clear up. Now go on. You too," he said to the men with the trunk. "I shall be along as soon as possible."

As the three assistants went in search of a cab, Kavanagh said to Holmes, "You had better come inside. Let's get this straightened out."

Chapter Sixteen

A HUNGER FOR THE UNCANNY, A LOVE OF THE SINISTER

In a dressing room, Kavanagh slumped into a chair. Any composure he had had left was gone. His face had taken on an ashen pallor, made worse by the harsh glare of the electric bulbs that surrounded the makeup mirror.

"I suppose I should ask you who you are," said he to Holmes.

"This is my colleague Dr Watson, and I am Sherlock Holmes."

"Ah. The detective. Yes."

"I take it Mrs Agius did not mention me when she came to visit you at your boarding house a few days ago."

"Not a word."

"Well, there is no reason why she should have, I suppose. She could not know that I have been looking into her husband's death. I just thought she might have referred to us meeting and told you to be wary in case a certain consulting detective started nosing around your business."

"She said nothing whatsoever on the subject. But how do you know she visited me?"

"I have my spies."

"And my identity?" said Kavanagh. "How did you ascertain that?"

"By much the same process. As I said just now, your look is distinctive. Not only does it give you an imposing, memorable stage presence, it permits your male assistant to impersonate you with ease. Not many will look past that moustache, that hair, to the face. They will certainly not notice the substitution when your assistant appears onstage so briefly, there then gone in a trice."

"So?"

"So, having been furnished with a physical description of you by my spy, my thoughts immediately went to the posters that are up all over the West End, advertising the Tivoli variety show. Your image is featured prominently on those. I was already half of a mind that Mrs Agius had enlisted the help of a stage illusionist in her endeavours. Now I knew exactly who that illusionist was."

"And you are here to – what? Unmask me as some kind of villain?"

"That all depends."

"On what?"

"Whether you *are* a villain."

"I am not," said Kavanagh stiffly. "At least, I don't think I am. All I did was help the woman. She said she wished to put the frighteners on her husband who, she told me, was an utter beast. She wished him to experience some of the misery and terror she had been living under all her married life. Let me tell you, Mr Holmes, Faye Agius is very persuasive. When she first came to me a few weeks ago – buttonholing me at the stage door, rather as you did – I found her disarmingly polite and more than a little intriguing."

"She is good-looking, too," I said.

"That cannot be denied," said Kavanagh. "I am as susceptible to feminine charms as the next man. Of course, I had no idea where it all would lead. Mrs Agius did mention, when she and I last met, that her husband had passed away suddenly. I did not ask how, and she did not volunteer any details. In the back of my mind, I wondered whether the event might be connected in some way to the little bits of trickery we had devised together, but I could not for the life of me see how that could be possible. Perhaps... Perhaps I simply chose not to think about it too hard."

"I would not be wrong in assuming, would I, that money changed hands?" said Holmes.

Kavanagh the Great nodded. "A decent sum. Her husband gave her an allowance, for buying dresses and suchlike, and she had saved up. Mine is not an especially lucrative line of work, Mr Holmes, and I will take income where I can get it. All Mrs Agius required of me was a few props, a little instruction, and a certain apparatus that I built specially for her."

"One of those props being the potassium perchlorate mixture known as flash powder."

"Indeed."

"Which she used, in tandem with a long, slow-burning fuse, to generate a cloud of smoke in a cupboard in her husband's study, one that left no trace of its origin. She also borrowed your magic lantern and 'wall of fire' slides in order to project an image of flames onto her husband's bedroom window from below in the back garden, extinguishing it the moment he threw back the curtains. As for the 'certain apparatus' you refer to, I imagine it is not unrelated to the finale of your act, in which young Elsie seemingly floats upward beneath a sheet, only to vanish into thin air."

Again, the illusionist nodded. "I thought the gimmick I came up with for Mrs Agius was a rather nice piece of work, if I do say so myself."

"It was that gimmick," Holmes said, "that she returned to you the other day, in a Gladstone bag."

"You are very well informed."

"Well informed but, equally, well capable of making analytical deductions based on evidence. Do you still, by any chance, happen to have the item?"

"It is among my effects at the boarding house."

"Might I be permitted to collect it from there?"

"When? Now?"

"Yes. I should very much like to have a look at it."

"I could write a note to my landlady, giving you permission to enter my rooms."

"I would be obliged if you did."

"Mr Holmes." Kavanagh wrung his hands beseechingly. "Whatever Mrs Agius did, whatever fatal mishap befell her husband, I had nothing to do with it. You must believe me when

I say that. My involvement begins and ends with helping her scare him. She wanted him to believe that he was being haunted by a ghost – the ghost of someone who died in a fire. I provided the means, and was paid for it. It was a job, no more, no less. If the woman had some nefarious ulterior motive, it was unknown to me."

"It never occurred to you to question why she was doing this thing?"

"Maybe it should have, but her desire for revenge seemed justification enough. The way she laid it out to me, it seemed little more than a prank. The intent might have been vicious but the end result, I thought, was harmless. After all, in my performances I perturb people just as much as I enthral them. It is part of the appeal of stage magic. The illusionist toys with notions of life and death. We lay claim to unearthly powers. Even if the audience knows what we are presenting them with is a trick, nevertheless it touches some deep, dark part of their souls. It satisfies a hunger for the uncanny, a love of the sinister. With Mrs Agius, I took that principle to extremes, but it was all in a good cause, or so I thought."

"She was a damsel in distress," said Holmes, "a woman wronged, and you came to her rescue."

"Yes, that's it. That's precisely it. She seemed wholly sincere. She implored me to lend her the benefit of my expertise. She dangled money in front of me. How could I reasonably say no? How could any man?"

"And hence I do not deem your actions criminal, Mr Kavanagh. I could censure you for your cupidity and your wilful blindness, but neither of those faults warrants a jail sentence. The death of Eustace Agius was not a foreseeable consequence of your endeavours."

"So you are not going to give me up to the police?" said Kavanagh.

"That has never been my intention."

"But you said something earlier about murder, and me being an accessory."

"An unwitting one," said Holmes, "and if it comes to it, I will put in a good word for you with Scotland Yard, where I wield some influence. I very much doubt you will have any trouble with the law over this."

The colour began to return to the illusionist's face. "Thank you, sir. And here, let me return the favour by writing you that note I promised."

Kavanagh gave Holmes the piece of paper on which he had written a few lines addressed to his Frith Street landlady and appended his signature at the bottom. "You'll find the gimmick in the wardrobe, stored inside a cardboard box. I was rather pleased with it and kept it with a view to perhaps utilising it in some future illusion. Seeing as it is now associated with a man's death, however, I can assure you that that will never come to pass. My conscience would not allow it."

"That speaks well of you."

"If only I could wave a wand," said Kavanagh the Great, with feeling, "and make it as though none of this ever happened."

"For that," said Holmes, not unsympathetically, "you would need genuine magical powers."

Chapter Seventeen

DEATH BY SUPERNATURAL CAUSES

Kavanagh's letter gained us entry to the boarding house and his rooms, and we found a large cardboard box stowed in the wardrobe, as promised. Holmes lifted the lid, glanced inside, and shut it again, seeming satisfied. I caught a glimpse of black fabric and glinting metal, but that was all.

Thence we drove to Knightsbridge, Holmes with the box on his lap. Its contents clinked softly with the motion of the cab.

Tarleton Crescent was our destination, and it was nigh on ten o'clock when our hansom pulled up outside. As we stepped down, I cast a look towards the small park in front, trying to descry a figure or two hiding among the trees. I assumed there were still Irregulars on watch duty there. If so, however, they were well concealed.

"It's rather late to be calling, don't you think?" I said as Holmes and I ascended the steps to the porch.

"Late suits my purposes," Holmes said. "This is not a social call, anyway."

"No, we are here to confront Mrs Agius with proof that she killed her husband. Yet I still cannot see how she can be a murderer. For one thing, should you want a man dead, scaring him is an inordinately elaborate and uncertain way of achieving that result, even if he does have a weak heart. As Mrs Agius herself said, there are many simpler and more reliable methods."

"Unless one is hoping to deflect suspicion away from oneself, of course."

"Of course. Death by apparently natural causes."

"Or by supernatural causes, one might say."

"But then why, when Agius had his heart attack, did Mrs Agius do her utmost to save him?" I said. "She used three amyl nitrite pearls on him. That is not the behaviour of a murderer."

"Mr Agius's dying word would suggest otherwise."

"His dying word? But that was his wife's name."

"Was it, Watson? Was it? And what of the broken wineglass on the hallway floor? How did that get there?"

"I had almost forgotten about the wineglass," I said. "Aren't we to assume that it was transported thither by the ghost? There is a certain type of phantom, a poltergeist, that is reputed to move physical objects around, sometimes quite dynamically."

"We may well be expected to assume as much. The wineglass remains, however, a telling detail, if for no other reason than that it is so out of keeping with other aspects of the haunting."

So saying, Holmes rapped on the door, and shortly the butler arrived.

"Mrs Agius is not expecting us," Holmes told him. "However,

if you tell her that we have lately been at the Tivoli Theatre, I believe she will agree to see us."

So she did, for not three minutes later we were warming ourselves by the drawing room fire, in the company of both Mrs Agius and young Vernon.

"I am not sure that what we are about to discuss, madam, is for your son's ears," said Holmes.

"Vernon is old enough. He stays."

"Very well. Let me get straight to it, then. I know who is responsible for the supposed haunting that ultimately cost your husband his life. It was not some cotton mill ghost. It was you, Mrs Agius."

"Mr Holmes—"

"Kindly do not try to deny it."

"I was not going to," she said. "I freely admit I am the author of those events. You must know that already, since you referred to the Tivoli."

"Mama?" said Vernon, aghast. "*You* did it? The prints? The flames? The… thing that Papa and Sturridge saw?"

"I did it all, my boy." Mother and son were seated side by side on the sofa, and she patted his knee. "I should have known Mr Holmes would find me out. I hoped I had got away with it, but, as you yourself have been keen to point out on many an occasion, Vernon, he is a very perspicacious man. If only your father had not hired him."

"Quite so," said Holmes. "Without realising it, Eustace Agius set in motion the solving of the mystery of his death, before he had even died."

"I could have refused to speak to you when you came, Mr Holmes," Mrs Agius said, "but I felt sure that would arouse your suspicion. Instead, I thought it better to meet you and put on a bold front."

"You were convincing, madam, not least in the image you presented of a woman who did not greatly regret becoming a widow. You could have resorted to tears and histrionics in order to persuade us that you were labouring under the weight of a grief you did not truly feel, but rather you played it straight. Your honesty was refreshing and credible, and made you seem almost too obvious a candidate to be the guilty party. Brava for that."

"Thank you, sir."

"It was a smart ploy, too, showing us the letters. They certainly directed my attention elsewhere. Yet they proved a false trail. Do you even know who wrote them?"

"I don't," said Mrs Agius. "I assumed they came from the widower of an employee of my husband's. They did not?"

"They came from Danvers Lockforth."

"I do not know the name."

"A man whom your husband swindled."

"That would make him one among many. What did this Danvers Lockforth hope to gain by sending them?"

"I believe it was a form of revenge."

"Then it was a pretty futile one, was it not?"

"As Lockforth himself doubtless realised, eventually," said Holmes. "At any rate, the letters dried up after a few months. His rage must have spent itself."

I should note here that Holmes wrote to Danvers Lockforth later in order to verify this supposition of his, going to some lengths to reassure the fellow that nothing he said would be used as incriminating evidence and the police would not be contacted; this was for Holmes's personal satisfaction only. He gave his word on that as a gentleman. Lockforth replied, and it turned out that Holmes was almost but not entirely correct in regard to his reasons for abandoning the whole letter-writing enterprise. Lockforth said that the mere act of putting those words down on paper somehow served to purge him, little by little, of his hard feelings towards Eustace Agius. There came a time when his heart was no longer in it, and he felt lighter and freer, and so he gave it up. In this regard, the letters can be said to have served a worthwhile purpose, as a kind of cure for animosity, for they had put Lockforth in a position when he could almost forgive Agius for cheating him. However, in a postscript, he did admit that he had not been particularly saddened to hear that Agius was dead.

My friend continued his address to Agius's widow. "Nonetheless, the letters gave you inspiration, did they not? They were what set you onto the idea of 'haunting' your husband. The letters may have stopped coming but you saw how they had distressed him, how they preyed on his mind, and you decided to capitalise on it. The handprints and footprints made of soot were a start. They were easy enough to manufacture, and as the mistress of the house you could move around the premises with impunity. You could enter your husband's study, or his bedroom, and leave a print using your own hand or shoe sole, caked in soot from the nearest fireplace; and should you be seen entering or leaving the room, nobody would question why you were there, the way a servant might be questioned. I can only presume you wiped the affected hand or shoe clean immediately after carrying out the deed, using a handkerchief which you would later dispose of."

"Not a handkerchief," said Mrs Agius. "Each time it was a rag, which I would keep on my person for just that purpose, and then afterwards burn."

"I see. Yes, much more economical that way," said Holmes. "The effect of the prints on your husband's mental state told you that you were on the right track. Now it was time to escalate matters, and that is where Kavanagh the Great came in."

"Who is Kavanagh the Great?" Vernon Agius asked.

"A stage illusionist," said Holmes. "I imagine your mother saw one of the posters for the variety show at the Tivoli in which he appears on the bill. They are all over town. She realised that an illusionist might be able to help her concoct more extraordinary and compelling ghostly effects than mere sooty prints. Perhaps she may even have read a review of his performance, citing the 'wall of fire' trick. Kavanagh proved not just the man for the job, but eager to help. Hence the flames at the bedroom window, the smoke in the study. He supplied you with everything you could need, Mrs Agius, and received handsome recompense for it."

"Did he confess all?" said the widow.

"Without much prompting."

"He seems the type. All that money I paid him, and he gave me up just like that."

"He feared the hangman's noose. As should you."

"Mr Holmes!" Vernon cried in alarm. "Surely not!"

Mrs Agius was somewhat more composed than her son. "Why might I be hanged?" said she, looking at Holmes levelly. "I meant only to scare Eustace. To humiliate him. To teach him the error of his ways. I did not mean him to die."

"I see," said Holmes. "Rather in the manner of Dickens's *A Christmas Carol*, then? Ghosts transforming your Ebenezer Scrooge of a husband from cruel misanthrope to kindly philanthropist?"

"That's it. I thought it might bring about a change of heart."

"And it did, if not in the way you intended. What, after all, could more radically change a man's heart than its ceasing to beat altogether?"

"Harsh, sir."

"I beg your pardon. That could have been more tactfully put. All the same, you are not being wholly honest here, Mrs Agius. Not in the least. And if you will allow me to stage a small demonstration, I shall make clear how I have come to that conclusion."

"A demonstration?" said Mrs Agius.

"Give me a few minutes to set everything up," Holmes said. "I am going to recreate the events of the night your husband died, and by this means prove that the cause of his death was not sheer terror, but you."

Chapter Eighteen

AN ANGEL OF DEATH

It was an awkward ten minutes I spent alone in the company of Faye and Vernon Agius. Holmes had gone out into the hallway with express instructions that he was not to be disturbed. He had taken the cardboard box with him, and I heard him out there, moving around, going up and down the stairs a couple of times. Meanwhile, mother and son, clasping hands, simply stared at me. Polite conversation seemed inappropriate. I felt as though I was somehow the agent of their misfortune; I was an angel of death, there to escort Mrs Agius on the first steps of her journey towards the scaffold. I did not know where to look, so I fell to studying my own fingernails.

Eventually Holmes summoned us to join him. I all but leapt out of my seat in my eagerness.

In the hallway, the lights were now out. The only illumination came from an oil lamp Holmes had found from somewhere. This he passed to me to hold.

"Watson, you are going to play the role of Eustace Agius in

this little re-enactment of mine. Vernon, I would very much like it if you were to serve as a substitute for Sturridge."

"I shall do no such thing," said the lad, "and you can't make me. It's absurd, all of it. Absurd."

"Oh, go on, Vernon," said his mother. "It can't do any harm. I'm sure Mr Holmes knows how I pulled off the stunt with the ghostly black figure, but there lies the limit of his knowledge. I did not kill your father, not on purpose. How could I have? His heart gave out thanks to the strain imposed on it by fear. I am not sad that that was the outcome. I don't think you are either. And let's not forget, I tried to revive him. I told you as much."

"And Sturridge has confirmed it."

"You have spoken to Sturridge? Obviously you have."

"I conducted a thorough interrogation of the fellow, although he may not recall it as such."

"Well then, there you are," said Mrs Agius. "You know I am telling the truth. When Eustace collapsed, I administered amyl nitrite. Thrice. I did everything I should have. It is not my fault it did not work."

"Still, I am not going along with this… this charade," said Vernon Agius vehemently.

"Do it, Vernon," said Mrs Agius. "Indulge Mr Holmes. He is your hero, isn't he? Do it for that reason, then, if not for my sake. Then this will be over with and we can all go to bed."

Vernon lifted his shoulders and let them fall. "All right, Mama."

"Good of you, my lad," said Holmes. "I myself will play the one remaining part in our dramatis personae, that of Mrs Agius.

We shall, the three of us, go up to the first-floor landing. Mrs Agius, you stay where you are and observe. Please be so kind as to let me know if I misrepresent the sequence of events in any way."

On the landing, Holmes retreated into the shadows at the foot of the next flight of stairs, beside a large ornamental Chinese vase that rested on an occasional table.

"We open the scene as Mr Agius and Sturridge begin to descend to the hallway," said he. "Sturridge has the lamp. Watson, pass it to Vernon. Now, Sturridge goes first, Mr Agius following. Down you go. Slow and wary. That's it. Meanwhile, here I am, as Mrs Agius, who has just come out of her bedroom on the second floor and tiptoed downstairs to this landing. She is prepared. She, after all, is the one who made the crash in the hallway a short while earlier, by dropping a wineglass over the banister from just outside her bedroom door so that it plummeted through the stairwell all the way to the floor. Then, having thus successfully disturbed her husband from his slumbers, she hurried back into her room to hide. Her trap is set. Lying in wait amid the shadows, she watches the two men. They reach the foot of the stairs. They are in the correct position. Sturridge notices the broken glass but does not have time to ponder it, for now Mrs Agius makes her move."

Vernon and I stood side by side. The lamp's nimbus of light did not spread far. I could make out Mrs Agius by the doorway to the drawing room. The rest of the hallway was in gloom.

Then, all at once, out of nowhere, a black shape arose. The hair on the back of my neck stood erect. My heart jumped in my ribcage. Even though I had known something of the sort was imminent, the phenomenon gave me quite a fright. I could only imagine how horrifying it must have been to Eustace Agius and Sturridge, who had had no forewarning of its appearance.

The ragged black phantom hung in the hallway, hulking and ominous. Slowly, forbiddingly, one arm rose to horizontal. This was the "finger of blame" Sturridge had spoken of, and it was pointed straight at me, or rather at Eustace Agius.

The baleful apparition hovered like that for another few seconds, and suddenly it shot ceilingward, vanishing from view. Though I knew it to be no real phantom, only a hoax, I was rather relieved to see it gone.

"Now then," said Holmes, "if you would be so good as to ignite the gas jets, Mrs Agius, I can reveal the mechanism behind this frightful figure."

As the hallway chandelier bloomed with light, Vernon extinguished the lamp in his hand. Holmes then carefully lowered a long, thin swathe of black cloth through the arms of the chandelier on the end of a piece of fine wire. The filmy material – cheesecloth or muslin, I thought – puddled on the floor, merging with the dark rug below the chandelier. The wire, even amid all that brightness, was almost invisible.

"Let me do it again," said Holmes, "this time with full illumination so that the artifice is laid bare. At first, the presence of the cloth on the floor is disguised by the rug. The wire cannot be seen at all in the dark."

He tugged on his end of the wire and the cloth began to rise. It took shape, some kind of metal armature within it forming a rough approximation of a head and shoulders. The rest of the tattered fabric hung loose from this framework, creating a spectre-like outline.

"Kavanagh has hinged the armature cleverly so that its pieces slot into place under their own weight as it rises," Holmes said. "When fully activated, this gives the upper portion of the figure a three-dimensional solidity. It's the same principle by which he makes his assistant Elsie appear to float upwards onstage. He drapes a sheet over her as she lies across the trestles, where she is maintaining her supine position through sheer bodily self-control. She is much stronger than she looks. Within the sheet, however, is an armature mimicking her outline. It slots on top of her, Elsie slithers out from under it while Kavanagh is misdirecting the audience with a lot of arm waving, and then sheet and armature are hauled up into the flies by another assistant."

The figure's arm began to rise, as before.

"Here, we see how a second wire, running parallel to the main one, lifts our ghost's arm to produce a gesture of recrimination. Then, if I pull swiftly on the main wire again like so, the figure slips upward between the arms of the chandelier. The narrowing puts extra pressure on the hinges of the armature, with the result that it collapses, thus."

The apparition flattened out, becoming a shapeless swathe of black cloth again as it passed through the chandelier.

"Similarly, Elsie seems to vanish when the sheet is whipped away," Holmes said. "But that is only because she is not even there. It is only the collapsible armature mimicking her body. The real Elsie, in the interim, has been busy running all the way round from backstage to the front of house so that she can make her grand entrance in the stalls. In our case, no such re-manifestation is needed. The ghost has done its bit. All Mrs Agius need do is bundle up the apparatus and secrete it somewhere. Inside this large vase, most likely, where it will remain unnoticed until she retrieves it later. Is that what you did, madam? I am correct on every count?"

Mrs Agius nodded.

"Quite ingenious, really," Holmes opined. "As was what came next, the final part of your scheme. The last twist of the knife, as it were."

Chapter Nineteen

A BLANK ROUND

"Y ou may not have known for certain, Mrs Agius," Holmes said, descending the stairs, "that the appearance of the ghost would precipitate a heart attack. Such was the fragility of your husband's condition, however, that you knew one might well occur sooner or later, whether through your doing or not, and so you made provision for that eventuality."

"What are you talking about, Mr Holmes?" said Vernon Agius.

"I am talking about an amyl nitrite pearl. Or rather, a pearl purporting to contain amyl nitrite but actually filled with nothing more potent than plain water."

"No! It can't be true," said the boy.

"It is. For proof, I have the eyewitness evidence of none other than the man whom you have been standing in for, the valet Sturridge. I interviewed him a few days ago, although he could not have known it was I."

"You were in disguise. Just as in that episode Dr Watson

depicts in *The Sign of Four*, when you dress as an elderly master mariner."

"That is so," said Holmes. "Sturridge described how he went to fetch his master's pillbox of amyl nitrite pearls. He encountered you on the landing, Mrs Agius, and you took the box from him and went down to minister to your husband. Sturridge saw you break three pearls, one after the other, beneath Mr Agius's nose."

"Precisely as I myself recounted to you," said Mrs Agius. "I may have borne little love for my husband, Mr Holmes, but I am not inhuman. I used every means available to keep him alive."

"Did you? Sturridge reported that you dropped the first pearl you took out from the box and had to retrieve it from the folds of your nightgown. That, I submit, was no accident. Your act of seeming clumsiness gave you the perfect opportunity to exchange the real pearl for a doctored one – swapping a live bullet for, so to speak, a blank round. It would not be too difficult to undo the end of a pearl's sleeve and insert a glass capsule of similar size, one containing nothing more innocuous than water, then fasten the end back up. You may already have had this doctored pearl concealed in your hand. Conjurors like Kavanagh call this 'palming'. That or it lay in a pocket of your nightgown and you were able to swap it surreptitiously for the real one. You had a doctored pearl with you that night because you knew that, with all you had planned, you were very likely to have the opportunity to use it. In either case, whether you palmed it or took it from your nightgown, Sturridge did not see the substitution, and thus you were able to give your husband not the pearl with the inhalant that might have saved him, but a water-filled dud, which as good as doomed him."

Mrs Agius gave a hollow laugh. "That is not true. That is not true at all. I freely admit to everything you have said up until now, Mr Holmes. Your little piece of showmanship, laying bare the whole business with Kavanagh's ghost apparatus, all of that is accurate. But this? A doctored amyl nitrite pearl? No. Where is your proof? You have none."

"I do," said Holmes. "Your husband's last word. He spoke your name. 'Faye'. Or, to be more accurate, he spoke your name followed by a guttural gurgle in the back of his throat. Sturridge assumed this to be some kind of death rattle, but what if it was not? After all, 'Faye' and a pharyngeal fricative might, when put together, be construed as the word… 'fake'."

"Fake," I echoed, bemusedly.

"Fake," said Vernon Agius too, his eyes widening. He turned to his mother. "Mama, surely that isn't what happened. It cannot be."

Faye Agius fixed her son with a long, complicated look. To my way of thinking, she was making up her mind what to say to him, debating whether or not she should come clean and confess her murderous deed. Neither she nor Vernon had loved Eustace Agius. They had hated and feared the man. Nonetheless, if Holmes was right, Mrs Agius had killed her husband. How could a son be expected to take news like that? How could he ever look his mother in the eye again?

Mrs Agius's shoulders sagged. The air of lofty certitude she had maintained up until now cracked and fell away, like a brittle crust.

"You have me, Mr Holmes," she said in a low, defeated murmur. "I did it, just as you say. I gave Eustace a doctored pearl. Please, though, before you turn me in to the police, allow me to say one or two things in my defence."

"I should expect no less," said Holmes.

"First of all, it was only the first pearl that was doctored. The next two I gave to Eustace were the genuine article, straight from the pillbox. I... I was overwhelmed by remorse. I could scarcely believe what I had done, and I wished to make things right. I thought – I prayed – that the subsequent pearls would compensate for the false one. They did not. Evidently the damage was already done and no amount of amyl nitrite could undo it. Is that not likely, Dr Watson?"

"The sooner the drug is administered, the better," I said. "In situations like that, every second counts and any delay can be fatal."

"Yes. Yes." Mrs Agius was quivering with emotion, her voice merely a wisp of sound now. "Another mitigating factor is this. Eustace was running his business into the ground. He was on the verge of insolvency. In order to shore up the mills, he was dipping into private funds."

"Your inheritance," said Holmes.

Some animation returned to the widow. Her mouth tightened and her eyes flashed. "Yes! *My* money. Money my father bequeathed me. Eustace's by law, but mine by rights. Even though Eustace was close to losing everything, I felt sure that he would leave my inheritance untouched. Then at least there'd be *something* to pass on to Vernon in due course. Instead, it looked as though he was going to squander it all, to the last penny. I could not let that happen. I couldn't!"

"And your only recourse, as you saw it, was to take his life."

"I know. I know." She shook her head dejectedly. "But I am a mother, and a mother protects her offspring. She will do anything to ensure her child's wellbeing. I could not have Vernon go out into the world penniless, the son of a bankrupt. How would he ever get on in life? He might not even have been able to finish his schooling at Harrow, such was the level of impoverishment that Eustace threatened to get us into. If what I did seems drastic... well, so be it. But I did it for the right reasons, and if I must take the consequences, then I shall. But, Mr Holmes..."

"Yes, madam?"

"It is in your power to prevent that." Mrs Agius fixed her tearful gaze on him. "I surely don't have the right to ask this of you, but you needn't tell the police everything, need you? I will happily acknowledge that I carried out the haunting. Kavanagh obviously cannot be guaranteed to keep his mouth shut about that, and so all I can do is own up to as much as he himself knows of the matter and pay whatever penalty awaits me for it. It is involuntary manslaughter, isn't it? If someone dies as an unintended consequence of your actions? And involuntary manslaughter, unlike murder, is not a capital offence."

She took a step towards my friend.

"I am throwing myself on your mercy, Mr Holmes," she said. "Consult your conscience. Look in your heart. Do I deserve the rope? Really? Truly?"

Chapter Twenty

EXORCISED

We left Faye and Vernon Agius in the hallway of 23 Tarleton Crescent and ventured out once more into the night air that was filled with a hurly-burly of snow. My last sight of mother and son, as we closed the front door behind us, was a piteous one. They were embracing, both sobbing.

"Holmes," I said, "for what it's worth, you made the right decision. Sometimes I question the way you take the law into your own hands and choose whether a criminal should face justice or get away scot-free. Our country's judicial system is there for a reason, and it isn't for you or me to circumvent it. Last winter, however, with James Ryder in the blue carbuncle case, and now with Mrs Agius, you have exhibited clemency where clemency is due. Eustace Agius did not deserve to die at his wife's hands, but at the same time he did not deserve to live. It is not as if Faye Agius will go on to kill again. What she did, she did out of sheer desperation, and God forbid she should ever find herself once more in a similar predicament. That would be just too cruel."

"The gallows would have made an orphan of Vernon," said Holmes, "and I could not deprive a son of his mother as well as his father, not when it was in my power to prevent it."

"Moreover, Vernon now has a chance at leading a decent, productive life. In time, he will shake off the shadow his father cast over him. He will make something of himself."

"That is to be hoped. I would not call it an easy decision, though, Watson, and if it proves to be a misjudgement, that is something I shall have to live with. One last loose end to tie up now."

Holmes placed thumb and forefinger between his lips and blew a shrill whistle.

"Wiggins?" he called out. "Is that you and a cohort I spy, lurking in the park there?"

Through the hectic tumble of the snow I saw a head poke out from behind the trunk of a tree, followed by another.

"Mr Holmes," came a voice that was unmistakably that of Wiggins. "I thought it was you we saw going in earlier. I said to Stanley here, 'That's Mr Holmes, I could swear to it, and Dr Watson too.'"

"Consider yourselves relieved of duty. The case is closed."

"And I'm right glad to hear it, sir." The Irregulars' de facto leader came fully into view, clambering agilely over the railings and lowering himself onto the pavement on the other side. "This blinkin' snow. It was getting to be a struggle just to keep my teeth from chattering."

He was joined on the pavement by the other Irregular, Stanley, and the two of them crossed over to Holmes's and my side.

Neither was wearing what I considered sufficient clothing for the weather, and I marvelled at their hardiness. Few could have endured long in such conditions with only a shirt, a pair of holed shoes and a patched, threadbare jacket to keep them warm.

Holmes fished in his pocket for money for them.

"Might I ask, Mr Holmes," said Wiggins, "what these toffs were up to, that we had to keep an eye on them? Although, if it ain't none of my beeswax," he added quickly, "just say so."

Holmes deliberated, then said, "There was a malign spirit dwelling in that house, Wiggins. It has been exorcised. That is all you need to know."

With that, the two Baker Street Irregulars scurried off to whatever nook or rookery they called home, while my friend and I turned our footsteps towards the nearest main road, where we might find a hansom.

As we walked through the dense pall of snowflakes, I could have sworn I heard Holmes mutter under his breath, "Exorcised for now and, I trust, for good."

I did not understand the meaning of the remark. I was not even sure I had heard him correctly. That was why I said nothing.

Only later, much later, would I discover just what he meant.

The Third Terror

THE YUKON CANNIBAL

1894

Chapter One

A KIND OF REVENANT

Between 1891 and 1894 my life changed markedly. In the course of those three years I lost a friend, buried a wife and regained said friend, in that order. To call it a turbulent time would be an understatement.

The friend, of course, was Sherlock Holmes, who in the spring of '91 perished at the Reichenbach Falls in mortal combat with that archfiend Professor Moriarty. So I believed, at any rate, and I mourned his death as deeply as it is possible to, for weeks on end. The one redeeming feature of this dismal period was the fact that Mary had fallen pregnant and we were expecting delivery of the baby soon. This helped anchor me. It was something to look forward to, the proverbial light at the end of the tunnel.

Complications with the birth doused that light once and for all. Not only was my unborn child taken from me, so was Mary. In the space of a few short months, the very greatest treasures that I could call mine were stolen away – Holmes, wife, the prospect of fatherhood – and I lapsed into utter despair. I regret to say that I found solace in the bottle, following a path which my older brother had taken and which had led ultimately to his ruin. It almost led to my own. I shunned society. I neglected work, which put my practice in danger of failing. Many a night I would sit up alone, in a drunken stupor, and contemplate my service revolver and the ends it might be put to, by which I mean putting an end to me. More than once I even placed the barrel against my head. I think all that stopped me from going any further was my inner numbness. If I had felt something, anything at all, I might have found the wherewithal to pull the trigger. Instead I felt nothing whatsoever and, devoid of pain or motivation, sooner or later I would lower my arm and let the gun slip from my fingers to the floor.

It does not fill me with pride to recount these things here, yet I would defy any man, no matter his strength of character, to experience such a litany of calamities as I did and not wonder whether it was worth persevering with life. In time, I pulled myself out of my slough of despond. It was slow going, each day a struggle, but by late '93 I was more or less back to my old self. So others told me, at any rate, although their sole point of reference was the impression I gave. They could not see through the façade to the John Watson beneath, who was still prone to quiet sorrow and the occasional bout of hopelessness.

Then, in April of 1894, came a miracle. Holmes was back from the dead. A theme of this present narrative is beings who live on beyond the grave in one form or other; and I might apply it to Holmes himself, for with his return from seeming death, what was he but a kind of revenant? A ghost made flesh?

Joy found a place in my world once more. I had renewed purpose and vigour, and soon Holmes and I were adventuring together like before, as if there had never been any hiatus in our partnership. We were even called upon to revisit the scene of one of my friend's greatest triumphs, Dartmoor, where five years earlier we had confronted the notorious Baskerville Hound. On this second occasion we were forced to deal with the repercussions of the previous case, in a chronicle I have published under the title *The Beast of the Stapletons*.

That episode took place not long before the one I am now about to relate, which began, as Holmes's investigations almost invariably did, with the arrival of a client at our lodgings. I say *our* lodgings because by that point I had put my house in Paddington up for sale and moved out, happily reinstalling myself in my former quarters at 221B Baker Street.

The client was a journalist, Hitesh Basu by name, and he arrived on a stormy night in mid-December when rain was lashing down on London and thunder stalked the skies above the city like a bellicose god. It was weather into which only the foolhardy or the very desperate might venture out, and Basu belonged in the latter category.

Having briefly introduced himself, he stood in our drawing room, sopping wet and shivering, his hair plastered to his head. I offered him a brandy to warm him up internally while, to do the same for him externally, Holmes stoked the fire. Basu's clothes steamed as they began to dry.

"Thank you both, kind sirs," said he when he had shaken off the worst of the damp and chill. He looked to be in his late twenties and had fine features, particularly his eyes, which were of an almost luminous tawny hue and had an appealing gentleness about them.

"This rain must remind you of the monsoons back home," I offered cheerily.

No less cheerily, Basu replied, "I wouldn't know about monsoons. I'm from Muswell Hill."

"Come along, Watson," Holmes chided me. "The man doesn't have a trace of a subcontinental accent. He is as native an Englishman as you or me. He is an Oxford graduate, as well, and the recipient of a Half Blue from that university, earned for boxing."

"How do you know all that, Mr Holmes?" said a somewhat perplexed Basu.

"Your tie, my dear fellow, your tie. Those are the navy-and-silver stripes of an Oxford Half Blue, am I not correct?"

Basu glanced down at his tie, then up at Holmes. "Of course. But how did you know I got it for boxing?"

"At Oxford the 'noble art' is one of the sports which, even when practised at varsity level, is not accorded a Full Blue. This, in tandem with certain physiognomical traits, suggested boxing to me."

"Physiognomical traits? Oh, you mean my nose."

"I mean the slight thickening of your brow, but yes, mostly I refer to your nose. How many times has it been broken? Twice?"

"Three times," said Basu. "My mother says it's so crooked now, it looks like the letter 'z'. She never approved of me taking up pugilism. It just so happens I was rather good at it. The state of my nose might seem to tell a different story, but I came by that during my early days, before I learned how to bob and weave properly."

"And now you wield your fist in a different way, holding a pen to write sketches for the *London Weekly Cornucopia*."

"You know of my work?"

A peal of thunder crackled overhead, drowning out Holmes's reply. He waited until it had spent its anger before trying again.

"I read it avidly," said he. "Your byline is a watchword for journalism of the highest calibre. Not only is your prose concise and elegant, your sketches can be very combative. I say that as a compliment. You may not box any more but you are happy to fight on behalf of the underdog, through your articles. Your recent excoriating piece on registered common lodging houses, for instance, was most commendable. I daresay it was not a pleasant experience, posing as a vagrant and spending nights in an assortment of dosshouses."

"It most certainly was not," said Basu. "I still itch, thinking of the bed lice. They are dens of iniquity, those places. I do not mean simply that the accommodation is wretchedly shabby or that all manner of licentiousness goes on there. People sleeping cheek by jowl in overcrowded dormitories, men mingling with women, children with adults, innocents with criminals – that is bad enough. The real iniquities, however, are that the landlords charge four pence a head for such squalor and that the police, who are supposed to inspect all common lodging houses regularly, seldom do. If my article in the *Cornucopia* goes some way to changing that state of affairs, then I will be satisfied."

"Mr Basu is something of a crusader, Watson, as you can tell."

"So it seems," I said.

"I may have a university degree," said Basu, "but I come from lowly stock and know what it is to be poor and oppressed. My father was a Bengali lascar who, after years at sea, settled in England and found work at Tilbury Docks. My mother was an ayah for the family of a British colonel in Madras, who brought her back with them when his posting ended. The two of them met, married, had me, and then, when I was barely an infant, my father was killed in an accident. The cable of a wharf crane snapped and he was crushed by a falling cargo crate. My mother then found work as a nanny for various families. She did not earn a great deal, nor did she remarry, and I grew up in straitened circumstances."

"Yet still you gained a place at Oxford," said Holmes.

"That was in no small part thanks to Professor Isidore Carmody, the Surrey academic. My mother looked after his daughter for a time, when I was very small. The girl, alas, died of scarlet fever, aged nine, and the disease took Carmody's wife at the same time. Carmody remained fond of my mother and the two of them stayed in touch after she left his employ. He even helped her out financially from time to time with small donations. Through my mother, he followed my progress, and it was he who suggested I apply for a place at Oxford. He vouched for me to the admissions board at Balliol College, where he himself studied, and even paid for my fees and accommodation."

"A worthy benefactor, by the sound of it."

"He was a very good man. And in fact, it is about him that I have come to see you, Mr Holmes."

"Is it now?" said Holmes.

"Yes. Might I take a seat? I think my clothes are sufficiently dried out."

"Of course." Holmes motioned Basu to the chair that was regularly used by his clients. I, meanwhile, recharged his brandy glass.

"From your use of the past tense when referring to him, Mr Basu," I said as I handed him the drink, "are we to infer that Professor Carmody is no longer among the living?"

"He is not," said Hitesh Basu with a heavy sigh, "and his death was more than a tragedy, gentlemen. It was an atrocity."

Chapter Two

BITE MARKS

After a remark like that, Basu could not help but have our undivided attention.

"Since my graduation, the professor and I exchanged letters sporadically," he said. "I kept him abreast of my progress through the world of journalism. He would encourage me and every now and then furnish me with a critique of one of my published articles. He could be a hard taskmaster but his comments were always perceptive and seldom wrong. If, as you suggest, Mr Holmes, my prose has concision and elegance, it is down in no small part to him. He was a stickler for both accuracy and simplicity. Some found him pedantic, some curmudgeonly, and he could be both, but beneath this beat the heart of a man who wanted the best for everyone and who held himself to as high a standard as he held others. I am greatly saddened by his death. I feel the world has lost a shining light."

I was moved to pat the young fellow's shoulder in sympathy. Thanks to my own losses, which may not have been all that recent but still felt raw, I was sensitive on the subject of bereavement. Rarely did seeing another person suffering it fail to arouse a strong reaction in me.

"Professor Carmody was the nearest thing I had to a father," said Basu. "I have no memory of my real father at all, and Carmody, in the absence of any other, filled that role more than adequately. I felt his benign influence throughout my youth and young manhood, and our relations were always cordial. Therefore I was appalled to learn, just last week, that he had died – and had died horribly.

"The professor," the journalist continued, "lived near Haslemere, in a beautiful old house in the country, Grayshott Grange. I have visited there a few times. Most recently I went down to pay my respects to him and his new wife. He remarried last year, as it happens. She is a dignified lady with a son in his late teens, and the two of them, she and the professor, seemed to me a good match. I had a very pleasant stay, and that was the last time I ever saw him.

"Last week, I got the news. Carmody had been out walking one afternoon. It was relatively mild for the time of year, remember? The last breath of autumn. Nothing like the tempestuous fury of tonight. There are extensive woods surrounding the professor's estate, which he enjoyed strolling through, and this is where the awful event occurred. Carmody was… well, he was set upon savagely and killed. Something mauled him to death and… and consumed parts of his body."

As he said this, Basu gripped his empty brandy glass so hard that his knuckles whitened. I gently took the glass from him, filled it once again, and returned it to him. He took a trembling sip and seemed to recover some of his composure.

"You know," I said, "this is beginning to ring a bell. There was something in the papers the other day about a wild animal attack in Surrey that resulted in a fatality. Didn't you point out the article to me, Holmes?"

"I did," said my friend.

"I never got round to reading the piece myself, and I don't remember you mentioning the victim's name. I do, however, recall you saying something about a wolf or a rabid dog being responsible."

"I said that that was what the police had concluded," Holmes said. "Perhaps you also recall me saying that I found the rabid dog explanation just about plausible but the idea of a wolf being the guilty party was tenuous in the extreme. I still feel that way. There are no wolves in Britain, outside of zoos and menageries, and even if one were to get loose, it would be unlikely to attack a man. A solitary wolf, lacking the solidarity of the pack, is a timid creature. It would shun humans and sate its hunger on small animals such as rabbits. By the same token, if an entire wolf pack had been involved, there would have been practically nothing left of their prey, which is somewhat different from merely 'parts' of him being eaten. I believe, too, that a wild boar was also proposed as the culprit, and even an escaped circus lion."

"That is all true," said Basu. "So you were aware of Professor Carmody's death already, Mr Holmes?"

"I was. I said nothing because I wanted you to present your tale in your own manner, without trying to anticipate what I might or might not know and therefore second guessing yourself. That way, your account would be as pure and unadulterated as possible. However, Watson has put paid to that plan."

"I didn't realise I was meant to keep quiet about you showing me the article," I said.

"I am not censuring you, old friend. We are where we are. Please continue, Mr Basu."

"Naturally, it came as a terrible shock to learn of my benefactor's death," Basu said. "For a day or two, all I could do was wonder at the workings of a divinity that would take so virtuous a man from us, well before his time, while leaving countless scoundrels and villains still roaming the earth. I found out about the funeral arrangements and went down to Surrey for the ceremony. It was a sombre occasion, attended by many of the great and good from the world of academe, as well as Carmody's friends and immediate family and prominent members of the local community.

"At the wake, which was held at the Grange, I fell to talking with Carmody's GP, Dr Burnell, who happened to be the one who had examined the body to determine cause of death. He had contrived to get himself a little tipsy at the wake, which would normally be regrettable but in this instance, as it turned out, was not. His tongue was loosened, you see, and he told me something he might otherwise not have."

"Namely?" said Holmes

"Dr Burnell confided that the bite marks on Carmody were inconsistent with the bite of an animal. He had refrained from mentioning this in his report at the inquest for fear of causing unnecessary upset to the widow and others close to the deceased.

He was reluctant to say any more, but I am, by dint of professional experience, quite adept in getting people to open up. I plied him with a fresh glass of wine, asked a few subtly probing questions, and soon Burnell was telling me that he would not swear to it, but the bite marks, to his eye, had looked human."

"Human!" I exclaimed. "Surely not."

"That's what I thought," said Basu. "My feeling was that he must be mistaken. And yet, as I pressed him, Burnell grew insistent. The wounds on Carmody, he said, did not bear the jagged, slashing tears that denote the depredations of a carnivorous animal whose jaws are equipped only with canine teeth. There were impressions in the flesh exactly such as a set of human teeth might cause. And that led me, inexorably, to a terrible inference."

"Which was?" said Holmes.

Lightning flashed behind the curtains, sending jagged streaks of illumination into the room. Thunder rumbled a moment later, so loud and reverberant it made the window casements rattle in their frames.

"For that," said Basu, "I am going to have to tell you about Jonah Denbigh. Denbigh, also known as the Yukon Cannibal."

Chapter Three

ANTHROPOPHAGOUS WAYS

"I first learned about Denbigh three years ago, on a previous visit to Grayshott Grange," said Basu. "Carmody himself mentioned him to me.

"'I don't suppose you've ever heard of him, young Hitesh,' said he. 'Few outside this area have. He is a recluse, living in a hut in the depths of the woods, not far from here. He refuses to consort with civilisation and spends his days trapping and skinning woodland mammals and curing their meat, for his private consumption. There's a fascinating, if rather gruesome, story attached to him. I don't know how much truth there is to it, but anyway...'

"Carmody proceeded to tell me how, back in the mid-1870s, Denbigh was stuck halfway up a mountain in the Yukon for an entire winter, along with two companions. They were gold prospectors, the three of them, all from England, who had emigrated to Canada to seek their fortune. When spring came, Denbigh alone descended from the mountain, dazed, emaciated, starving. The remains of the other two men were discovered later, unburied. They had been ravaged and eaten by wild beasts, or so it appeared, but then rumours began to swirl. People began to wonder how Denbigh had survived when neither of his colleagues had. People began to put two and two together...

"'Well, at any rate, it's just a story,' the professor concluded. 'Perhaps it might be of interest to you, though. You could write about it.'

"The idea lodged in my brain. Carmody was right, it *was* interesting. And just then – I will admit this to you, gentlemen – I was in need of something that would really make an impression, something sensational. I hadn't yet found my comfortable berth with the *Cornucopia* and was scratching a living through freelance assignments for various lesser organs. A true-life tale of cannibalism in the Canadian wilderness – call me cynical, but it would certainly get me noticed and boost my career.

"So I went in search of Denbigh's hut and, following directions given to me by a local gamekeeper, found it. It was not a pretty place, and its inhabitant was none too pretty either, nor any too welcoming. I was able to gain his trust, however, and in time he overcame his reticence and gave me his version of events.

"Denbigh hotly denied he had ever resorted to cannibalism. It was a grizzly bear that had killed and eaten the other two prospectors, he said. This had happened not long after the snows came unexpectedly early and trapped the three men in their camp, cutting them off from the rest of the world. Thereafter Denbigh had eked out their remaining food supplies, which proved just enough to live on until spring arrived and the snow thawed sufficiently that he could leave.

"He would have remained in Canada and carried on his prospecting, but the suspicions that had become attached to him would not go away. He was spurned, spat upon, vilified, until at last he could take it no more. He returned to his native England and attempted to start afresh. However, his ordeal in the Yukon had left him a broken man. His health was ruined and his mind was disordered. He could not hold down a job, and in the end he retreated to the woods near Haslemere and withdrew from the world."

Basu paused as thunder yet again made its deafeningly loud complaint. Rain, meanwhile, lashed the windowpanes, attacking them as though trying to break in.

"Even leading the life of a hermit, however, Denbigh could not escape his past," he resumed. "Some years ago, before I met him, the locals got wind of what he was alleged to have done in Canada. God knows how, but I suppose nowadays news is international, and an accusation like that is hard to shake. Someone must have learned of his name, remembered a Jonah Denbigh who was accused of being a cannibal a couple of decades earlier, and made the connection. As a result, Denbigh suffered persecution. His hut was vandalised. He was beaten and shot at. The ill-treatment lasted several weeks, and he endured it, until eventually it ran its course and people stopped bothering him.

"I told him I could help him. I would write an article, telling his story from his viewpoint. I was quite certain that Denbigh was innocent. The way he spoke about his time on that mountain had, as far as I was concerned, the ring of truth, and that was the approach I would take in my piece. My aim was to exonerate him.

"Denbigh did not want me to write the piece. He said it would simply rake over old coals and rekindle the flames. I assured him it would have the opposite effect. The fire would be damped out once and for all.

"Gentlemen…" Basu shook his head ruefully. "How naïve I was. I kept up the pressure, and Denbigh finally consented. I penned my article. It appeared in the *Surrey Oracle*. It made a minor splash and brought me to the attention of the editor of the *Cornucopia*, who offered me regular work. But whereas the article's effects on me were almost wholly positive, its effects on Denbigh, by contrast, could scarcely have been more negative. Once more the persecution began. He was hounded and victimised. This time it persisted for months until, as before, the locals wearied of it and left him alone again.

"As soon as I heard about these unintended consequences, I called on Denbigh at his hut to apologise, but he refused to listen. He just cursed me and drove me off at knifepoint.

"And that was the end of the rather sorry affair, or so I thought. Now, however, I am beginning to think I may have been wrong. What if Denbigh lied to me? What if his account – which had seemed perfectly credible, to me at least – was false and he really did survive by eating the other two prospectors? And what if, having gained a taste for human flesh, he has indulged it once more?"

Basu threw up his hands in anguish.

"Denbigh knew I was close to Professor Carmody," he said.

"I told him as much, when explaining how I had come to know about his existence. Perhaps, in order to get back at me for the trouble I caused him through my well-meaning attempt to clear his name, he attacked and killed the professor. Then, falling back into his anthropophagous ways, he consumed portions of him. I was not available, so Carmody was the next best thing. It is a disgusting thought but I cannot get it out of my head."

"You say it was three years ago that you wrote your article about Denbigh?" said Holmes.

"Yes."

"Three years does seem rather a long time to wait before enacting vengeance."

"Don't they say revenge is a dish best served cold?"

"An unfortunate choice of words, under the circumstances, but I take the point. Tell me, does anyone else, save you and Dr Burnell, know that the bite marks on Carmody's body appeared human in origin?"

"Not as far as I'm aware."

"That is something. I imagine if the police had been informed that there was foul play involved, it would be common knowledge by now. Her Majesty's Constabulary have many virtues, but continence is not one of them. Then there is Burnell himself, who may, were he to get drunk again, carelessly reveal to another what he has hitherto shared with no one but you, Basu. All I'm saying is that, should word get out about the nature of the bite marks, Denbigh can expect further and perhaps greater trouble."

"And if what I fear about him is true, it will be no more than he deserves," said Basu.

"Let us reserve judgement on that for the moment," Holmes counselled. "If there is to be an execution, I would rather it is the product of a fair trial in a court of law than the work of a mob meting out summary justice."

"You reckon it might come to that?" I said. "A lynching?"

"Abuse came Jonah Denbigh's way the first time simply on the strength of unsubstantiated rumour, Watson. It came his way a second time after an article was published that should, by rights, have repaired his reputation. You can imagine the response from people in the vicinity if they are led to think that he murdered Professor Carmody, a local dignitary, and cannibalised his body. One should never underestimate the vindictiveness of crowds, nor their willingness to believe the worst."

"Then you will follow up this matter?" said Basu.

"Urgently," said Holmes, "before it is too late."

Chapter Four

THE SYLVAN HEART OF SURREY

The storm was gone by dawn, having raved and stamped its foot well into the small hours. Out of the windows of our train from Waterloo to Haslemere, Holmes and I saw its effects everywhere, in downed trees, missing roof slates and inundated fields. The world seemed ragged and exhausted in its aftermath, as though earth and sky had wrestled violently before declaring a draw.

At Haslemere Station we hired a dog-cart to take us to Grayshott Grange. Basu had caught an earlier train, and we had arranged to meet him at the house, at his suggestion. He had said it would afford a useful base of operations and he would wire Professor Carmody's widow ahead to inform her of his intentions. She was a gracious woman, he had averred, and would not mind the imposition. She knew of the esteem in which her late husband had held him, and vice versa, and she had told Basu at the funeral that he remained welcome at her home at any time.

On the way to the house, we drove through a small town, name of Betchfield, and then entered dense woods that sprawled across undulating countryside. Surrey is the most forested county in England, and we were in its sylvan heart. The storm had stripped the trees their few remaining leaves, plenty of which now lay scattered across the road, forming a damp, mushy carpet that muted the clop of the horse's hooves and the rumble of the cart's wheels. Bare branches dripped with accumulated rainwater, so that all around us there was a constant pattering susurration. The morning's weak sunlight glinted off the droplets as they fell.

After a mile or so of this we came to Grayshott Grange. The house stood at the end of a long drive and proved to be a venerable Jacobean manor that seemed to sprawl in a dozen different directions at once. There were countless gable ends and roof pitches, while the outer walls consisted of square timber frameworks painted black and filled in with bricks in a neat herringbone pattern. Stocky chimneys rose in groups of two or three and diamond-leaded windows peered out in little irregular clusters. In all, the place was a mix of symmetry and asymmetry, giving an impression of ordered chaos, as if it had been built all those years ago to no particular design but a great deal of care and attention had gone into its construction nonetheless.

A broad, arched wooden door opened as the dog-cart pulled up, and out stepped a man in butler's livery. He was well over six feet tall and gaunt, with a pinched, almost cadaverous face. He waited until we had alighted before speaking to us.

"Mr Holmesh, Dr Watshon, I preshume," said he, as the cart rattled away.

"That is us," said Holmes.

"Mishter Bashu awaitsh in the library. Thish way."

Unsmilingly, the butler beckoned us to follow him. His lugubrious demeanour was offset somewhat by his unfortunate sibilant lisp. He also had a habit of working his jaw from side to side, doing this several times as he led us across a galleried hallway and down a corridor, the action issuing an audible click each time. I presumed he suffered from some disorder of the temporomandibular joint, perhaps arthritis. This would also account for the lisp, in as much as full range of movement in his mouth was inhibited.

His height was another affliction, at least in a house of this vintage, for every doorway had a low lintel and he was obliged to duck in order to pass through. Even in the library, when we reached it, he stooped so that the top of his head did not scrape the ceiling beams.

"Your gueshtsh, shir," he said to Basu.

"Thank you, Fitch. Gentlemen? Would you care for refreshments after your journey? Some coffee, perhaps?"

Holmes nodded assent, as did I.

"Fitch, coffee for three, please, if you'd be so kind."

"Of courshe, shir." The butler bowed out of the room.

The library, as with the rest of the house, bore the customary indicators of mourning: the turned pictures, the stopped clocks, the half-drawn curtains, and so forth. I recalled how I had followed these practices at my own home in the wake of Mary's demise, and, more dimly, the various other instances when I had encountered them, for example at 23 Tarleton Crescent.

For me, they now carried added poignancy and perhaps would do so forever.

To distract myself from these glum musings, I took a moment to gaze around at the bookshelves, which were plentiful and stocked with an enviable array of tomes. Mostly these seemed to be philosophical treatises, academic textbooks, and works of reference running to multiple volumes, along with a smattering of atlases, dictionaries and almanacs. I spied, too, some incunabula that were kept behind glass, under lock and key. Their bindings showed their age, the leather dilapidated, the Latin titles so faded that they were hard to decipher.

"I see you're admiring the professor's collection, Doctor," said Basu. "Isidore Carmody was a student of just about everything. Biology, botany, chemistry, physics, mathematics, history, you name it. He had no particular specialism, unless you call a fascination with how people work a specialism. He was interested in anything that expanded his understanding of human nature and the ways we live and behave. In that respect I think you and he, Mr Holmes, would have got along famously."

"I imagine we might have," said Holmes. "Money was no object for him, I take it."

"Family wealth, going back generations. He was not an acquisitive man. Money, to the professor, was simply a means to an end. It enabled him to pursue his studies freely and contribute to causes he deemed worthwhile."

"Among which," said a female voice, "he counted you, Mr Basu."

Holmes and I turned, and there, framed in the same doorway by which we had just entered, stood a woman.

It took me a moment to realise who this was. Her face was very familiar but I had last seen it some years earlier, in a somewhat different setting. What helped me identify her was the fact that she was dressed in mourning, as she had been on that previous occasion.

"Mr Holmes, Dr Watson," said she whom we had formerly known as Faye Agius. "We meet again."

Chapter Five

TWICE A WIDOW

"Your servant, madam," said Sherlock Holmes, with a slight inclination of the head that might just be called a bow.

"My goodness," I said. "What a remarkable coincidence. Mr Basu told us Professor Carmody had remarried, but…"

"But evidently he neglected to say to whom," said the professor's widow.

"You three already know one another, Mrs Carmody?" said Basu. "I had no idea."

"These gentlemen and I were briefly acquainted some years ago. I have cause to be grateful to them."

"I told you in my telegram that Sherlock Holmes was coming down, but when I arrived this morning you did not allude to your connection."

"I assumed you were aware of it, because I thought you would have mentioned me to Mr Holmes when discussing Isidore with him."

"And indeed I did, if only in passing."

"But you neglected to tell him the name I used to go by," said the one-time Mrs Agius, now Mrs Carmody.

"I did not go into any great detail about you."

"Am I so forgettable, Mr Basu? So easily consigned to the margins?"

Basu looked abashed. "Mrs Carmody, I apologise."

"Oh, stop," said she with a small, amiable smile. "I am only teasing."

"Mr Basu did say something to us about Professor Carmody's new wife having a son in his late teens," I said. "Clearly that would be Vernon. How is the lad?"

"He finished with school in the summer, Doctor. I'm pleased to relate that he did exceptionally well in his exams and was offered a place at university. Cambridge, no less. However, he deferred, at Isidore's insistence. Isidore – my poor Isidore – suggested Vernon might benefit from a year at home. He offered to be his mentor and share with him some of his vast knowledge. I, too, thought this a good idea. Vernon would learn things under his stepfather's tutelage that he might not elsewhere."

"I should like to see him again, if possible. I imagine he is much grown."

"He is somewhere around. He does not get up early, in common with many a boy his age, but I'm sure he will show his face soon."

At that moment, Fitch reappeared, bearing a pot of coffee and three cups on a tray. He served Holmes, Basu and me, then asked his mistress if she required anything. She shook her head, and he quietly withdrew.

"It would appear, Mrs Carmody," said Holmes, "that we are once more in the position of having to offer you condolences on the death of a husband."

"I have been, one might say, less than fortunate in that regard," she replied equably. "Isidore and I were not together long. All the same, I feel the loss more keenly this time than I did the last, as you may well appreciate. And then there is the awful nature of his passing…" She shuddered. "I am still having trouble believing it, to be honest. Ours was not a conventional marriage. Isidore was a man who lived very much in his own head. Intellectual pursuits were his all, and everything else came a poor second. Yet he was affectionate towards me, and towards Vernon too, and we neither of us had cause to grumble. He took us in. He paid for Vernon's last few terms at school. He showed us kindness, where others were less charitable. It may not surprise you to learn, Mr Holmes, that after Eustace died, life became rather difficult for my son and me."

"In what way?"

"I really shouldn't bother you with it."

"No, please. Go ahead. I insist. It isn't often that I am privy to the sequel to a case, once the case itself is over."

"Well, for one thing, that man left a terrible financial mess for me to sort out," Mrs Carmody said, lowering herself with decorous grace into a wing-backed reading chair. "The banks called in his business debts. Every one of his mills had to be sold in order to clear the deficit. This took time and cost an exorbitant amount in lawyers' fees. By the end of it, Vernon and I were, if not destitute, then certainly living in less favourable circumstances than we had been accustomed to. There was still my inheritance – what was left of it after Eustace had had his way with it; but that, along with the rest of his estate, was put into trust for Vernon. He will come into it when he turns twenty-one. We were able to live off the interest on the capital in the meantime, but it was a relative pittance. We had to reduce our outgoings by moving out of London, trimming our domestic staff to the bare minimum, and generally pinching the pennies, which included withdrawing Vernon from Harrow and sending him to a less expensive school. This is not to complain, merely to explain."

"I understand."

"Haslemere seemed as nice a place as any to relocate to. I have family around these parts. We rented a little villa on the outskirts of the town, and we were content. We were even happy. My previous husband, you see, Mr Basu, was something of an ogre."

"The professor did once suggest something to that effect," said Basu. "I am sorry it was so."

"Dying was one of the best things Eustace Agius ever did," Mrs Carmody went on. "But it brought complications in addition to the financial ones I have just enumerated. I might as well admit this to you now, since doubtless you will learn of it from Mr Holmes later, but there was talk that I somehow had a hand in his death."

"Oh, my!" Basu declared.

"It is a long, involved tale. I will tell you it sometime. That is how Mr Holmes and I were drawn into each other's orbit, at any rate. He and Dr Watson came to look into the matter, for although a heart attack carried Eustace off, there were extenuating circumstances which made it appear as though it might have been caused deliberately."

"How is that even possible?"

"Again, I will tell you all about it sometime. The main thing is, Mr Holmes showed that, while certain activities of mine may not have been conducive to Eustace's overall wellbeing, his death itself was pure happenstance. My intent had not been to kill."

Mrs Carmody said these words, at the same time directing a very pointed look at both Holmes and me. I kept my expression as neutral as possible, while my friend's face was as impassive and unmoving as a death mask.

"The police chose not to prosecute," she continued, "and the press, thank God, did not get wind of the story. That would have been beyond awful. My name, then, would truly have been mud."

"The press," said Basu wryly. "Those wicked folk."

"Not you, obviously, Mr Basu. You are the exception that proves the rule. But you know how most journalists are."

"I do, I do, more's the pity."

"We got off lightly, I am aware of that," said Mrs Carmody. "It could have been much worse. Nevertheless, in certain circles, tongues wagged. Those who knew how vile Eustace had been to Vernon and me drew their own erroneous conclusions, and that was another good reason for us to quit London. In society, when a whiff of scandal attaches itself to you, it becomes a miasma worse than the Great Stink of 'fifty-eight. Surrey afforded us an opportunity to start over. Soon enough, Isidore and I met.

I could claim it was a whirlwind romance, but I would be lying. Isidore was formal, even stuffy, and for several months we enjoyed high teas and gentle perambulations, during which he would lecture me on whatever scholarly topic was currently obsessing him, and I, in the role of audience, would listen. I was not even sure he had any amorous interest in me, right up until the day he proposed. Talk about a bolt from the blue. But what else could I say in response, apart from yes? I sensed the goodness beneath that crusty exterior and knew he would never ill-use me. And I was right. Isidore has been – *was* – a model husband. Passionate ardour may not have been among his qualities, but I was willing to forfeit that in the name of security. He was likewise an exemplary stepfather to Vernon, stern but benign, generous with his time. I felt that my son and I had, after a period of turbulence, found a safe harbour."

She downcast her gaze.

"It seems that fate has decreed otherwise," she said, stifling a small sob.

At that moment, a dog came into the library. It was her small pug, and I dredged my memory for its name.

"Is that little Otto I see?" I said merrily as the pug ambled up to its mistress's side. I still felt no great fondness for the creature, but I was willing to feign it for Mrs Carmody's benefit.

Mrs Carmody scooped the dog up off the floor and clasped it to her breast. "No, Doctor. Alas, Otto went missing during the summer, a few months after we moved into the Grange. He must have wandered off into the woods one day and got lost, never to return. He wasn't the brightest of dogs. We called and called for him, but never found him. No, this is Hugo. He's barely more than a pup, and he is a delight." She nuzzled the pug's head with her nose. "He fills the gap Otto left in my life."

"Does he boast a royal pedigree, as Otto did?"

"Sadly not. Isidore bought him for me, though, and that, as far as I'm concerned, makes him just as cherishable." Again, she fought back a sob. "Mr Holmes," she said, "it seems that Mr Basu is unconvinced by the police's explanation for my husband's death. He says he has information – he won't tell me what – that leads him to think Isidore was not killed by a wild dog or a boar. This, in turn, leads *me* to think he must have died by human hand. If that is the case, if there is even the remotest possibility that Isidore was murdered, I wish you to find out who did it. Whatever your usual rate is, I will double it. Treble it, even."

"Mrs Carmody, I am happy to pay Mr Holmes's fee," said Basu.

"And I am more solvent than you, Mr Basu, and Isidore was my husband, and there is an end of it. What I fail to comprehend is why anyone might have wanted him dead. He had no enemies that I know of. He could rub people up the wrong way sometimes, but it was never malicious. Usually it was when someone said something ignorant or wrongheaded and he would take it upon himself to correct them. In that situation, his manner could be so peremptory that the other person might easily take offence. There was not a mean bone in his body, however. Anyone who would wish harm on a man like Isidore Carmody is the vilest villain on earth, and if he *was* murdered, you must catch the culprit, Mr Holmes, and you must see to it that justice is served!"

Chapter Six

A SERIAL DISPATCHER OF SPOUSES

Holmes, Basu and I left the library with Mrs Carmody's impassioned injunction ringing in our ears.

"Holmes," I said in a quiet voice as we retraced our steps to the hallway, "are you thinking what I am thinking?"

"As a general rule, I should hope not," said Holmes, "for then I would never solve a single case."

I smarted somewhat at that. "You never tire of disparaging my intellectual capacity, do you?"

"Only in jest, old friend. You know how greatly I respect you, in all your many parts. I would never chaff you in the way I do if I did not think the world of you."

"Well, I suppose I believe that. At any rate, what I was going to say was this. Does it not strike you as odd, if not downright suspicious, that that woman should become a widow twice in relatively swift succession?"

"Are you implying, Doctor," said Basu, "that Mrs Carmody is a sort of serial dispatcher of spouses?"

"Without wishing to go into the full facts of her previous husband's demise, Mr Basu, there undoubtedly would be grounds for thinking that way."

Basu seemed both saddened and disconcerted by my words, but at the same time I saw a spark spring to life in his eyes. I thought I recognised it and wondered if a similar spark appeared in mine whenever a fresh escapade with Holmes beckoned. Basu and I might practise different forms of writing, but we were, all said and done, both writers, and nothing was more appealing to those in our trade than the prospect of a juicy story.

"If you are thinking of turning this into one of your sketches," I said to him, "please at least wait until Holmes has resolved it fully before putting pen to paper."

"Better yet," said Basu, "I shall do nothing about it at all. This is your territory, Dr Watson, not mine. Of the two of us men of letters, you are by far the more celebrated, and after… how many books is it now?"

"Four."

"After publishing four books of Mr Holmes's adventures, your association with him is well-entrenched. You are the chronicler of his deeds, not I, and I would not wish to tread on your toes."

It was the right answer, and I was glad that Basu and I had come to an accommodation amicably.

"You raise a fair point, Watson," said Holmes. By now we had regained the hallway. "It does look, on the face of it, as though Mrs Carmody is making a habit of marrying, only for her husbands to meet untimely and unusual deaths. Such a pattern of behaviour must inevitably arouse suspicion. Yet we should consider the differences between the two situations as much as the similarities." He ticked them off on his fingers. "First of all, Eustace Agius and Isidore Carmody were wholly unalike in temperament, the one a violent, bullying egotist, the other a crotchety but good-natured intellectual. Second of all, Agius was ailing physically and died through, shall we say, a hastening of the inevitable. Carmody, by contrast, died while in good health – as a man who enjoyed regular strolls as exercise would be – and in a manner both unexpected and brutal. Third of all, the one left behind vast debts, the other a sizeable estate."

"That third difference is surely the crucial one," I said, "and it reinforces rather than invalidates what I am getting at. The first time around, Mrs Carmody – Mrs Agius as she was then – ended up poorer and a pariah as a consequence of her widowhood. However, she was also free from the yoke of oppression Eustace Agius placed upon her and their son, and to her that may have been a price worth paying. This time around, she finds herself very comfortably off, does she not? As Professor Carmody's widow, everything that was his is now hers. In both instances the death of a husband was advantageous to her, just not in the same way."

"In other words, a woman who has committed mariticide once and profited from it is liable to do it again. Yes?"

"Yes. It stands to reason."

"Mariticide?" said Basu. "You are painting the lady in a very dim light, I must say. I do not know Mrs Carmody at all well, but now I'm thinking that, for all her gentility and charm, something very dark lurks within."

"She is not an unwily woman," said Holmes. "One might even go so far as to call her devious. On this occasion, however, I am sceptical that she could have savaged Professor Carmody in the way you described to us yesterday, Basu. What do you think, Watson? Did she stalk him in the woods and then set upon him, tooth and nail? Perhaps she and her pug did it together, a conspiracy of canine and female. The dog gnawed his ankles while Mrs Carmody tore him apart with her bare hands."

"You are ridiculing me again, Holmes."

"Only somewhat. Well, quite a lot, if I'm honest."

"I must say I find your remarks somewhat distasteful, Mr Holmes," said Basu. "I would be grateful for a little more sensitivity when talking about the killing of a friend of mine."

"And I deeply regret having caused offence," Holmes said, with sincerity. "I sometimes forget, especially when I am in the thick of a case, that human beings are involved. I have a tendency to treat people as data. Watson despairs of that quality in me."

"Apology accepted."

"I agree with you, Holmes," I said, "that no one in their right mind would think Faye Carmody capable of bloodthirsty violence. However, she could always have paid someone to attack and kill the professor on her behalf. That, certainly, would not be beyond her."

"The someone in question being Jonah Denbigh, I suppose."

"Why not?"

"Who then incriminated himself by reverting to his erstwhile Yukon ways and dining on the body."

"Again, why not?"

Holmes shrugged his shoulders. "Let us lodge that theory in the pigeonhole marked 'Possible But Not Probable'. But hark! Who is this?"

Footfalls sounded from the gallery that overlooked the hallway, announcing the presence of a resident of Grayshott Grange. Next moment, who should come into view but Vernon Agius himself.

As he descended the stairs, blearily rubbing his eyes, I marvelled at the vast difference four years can make in a youngster's appearance. Vernon was now far more man than boy. His shoulders had broadened, he was as tall as me, and his face had lost every last trace of softness. Downy stubble coated his upper lip, and his chin was firm, with a pronounced cleft. His hair, still tousled from sleep, had been grown long in that way that fashionable young men seem to like, reaching almost to his collar at the back, and sideburns were beginning to sprout at his temples.

His surprise at seeing Holmes and myself in the hallway was manifest.

"Good heavens," he said. His voice, of course, was deeper in timbre than ever before, and rather reminiscent of his father's. "Well I never. Sherlock Holmes and Dr Watson. Mr Basu, are you the reason these old friends of mine are here?"

"Guilty as charged, Vernon."

"Then I cannot thank you enough. How wonderful it is to

see you both again." Vernon bounded over to us and shook our hands enthusiastically. "Were we expecting you?"

"I sent your mother a telegram late last night, advising her that all three of us were coming," said Basu. "It arrived first thing this morning."

"While I was still in the Land of Nod," said Vernon.

"Apparently so."

"And…" Vernon's expression clouded. "Oh dear. I can only assume some dark errand brings you to Grayshott Grange. Is that right, Mr Holmes? It must be to do with my stepfather. Am I to infer that he is dead through some means other than the obvious? Can it be that felony was involved? No, surely not."

"That is what I am here to establish," said Holmes.

Vernon staggered back to the staircase, where he sank down on the bottom step and put his head in his hands. "Oh God. It is like a nightmare. Bad enough that Professor Carmody died, and horribly too. Now we have to consider that he was slain deliberately? But who would do such a thing?"

"Your mother tells us he had no enemies. Is that the case?"

"Enemies?" Vernon searched inwardly. "I can't think of any. Perhaps he had rivals in the academic world. Perhaps there was a longstanding feud with another scholar over some obscure point of knowledge. I don't know. He could be abrasive at times, that is for sure, which may have earned him the enmity of others."

"You liked him, though. Your mother said as much."

"Liked him?" said Vernon. "Looked up to him, certainly. He wasn't the sort of man who aroused warm feelings in one. He could be very cold. Distant."

"But you postponed taking a place at Cambridge in order to spend time with him instead."

"Is that my mother again? She has not been stinting with the facts, has she? Yes, I did. Professor Carmody proposed becoming my unofficial tutor, and I agreed. I felt unready to go up to university yet. I thought a year out might give me some perspective on things and allow me to mature a little."

"Mature?" I said. "To me, my boy, you seem wise beyond your years."

"Thank you for saying so, Doctor. In truth, I hoped to develop my brain further and broaden the scope of my knowledge, before embarking on a degree. This was a house of great learnedness, gentlemen, if nothing else. Professor Carmody was always instructive. It was his great joy in life, sharing his erudition with others, and it would have been foolish of me not to take advantage of that. What are your plans now, might I ask? I assume, Mr Holmes, you are formulating certain lines of enquiry."

"I am."

"Can I ask in what direction they lead?"

"It is too early to say."

"Might I offer some advice? You speak of 'enemies'. But what about dangerous friends?"

"I'm not sure I follow."

"The hermit in the woods – what is his name? Denbigh. Do you know about him?"

"I do," said Holmes. "What of him?"

"It might interest you to learn that my stepfather had lately taken to visiting him."

"He had?"

"Yes. In fact, that was where he went, the day he died. He had become fascinated with him, you see. Denbigh is notorious around this area. You probably know why. You must do if you know about Denbigh at all. I would be amazed if Mr Basu has not already told you everything about him, given that it is the story that made his career. I'm sorry, Mr Basu. That came out sounding more scornful than I intended."

"No offence taken, Vernon. You are not far from the truth."

"I am aware of Jonah Denbigh's past experiences," said Holmes, "and the allegations that have dogged him since. It does make him a person of interest in the case."

"To Professor Carmody he was a person of interest too," said Vernon. "He decided to turn him into an object of study, and so he made frequent trips out into the woods to see him at his humble abode. He brought him food, gained his trust, and began interviewing him. I think he planned on writing a monograph about him. He wanted to explore, from a psychological standpoint, not only the ordeal Denbigh underwent in the Yukon, but its legacy. He was still in the preliminary stages of this endeavour. He had not made any notes yet. It excited him nonetheless. 'Denbigh endured a spell of unimaginable privation and hardship,' he said to me, just a few weeks ago. 'Twenty years on, he has still not recovered. He lives now rather as he did during his winter on that Canadian mountainside, hand to mouth, in the most meagre of dwellings, remote from his fellow men and the appurtenances of civilisation. Is he trying to escape the terrible event? Or is he forced by some unknowable compulsion to relive it, day after day,

perhaps as a form of penance? That is what I intend to discover.'
I fear, however, that my stepfather's pursuit of enlightenment
proved, in this instance, disastrous."

"Denbigh turned on him, you mean?"

"The man is like a wild animal. You'll see, when you meet
him. His living conditions are as crude as any caveman's, and he
has developed an outlook to match. I doubt I can dissuade you
from going out there to speak to him, Mr Holmes. All the same,
I would advise you to take every precaution. My stepfather may
well have fallen foul of Denbigh's feral temperament, and I would
hate for the same thing to happen to you."

Chapter Seven

AN OMINOUS ORNAMENT

"We would do well to heed Vernon's warning," said Holmes as he, Basu and I sallied forth from Grayshott Grange shortly afterwards. Basu had invited us to take luncheon with him, and we had enjoyed a cold collation in the dining room that left me feeling fortified for the afternoon ahead. Neither Mrs Carmody nor Vernon had joined us for the meal, which, under the circumstances, was perhaps understandable. Grief and sociability do not always go hand in hand.

"Watson," my friend continued, "before we left Baker Street this morning, I enjoined you to fetch your service revolver from its drawer. You did as I asked, I hope."

"Fetched it, cleaned it, loaded it," I said. "It is right here." I patted the pocket of my greatcoat, where the revolver formed a bulge. A box of Eley's No. 2 ammunition formed a complementary bulge in the pocket on the other side.

"Excellent. Between my baritsu, Mr Basu's proficiency at boxing and your background in soldiering, I am confident that we are equal to any challenge that Denbigh may present, but a Webley Pryse top-break will give us an edge if needed."

We crossed the Grange's extensive lawns and arrived at a low wall that marked the boundary of the property. A little gate afforded access to the woods beyond, and we passed through it.

We had not gone far before we lost all sight of the Grange. The trees' black trunks seemed to close in around us, and their branches overhead clustered so thickly together that, even though leafless, they dimmed the daylight to half its customary brightness.

For a time we followed a narrow, winding footpath, Basu leading the way. All was stillness and hush, save for the pitter-patter of the trees shedding the last few droplets of rainwater and the soft crackle of damp loam settling. Soon the footpath petered out, but Basu seemed to know where he was headed. Distantly a rook cawed, that forlorn sound, and not long after that another bird – it moved too fast for me to identify it – took flight noisily from its perch high in a sycamore, whisking away from us in fright. We traversed a rushing rivulet by means of a fallen beech tree whose moss-covered trunk acted as a kind of bridge, and pressed onward, deeper into the woods.

A couple of months earlier, Holmes and I had returned from Costa Rica, whither we had travelled in pursuit of a kidnapper, in connection with the second Baskerville case. We had under-taken a river journey deep into that country's interior, voyaging through lush, primordial rainforest; and here, now, I was filled with a sense of isolation and insignificance not dissimilar to that which I had experienced there. It seemed remarkable to me that we were in Surrey, one of the Home Counties, a mere forty-odd miles from the epicentre of the civilised world, London, and yet the landscape was so wild, ancient and untamed. The trees sang with the raw majesty of nature, and their song was not altogether a friendly one. We three were intruders. Fanciful though it might sound, that was how it felt. Intruders, setting foot in a domain where we did not rightfully belong and where our considerations came second to those of a numinous force that was both immeasurably older and immeasurably vaster than men. Elsewhere our kind might be top dog, but in these woods we were far from it.

Then we came upon the skulls.

Basu had just announced that we were not far from Denbigh's hut. "It can't be more than a quarter-mile more," said he, and a moment later, rounding a hawthorn thicket, we were confronted by an assemblage of small white skulls. They hung at roughly head height from the lowest limb of a towering oak, suspended on varying lengths of twine. There were about a dozen of them all told, the smallest no bigger than the tip of my thumb, the largest equivalent to my fist. In the wintry breeze that stole between the trees they twirled and spun slowly, languidly. In a way they resembled a child's toy, one of those paper mobiles that dangles from a playroom ceiling, depicting clowns or jungle animals or the like. Yet there was nothing delightful or enchanting about them. Their empty eye sockets stared at us with contempt. The skulls' very presence – the fact that someone had thought to decorate this spot with such an ominous ornament – spoke of a dark imagination at work.

Holmes moved in to inspect the things, putting his nose right up to them.

"The full panoply of British woodland mammals is represented, it seems," he opined. "This, if I am not mistaken, is the skull of a vole. This one came from a fox. This, a badger. And this one, judging by the sharp teeth fringing the upper jaw, all of similar size, is a hedgehog's. I could go on."

"This is new to me," said Basu. "The last time I visited Denbigh, I didn't come across anything of the kind."

"That was three years ago," said Holmes.

"Admittedly."

"Much can change in three years. However, this display of animal crania is a very recent addition to the woods. It can't have been in place more than a fortnight. The twine shows next to no weathering and is free of mould, and the cut ends look fresh. The skulls themselves are still clean. If they had been here for, say, even a few months, lichen would have started to grow on them."

"But whose handiwork is it?" I said. "Denbigh's?"

"We are near enough to his home for that to be likely."

"What is it for?" said Basu. "That's what I want to know."

"Not to beautify the place, certainly," Holmes replied. "No, ask yourself, 'How does seeing these skulls make me feel?'"

"Unnerved," Basu said.

"Unwelcome," I said.

"Precisely. I'm reminded of the practice common among headhunter tribes all over the world, from the South Seas to India to the Americas. They set the shrunken heads of their enemies on posts around their villages in order to ward off other enemies and outsiders in general. The intention here is much the same. The casual rambler, were he to encounter this sinister little collection, would doubtless deviate from his course and indeed give the entire area a wide berth. We, however, are not the casual rambler. We go on."

Holmes motioned to Basu, inviting him to resume guiding us. After a moment's hesitation, the journalist complied. He stepped around the dangling skulls and proceeded along much the same course we had just been taking, albeit with a much more hesitant air than before. Holmes and I followed.

A hundred yards further on, Basu halted. "I just need to take my bearings," said he. "I was once very familiar with the route, but it's been a while, as you know. It isn't as though woodland comes with a street map, and nature is in a perpetual state of flux. But I think... Yes. That stand of silver birches is familiar. A definite landmark. See that ridge? Denbigh's hut lies just beyond."

He began to climb the shallow slope to the ridge, until all at once Holmes hissed, "Basu! Stop!"

Such was the urgency in my friend's voice that Basu halted immediately, poised in the gap between two trees.

"Not one step further," Holmes said. "Do not even move a muscle. You are in the gravest danger."

Chapter Eight

HOVEL

olmes strode carefully up to Basu, who was holding himself as still as a statue. I myself could not discern any imminent threat to the journalist, but I trusted Holmes's judgement. His eyesight was sharper than mine, his instincts keener. If Holmes claimed Basu was in danger, then he was in danger.

Saying nothing further, Holmes crouched down. He focused his attention on the patch of ground directly in front of Basu. Reaching out a finger, he gently lowered it, as though depressing some invisible lever. Then, withdrawing his hand, he ran his gaze laterally along the forest floor, before diverting it upwards to the trunk of the nearest tree. He crawled towards this on hands and knees over the muddy ground, straightening up beside it. His expression was grim throughout this procedure, and became grimmer still as he studied the tree.

"What is it?" Basu asked. "What –?"

Holmes held up a forefinger to silence him, without looking round. He pursed his lips pensively, then fished in the pocket of his Inverness cape and took out his penknife. Unfolding the blade, he turned to Basu and said, "Walk backwards. Steady as you go. Three or four yards should do it."

Basu did as bidden, whereupon Holmes applied the knife to something attached to the tree trunk.

Next instant, a branch lashed out sideways, quick as a whip, coming to a halt where Basu had been standing. It quivered in the air, parallel to the ground and some four feet above. Attached to it were three short stakes positioned horizontally. Each was set a few inches apart from its neighbour and whittled to a sharp point.

"My God," Basu breathed. "What is it? Some kind of booby-trap?"

"A boobytrap is precisely what it is," said Holmes. "These stakes would have penetrated your chest to a depth of an inch or so. Not necessarily a mortal injury, but a crippling one nonetheless."

"It has the potential to be fatal," I pointed out, "were infection to set in."

"That is certainly true," said Holmes. "And if Basu were a head shorter, he might have lost an eye. This is a very nasty setup, all in all, but also neatly contrived. A length of fishing line, set at ankle height and all but invisible to the naked eye, serves as a tripwire. One end is secured with a peg made out of a twig, inserted into the earth, there. It is looped around this other peg, here, which is embedded less firmly. Thus, a tripwire. Then the other end of the fishing line is attached to the branch, here, holding it back. When the action of a passing foot pulls the looser of the two pegs out of the ground, the line goes slack and the tension on the branch is released. Thanks to its natural elasticity, the branch swings out at velocity and with some force. You were lucky I spotted it in time, Mr Basu."

Wan and shaken, Basu nodded. "I am forever in your debt, Mr Holmes."

"From here on, I shall be in the vanguard. I trust you have no objection?"

"None at all, sir."

"Tread with caution, both of you."

So we did, and so did Holmes himself. He placed his feet in a gingerly fashion, one directly in front of the other. His entire body was tensed, as if at any moment the ground might give way beneath him and he would need to leap back. Basu and I, meanwhile, imitated him step for step, going exactly where he had gone and adopting the same wary attitude even though he was, in a manner of speaking, clearing the way for us.

Presently I caught sight of a mean little dwelling, nestled in the lee of a mossy rock outcrop. Although Basu had dubbed it a hut, that was really too grand a word for it. Rather, it was a hovel made of timbers propped upright and fastened together with cords. Fronds from some evergreen tree had been placed on top to form a roof, interwoven perhaps just densely enough to keep out the rain.

In front of the ramshackle dwelling, a cooking fire smouldered within a ring of stones, sending up a thin skein of smoke. A couple of filthy black saucepans sat beside it. All around the place, animal carcasses lay in various states of decay and dismantlement.

Strips of meat hung from a line, drying in the air. Bones were heaped in small piles.

I could not get over how sordid it all looked. It seemed incredible that a born Englishman could live this way, like some sort of primitive from one of the most benighted corners of the globe. What with this, the skulls and the boobytrap, I began to think that Denbigh was not in full possession of his faculties. Might, then, his cannibal reputation have some basis in the truth after all?

No sooner had I entertained this thought than there came a bloodcurdling cry from above, like the ululation of a wild beast. Next thing I knew, a shape hurtled down from the trees – a man clad in rags, brandishing a knife. He landed beside Holmes, who reacted swiftly but not swiftly enough. Even as my friend pivoted, his hands curling into fists, the man levelled the knife at his throat.

"You so much as move," the fellow growled, "I'll slit your throat."

Chapter Nine

A RIGHTER OF WRONGS AND AN ADJUSTER OF INEQUALITIES

Holmes stood stock still, with the knife hovering at his Adam's apple. I recognised the weapon as a military-issue bayonet, the kind you might buy cheaply at any pawnbrokers. It was as chipped and rusty a specimen as I had ever seen.

"Same goes for you two," said the man wielding the bayonet, not taking his eyes off Holmes. "Either of you tries anything, your friend dies."

"Mr Jonah Denbigh, I presume," Holmes said. He was far calmer than I might have been in his position.

"That's me. What of it?"

"We have come here to talk to you. We mean you no harm." Holmes spread out his hands, as if to prove the point.

"Yes?" said Denbigh, unpersuaded. He was thin as a rake, with eyes that loomed whitely from a grubby, mud-smeared face. He wore a makeshift turban on his head, fashioned clumsily from a bolt of linen, and from beneath this his hair poked out in long, matted rat-tails. His clothing was so old, shabby and threadbare that the average Baker Street Irregular's garb looked like Savile Row finery by comparison.

"Yes," Basu piped up. "Remember me? Hitesh Basu. I wrote an article about you."

"Oh, I remember you all right, Mr Hitesh Basu," Denbigh snarled. "I remember your article, as well. Caused me no end of nuisance, that did. You've got some nerve, coming back. Last time you were here, I sent you away with a flea in your ear. I might not be so restrained this time around."

Even as he spoke, my hand was stealing towards my pocket. I fancied I might be able to draw, cock and fire my revolver quicker than Denbigh could make good on his threat and slash Holmes with the bayonet. All I needed was for him to be distracted, just momentarily.

Almost straight away, my chance came.

Basu appeared to have been having similar thoughts to mine. Out of the corner of my eye I saw him begin to creep towards Denbigh, his arms coming up into a pugilist's pose. I think he intended to break into a run and charge at the man, hoping the element of surprise would work in his favour. Holmes had just saved Basu from a stabbing; evidently Basu wished to return the favour.

Denbigh spied him. "What did I just say?" he roared, jabbing the bayonet outward in Basu's direction. "I said don't try anything funny. You keep where you are, Basu. D'you want this man's death on your conscience?"

It was the opening I had been looking for. Denbigh's focus

was entirely on Basu, and the bayonet was no longer poised adjacent to Holmes's throat, although it remained close enough to my friend that it could still be deployed against him easily. I delved into my pocket and whipped the revolver out, thumbing the hammer back at the same time. I brought the gun up and aimed. I had a clear line of fire. At this range, a shade under six yards, I could not miss.

"Watson, no!" Holmes dived in front of Denbigh, putting himself between me and my target. His hands were held high. "Put your gun away. There is no reason why we can't all sit down and have a civilised discourse. Don't you agree, Mr Denbigh?"

Denbigh's face registered bewilderment. "You – you could have been killed!" he exclaimed to Holmes. "That man was ready to shoot. I saw him. You're damned lucky he didn't."

He was not wrong. I had been a hair away from pulling the trigger. I lowered the revolver. While Holmes remained in front of Denbigh, I was not going to keep the gun trained in that direction and risk discharging the weapon by accident.

"I know my Watson," said Holmes. "His reflexes are excellent. I was never in any real peril. Was I, old friend?"

"No. Not at all," I replied, wishing I felt as confident as I sounded. The thought that I had come so close to putting a bullet in Sherlock Holmes had brought me out in a cold sweat. It does still, as I recollect the incident now.

"All the same, Mr Denbigh," Holmes went on, "the fact that I would even consider putting my life on the line for you – a stranger and, more to the point, someone who is threatening me with a bayonet – ought to tell you that my intentions are honourable. Bear in mind, too, that I allowed you to ambush me."

"You... *allowed* me?"

"As we approached this spot, I knew you must be nearby. You had not extinguished your cooking fire, so you could not have gone far. Surreptitiously I looked for you, and spied you lurking up there in the branches of the tree. You were not as well concealed as you thought. I then deliberately walked beneath you, leaving myself open to assault."

"But I could have hurt you."

"If, after pouncing, you had made a move that I deemed potentially injurious to my health, I would have retaliated," Holmes said. "In that event, you would now most likely be nursing a broken arm. As long as you confined yourself to holding me at knifepoint, however, I was prepared to keep any interaction between us purely verbal, trusting that you could be reasoned with."

"Why should I believe you?" said Denbigh. "You are here in Hitesh Basu's company." He jerked his head towards the journalist. "That man is no friend of mine, and therefore neither are you."

"You know how sorry I am for the trouble that arose from my article, Denbigh," said Basu. "I swear I didn't mean for it to fall out that way. I did my utmost to be fair and sympathetic. My only goal was to make life better for you."

"Whereas you ended up making it worse."

"Is it my fault if people happened to read not what I wrote, but what they wanted to read?"

"You should have left me alone. You should all leave me alone. Everyone should." The bayonet, which Denbigh had let sag in his grasp, came up again to menace Holmes. "Isidore Carmody is dead. I know about that. There's not much goes on in these woods that I'm not aware of. Your friend, Mr Basu. *My* friend too. I know he died and I know the manner of his death. And I can tell you for free who's going to get the blame for it. Mad old Denbigh the cannibal, that's who."

"Hence that little spectacle you arranged with the animal skulls," said Holmes.

"Found that, did you?"

"And the boobytrapped branch, with the stakes affixed. You have erected these and doubtless other deterrents around your homestead, for fear that a mob will soon be stampeding hither, baying for blood."

"You think they won't? It's only a matter of time."

"I concur. It *is* only a matter of time," Holmes said. "If, however, you are innocent of Carmody's murder, as you seem to be asserting, we may be your only chance of avoiding the worst. You need to set aside your animosity towards Basu. At the same time, you must permit me to ask you some questions, and you must be as honest in your answers as you can."

Denbigh looked at Holmes sidelong. "Who in God's name are you, anyway?"

"This, Denbigh," said Basu, "is Sherlock Holmes."

The hermit's face was a blank.

"You know," Basu said. "Sherlock Holmes of Baker Street. *The* Sherlock Holmes."

"Never heard of him."

"I accept that my fame may not have reached this far into the bosky depths of Surrey," said Holmes with an ironical sigh. "To the world at large, I am renowned as a righter of wrongs and an adjuster of inequalities. If you are a lawbreaker, I am your worst enemy, but if you have committed no crime, then you have nothing to fear from me. As things stand, it is possible that I can help prevent the onslaught of enraged civilians you anticipate, Mr Denbigh. But that is only if you are cooperative."

Emotions warred in Denbigh's face, doubt vying with hope. Eventually he said, "All right. I'll grant you a hearing. But I'm not putting my knife away. It stays by my side, whatever."

"That is acceptable," said Holmes.

"Any funny business, anything at all, you'll feel its edge. You see if you don't."

"In that same spirit," I said, "my gun stays in my hand."

Denbigh eyed me, weighing up my proposition.

"It is not open to negotiation," I stated.

After some further deliberation, he relented. "Well, it shall have to do, I suppose."

"Perhaps you might prepare us something to drink?" Holmes suggested. "Tea, maybe?"

"I can't do the kind of tea you're thinking of," said Denbigh. "I can manage nettle tea, though."

The corners of Holmes's mouth twitched. "Well, it shall have to do, I suppose."

Chapter Ten

A SPECIMEN UNDER GLASS

Nettle tea tasted more or less as I suspected it might, grassy and astringent. I sipped mine from an earthenware mug with a broken handle, making what I hoped were appreciative noises. Holmes drank his from a battered enamel cup, while Basu was obliged to use a jam jar. From the quality of each of our respective receptacles, one might infer that Denbigh was ranking us according to preference. He himself had an enamel cup near identical to Holmes's, if in somewhat better condition and more capacious.

"Often entertain guests, do you, Denbigh?" Holmes said.

"Hardly. What makes you think I would?"

"You have more drinking vessels than a solitary man requires."

"Ah, as to that, I'm a bit of a scavenger, see. I roam the woods, picking up whatever others leave behind. You never know what might come in handy. Just because someone doesn't have a use for a thing any more, doesn't mean nobody does."

"It can't be easy," I said, "living off the land."

"After close on twenty years, I reckon I have the measure of it."

That might have been the case, but Denbigh nevertheless looked in poor physical condition. Aside from his near-skeletal thinness, he lacked several teeth, and his skin bore patches of inflammation that were either ringworm or scabies. His personal hygiene left something to be desired, too. I can attest to this by simple virtue of the fact that I was sitting downwind of him and it was not the most aromatic place to be.

"Nature provides," he went on. "The fowl of the air, the fish of the stream, the four-footed creatures that burrow or forage or climb, the plants that grow in profusion – it's all there for the taking. A man does not have to be surrounded by other men to thrive. He does not need his life served up to him on a plate."

The cooking fire, which Denbigh had rekindled into full flame in order to boil water for our tea, gave a loud crackle. As if this were a spoken invitation, Denbigh laid a handful of dry twigs on it, and the fire consumed these greedily.

"You want to know if I killed Carmody," he said, staring into the blaze. "That's what you've come all this way after."

"Can you assure us that you did not?" said Holmes.

"Categorically. I told you, he was my friend."

"Friends have been known to turn on friends. Positive strong feelings towards another person can sour and become strong feelings that are negative to an equal degree. The two are opposite poles of the same magnet."

"Carmody peeved me, did he?" said Denbigh. "Betrayed my trust, maybe, or made some caustic remark, and I lost control, set upon him and tore him apart?" He sneered. "Whatever you may think of me, that is not the sort of man I am."

"You can understand how people might make that assumption, though."

"I can, given my lifestyle. And my history."

"According to the doctor who conducted the autopsy, there were bite marks on the body. Human bite marks."

At this, Denbigh reeled. Beneath the patina of dirt on his face, he visibly paled. He put a hand to his brow, rubbing distractedly.

"You did not know?" said Holmes.

"How could I? Never saw the body myself. I heard all the fuss when it was found. People shouting and crashing through the undergrowth all day between here and Grayshott Grange. I went to take a look, to see what was up, but by the time I got there, the body had been removed. All I saw was the aftermath, the earth churned up where he'd fallen, the blood spatters. I didn't even know it was the professor who'd been killed until I eavesdropped on a couple of policemen who were poking around the spot and heard them mention his name. That fair discombobulated me, that did. Carmody had come out this way just the previous afternoon. We'd had a nice long chat, him and me, and then as the sun started to set, off he'd gone, into the gloaming, with a fond farewell. I can't think for the life of me who'd want him harmed, nor why so violently. It beggars belief."

"He had taken a professional interest in you, hadn't he?"

"He had a curious mind, and to him I was a curiosity. He called me a 'case study'. I didn't take to that at first. It made me feel like a specimen under glass. But that was just how Carmody was. Everything was science to him, even people. I grew to understand that he wasn't being nosy. Rather, he genuinely wanted to learn from me."

"Learn what?"

"What do you think? About my past. About my time in the Yukon. About whether I had done what I'm alleged to have done. I asked him once why it was so fascinating to him. He said, 'I am making an inquiry into evil.'"

"An inquiry into evil?"

"His very words. He told me he was becoming more and more intrigued by the subject. 'Evil is all around us,' he said. 'Evil can wear many guises. Sometimes it can reside in your own home, hiding behind the sweetest of faces. You can invite it in without realising.'"

I cast a glance at Holmes, who briefly met my eye before looking back at Denbigh. I was thinking of Faye Carmody. Could she have told her new husband that she had been instrumental in her previous husband's death? Or had Carmody perhaps worked it out for himself? Had he become concerned that the woman he'd recently married, in good faith, was tainted? Was he afraid he himself might go the way of Eustace Agius, a victim of her homicidal tendencies?

"He got the full story out of me eventually," Denbigh said. "He got the lot. More than even you did, Basu. You I gave the sanitised version, just half of the truth, the palatable stuff. Carmody winkled out everything. Evil did take place on that mountain. Not the evil you're thinking of, but evil nonetheless. It felt good, admitting it all to him, and when I was done telling him, he didn't just abandon me, the way some did." The hermit directed a glare at Basu. "Over the next couple of months he continued visiting, bringing little gifts with him, things to help make my life that bit easier – cigarettes, a tot of rum, some boiled sweets as a treat – and we'd just talk, him and me, about this or that, anything, everything. He liked to hear my observations about the natural world, the changing of the seasons, things of that sort. He'd even make notes."

"Did evil ever get mentioned again?" said Holmes.

"Now and then, in passing. He seemed troubled, did the professor. The more so as time went by."

"Perhaps you would share with us what you shared with him."

"You want the full story too? What for?"

"It may be pertinent," said Holmes simply. "Surely, having unburdened yourself once, you can do so again."

Denbigh ruminated, gazing darkly into the fire. At last, coming to a decision, he said, "Very well. If it will help catch whoever killed him…"

Chapter Eleven

A SHINING, LUSTROUS DREAM

Jonah Denbigh crossed the Atlantic in the spring of 1873 with two companions, friends from his hometown of Farnham in Surrey. He was a young man then, eager to make his way in the world. North America beckoned, a place where fortunes were being made, almost overnight, by those prospecting for gold.

Gold rushes had occurred at intervals in the United States since the turn of the century, with fresh motherlodes of ore being discovered all the time. Drawn by the allure of instant riches, Denbigh and his friends scraped together everything they could to pay for the sea voyage, with enough left over to buy necessities once on American shores. Arriving at Boston, they disembarked and journeyed inland by train. Along the way they kept an ear out for rumours. They did not want to try any of the old, played-out goldfields. They were keen to find somewhere new and unexploited.

Denbigh's friends were Jack Travers, known as "Black Jack" on account of his swarthy complexion, and Ned Craddock.

Travers and Craddock were half-brothers, and were fond of each other but squabbled often, just as though they had been real brothers. Travers had a particularly foul temper, which was a further justification of his nickname, for when he was roused to anger his mood could be of the very blackest. At other times he was kindness personified, polite in his dealings, generous to a fault. It was as though two contrary individuals lived within the same body, competing for dominance.

Westward they went, these three, with their money rapidly diminishing. Nowhere did there seem to be the news they were hoping for. The California gold seams had been mined to exhaustion. The same was true of Fraser Canyon in British Columbia, sites in the Rocky Mountains and the Territory of New Mexico, and along the Colorado River. All they heard, in response to their enquiries, were tales of a few who had struck lucky and were now set for life, and countless others who had toiled hard and come away empty-handed. Yet men were still out there, tirelessly panning riverbeds, digging into the earth, dynamiting hillsides, driven on by a shining, lustrous dream. Denbigh, Travers and Craddock shared that dream, and refused to be daunted.

Then their luck turned, or so it seemed. At a bar in an Idaho settlement known as Eagle Rock, a hollow-eyed, beaten-looking old timer told them that the Klondike region of the Yukon, up in north-west Canada, was the next likely spot for a gold rush. For years the indigenous tribes around there had spoken of extensive gold deposits, but since those people preferred copper, the other precious metal had no value to them and so they had not troubled to excavate it. Furthermore, the European pioneers who were now making inroads into the area were more interested in fur trading, since the profits from that were easier and more immediate than from gold mining. The old timer insisted that if the three Englishmen wanted to steal a march on their rivals, the Yukon was where they should go.

By then, late in 1873, the threesome were growing desperate, not to mention perilously low on funds. They decided on one last roll of the dice. They would follow the old timer's tip.

Winter was setting in as they made their way towards Canada, joining a trickle of other prospectors bound for the Yukon. The true Klondike gold rush would not occur until much later – indeed, it only really began two years after the events of this very narrative, when word got out about a huge find made by a certain George Carmack and his party on the aptly named Bonanza Creek – but prior to that a handful of men had begun opening up routes along the White Pass and the Chilkoot Pass. Back then, the Canadian authorities were not nearly as stringent as they would later become about the rules prospectors must follow. Such items as sufficiently warm outerwear, proper camping equipment and an adequate supply of food were yet to be made mandatory. In the early, unregulated years, all that was required was the desire to go and a willingness to brave the elements.

Our trio had both. They also had simply no clue what faced them. With the very last of their cash reserves they purchased a pack mule, a flimsy tent, supplies of hardtack and jerky, a camping stove, mattocks, sieving pans and a map of the territory. Then, with the first snows beginning to fall, they set off from

Skagway in the southernmost tip of Alaska, crossing the border into Canada and following the White Pass trail through the mountains. The fact that nobody else was making the journey at that time of year should have been a warning sign, but even if someone had expressly advised them against going, it is doubtful they would have listened. Their plan was to reach Bennett Lake, where they would build themselves a raft and paddle thence along the Yukon River towards the lands where the gold was said to be the most plentiful. The winter had other ideas.

A British winter is bad enough, but it is nothing compared with the winters of the frozen north. Denbigh, Travers and Craddock had not gone more than twenty miles before the snow, initially gentle and tolerable, became unending and relentless. It fell and fell and fell, but still they forged onward along the pass. The going became treacherous and slow. Snow piled up until it was knee-high, then thigh-high. By the seventh or eighth day, Denbigh proposed that they turn back. Travers bristled at this, calling him a coward and a weakling, while Craddock was broadly in agreement with Denbigh's idea but deferred to his half-brother. Travers was not only the older of the two by eight years but also the larger and more imposing by far, and Craddock tended to do whatever Black Jack said.

The mule became stubborn. It bucked and baulked beneath the layer of snow that covered its pelt like a white carapace. Only by the repeated application of a switch to its hindquarters could they get it to move. Meanwhile, greater and greater desolation surrounded them. In the rare intervals of clear weather between snowfalls, the emptiness of the mountains yawned around the three Englishmen. The vista was both majestic and terrifying: saw-toothed, snow-capped peaks stretching endlessly to the horizon like gigantic white waves in a stormy sea.

After a fortnight more of slogging along that narrow trail through the ever-deepening snow, even Travers had to admit that they should give it up and head back. If they managed five miles in a day, it was a triumph. Huddled in their tent at night beneath thin blankets, they were so cold they could barely sleep. They were losing weight at an alarming rate and their strength was ebbing. The shining, lustrous dream was becoming a tarnished nightmare and might well kill them if they did not abandon it soon.

On the afternoon of the day they turned around, they heard an ominous rumbling from somewhere ahead, down the trail. It lasted several minutes, and none of them realised what it portended. The next morning, they discovered its cause. An avalanche had closed off the steep-sided pass. There was no way around the blockage. The route back to Skagway was impassable.

An unenviable choice faced them. They could continue along the pass as before, or they could stay put for the rest of the winter and carry on when spring came and the snow melted. Travers was in favour of the former alternative. For once, Craddock went against his half-brother's wishes and voted for the latter. So did Denbigh. They were all of them exhausted, Denbigh pointed out. To continue going would gradually sap whatever strength remained to them, and there was no guarantee they would make it to the other side of the White Pass before they collapsed from fatigue, unable to carry on. It seemed prudent to conserve their energies and wait out the winter. It would be two months at most, surely, before conditions improved and the way became clear once more. They could hold out for two months, couldn't they?

Travers grudgingly saw the wisdom of this, and so began their time of grim, gruelling tribulation. Day after day was spent cloistered in the tent, with the three parcelling out their meagre food rations between them. Sometimes there were blizzards, other times merely heavy snow. They had to keep digging a path out from the tent flap, lest they be buried completely. There were frequent arguments, most of them initiated by Travers. As their tempers frayed, so did their sanity. It was hard to keep track of time. The days shortened, the nights grew ever longer, until the darkness seemed almost perpetual.

Then the mule died. This was not unexpected. The beast had begun wheezing and braying discontentedly and growing ever more listless. One morning, they found it standing at its tether, head bowed, unmoving, frozen through. For the animal it was, in a way, a mercy. For the men too, for they now had a source of fresh meat. Travers had been hinting for some while that they should kill and eat the mule, while Denbigh and Craddock had argued that they would need it for the journey back to Skagway. Now the point was moot. Fate had taken the matter out of their hands.

They carved the mule up and ate the flesh raw, chewing on the frozen meat until it was pliable. They cooked the internal organs on the camping stove, using the little fuel they had left, and ate those too. Travers took the hide and made a jerkin of it. Craddock sewed the scraps left over into crude mittens. The carcass, little more than a heap of bloodied bones and hooves, lay a few yards from the tent, preserved from decomposition by the freezing cold.

The mule meat kept them going for several days, and even raised their spirits somewhat. But they were still hopelessly ill-equipped and understocked, and soon they were again meting out the hardtack and jerky, in ever smaller portions, and their hunger was mounting. A vicious row broke out between Travers and Craddock, the one accusing the other of taking more than his fair share of the victuals. If Denbigh had not played peacemaker, it would have come to blows, and perhaps worse. Nevertheless, the half-brothers spent the next week glowering at each other and muttering oaths. The atmosphere in the tent was poisonous.

Not long after that, while mutual resentment still simmered between Travers and Craddock, the bear came.

Chapter Twelve

THE CALCULATION

Lured out of hibernation by the smell of the carcass, the bear – a great black grizzly – descended on the campsite one morning and proceeded to dine on the mule's remains. Denbigh, Travers and Craddock spied it coming and hid in their tent, transfixed by terror. They heard the creature crunch bones between its powerful jaws. They heard it grumble contentedly to itself. They prayed that, when sated, it would shamble off back whence it came, never to return.

The bear, however, was inquisitive. After its feast it began sniffing around the tent. It knew there were people within. Its short, snuffling breaths sounded, to the three men, as loud as gunshots. They flinched as the bear began to test the tent's canvas with one paw. Yet another casualty of their ill-preparedness was their failure to bring a rifle or similar weapon. They had simply had no notion how wild the wilderness could get.

Now the grizzly raked its claws down the canvas in an exploratory, almost playful fashion. By this means it created a set of narrow parallel rents in the material, through which it peeped a gimlet eye, surveying the tent's quailing occupants. Each man believed his hour had come and a terrible death loomed.

The bear studied them for several minutes, grunting softly, until at last, seeming to tire of the sport, it departed. Or so the three men thought, although none was any too enthusiastic about going out and checking.

"You do it, Ned," Travers insisted to Craddock.

"If you're so blasted keen, why don't you?" came the retort.

The argument escalated fast, and another fight seemed on the cards, for all Denbigh's efforts to calm tempers. Ultimately, Travers simply grabbed Craddock by the scruff of the neck and thrust him, flailing and protesting, out through the tent flap.

Denbigh waited with bated breath. Then, in a reedy, quavering voice, Craddock announced that it was all clear. No bear. The other two emerged from the tent. The grizzly had left behind precious little of the mule's carcass, just a few half-chewed splinters of bone. Its musky scent still hung in the air, but of the bear itself there was no sign.

"I can't do this," Craddock said. "I can't stay here any longer. What if it comes back? It might."

"Stop your snivelling," his half-brother snapped. "I know enough about bears to know that it should be sleeping throughout winter. It'll have returned to its cave and its nap, and we shan't hear from it again."

No sooner had he said these words than there was a deep, hackle-raising roar from close by. The grizzly sprang into view from the ridge overlooking the pass. Either it had been lying in wait there, the cunning thing, or it had climbed over the ridge when the men's voices attracted its attention and brought it back. It came lumbering down the slope, slithering in the snow in its eagerness to reach them. It was making a beeline for the nearest of them, Travers, doubtless drawn to him because of his mule-hide jerkin, which smelled the same as the carcass the bear had earlier so enjoyed.

Denbigh saw the moment of decision in Black Jack Travers's dark eyes. He saw his friend make the calculation: his own life or another's. He chose another's. He chose that of the person who, between Denbigh and Craddock, happened to be closer to him just then: his own half-brother.

Travers seized hold of Craddock, picked him up bodily and hurled him with all his might towards the bear. Craddock landed sprawling in the snow just a few feet in front of the oncoming beast. He had time to clamber to all fours and begin to scramble away. He did not get far. The snow was too deep, his terror too debilitating. The grizzly was upon him and made short work of him. It clamped its maw around his neck and lifted him high in the air, Craddock screaming and gibbering. It shook him from side to side, and Denbigh heard the sharp *crack* as skull parted company with upper vertebrae. Craddock's wails of distress were instantly silenced.

The bear dropped the body to the ground and set to work, gnawing and rending. Denbigh could not stand to watch. He dived back into the tent. He knew it was not a place of refuge. The bear could tear the canvas to shreds with ease. He was no safer within than without. The tent offered the illusion of protection nonetheless, and that was better than nothing.

Travers felt the same way and joined Denbigh inside. They clung to each other. Although Denbigh feared and abhorred Black Jack Travers at that moment, he also needed the comfort of human contact. Meanwhile, outside, the grizzly slobbered as it made the most of its kill.

After it was done eating, the bear did not harass them. For hour upon hour Denbigh and Travers did not move. It seemed that at any second the bear might burst into the tent and extract the tasty morsels within. Night fell, day broke, and only then did they begin to believe the grizzly had gone, and gone for good. It wasn't until late in the afternoon, however, that Denbigh dared poke his head out through the flap. He had a knife in his hand, a small serrated implement designed for nothing more than culinary purposes. Against the bear it would have been utterly useless. He might as well have wielded a sewing needle. He drew some tiny measure of reassurance from it all the same.

He could not see the bear. All he could see was the mangled skeleton of a man, encircled by a butcher's shop of offal, which was in turn encircled by an expanse of ruddied snow. He had had no idea how much blood the human body contained. So much of it.

He drew his head back in, swallowing down his gorge.

"It has left us alone," he said to Travers.

"You sure about that?"

"As sure as I can be."

"Well, thank God. Now listen, Jonah. About what happened

out there, with the bear and Ned... We must get our story straight. Anyone who wants to know what became of him, we say that Ned went outside alone to answer the call of nature. We had no idea about the bear. It took him unawares. We heard his cries but there was nothing we could do. Got that?"

"But he was your brother, Jack."

"Half-brother," Travers corrected him. "I was seven when my mother remarried, eight when Ned was born. You could not say we grew up together. We just happened to live in the same house."

"I, for one, never thought of you as anything but full brothers," said Denbigh. "When I first met you, you seemed quite alike."

"We had our differences."

"But to kill him, Jack..."

"I did not, Jonah, remember? The bear did. That's the truth of the matter, and you'd do well to remember it."

Travers's gaze was fierce and unwavering. Denbigh cast his mind back to the moment the other man had hurled Craddock towards the grizzly. He knew he was in the presence of someone who was not bound by any sense of commonality with his fellow humans, not even the ties of blood. Travers had sacrificed his half-brother's life without qualm, simply because Craddock had handily been within reach at the time. He might, just as ruthlessly and unhesitatingly, sacrifice his friend's. Denbigh would have to tread very carefully from here on.

"It was a dreadful shame," Denbigh said, choosing his words, "that the bear caught Ned. Would that we could have gone to his assistance, but by the time we stirred ourselves to leave the tent, it was already too late."

"That's it," said Travers, beaming sunnily. "You're getting it. Keep to that version of events, and all will be well. And look on the bright side. One less mouth to feed means our rations will go further. We'll get off this damned mountain yet, Jonah. Just you wait and see."

Denbigh nodded, while wondering how long he could abide in the company of someone who, he now knew, was wicked beyond redemption. The geniality that Travers sometimes exhibited, as then, was a mere front. The man was rotten to the core.

Chapter Thirteen

EVIL INCARNATE

Day after day after day passed. Denbigh and Travers sat in the tent, leaving it only occasionally. Sometimes they could go whole hours without exchanging a single word. Travers brooded darkly. Denbigh had no way of fathoming his thoughts, nor any great desire to. Again and again he recalled how the other man had tossed Craddock to the bear with scarcely a second thought. And that was his own relative. Would he feel any compunction about doing the same to Denbigh if the situation arose?

Around Farnham, Travers had been notorious for getting into fights and doling out vicious beatings. It did not take much to provoke him to violence, especially when he had had a skinful. Denbigh had quite liked having a friend who was so disreputable. It had conferred on him a certain cachet. Local toughs never bothered him, knowing that he was associated with Black Jack Travers.

Now, Denbigh was beginning to regret ever meeting the man. Travers, and to a lesser extent Craddock, had been ne'er-do-wells, taking whatever casual, low-paid jobs came their way, whereas Denbigh had been employed as a groom for a successful racehorse owner. "I have a stable income," as he liked to joke. It was Travers who had proposed the three of them should seek their fortune in America, and he had worked on Denbigh tirelessly, overcoming his resistance, wearing him down, until finally he agreed. Denbigh had put up most of the money they needed, his contribution comprising all of his savings and a modest legacy from an uncle, with Travers and Craddock between them supplying only a quarter of the total. For all that, there had never been the suggestion that the profits from their gold-prospecting endeavours would be split anything other than equally, three ways, and with hindsight Denbigh could see that Travers had used him. He and his money had been merely a means to an end. Travers took what he could from others and never gave a damn.

Trapped in that tent with the man, forced to breathe the same air as him day after day, night after night, Denbigh felt increasingly sickened and repulsed. He despised himself as much as he despised the other. Why had he been so biddable, so easily led? If not for Black Jack Travers, he would still be in England – wonderful, temperate, *safe* England – with a life that, if unexciting, had prospects. His abiding emotion, in the depths of that Yukon winter, was loathing. Sometimes there was despair, sometimes anger, but mostly there was loathing.

It didn't help that their food supplies were nearing depletion, nor that he was beginning to suspect that Travers was stealing extra rations for himself while he, Denbigh, slept. For although they were both growing dangerously thin, Denbigh was doing it at a faster rate, and he could only assume that Travers was maintaining his bulk by underhand methods.

And always Travers was there in the tent, in that stinking mule jerkin of his, uncommunicative, deep in his own thoughts. Always, inescapably, Denbigh had to endure his presence, which was as festering and malignant as any cancer. At times it seemed that he had been consigned to some kind of purgatorial limbo, perhaps Hell itself, albeit the coldest, least infernal Hell imaginable. There was only this ice-rimed tent, there had only ever been this ice-rimed tent, and Black Jack Travers inhabited it. He was a demon, or possibly even Satan, put there to torment him – the embodiment of every sin, evil incarnate.

In his more lucid moments Denbigh considered certain practicalities, but even these musings led him down dark alley-ways. What would they do if their food ran out and the snow had not started to thaw? What might they find to eat, out here in this empty, treeless nowhere? A quarter of a century earlier, a group of pioneers following the Oregon Trail west had become snowbound in the mountains of the Sierra Nevada, much as he and Travers were snowbound, and had resorted to eating their dead to survive. The story of the so-called Donner Party, which had been reported internationally, was an object lesson in hubris and lack of foresight. They had ignored advice and spurned aid, and paid the price for it in the end by being forced to break the ultimate taboo.

Might it come to that for him and Travers, here in the Yukon?

Might one of them wind up using the other's corpse as a source of nutrition? Denbigh, in spite of his aching, growling stomach and the dreams of pies, puddings and stews that plagued him in his sleep, could not see himself eating Travers. He could, on the other hand, see Travers eating him. Travers had no conscience, no motivation save self-interest. Travers would do what was best for Travers, and if that meant cannibalism, so be it. Denbigh did not think the other man would wait for him to die first, either. Once the compulsion to eat him became strong enough, he would simply kill him.

Denbigh kept the kitchen knife close at hand, just in case. It was not the only knife in the tent, however.

The nights were discernibly shortening, the days lengthening, but still the snow would not let up. Every time the skies cleared and there was a lull, every time it seemed that the winter was at last drawing to a close, in would come the next phalanx of heavy cloud and the next few inches of snow. Spring remained an impossibly distant prospect, an eternity away.

It was during one of these tantalising interludes between snowfalls that Denbigh came to a fateful decision. Night had fallen and he had stepped out of the tent to get some air, and also to take a break from the constant proximity to Travers. The firmament was filled with thousands and thousands of stars. The moon was a disc of purest white light whose brightness cast everything into sharp relief. There was not a breath of wind, no sound, only an awesome, primordial silence. Denbigh felt as though he could have been the sole living thing in all of Creation. It was just him and God. A God who would surely not condemn him for what he was contemplating doing. A God who might even consider it a righteous act.

He returned to the tent, slipping back inside slowly, stealthily. Black Jack Travers was fast asleep, snoring a little. Denbigh drew the knife.

Chapter Fourteen

SOLITARY CONFINEMENT?

"I told you, Basu," Denbigh said, "that both Craddock and Travers perished as a result of a bear attack."

"You told everyone that," Basu replied. "You have also always maintained that it was the bear, not you, who ate them."

"The latter statement is partly true. The bear ate Craddock. It did not eat Travers. But then, neither did I. However…"

"However," said Holmes, "it was no bear that killed Black Jack Travers."

Denbigh bowed his head. Throughout his recitation he had scarcely once lifted his gaze from the cooking fire. Every now and then he would add a further twig or two to it.

"How could I suffer him to live?" he said at length. "How, given what he was, what he had done?"

"And what you feared he might do to you."

"That as well. Have you ever encountered someone irretrievably, unrepentantly bad, Mr Holmes? Someone without whom the world would be better off?"

Denbigh framed the question as though expecting the answer no. All Holmes said in response was a simple "Yes".

"Really?"

"More than once," said Holmes. "Watson will back me up on this. There is one example I can think of in particular, a man so corrupt and depraved that I took it upon myself to remove him from existence, lest his profane influence spread any further. The feat almost cost me my life, and even after his death, such was the stain he left behind that it was three years before it was erased fully. You called Black Jack Travers a cancer. Well, cancers need to be cut out."

"So you understand why I did what I did."

"Up to a point. I believe *you* believe Travers posed a threat to you. You may well be right. We shall never know. Perhaps, by killing him, you pre-empted his killing you. Perhaps not. Undoubtedly it helped you to survive, in as much as it meant there was enough of your food rations left to sustain one man for the remainder of your time in the mountains. You also, I might add, took the precaution of mutilating Travers's body so that it would look as though he too, like Craddock, was the victim of a grizzly."

"I did. I thought it a prudent action, should the body be found, as was possible."

"As, indeed, happened. And you clearly did a proficient job, since those who discovered it and the other body could not distinguish between the genuine article and the mimicry."

"I had the example of Craddock's cadaver to emulate. You could say I drew on life."

"Life, or life's opposite," Basu interjected.

"I defy anyone in the situation I was in to have done other than I did," Denbigh declared. "Unless you were there, facing Black Jack Travers every hour of the day and night, knowing his nature, knowing that he was surely plotting to kill you, you are in no position to judge. If it was anything, it was self-defence." His voice softened a little. "Anyway, now you gentlemen know the whole story. Of course, if it comes to it, I shall deny everything I have just said. I shall stick rigorously to my original claims."

"I think," said Holmes, "that sufficient time has passed that there is no reason to involve the police in the matter. You have effectively sentenced yourself to twenty years of prison, Denbigh. One might even go so far as to call it solitary confinement, even if your gaol cell happens to be the great outdoors. That is surely punishment enough. I thank you for being so honest with us."

"And do you believe me now when I say I did not kill Professor Carmody?"

"What I believe is irrelevant. All that matters is what I can prove." Holmes got to his feet. "Our next port of call should furnish me with that proof. Watson, Basu, will you join me?"

I clambered upright. My joints had seized up from sitting for so long on the cold, damp ground, and I eased out my limbs, grumbling inwardly. At the same time, I was conscious that I had little to complain about. Next to Denbigh's gruelling winter in the frozen wastes of Canada, a little stiffness was the mildest of inconveniences.

"Basu," said Holmes, "do you know where we might find Carmody's GP, Dr Burnell?"

"His practice is in Betchfield, I understand."

"The town we passed through on the way to Grayshott Grange. Do you think you can get us there?"

"I think so." Basu sounded hesitant. He looked around, then pointed. "I'm fairly certain that if we go in *this* direction…"

"*That* direction," said Denbigh irritably, pointing the opposite way. "North. Keep going for about two miles. You'll come to a meadow. Cross that to its north-west corner, where you'll find a beech spinney. Beyond lies a road. Follow the road due west for half a mile, and there's Betchfield."

"Excellent," said Holmes, and began walking.

"Listen, Denbigh," Basu said. "I just want to say again, I'm—"

"Save it," Denbigh cut in, with a dismissive wave of the hand. "I don't want to hear it. You want me to say I forgive you? I forgive you. There. It's been said. Take it with you. Doesn't mean I mean it."

In the face of this rather graceless offering, Basu simply nodded. There was a wounded look in his eyes. He had held out an olive branch more than once now, only to have it slapped aside. I doubted he would ever receive the absolution he craved from Denbigh.

He traipsed off in Holmes's footsteps. I turned and did the same.

"Keep an eye out," Denbigh called after us. "You'll come across a couple more of my little defensive measures that-a-way."

"Noted," said Holmes over his shoulder. "I'm sure I shall spot them in time."

"I hope that you do, for your sake."

After about thirty paces, I allowed myself a backward glance. Denbigh had not moved. He was still squatting in front of the fire, staring hard into it. The cups that he, Holmes and I had drunk out of sat before him. The jam jar Basu had used lay elsewhere.

I looked at those three empty cups, and I thought of Denbigh, Black Jack Travers and Ned Craddock winding their way laboriously up the White Pass, the lure of wealth dancing enticingly before them, not one of them realising the horrors that awaited.

Solitary confinement? No. Denbigh shared his squalid, hermit-like existence with others. The ghosts of his two dead friends were forever with him.

Chapter Fifteen

HINDSIGHT WEARS SPECTACLES

We arrived at Betchfield without mishap. Denbigh's directions were accurate, and Holmes possessed an inner compass of surpassing accuracy. Similarly, Holmes was able to navigate around the traps Denbigh had warned about. One of these was a set of stakes embedded at an angle in the ground and hidden beneath leaves, so that they might penetrate the sole of an unwary foot. The other was a length of fishing line tied at throat height between two trees and stretched so taut that anyone blundering into it would suffer serious laceration of the neck and possibly, if going at speed, a severed artery or windpipe.

As we approached the town, I mused aloud that I was not wholly convinced by Denbigh's protestations of innocence. "Seeing that he once killed a man in cold blood," I said, "I am more inclined, not less, to think that he might do it again. By the same reckoning, anyone who sets potentially lethal traps must have his grasp of morality called into question at the very least, if not his sanity."

"But what reason did he have for killing Carmody?" said Holmes.

"He had entrusted the professor with his great guilty secret. He might then have had misgivings and decided to do away with him so that Carmody could not share it with anyone else."

"He has just entrusted us with the same secret, and not unwillingly, either. But still," my friend allowed, "you make a valid point, and it leads me to speculate whether what we just drank was actually nettle tea after all."

"I beg your pardon?" said Basu.

"Maybe Denbigh knows his secret will be safe with us because he has made us consume something altogether less innocuous. A solution of monkshood, perhaps, or else belladonna, better known as deadly nightshade."

"Deadly...?"

"It could have been the death cap mushroom, I suppose. That's the one I would have chosen, although there are any number of plants, abundant in woods like these, that are fatal to humans if ingested. Whatever it was, we shall soon be feeling the effects."

The journalist gaped at Holmes, his mouth downturned in alarm. "You're not serious! Are you?"

"I must say I am beginning to feel a touch queer," said Holmes, putting the knuckles of one hand to his forehead.

"He's joking, isn't he, Watson?" said Basu. "I'm feeling fine myself. He must be joking."

"I rather suspect he is," I replied. "Holmes often rebukes me for my sense of humour, which can err on the mordant side. He appears to be exhibiting a similar kind of humour himself."

"Of course Denbigh has not poisoned us," Holmes said to Basu with some asperity. "You saw as clearly as I did how he steeped the nettles in the boiling water. More to the point, he drank the concoction himself."

"Ah. Yes. True."

"As to Watson's proposal that friend Denbigh slew Professor Carmody so as to ensure his silence, let us pin our hopes on Dr Burnell being able to settle the question, once and for all."

Betchfield was only a small town – a large village, really – and locating Dr Burnell's practice was easy, for his sign, an engraved brass plaque, hung prominently in front of one of a handful of houses that abutted on the central green. Like many a provincial GP, he worked out of a downstairs room in his own home. The front parlour served as a surgery, while an adjoining room, which could be reached from the outside via a side door, was both waiting room and reception.

There in that antechamber, a comely but rather vacant-looking girl sat at a clerk's desk. If this was Burnell's receptionist, she plainly did not have much to do, for she was alone and, as the three of us entered, was perusing the latest edition of the women's fashion magazine *The Queen*. She closed the magazine and looked up indolently.

"Do you gents have an appointment?" she enquired. Her dress was of a gaudy hue and elaborate design, bordering on flamboyant, while her face was somewhat over-rouged.

"We do not," said Holmes.

"Can't see the doctor without an appointment."

"Does he have a patient with him now?"

"No."

"And is he likely to be busy in the immediate future? I ask, confident that this cannot be the case, for there are a half-dozen chairs for patients in this room and none is occupied."

The receptionist consulted a diary. "He has a three o'clock."

"It is only just gone two. He will see us."

"All three of you at once?" the girl said with a frown.

"All three at once."

"Are you registered with him? Can't see the doctor if you're not registered."

Holmes gave clear signs of a man straining at the reins of his patience. "We have come in connection with the death of Professor Isidore Carmody, at whose autopsy Dr Burnell officiated. We would like to discuss certain irregularities in his report."

This was a lie, obviously, but not as great a lie as the one Holmes tendered next.

"Are you police?" the receptionist asked.

"We are. We have just this morning travelled down from Scotland Yard."

The receptionist appeared both impressed and intimidated, which was the desired effect. "And you're saying there were… irregularities? What sort of irregularities?"

"With all due respect, my girl, that is not a matter for your ears." I noticed that Holmes was adopting certain police inspector mannerisms for his little charade, not least his choice of language. In particular he was aping the officious bearing of one G. Lestrade, right down to that fellow's narrow-eyed, ferrety way of looking at people and his rather nasal intonation, not to mention his habit of clasping his hands together behind his back and rocking to and fro while conducting an interview.

"You mean about the bite marks on the body being human ones?"

"I am not at liberty to divulge any further information. Now, are we going to shilly-shally here all day, or are you going to inform Dr Burnell of our presence?"

Without further ado, the receptionist stood, knocked on the door connecting the waiting room to the surgery, and went in. We heard a muffled conversation from the other side of the door, and presently she returned and motioned us to enter.

Dr Burnell was in his late sixties if he was a day, with a horseshoe of grizzled, curly hair that sat perched around his bald pate like a Roman emperor's laurel wreath. His shoulders were perpetually hunched, and he wore thick-lensed spectacles through which he peered blinkingly. I knew his type well, the country doctor who had been snugly ensconced in his practice for decades, with no other ambition in life, no need or wish to go further afield. Tirelessly he had tended to successive generations of local families, addressing the ailments of children he had helped birth, and their children, and *their* children. He was in every sense reliable, yet in his dotage he was beginning to lose a step, or so I adjudged, for I observed a tiny tremor in his left hand, the onset of some sort of palsy, and through the spectacles his eyes looked weak and watery, more so than mere myopia could account for. I suspected he had no more than a year or two left in him before infirmity obliged him to retire.

"Scotland Yard, is it?" said he querulously as the receptionist withdrew, closing the door behind her. To the rear of his desk were several filing cabinets which, if they were anything like mine, were crammed with patient files and case histories. "No, wait, it can't be." Dr Burnell was squinting at Basu. "I know you, sir, don't I? We met at Professor Carmody's funeral. You're no policeman. You're a journalist."

"I regret the imposture," said Holmes. "It was necessary in order to circumvent a certain level of, shall we say, bureaucracy."

"You mean Flossie."

"If such is your receptionist's name, then yes, that is what I mean."

"She is a stickler for the rules, that girl. It gives her a modicum of power over others which, elsewise, she does not have. Who are you, then?"

Holmes introduced himself and me. "Mr Basu, of course, you are already acquainted with."

"Holmes the private detective? Ah. I see. Mr Basu has brought you here regarding the detail about the body which I unfortunately let slip to him at the funeral."

"The human bite marks."

"I knew I shouldn't have said anything," Dr Burnell said. "Discretion is paramount in this profession. Don't you agree, Dr Watson?"

"Indubitably," I said. "It is enshrined in the Hippocratic Oath. 'And whatsoever I shall see or hear in the course of my profession, as well as outside my profession in my intercourse with men, if it be what should not be published abroad, I will never divulge…'"

"'…holding such things to be holy secrets,'" my fellow medic finished. "My tongue does run away with itself sometimes, especially in off-guard moments. It does not matter so much with reference to the dead, rather than the living, but even so." He sighed. "Ah me!"

"Basu tells us you were quite insistent that the bite marks were not those of an animal," said Holmes.

Dr Burnell pondered for a moment, then said, "Well, the cat *is* out of the bag, after all. Yes, they were human. I am almost sure of it."

"But not sure enough to put it in your report."

"Can you imagine the upset it might have caused? Bad enough that the man died in so foul a manner. If I had been completely certain it was a person who had killed him and not an animal, I would have said so. But I could not be, not beyond a shadow of a doubt. If my vision were a little sharper, perhaps that might have helped. I erred on the side of caution, anyway. I realise, too, whom all eyes would have turned to, had I aired my suspicions publicly. That fellow in the woods, the supposed cannibal."

"Jonah Denbigh," said Basu.

"That's him. People around here despise him and are terrified of him in equal measure. Twice, in my memory, he has been hounded and harassed. Inhabitants of this very town were responsible both times. They are normally law-abiding folk, but once they get their blood up… Well, you know how mobs are. There is no wisdom in crowds. They seek an outlet for their fears and insecurities. They look for scapegoats and focus their hostility there. When a man is already an outcast, it doesn't take much for him to be turned into a pariah. I was loath for that to happen again to Denbigh. I regret my decision now," he finished, with a self-deprecatory shake of the head. "It was poor judgement on my part. I ought to have had the courage of my convictions."

"At the very least, you could have tipped off the police first," said Basu. "They could have got to Denbigh before anyone else and taken him into custody, for his own protection as much as anything."

"Hindsight wears spectacles," Dr Burnell lamented. "As do I, for all the good they do." He removed said item, huffed on the lenses and gave them a polish with a handkerchief. Without the spectacles on, he looked positively mole-like.

"It may be that Denbigh was responsible for the attack," said Holmes. "Then again, it may not. You can resolve that, Doctor, simply by providing a sketch of the bite marks as best you can remember them."

"I'm not sure that's possible," Dr Burnell said. "It was a good fortnight ago that I examined the body."

"The sketch does not have to be perfectly accurate. Just as accurate as you can manage."

"Very well. I suppose I can try."

Dr Burnell took out a pencil and a sheet of blank notepaper from his desk drawer, and commenced drawing, head bent low over his work.

"This is the closest approximation," he said when he was done. "It is pieced together from the various partial bite marks I saw on the body. I have amalgamated them into a single whole. I hope it is of some use."

He passed the sheet of notepaper to Holmes, who examined it attentively.

"You have assisted us a great deal, Doctor," said he. "Denbigh is exonerated."

"You're sure?" I said.

"Never surer. Look."

Holmes showed me the sketch. It depicted a perfect semi-circle of tooth marks.

"How do these differ from Denbigh's teeth?" he said.

"They all are present and correct."

"Quite so. In his upper jaw alone, Denbigh is missing an incisor, both canines and a bicuspid."

"Whoever did it, definitely a full set of teeth was involved," said Dr Burnell. "What a relief, to know that Denbigh had no part in the crime."

"A crime has still been committed, however," said Holmes. "And another may yet be. Doctor, is there anyone you told about the bite marks being possibly human, other than Basu?"

"No. Nobody."

"You would swear to that?"

"I would."

"Then how is it that your receptionist, the winsome Flossie, is aware of it?"

"She is?"

Holmes nodded.

Dr Burnell's face coloured. "Oh, that wretched girl!" he said through gritted teeth. "She is new. My previous receptionist quit the post to get married several months ago. I am still training Flossie up, and I've been feeling for a while that she is not best suited to the job. She is incorrigibly nosy. I've caught her, more than once, poring over a patient's notes. I've told her that they are none of her business, and she has acted suitably chastened, but that doesn't seem to stop her. She listens at the keyhole to that door sometimes, too, while I am in consultation. I'm sure of it."

"How might she have found out about the bite marks, though?"

"Let me think. A-ha. Yes, I have it. I included a mention of them possibly being of human origin in a first draft of the report. I then rejected the notion and rewrote the report, this time omitting that reference. The first draft went in the waste-paper bin. One of Flossie's duties is emptying the bin every week. Doubtless she came across the draft and took the opportunity to look at it. I shall have to sack her over this."

We heard a gasp from the other side of the door, whereupon Holmes sprang to his feet, grasped the door handle and wrenched it open. There stood Flossie in the doorway, in a half-crouch, with an aghast expression on her face.

"I knew it!" Dr Burnell cried. "You appalling creature. Caught in the act! Eavesdropping! And after I gave you this opportunity, too. I could easily have gone for someone more qualified. I only even considered you for the position because you are a friend of my granddaughter."

"Oh, sir, sir!" Flossie declared. "I am sorry! Do not sack me!"

She sank to her knees, looking up at Dr Burnell imploringly. "I never meant to pry. Can I help it if I am curious by nature?"

"You know how important confidentiality is in a doctor's surgery. I have drummed it into you countless times."

"I shall do better in future." Tears were welling in her eyes. "Give me another chance, I beg you."

"Silly girl. Why should I?"

It was a comical tableau, like a scene from a farce, or a melodrama, or even one of the Savoy operettas so beloved by my late wife: Flossie genuflecting before her employer, hands clenched together in remonstration; Dr Burnell leaning over her, wagging a finger in reproof. I was tempted to chuckle, and might have done, had I not observed the grim expression that had stolen over Holmes's face. Something about it all, evidently, was no laughing matter.

"Flossie," said Holmes. "Answer me this, and be truthful, for a man's life may depend on it."

"Yes, sir," sniffed the girl, whose copious outpouring of tears had scored pale lines through the rouge on her cheeks.

"Have you told anyone that the bite marks on Professor Carmody's body may not have been made by an animal?"

"No, sir. I mean, I suppose I told you, didn't I? But that was after you had said you were policemen, so I assumed it would be all right."

"Are you quite certain about this? No one other than us? No one whatsoever?"

Flossie gnawed a thumbnail. "I may have spoken about it to Ginger."

"And who is Ginger?"

"Ginger is my man. Ginger Hesketh."

"One of Betchfield's gallant young bucks," said Dr Burnell with a hint of disdain. "Real name Gabriel, but known to all and sundry as Ginger on account of his red hair. He and his cronies are great roisterers, forever falling into, and out of, the pub. And indeed into, and out of, trouble. His father Patrick is a blacksmith, and he was something of a roisterer, too, back in his day. Like father, like son. As I recall, it was Patrick Hesketh who led the persecution of Denbigh the first time around. He likewise incited the more recent spate of attacks on the fellow that were prompted by Mr Basu's article, and son Ginger abetted him in those."

Holmes's expression grew grimmer. "How recently was it, Flossie, that you told your Ginger that the bite marks might be human?"

"Yesterday, sir."

"But you would have known about it for longer than that. Dr Burnell prepared his report a fortnight ago, and he tells us you empty his waste-paper bin once a week."

"Oh yes. I found out about it last Friday. I kept it to myself for a time. I was trying to be good and do my job the way I ought. But then yesterday Ginger was talking about Jonah Denbigh, and it just sort of slipped out." She shrugged her shoulders helplessly, as though somehow this was not her fault.

"And how did he respond?"

"He was angered, sir," said the girl. "Muttered about it something fierce, he did. Said he would let his father know."

Holmes drew in a breath. "This is as I feared," he said to me and Basu. "Now that word has leaked out, it surely won't be long before Hesketh senior gathers together what the Americans would call a posse. He may be doing it right now, even as we speak. This is surely the excuse he has been looking for to assault Denbigh for a third and perhaps final time. We must hurry. Jonah Denbigh, his defensive measures notwithstanding, is in peril of his life, and it is incumbent upon us to get him to a place of safety."

Chapter Sixteen

STOKED UP WITH SELF-RIGHTEOUSNESS AND ARMOURED WITH ANGER

The return journey to Denbigh's hovel took us less than half the time, such was the pace Holmes set. I struggled to keep up, and even Basu, though young and fit, began to flag after a while. We did not even slow down during the last stretch of the journey, as a precaution against inadvertently springing any of Denbigh's various traps. Holmes had memorised the whereabouts of these on the way out, so that bypassing them now presented no obstacle.

By the time we arrived back at the hovel, the sky was beginning to darken, the woods growing shadowy around us. To our great relief, Denbigh was alone. No mob had paid him a visit yet.

"Denbigh, you must accompany us," Holmes said. "No ifs or buts. You cannot stay here."

"Why ever not?" Denbigh snapped.

"There is good reason to think you are in imminent danger."

Briefly Holmes outlined the situation to him. "*We* know you did not kill Professor Carmody. Others may have reached a different conclusion."

"This is my home." Denbigh gestured around him at his particularly humble abode. "I can't just leave it. I *won't*."

"Remain, and the consequences will almost certainly be grievous. I do not expect Patrick Hesketh and his fellow towns-people to be as lenient with you as before. It is no longer a question of hearsay and innate bigotry. To them, it appears as though you have finally confirmed their worst suspicions, and on their very doorstep, too."

"I've withstood their attentions before, and I am prepared, as you know."

"This time it is different," Holmes insisted. "You must realise that. There is no telling what these folk, with their hooligan mentality, will do. I would not put it past them to—"

He broke off. Distantly, through the trees, we could hear a commotion. Voices burbled. Footsteps crashed. The noise was coming from the direction of Betchfield.

"That can only be them," Holmes said. "A dozen of them, by the sound of it, and making no secret of their presence, which suggests men stoked up with self-righteousness and armoured with anger. I had hoped the grace period might be a little longer than this. Then again, we are lucky to have beaten them to it at all. Now, Denbigh! There is not a moment to lose."

Still the hermit prevaricated. "If they are after me, I can make a stand here."

"Even with your traps, and our assistance, there is no guarantee of victory and every chance of an adverse outcome. We must get you to a place of sanctuary."

"And where would that be?"

"Grayshott Grange is not far," said Basu.

"An excellent idea," said Holmes. "Just what I was going to suggest."

"I won't be welcomed there," said Denbigh. "Not if they think I killed Carmody."

"If you are with me, and I vouch for you, they will let you in."

"And no mob, surely, would go so far as to set foot on private property," I added.

"We have no assurances on that front," said Holmes, "but let us trust you are right."

The noise was getting louder. Now, one could make out individual voices offering gruff exhortations such as "This way!" and "Not far, lads!" and "He's had this coming a long time!" Unmistakably it was a small group of men bent on troublemaking.

At last Denbigh was galvanised into action. "You promise you can protect me, Mr Holmes?"

"As long as it is in my power to do so, yes."

Denbigh took a look around his little encampment, as if fearing he might never see it again. "Then let's go," he said heavily.

As we began to move, I caught my first sight of the approaching "posse", to use Holmes's descriptor. They were visible amid the gloom between the trees, and it was clear that they were headed our way and that they outnumbered us at least three to one. Their intent was obviously hostile, too, since several of them brandished some kind of weapon such as a knife or an agricultural implement; one was even carrying a gun. Our only recourse was to make off in the opposite direction, which by great good fortune happened to be the direction in which Grayshott Grange lay, more or less.

"Hey!" came a yell from behind us. "I think I see him!"

"Me too," said someone else. "He's with some others. Looks like they're trying to escape."

"Hurry, then!" shouted a third. "Doesn't matter who's with him. We'll grab 'em too. They'll give him up to us, if they know what's good for them."

We four broke into a run, as did the posse.

Next thing we heard was a sudden wail, followed by some agonised cursing. "My foot! My damned foot! Something's stuck it. Gone all the way through. Ah, for the love of God, it hurts!"

One of the men had, it seemed, discovered the set of stakes planted in the ground by Denbigh.

I saw a quick grin flash across Denbigh's face.

"Never mind that!" someone else bellowed. It was the same voice that a moment earlier had urged everyone to hurry, and I could only assume it belonged to the posse's ringleader. "Leave him. We can't let that man-eating fiend get away."

We increased our speed, while our pursuers likewise stepped up their pace. There were perhaps fifty yards between us and them.

Then came the sharp, resonant *crack* of a shotgun. Instinctively, the four of us ducked.

"That was just a warning," said the ringleader to us. "Halt right there, or next time Barnaby won't be aiming in the air."

I whipped out my revolver, whirled about and loosed off a couple of rounds. I, too, aimed high. I heard one of the bullets whine as it ricocheted off a tree bough.

"Two can play at that game," I called out.

My return fire sowed consternation among the posse.

"They're armed, Patrick," one man groused. "I didn't come here expecting I'd get shot at."

"What of it?" said the ringleader, who I now knew for certain must be Patrick Hesketh, town blacksmith. "We're armed as well. Barnaby, a quick reminder of that?"

Accordingly, a second shotgun blast came our way from the man addressed as Barnaby. This time, the little cluster of pellets zinged not far above our heads, sending down a shower of twigs broken off by its passing. I answered with another round from my revolver, well aware that this served a deterrent purpose only. Unlike the fellow with the shotgun, I had scant hope of hitting anyone at a range of fifty yards with a pistol.

Running on, we arrived at the rivulet which we had crossed earlier using the fallen beech tree. We could not afford to pick our way along that mossy, makeshift bridge this time, for we would have to go single file, painstakingly, and it would slow us down too much. Instead, following Holmes's lead, we waded through the water. It was bracingly cold and came up above our knees where the rivulet was deepest.

This still enabled the posse to narrow the distance, if not as much as our using the beech bridge would have. As I clambered up the bank on the other side, I darted a look over my shoulder. Our pursuers were now less than twenty yards away. The man with the shotgun stopped, sighted down its side-by-side pair of barrels, and pulled the first trigger. Soil exploded beside Denbigh's foot, a small crater appearing in the ground. Denbigh yelped in fright.

Barnaby let out a gloating laugh and curled his finger around the second trigger. He had his eye in now. He wasn't going to miss.

Unfortunately for him, neither was I.

My revolver barked. I winged Barnaby in the arm, as I had intended. He tumbled to the ground with a shrill howl. At the same time, his finger convulsed on the trigger and he peppered the leg of a man a few yards away. The other man also howled and went hopping round in a circle with a thigh full of shot, swearing liberally.

"Bravo, Watson," said Holmes. "But we do not have the luxury of pausing to congratulate ourselves. We have enraged our foes, not confounded them."

Never was a truer word spoken, for the remaining members of the posse came after us with a vengeance. They forded the rivulet as we had and continued the chase on the other side, uttering threats and insults in profane profusion. Hesketh, a heavy-set, sandy-haired man, had snatched up the shotgun dropped by Barnaby and taken a handful of cartridges off him. He had not yet reloaded, but surely would at the first opportunity.

It was then that I realised Denbigh was not uninjured, as I had thought. The shot that had hit the ground by his foot had hit him also. He himself seemed to perceive this only belatedly. After running a dozen or so yards he began to limp. Then he drew up short with a hiss of pain and peered down at his foot.

I saw that part of the heel of his boot was torn away, and blood was oozing out through the hole.

Without hesitating, Basu drew Denbigh's arm around his shoulders and slipped his own arm around the other's waist. "Give me your weight. I will support you."

Denbigh looked at the young man askance and seemed for a moment to be debating whether to accept his help.

"Don't go thinking this makes us quits," he said.

"I would do the same for anyone," replied Basu.

"Good. I don't want you getting any ideas, that's all."

With Basu's aid, Denbigh hobbled along. Their speed was decent, all things considered. Nevertheless, the four of us as a whole were hampered now by Denbigh's wound, and our pursuers seemed more determined than ever to catch us. Hesketh made this clear as he yelled, "We've got 'em, boys. Ginger, take your two friends and move around the side of them. They're not going nearly as fast any more. You can cut them off ahead."

Sure enough, three of the younger men in the group broke off and veered to the right in a flanking manoeuvre. They sprinted past, outpacing us easily. We four stumbled into a hollow, and as we came up the other side, there stood the trio of youngsters at the top of the slope, looking down at us with feral grins. One of them, a fellow with a shock of fox-coloured hair, could only be Hesketh's son and Flossie's beau, Gabriel, popularly known as Ginger. He was the spitting image of his father, if a little less coarse-complexioned and not so thick around the middle.

Holmes went straight to confront them. Ginger had a forging hammer in his hand, one of the tools of his father's trade. Another of the three wielded a long sheath knife, while the third was bare-handed. Holmes tackled the one with the knife first, reckoning, as did I, that a man with a bladed weapon constituted the greatest danger. He disarmed him with a strange, complicated twist of the wrist, then brought him to his knees with a jab to the solar plexus and dispatched him into unconsciousness by means of a roundhouse punch to the head.

Ginger Hesketh lunged at him from the side, swinging the square-ended hammer viciously. Holmes parried by sliding his open hand along Ginger's forearm. He then wrapped his arm around the other's arm and bent it back against its elbow with considerable force. There was a just audible *crunch* as the joint was dislocated, and after that a very audible shriek of pain from the throat of the injured party.

The third youth all at once looked a good deal less confident about his prospects. He had just watched Holmes swiftly and ruthlessly incapacitate his two associates, all in the space of ten seconds. He put up his hands in submission.

"I am a merciful man," said Holmes, "and would not hurt someone who has surrendered."

The other looked relieved.

"On most days," Holmes added, accompanying the remark with an uppercut to the jaw that rocked the young man back on his heels and sent a tooth flying through the air. The recipient of the punch tottered, then collapsed in an insensible heap.

This delay cost us dear. The rest of the posse, their complement now halved, were almost upon us. I let loose another warning shot, and they recoiled and backed away. Yet, as we resumed our progress, so did they. Patrick Hesketh was incensed by the punishment Holmes had meted out on his son.

"We're getting Denbigh, don't you worry about that," I heard him snarl to his comrades. "That lanky beanpole of a bloke, though, is mine. Nobody does that to my own flesh and blood. I'll tear the scoundrel apart with my bare hands!"

I was panting hard. Denbigh was limping worse than ever. Basu was bearing more and more of Denbigh's weight, and this was taking its toll on him. Holmes, for his part, was perhaps a little short of breath but his vigour was otherwise undimmed. There were times when my friend seemed indefatigable, possessed of a stamina so great it was almost superhuman.

We hurried onward as best we could, with Hesketh and his fellow hounds ever at our heels. Hesketh had slotted fresh shells into the shotgun and sent a couple of shots our way, neither finding its mark. There remained two rounds in my revolver, but rather than shoot back I elected to conserve them until they were absolutely needed. I had the box of Eley's, but reloading the gun required a moment of respite, which was not available just then.

I began to despair of ever making it out of those woods. The world seemed to be just trees and more trees, and slippery wet ground, and branches that slapped one in the face and clawed at one's clothing. Were we even going in the right direction any more? Might we, in all the chaos and confusion, have got lost? I presumed that Holmes had stored the original route in that remarkable memory of his and would not lead us astray. Failing that, Denbigh would surely point out if we were going the wrong way, for he must know these woods like the back of his hand.

Yet, given that he was wounded, he might not be thinking clearly. As for Holmes, even he was not infallible, and it was possible he might have become disorientated and be unwittingly taking us round in circles.

Such lack of faith! For no sooner had I entertained this doubt than, up ahead, I glimpsed black-painted wooden beams and the redness of brickwork. It was Grayshott Grange, and rarely have I been so glad to see a building. With a soft chuckle of triumph, I redoubled my efforts. Basu and Denbigh were likewise reinvigorated by the sight of the house. Coming to the boundary wall, we dashed through the gate one after another in quick succession and across the lawn. I was last in line, and I stole a backward glance as we neared the place where we hoped to find asylum.

Patrick Hesketh and his band of cronies, what was left of them, had arrived at the gate and were vacillating. Did they dare go on? Inflamed with outrage and rancour though they were, might trespass be taking things a step too far?

I saw Hesketh come to a decision. He loaded the shotgun dextrously with two fresh cartridges and brought it up to his shoulder. Denbigh and Holmes were close together. He could have been aiming at either one of them, and he had ammunition to take out both.

"Hesketh!" I called out. My own firearm was raised.

He looked over at me. He looked back along the length of the shotgun.

"Shoot, and you are a dead man," I said. "I mean it."

"You could miss."

"And just as easily I could not. Are you willing to take that chance?"

Holmes, Basu and Denbigh were now at the front door. Holmes tried the handle and it turned. As is common at many a country residence, the front door was never locked during the daytime.

Hesketh had just seconds to make his choice before his targets disappeared inside. He half-closed one eye in order to improve his aim with the other. I did the same. I genuinely felt I might have to kill this man. I might even have to take a pre-emptive shot, to prevent him killing another man.

It was no small relief to me when I saw his shoulders slump and the shotgun decline towards the ground. He directed a look at me that was pure spite.

"Whoever you are, you have bought yourself a reprieve," Hesketh said, "nothing more. You can't keep Denbigh in that house indefinitely. Sooner or later, he will have to return to his lair in the woods. And I shall be waiting. His kind cannot be allowed to live. He is an abomination, an affront to all that is proper and decent."

"Tend to your wounded and forget all about Jonah Denbigh," I replied. "He is not the monster you think he is. He is a man much maligned and misunderstood. And should any harm come to him in future," I went on, "you personally will be held to account for it, Mr Patrick Hesketh. You have my word on that as an Englishman and a gentleman."

Hesketh and his cronies went away muttering, and I exhaled, the tension ebbing out of me. I turned, pocketed my revolver, and trudged towards the Grange. Sherlock Holmes was holding the door open for me, and his smile was broad and approbatory.

"Watson, my dear fellow," he said, patting me on the back as I went in. "My dear, dear fellow." It was all he needed to say and all I needed to hear.

Chapter Seventeen

MOUSETRAPS AND OLD DENTURES

The butler Fitch was the first occupant of the house we encountered.

"Goodnesh grashioush!" he exclaimed, surveying our small gathering in the hallway. "What on earth hash happened?"

"We have been set upon by a group of irate locals," said Holmes. "This house affords us a safe haven, and for that, Mr Fitch, we are most grateful."

Fitch nodded. Our dishevelled, fatigued condition, not to mention our muddy trousers and squelching shoes, surely corroborated Holmes's claims.

"I musht shpeak to Mishish Carmody. She should be informed of your arrival."

"Of course, my good man. First, however, one of our number is injured, as you may or may not have noticed. Might you show us to the kitchen, where my friend Dr Watson will effect repairs?"

Sympathy to another's plight overcame Fitch's sense of

protocol. "Shertainly," he said, working his jaw from side to side in that odd way of his.

Moments later we were in a spacious, well-appointed kitchen, where a cook was making a start on the preparations for supper while a scullery maid washed the lunch dishes. I sat Denbigh down, helped him take off his boot, and set about cleaning and binding his wound, using water, alcohol and strips of a dishtowel. He had lost a fair amount of flesh from his heel, but his Achilles tendon was intact and he would, in my opinion, walk more or less as normal once healed.

Fitch had gone in search of the lady of the house. The cook and scullery maid, meanwhile, looked on as I ministered to Denbigh, as did Holmes and Basu. Neither woman appeared delighted at their workplace being turned into a temporary surgery.

Holmes felt moved to apologise. "Miss. Madam. This is a gross imposition, I understand. Please be assured, we shall be out of your way as soon as possible."

"I should be much obliged, sir," said the cook.

"While I am here," Holmes went on, "might you satisfy my curiosity on a couple of small matters?"

"I can try, I suppose," the cook replied warily.

"I see an unusual quantity of mousetraps on the floor. There is one in each corner, and another beneath the carving table. Has there been an infestation lately?"

My ears pricked up. Holmes was not making idle chitchat, that much I knew, not least because he found idle chitchat abhorrent. He could only be asking about the mousetraps for a specific reason.

"There are always more mice around the house during winter than at any other time," the cook said. "They come indoors where it's warm and where food is plentiful."

"Even so, *five* traps?"

"And three more in the pantry," said the scullery maid.

"Don't you have a cat?" said Holmes. "That would be a simpler and more hygienic solution, surely."

"We did have a cat," said the cook. "A little brindled thing, Queenie. She was an expert mouser."

"What happened to her?"

"We don't know. She disappeared in the spring. April, it was. Here one day, gone the next. Not like her to just wander off, but then that's cats for you. They're a law unto themselves, especially the females."

Holmes was pleased with this answer. I could see it in his eyes. Something he suspected had just been confirmed.

"We've been meaning to get a replacement," the cook went on, "but then Mrs Carmody's dog disappeared too, and she wished to get her new dog settled first before we brought in a cat. We will get round to it eventually, although everything is a bit up in the air at present, as you can imagine, what with the professor being gone." She looked downcast. "The poor professor…"

"Yes, it is a pity," said Holmes, a tad too briskly. He was onto something. He had the scent in his nostrils, and that, as far as he was concerned, meant little time for niceties. "On an unrelated topic, your Mr Fitch seems to be having trouble with his dentures."

"You noticed that, did you?"

"They seem very uncomfortable. He is forever moving his jaw in order to make them sit better; and then, of course, there is that lisp of his."

Dentures, I thought to myself. This explanation for Fitch's speech impediment and habit of shifting his jaw around had not even occurred to me. An ill-fitting set of dentures. How had I not realised?

"That's because they are Fitch's old dentures, from years back," said the cook. "They make his gums dead sore, although he has no choice but to wear them because his newer set went missing."

"When was that?"

"That they went missing? Not very long ago. Back in October, I think it was. Isn't that so, Mabel?"

Mabel, the scullery maid, nodded. "Thereabouts."

"He kept them in a glass by his bedside overnight," said the cook. "One morning, he woke up and they weren't there. He must have misplaced them, but heaven knows where. It was all very queer. Good thing he still had his old set, otherwise he'd have been lost. He'd have been able to eat nothing but soup. He's entirely toothless, you see."

"I presume he cannot afford a new set."

"He is saving up for them. The professor offered to buy them for him, but Fitch wouldn't hear of it. He has his pride, does our Fitch."

Holmes looked more than satisfied now. With his disarming charisma and artfully posed queries, he had extracted nuggets of data from these two women, although at that precise moment I could not quite see what use any of it was. A vanished cat?

A missing set of dentures? Knowing Holmes as I did, these things must be of relevance, but as yet their meaning eluded me. I noticed Basu looking my way with a question in his eyes. I shrugged my shoulders at him, to show that I was similarly nonplussed.

"Watson, Basu," said Holmes.

We both snapped our heads round.

"It is by no means a misfortune that we have found ourselves back at Grayshott Grange," Holmes said. "One might almost discern the hand of providence in all of this. I am now entirely convinced that I know who killed Professor Carmody and why. It is," he added sombrely, "one of the more disturbing cases I have come across. Its implications are dire, and range back across recent history. I am very much concerned that my own past mistakes may have played a part in what has transpired here. It is too late to change what I have done wrong, but not too late to set things right. We must gather the professor's immediate next of kin, such as they are. Both Mrs Carmody and her son will want to hear what I have to say."

Chapter Eighteen

THE UNPALATABLE CONCLUSION

M rs Carmody and Vernon agreed to meet with us in the drawing room, which was large and lavishly furnished. Mrs Carmody's pug Hugo lay snugly in her lap, issuing wheezy breaths like an asthmatic. She fondled the dog's ears in an absentminded fashion. Her son, meanwhile, rested with one hip on the arm of her chair, his arms folded. His manner was, I thought, protective.

Basu, naturally, was present. He had sparked the investigation into Professor Carmody's murder, so there was no reason why he should not be in on the denouement. Denbigh had asked to attend too, and given that he had regarded Carmody as a friend and had for a while been chief suspect in the murder, we could not in all conscience refuse his request. He sat apart, in a window seat, keeping his bandaged foot elevated per my advice. With his ragged clothing and shambolic hair, he looked out of place in these opulent surroundings, a starveling crow in an aviary meant for sleek exotic birds.

"I come before you today," said Sherlock Holmes, "a chastened man. It is not so much a matter of what I overlooked as what I chose to ignore. I deliberately turned a blind eye to certain dark doings, and the ramifications have proved severe – more so than I could ever have predicted. Had I but been a little more judicious, a little less magnanimous, Professor Isidore Carmody would still be alive today. I shall carry the shame of it to my grave."

"What on earth do you mean, Mr Holmes?" said Mrs Carmody. "You never knew Isidore. I doubt you had even heard of him before Mr Basu came to you. How, then, could you have prevented his death?"

"By nipping things in the bud before they went further. By strangling his killer at birth, as it were."

"What I want to know," said Vernon, "is what this *creature* is doing in our house." He flicked his fingers at Denbigh. "Bad enough that he is grimy and malodorous. He is also my stepfather's murderer. He killed and consumed a harmless old academic. There's no question about it. Who else could it have been? Not a wild animal, that's for sure. It must have been him. He is the Yukon Cannibal, after all. Why are the police not on their way to clap him in irons? You are the great detective, Mr Holmes. A foe of crime. A staunch advocate of justice. What are you doing? Why let him just sit there, stinking up the place? At the very least he should be bound to a chair. He could flee at any time."

"Denbigh is going nowhere, Vernon," Holmes said evenly. "And would you please refrain from further such outbursts. Your chest-beating intimidates no one and changes nothing."

Bristling, Vernon leapt to his feet. "That is quite enough," he said with an imperious air. "My mother is in mourning, and you are upsetting her greatly with this whole rigmarole of yours. For her sake, I invite you all to leave."

"Vernon…" said his mother.

"No, Mama. I am the man of the house now, and as such, I make the decisions. Mr Holmes, you and your associates are no longer welcome on these premises. I am asking you to go quietly, but if you refuse, I am quite prepared to have you thrown out."

"Vernon." This time Mrs Carmody's voice was more emphatic. "Sit back down. You are making a fool of yourself."

"But, Mama…"

"Sit and hush. Let us hear Mr Holmes out."

With a sullen pout, Vernon resumed his place on the arm of her chair. He had just tried to behave like a full-blown adult, and it had resulted in him looking like a callow child.

"Thank you, Mrs Carmody," said Holmes. "I shall state the facts of the matter as simply as I can. You may not be aware that the bite marks on the professor's body appear to have been inflicted not by an animal, but by a human being."

Mrs Carmody's face registered surprise and alarm.

"It is not common knowledge," Holmes continued. "However, they were not inflicted by Jonah Denbigh. Likely though that possibility may seem, in light of his reputation, it cannot be the case. Denbigh lacks several teeth, whereas whoever made the bite marks has a full set. Or rather, that person used something in order to give the impression of someone who has a full set. By this I mean that a tool was employed to deflect suspicion towards a reputed cannibal living nearby. It was all a cunning stratagem."

"A tool?" said Mrs Carmody.

"A set of dentures. Owner: one Fitch, butler of this household. They were stolen at night from beside his bed while he slept."

"Stolen? I know Fitch lost the dentures, but everyone assumed they had just been mislaid."

"Stolen, with a view to using them for the very purpose I have just specified. With someone holding one half of the dentures in one hand, the other half held in the other, they could be manipulated in such a way as to mimic the effects of cannibalism, chewing, as it were, at the body."

"But who would do such a thing – kill Isidore and make it look as though a man had eaten him?"

"Someone who had reason to fear the professor and wished to get rid of him."

"Fear him?" said the widow. "But he was the most benevolent of individuals. A little abrasive at times, perhaps, but he meant well."

"Alas for the professor, he was close to unmasking a certain person as an out-and-out villain," said Holmes. "According to Denbigh over there, Carmody had recently begun investigating the subject of evil. It had become his latest line of scientific enquiry. 'Evil is all around us,' he told Denbigh. 'Sometimes it can reside in your own home, hiding behind the sweetest of faces.'"

"I knew nothing of this," said Mrs Carmody. "But then, Isidore's intellectual pursuits were his own affair. I left him to it and never got involved."

"The professor had recognised that something hideous was

taking place under his roof. He was a perceptive man. I think it must have begun when the resident mouser, one Queenie by name, went missing."

"The cook's cat."

"The very one. That was during the spring, and was followed in the summer by the disappearance of your dog, Otto, Mrs Carmody."

"Yes. So sad." She stroked Hugo harder, as if deriving succour from the presence of Otto's replacement. "Silly little Otto. He was a town dog, so he would not have appreciated the risks posed by country living. I can only think that a fox must have snatched him from the garden, mistaking him for a rabbit."

"No fox," said Holmes. "A human being abducted Otto, and Queenie the cat too, and killed them both."

"Why?"

"As a test of nerve. To see if it was possible. For the sick pleasure of it. There are many possible reasons. You would have to ask the culprit yourself. My own theory is that the deaths of Queenie and Otto were an expression of dissatisfaction, a way of purging an inner torment. Often, when a disturbed mind can find no other outlet for its frustrations, it visits them on defenceless animals, in sadistic fashion."

Mrs Carmody's face had begun to whiten. I believe she was reaching the same unpalatable conclusion that I myself was.

"And often," Holmes went on, "when a young man is very attached to his mother and sees her find happiness in a new husband, he feels enormous resentment."

All eyes in the room turned to Vernon Agius.

Chapter Nineteen

A MAELSTROM OF CONTRADICTIONS AND UNGUESSABLE URGES

"Yet he is unable to voice that resentment, this young man," Holmes said. "How can he, without upsetting his beloved mother? Without inviting accusations of jealousy? Without seeming a bad son? So he must bottle it up inside and keep it there. Keep it while it stews and bubbles and festers like bad beer, until he can contain it no longer and must somehow vent the pressure."

Vernon stared back at us mildly, blandly.

"But did it alleviate anything, Vernon, killing those pets?" Holmes asked him. "Did it assuage your turmoil, or did it instead only fuel it?"

"I don't know what you're talking about, Mr Holmes," said the lad.

"Did it perhaps answer some dark craving that has lain within you for a long time? Was it just another manifestation of certain grotesque impulses which you have indulged in, to my knowledge, at least once before, if not twice?"

"This is quite preposterous. Mama, are you going to let him talk to me like that? Your own son?"

"Be quiet, Vernon," said Mrs Carmody, purse-lipped.

"No, Vernon," said Holmes, "your mother knows as well as I do what sort of person you truly are. Possibly she has denied it to herself. I would not blame her for that. A mother cannot think the worst of her own child. It goes against the grain. She might even consider that the tendencies which led you to kill your actual father were noble."

"Kill my...?"

"It was not your mother who replaced your father's amyl nitrite pearls with ones filled with water. It was you. When he suffered the heart attack that was ultimately to prove fatal, she administered three of the pearls to him in the honest belief that they were the genuine article. Afterwards, when I confronted her about it, she played along with the idea I myself had proposed, namely that she substituted the first pearl with a fake one which she had already secreted in a pocket of her nightgown. In the event, what the valet Sturridge had observed – your mother dropping the pearl, then retrieving it – was just as it appeared, an accident. Only after I had talked of 'palming' did she realise she could pretend it was a deliberate move on her part. She knew by then that all the pearls in the pillbox were doctored ones, and furthermore she knew that the person who had done the doctoring was you. It could only have been you. Yet when I proposed that a substitution had taken place, with you feigning ignorance, what else could she do other than claim it was all her handiwork? She was covering for the true culprit. She risked being sent to the gallows for the sake of her son. She put her own life in jeopardy, as any good mother might, to keep her child safe."

"My mother wanted my father dead just as much as I did," Vernon said. "She meant to kill him. She devised the 'haunting' at our house in Knightsbridge with that express purpose in mind."

"But the doctored amyl nitrite pearls were your touch, Vernon. You had twigged what your mother was up to, and had filled your father's pillbox with fake pearls. These should not have been too difficult to create. All you would need to do was unpick one end of the mesh sleeve, take out the capsule, bore a tiny hole in it, empty out the amyl nitrite, replace it with water, seal the hole, slide the capsule back into the sleeve and refasten the end. Then everything would be ready for your father's seemingly inevitable heart attack. When it came, the fake pearls would not mitigate its effects."

"My mother could have done that just as easily as I. You have no reason to think she wasn't responsible for the fakes, as she maintained."

"I do have reason to think that, simply because she broke three pearls under your father's nose. Not one. Three. She claimed that only the first was a fake and that with the next two she tried to compensate for that pearl's failure to work. But why would she do that? Had she known that the first pearl would not work, had that been her plan all along, she could simply have applied that single adulterated pearl, allowed it to be unsuccessful, and left it at that. No one would be any the wiser, certainly not the witness to the event, namely Sturridge. Rather, she tried two further pearls, both of which were also doctored, unbeknownst to her. The truth is, your mother did not want your father to die. Or at least, she had a change of heart at the last moment. Is that not so, madam?"

Mrs Carmody lowered her head. "I wanted Eustace to suffer. I wanted to hurt him. Perhaps, deep down, I did even intend to kill him. But when I saw him lying there on the hallway floor at Tarleton Crescent, red-faced, gasping, writhing in pain… well, I was filled with an overwhelming sense of shame and regret. When Sturridge – that good man – went to fetch Eustace's pillbox, I knew that that was the right thing. I was committing murder, as good as, but Sturridge was bringing me salvation. I still had a chance to prevent Eustace dying. My hand was indeed trembling as I took out the first amyl nitrite pearl, and that is why I fumbled with it and dropped it. But the tremble was as much hope as anxiety. I still could redeem myself, I thought."

"You tried to remedy what you had done. Alas, even though you didn't know it then, your son had already deprived you of that possibility." Holmes turned back to Vernon. "You, my lad, by replacing all the pearls with fakes, had undermined your mother's efforts in advance. She, having realised this subsequently, was then left with no alternative, as she saw it. When challenged by me, all she could do was pretend she had substituted the first pearl with a fake one, making her the agent of your father's death, not you. Prior to that, she had taken the precaution of replacing the remaining doctored pearls in the pillbox with real ones, a further measure to conceal your crime and protect you."

"But if you knew all of this at the time," said Vernon, "why didn't you say anything?"

"Because I *didn't* know, not with any certainty. To quote one Dr Burnell, general practitioner of Betchfield, 'Hindsight wears spectacles.' I had an inkling of the truth, but even then I believed your actions were to some extent justified by circumstances. Eustace Agius was a dreadful villain, and if the two people closest to him, the two who were affected daily by his constant bullying and haranguing, had contrived between them to bring about his death… well, was that not justice in some form? A justice which surpassed any that the law of the land might have provided?"

Holmes paused, his expression sober and rueful.

"Of course," he said, "with that same blurry hindsight now corrected by the lenses of subsequent developments, I am able to see clearly that you also played a part in an earlier incident, Vernon. My focus on the case of Hector Robinson is sharpened. Watson, if you cast your mind back to our sojourn at Saltings House School in 'eighty-nine, you will recall how I had you try to break your way out of the boathouse in which the ill-fated Robinson was imprisoned."

"I remember it well," I said. "I was able to push the door open eventually, if not without some difficulty."

"And I wondered aloud whether Robinson might not have been able to do the same. Perhaps he might have, if somebody had not hindered him."

"Somebody? Do you mean…?"

"Suppose Robinson's pitiful cries for help did not go unheard after all. Suppose a fellow pupil went out to the boathouse and, when Robinson attempted to free himself, decided to hold the door shut from the outside. Robinson shoved and strained in vain while this other, stronger pupil steadfastly resisted him, until at last the captive gave it up, succumbing to hypothermia and exhaustion."

"Why would that have necessarily been me?" Vernon said. "What would even lead you to make that assumption?"

"Nothing much," replied Holmes, "other than a tiny detail which, at the time, did not strike me as important. It was something your teacher Wragge said. He mentioned he found your rugby kit hanging on the end of your bed, still damp, on the morning after you and Robinson were made to run laps in the rain. In itself, perhaps of no consequence. Now, however, I am minded to think it is of great consequence. Surely, some sixteen or seventeen hours after the event, the rugby kit would by then have dried. The fact that it had not would suggest that you had put it on again later and gone out into the storm wearing it."

"And why would I have done that?"

"In order to avoid returning to bed afterwards and having to sleep in soaking wet pyjamas," said Holmes simply. "As to why you went out at all, you shared a dormitory with, among others, Robinson. When games master Yeowell came to wake the boy after lights out, he would have been stealthy but perhaps he was not stealthy enough. He inadvertently roused one of the other sleepers, who pretended he was still slumbering but then, after teacher and boy were gone, got out of bed and trailed after them. His reason may have merely been curiosity, or else he realised Robinson was going to receive a further chastising and wished to witness it first-hand."

"So I was angry at Hector, is that it? But he wasn't the one who punished me. That was Mr Yeowell. Surely I should have been angry at *him*."

"You would not have been punished at all, Vernon, but for your noble gesture towards Robinson on the rugby pitch. Somewhere in your soul, you resented him for that. Perhaps you resented yourself, too. Nothing leaves one feeling foolish quite like being made to suffer for one's good intentions. Either way, there would have been a great deal of satisfaction in seeing Robinson on the receiving end of another punishment, this time on his own. It would have been a fine opportunity to gloat."

"Gloat? Then how come I defended Hector later, after he was dead, when Wyatt and Pugh mocked him? You were there. You saw it for yourself. I took a beating on his behalf. My actions were hardly those of someone who had revelled in his misfortune earlier."

"Given what you had done at the boathouse," said Holmes, "I would not be surprised if you were sensitive on the subject of Hector Robinson. Wyatt and Pugh touched a raw nerve, and you lashed out. You did not have full control of your emotions then, the way you seem to now."

"Even supposing all this were true," said Vernon, "and I am not saying it is, what would I have gained from holding the door shut on Hector?"

"I have no idea whether the motive behind the deed was pure malice or mere whim. The mind of a thirteen-year-old boy is a maelstrom of contradictions and unguessable urges. Cruelty is not alien to him. But do we not here see, with you, Vernon, the possible genesis of greater horrors? A foretaste of things to come?"

I returned my gaze to Vernon Agius. I was viewing him in a whole new light. He sat there, doing his utmost to appear insouciant and aloof, yet beneath it all, in those pale blue eyes of his, I detected shifting shadows, dark flickers, like the silhouettes of sharks in seawater; in that blithe smile of his, a smugness that bordered on contempt.

"Am I wrong, Vernon?" said Holmes. "Pray tell me I am wrong."

Vernon sighed deeply. "You are—"

"Not wrong," said his mother, before he could finish. "Vernon, my dear, there is no point dissembling any more. No point for either of us." Her mouth was a tight, grim line. "I know what you are. I have known for a long time. I have tried to ignore it. I have hoped against hope that it was all the fault of your father, and that in time you would outgrow the brutishness which he, whether by heredity or by example, instilled in you. You learned how to hide it and could make yourself seem appealing, even honourable. All said and done, though, you are still Eustace Agius's son. If anything, you are worse than he was. His cruel streak has, in you, curdled into a dark vein of wickedness."

"Mama, don't say that."

"I have no wish to say it, Vernon, but it's true. Did you, as Mr Holmes says, hold the door so that that boy, Hector Robinson, could not escape?"

"Mama, I…"

"Did you?"

She stared at him. Her son stared back. Then he dropped his gaze.

"Yes, Mama. I did."

"Why?"

"I… I honestly don't know. Mr Holmes is right. I woke up when Mr Yeowell came for Hector. I changed into my rugby kit and followed them out to the boathouse, keeping my distance. But I did not do this in order to gloat, Mr Holmes is wrong about that. Rather, my motives were pure, at least to start with. I had it in mind that Hector might need rescuing again. Really, that was my expectation and my intent. But then, when the time came, when Mr Yeowell shut him in the boathouse and walked away… something just clicked in my head. I thought… I thought, why not just leave the feeble little wretch where he was? Why did I keep saving him? Why did I keep putting myself to all that trouble, for no great purpose? Standing up to Mr Yeowell had, as Mr Holmes said, only earned me the same punishment Hector got, running round the playing fields for an hour in the rain. Why should I have to suffer just because he suffered? And why should he not suffer a little more? I stood there a long time in that downpour, thinking this through, and even as I did, Hector began pushing at the door, trying to get out. That decided me. He shouldn't be allowed to escape. He should stay there and see the thing out. Mr Yeowell would be back for him eventually, wouldn't he? But in the meantime, he should pay the full penalty. I had no idea that the water in the inlet was rising, or that Hector might die because of my actions. But nor do I regret what I did. Not wholly."

"And are you guilty of the recent abominations? The cat? Otto? Not to mention – God forbid – Isidore? Don't lie to me now, Vernon."

The look his mother gave him was searching, withering. Vernon seemed to shrivel before it, as a dry leaf before a flame.

"He saw it in me too," he said. "The professor. He saw what you saw. When he first asked me to defer my place at Cambridge and study under him for a year, I was flattered. I may not have liked him but I knew how respected he was in the academic world. I thought some of his lustre might rub off onto me. It soon dawned on me, however, that I myself was the object of study. He must have intuited who killed the cat and your Otto. He was trying to work out what I was, what manner of creature. All those hours the two of us spent together in the library, him ostensibly teaching me, but all along I was, to him, little more than an amoeba on a microscope slide. Every now and then I would catch him looking at me, staring hard, his brow furrowed. It was as though he could see through me. See *into* me. He was going to denounce me, I was sure. Sooner or later, he was going to reveal the truth about me to you, and then…" Vernon's voice became hoarse with emotion. "And then what would you think of me? You would despise me. You would reject me. I couldn't have that, Mama. I couldn't bear it. And so…"

"And so Isidore had to die," said Mrs Carmody.

"It was easy. After the cat and the dog – easy. He was coming back from one of his visits to Denbigh in the woods. I was lying in wait. He did not even see me. I had a knife. I leapt out at him from behind. It was over in seconds."

"And then you desecrated his body. Using Fitch's dentures, of all things."

"Mostly with the knife, in order to hide the initial wound and make it seem all part of a mauling. But yes, with the dentures too. I had appropriated them for just that purpose, to leave toothmarks."

Mrs Carmody shrank away from her son. It was as though she was seeing him for the first time – seeing in his outward appearance that which he had long harboured within.

"Mama," Vernon said, "he wasn't good enough for you."

"I think I should be the judge of that," she replied coldly. "For what it's worth, I felt Isidore was very much good enough for me. The man had his faults, but after Eustace Agius, he was a positive saint. He took us in. He showed us kindness. Oh, Vernon. What you have become – what you are – it is not what I would ever have wished for you. Not what any mother would wish. My son, my son!"

A pleading note entered Vernon's words. "Mama, you still love me, don't you?"

"How can I?" she shot back, her expression as stern as stone. "How can I now?"

The boy's face fell. He reeled, as though Mrs Carmody had landed a physical blow. He tottered to his feet. His eye roved around the room, alighting at last on Jonah Denbigh by the window.

"You," he hissed, jabbing a forefinger at him.

The hermit put a hand to his own chest, quizzically. "Me? What have I done?"

"I don't begrudge Mr Holmes his achievement here today. He has only carried out his professional duty, with his customary aplomb. I don't hold anything against Mr Basu, either. He followed his journalistic instincts and chased up a story. As for Dr Watson – well, he is Dr Watson, Boswell to Sherlock Holmes. The two are inseparable. But you… Why could you not simply play the part I assigned you? Why could you not just be the blasted Yukon Cannibal and take the blame for my stepfather's death, as you were supposed to? You've ruined everything."

Vernon was picking on the one person in the room he could still feel superior to. No longer was he the valiant opposer of bullies. In his moment of abject defeat, when every hope he had ever had was dashed and everything he held dear was crumbling away, he had become the bully himself. He was more his father's son than ever.

Suddenly he charged at Denbigh, snatching up a silver letter opener from a writing desk along the way. He was quick, covering the distance in just a couple of seconds. His intent could not have been more obvious, or more deadly.

Startled, I fumbled for my revolver. Holmes, who was further from Denbigh than me, moved to intercept Vernon.

Nearer to Denbigh than either of us, however, and faster off the mark, was Basu. He hurled himself between the young man and his target, adopting a boxer's stance, weight on the back foot, fists up. I barely saw the punch. It was as swift as a cobra's strike and as devastating as a mule's kick. All at once, Vernon was supine on the floor, out cold. The letter opener slipped from his uncurled, nerveless fingers.

Mrs Carmody calmly gathered up the pug from her lap and rose to her feet. With the dog clasped to her breast, she swept towards the door.

"When Vernon comes round," said she to Holmes, "kindly arrange for him to be removed from the house forthwith. I never want to see him again."

With that, and not even aiming a backwards glance at her unconscious son, she was gone.

Chapter Twenty

THE GHOST THAT NEVER RESTS

That evening, as a police wagon drove away from Grayshott Grange with a sullen, manacled Vernon Agius as its cargo, I was party to a brief exchange between Basu and Denbigh. They were standing by the Grange's front door, as were Holmes and I. Now that the affair had been resolved, we were all preparing to take our leave.

"You damned near got yourself stabbed back there, Basu," said the hermit.

"I know."

"That's twice now you've risked your neck to come to my aid."

Basu returned a shy smile. "I would do the same for anyone," he said, restating his comment from the earlier occasion.

"Would you, though?"

"Well, put it this way. I have no wish to make a habit of it."

Denbigh deliberated, then stuck out a hand. Basu shook it.

"You have earned my forgiveness, and more," Denbigh said.

"I am glad to hear it," said Basu.

"But no more articles about me, if you would."

"Not even one? I am keen to dispel any last connotations of cannibalism still clinging to you, and not only that but to proclaim your innocence in the murder of Professor Carmody, as established by no less a luminary than Sherlock Holmes."

"You don't think that that will only stir up further trouble?"

"Not if I do my job properly."

"Well, if you reckon it'll help…"

"The press has power, Mr Denbigh," said Basu, "which, if wielded wisely, can work wonders."

"I am going to take the precaution of moving to another part of the country anyway, if that's all right with you. Those wonders of yours may backfire, after all, as they did before. Also, I have no desire to tangle with the likes of Patrick Hesketh again."

"Let me know where you go, so that I can find you if need be."

"Maybe," said Denbigh. He turned, making as if to leave.

"Denbigh," I said, "are you sure it's safe to return to your cabin? Hesketh and the others might be lying in wait for you."

"Oh, I shan't go back there ever again, Doctor. I shall find somewhere else to spend the night, and in the morning I shall begin my quest for pastures new. Thank you for your concern, though. And my thanks to you, Mr Holmes, for your assistance in all this."

So saying, Denbigh strode off across the lawn, a dim figure in the moonlight. At the last instant, he looked round and lofted a salute to the three of us. We reciprocated, and then he was gone, his silhouette melting into the darkness of the woods.

The household four-wheeler had been put at our disposal and sat waiting to take us back to Haslemere, its twin lanterns aglow. While the three of us were clambering aboard, I noticed that Holmes looked preoccupied.

"Surely you can relax now, Holmes," I said as the driver whipped his horse's flank and the carriage got rolling. "Your work is done. You have scored another notable triumph."

"Have I, Watson?"

"I should say it is beyond dispute. A murderer is soon to be behind bars. An innocent has been cleared of blame. What more can you want?"

"A murderer who is scarcely eighteen years of age," said Holmes. "Old enough, if only by a few months, to be hanged for his crimes. It is hardly the most gratifying of outcomes." He heaved a sorrowful sigh.

"Mrs Carmody said it herself, Mr Holmes," Basu said. "How could you have prevented Professor Carmody's death? You are not a psychic. You do not have a crystal ball that can foretell the future."

"I should have trusted my findings, Basu. Vernon Agius was rotten to the core. He showed it both at Saltings House and, more overtly, a year later with his involvement in his father's death. On the former occasion I had no way of knowing for sure that he, or anyone, had held the boathouse door on Hector Robinson, and I can be pardoned for not pursuing the matter further. On the latter occasion, however, I gave Vernon the benefit of the doubt when both logic and instinct were telling me otherwise. While I was wandering the world afterwards, during that period when I was supposedly dead, my thoughts turned to the boy more than once. I hoped that the impulse which drove him to ensure the death of his father was a one-off. I liked to think that it had been consigned to the depths of his soul, never to resurface."

"You told Wiggins that a malign spirit had been exorcised from the Agius house," I said. "At the time, I assumed you were referring, metaphorically, to Eustace, but you actually meant Vernon."

"And the exorcism was not as thorough as it ought to have been."

"Vernon Agius was someone who gave every impression of virtue and decency. I myself did not see past that to the corruption beneath."

"Neither did I," said Basu. "I can hardly claim to have known the boy well, but he struck me as every inch the perfect, incorruptible youth."

"With all due respect to both of you gentlemen," said Holmes, "you are you and I am I. What may evade the scrutiny of others should not evade mine."

"You can castigate yourself as much as you wish, old friend," I said cajolingly. "It is, in my view, unwarranted."

Basu nodded in agreement.

Grayshott Grange receded behind us. Holmes looked around him at the gloom-hung woods, the rutted country road, the darkling sky.

"A man may not believe in the supernatural," he said at length, "but be plagued by phantoms nonetheless. Regret is the ghost that never rests. It rattles its chains and whispers its doleful complaint in one's ear at all hours, until one's dying day, and one cannot help but listen."

"Holmes…"

"No," he said more mutedly, as though not hearing me, "one cannot help but listen."

James Lovegrove is the *New York Times* bestselling author of *The Age of Odin*. He has been short-listed for the Arthur C. Clarke Award and the John W. Campbell Memorial Award, and reviews fiction for the *Financial Times*. He is the author of the Dragon-Award winning *Firefly: The Ghost Machine*, *Firefly: The Magnificent Nine*, and *Firefly: Big Damn Hero* with Nancy Holder. He has written many acclaimed Sherlock Holmes novels, including *Sherlock Holmes and the Christmas Demon* and a follow-up to *The Hound of the Baskervilles*, *Sherlock Holmes and the Beast of the Stapletons*. He lives in Eastbourne in the UK.